WHAT'S NEXT

WHAT'S NEXT

Geoffrey Keane

AuthorHouse™
1663 Liberty Drive
Bloomington, IN 47403
www.authorhouse.com
Phone: 1-800-839-8640

Published by AuthorHouse 01/25/2013

ISBN: 978-1-4772-7040-0 (sc)
ISBN: 978-1-4772-7039-4 (e)

This book is printed on acid-free paper.

CHAPTER ONE

IT IS THE 31ST century; the year 3017, to be exact. The whole world is a-buzz with the world government's mainframe computer release of January's monthly news briefing. The awareness prompt signaled us all over the world on Monday the 19th at precisely 10:01am eastern standard time in the U.S., but much of the world wasn't awake at the time, so it was much later in the day before many people in foreign countries had become aware of the details of the report and committed them to memory.

The report, received via wireless internet connection direct to each of our brains, through our brain retrofit computer chips, which most people nowadays had installed in their scalp as a young child, had been of enough interest, at least to most adults, to be called to their awareness.

This is so because when certain kinds of awareness prompts are delivered via the internet, we feel a sense of nagging curiosity, which moves us to direct our conscious attention to the information we are curious about. It's really no different from searching our minds to realize what's bugging us, the way we used to centuries ago when all we had was our natural minds; before the days of brain retrofitting.

The field of brain subsidy computer technology has developed considerably over the last several centuries, to the point where we think just as individually and independently as we did in the 20th century, but we also possess the capability to connect psychically to the Internet at will, and we have grown to become considerably more sophisticated in our education, and in our understanding of humanity.

The January report, on everybody's mind by the evening of the 20th, allowed us to become aware that today marks the 1,000th anniversary of the year the first world President Barack Obama, changed the course of human history, gaining widespread public support for a lifetime presidency term. Through Internet voting, the term of a Supreme Court judge was changed to four years. Internet voting, of course, led the way toward a single world government.

Of course, well over 100 presidents have been impeached since then, but many more have gone on to provide leadership for decades. The year 2017 marked the inauguration of the first life term president, at the end of the double 4 year term, which before that date was the maximum time an individual could serve as President in the U.S.

During his earlier term, Obama's administration instituted the first computerized employed citizen voting system, giving ultimate power to set laws and determine political decisions to the individual people of his nation. This was the advent of a world trend to follow suit, based on the overwhelming success of that empowerment of the people.

By the end of Obama's second 4 year term as U.S. president, politicians and political representatives nationwide were limited to acting according to the consensus polling results of necessity by law, concerning every issue; and the legal system had been overhauled considerably. Laws were appropriately modified, and were voted to become standardized among the 50 states.

The male heads of Major corporations were replaced with women, whom the consensus believed were less ruthless and dominating leaders, which later we discovered is absolutely true; and the cumulative effect of all these changes worked so much for the common good of the country that the U.S. became a model for the whole world to follow suit, in the years that followed.

Later, it was determined by polling, that it was Barack Obama's original campaign slogan "yes, we can!" which was largely responsible for the people's rise to power. During the course of history prior to that point, Presidents, Kings, Queens, Premiers, Ambassadors and other political leaders had always knuckled under to the rich and powerful, maintaining dominion over the people via ruthless domination. Politicians and the greatest leaders' hands were being forced in their decisions, to act as mere extensions of the most ruthless and powerful business leaders and financiers', including banks, which were privately owned, unlike now except on planet CAP, the capitalist society.

The slogan, "Yes, we can!" was repeated in public addresses by Obama as a response to different political heads and lawmakers contentions that the country's mainly unsophisticated citizens can't be responsibly charged with the task of setting and changing political policies and laws, governing themselves.

It was Obama's famous 2011 State of the Union Address which inspired employees to empower their employers nationwide to pass-on their consensus votes on several key issues to congressional representatives. On the first issue, it was voted in, that from that point forward, all political representatives must support the people's consensus views, and act consistently with the majority vote on any and all initiatives and amendments. On the second issue, it was formally recognized, that all of the people collectively had mandated the creation of a computerized voting system, which would educate, as well as qualify voters to exercise their voting privileges, via electronic testing of each individual prospective voter's awareness, of the factors surrounding each issue they intended to vote on.

To political leaders and lawmakers contending it was unethical for people to literally govern themselves having full weight to protect the country's interests, Obama shouted back in that famous speech, that "who were they kidding?!" Throughout the entire history of man, in terms of leadership, the fox has been guarding the hen house, and those charged with protecting us have acted like foes, having their way in a free for all, killing our resources our hopes and dreams, and our belief that justice might prevail; filling their overstuffed bellies and bank accounts with our hearts and souls, which they've ripped out of us with their vicious teeth, hoarding money and power through ruthless domination!

"No more!" he said; "no more will we be downtrodden by our leaders! No more will we sit back with broken spirits while dominating, oppressive forces saddle us with an increasingly unbearable burden of debt, in the process of plundering the economy, and decimating the network of small businesses and individuals who built this country brick by brick with their hard work and integrity."

"Let us now take the opportunity to initiate the first non-violent, bloodless revolution; putting real control into the hands of the people for the first time. We can only change the course of history in this manner for one reason: evolution. The evolution of our collective intelligence and wisdom to understand, that this is far better than being unfairly manipulated and dominated by subjective leaders; along with the evolution of our technology, which now gives us the capability to align ourselves as a people, and for each one of us to stand up and be counted, as a result of our advanced computer and communications developments."

It was then that the fledgling internet system was bolstered by the latest technology, and the addition of millions of voting terminals; which were police-protected privacy stations, powered by the latest computers connected to the internet. The stations could be used by adult workers who didn't already possess an internet-connected computer with an I.P. address specifically linked to their social security number. These stations were available by appointment on a first come, first serve basis.

On some of the larger issues, a wide range of background information was developed by expanded congressional committees, and made available to the general public via the new Federal government informational website. So many people went to that website, reading the material, and coming up to speed, so that they could pass the individual issue tests, qualifying them to vote on different issues, that as a result, qualified votes were cast by over 80% of the work force.

Then, later, in the year 2025, Barack Obama was named the first world president, his administration having assisted all 314 of the existing countries in the world to govern themselves by computerized popular vote; and also having developed the first model for agreeable compromise, signed by leaders of countries governed under the ideology of capitalism, communism, socialism, and religious order.

This first article of the world government rendered the world leaders who signed it physically powerless to take military or police action against any other country whose actions fell within the acceptable boundaries of agreeable actions under the compromise agreement. Any initiative started by a signing leader taking military action against another country without world government approval would subject that leader to arrest, conviction and permanent exile involving segregated confinement for life.

A large proponent for the successful enforcement of the terms of that agreement was the newly-developed DNA-GPS system which made it possible for authorities to locate anyone who's DNA had been input into the system, no matter where they were on the planet, even if they were hiding in a lead bunker. All known terrorists had been apprehended under that system.

Article one, of the world constitution, made it possible, for the first time in history, for countries running based on a variety of different ideologies, to peacefully co-exist, according to a contract which all of the world leaders signed, containing mutually agreed upon terms of compromise under all conceivable conditions. The article has been amended many times since, due to expanding possible conditions as discovered, and world authorities have had to intervene periodically to unseat various leaders, but this article is still a primary underpinning of universal society today.

Internet statistics showed that this text was saved in the individual memories of 72% of the worldwide public retrofitted with brain-internet connection capacity, including over 25% of minors under the age of 18. The rest of the report had a much lower rated memory retention factor, but that just indicated the high common denominator of human intelligence, in the current day and age, because it showed that the most important information had been sifted by individuals, from the much longer report. It has become widely known that it is counterproductive to store much non-essential knowledge, which can hinder our timely recall of the most important memories we will need to access.

Anyway, our story focuses in on a young married couple, Bill and Justina Symms, who have four-year-old boy and girl twins, whom they had decided to have, on their honeymoon 5 years earlier. Bill and Justina had met in 6th grade, just months before their class's college graduation; and they continued to date in Boston, where they both attended graduate school. They waited to get married until they were 18, having spent 3 years in the work force while living in separate apartments. They pooled their savings together and put down $30,000.00 global dollars on a $150,000.00 starter home in nearby Natick; which they had moved into after they returned from their honeymoon.

Bill had been offered a job out of college; in the marketing division of an android manufacturing company by the name of U.S. Android, and Justina had a job as a 3rd grade high school science teacher at Natick High, which was a global public school. Their combined earnings were under $60,000.00 annually, but they were young in their careers, and public servants didn't earn much either at the high school level.

However, Justina had been eligible for the global government lending program, as a public school teacher, and putting the loan in her name, they had gotten 80% financing at 4% fixed. The monthly payment on the standard 100 year loan was under $300.00 a month.

Their monthly expenses, including food and clothing, utilities, internet service and taxes left them with yearly savings of less than $5,000.00, but Bill would complete the apprenticeship program this year, and income for the average-aged mid-level executive at age 82 was nearing a million dollars annually. Bill had a good career to look forward to.

A company pension for a senior executive retiring at the 200 year mandatory retirement age often paid out over $200 million during the remaining two or three hundred years of retirement. It was great, what increased working career longevity did for retirement savings, especially when taking into account the extremely long-term investment earnings. A good percentage of the population was living beyond age 500 in the most recent generation, and many senior citizens interviewed were saying the retirement years were the best years of their lives.

I suppose a lot of that has to do with the "Benny" supplement, of which ingestion of the recommended daily amount, maintains your body tissue, bones and organ function at the "age 39" level perpetually until near death. The supplement was developed over 600 years ago, but is constantly being improved through continued research and development efforts. Of course, it was named after the late Jack Benny, as a joke.

Anyway, Bill earns a salary of $14,000.00 global dollars per year, under the Apprentice program; mere chicken feed. However, upon graduating from the program, he is due to receive a $100,000.00 bonus package, consisting of $20,000.00 in cash, $20,000.00 in stock options, and a pair of the latest "his and her" androids, being that he is married.

Being familiar with all the features and all of the attractive model types that he has to choose from, Bill is almost more excited by this prospect than anything else these days. He's been eligible to own a personal android since achieving adult status at age 18, but Justina has been apprehensive about how it might affect their relationship, and has asked Bill to hold off on getting a personal android for financial reasons too.

However, as the time approaches when he will receive the $30,000.00 models without cost, Justina too has started expressing excitement and optimism for their improved standard of living as a result of having these personal servants at their disposal. She's even joked about the probable sexual enhancement.

Justina came from mainly Swedish descent, and was 5'11 and 175 lbs. She was not curvy though; she had a very pretty face, and beautiful blonde hair, but she had small breasts, and a long upper body.

Bill on the other hand was shorter. He looked like a shorter version of Paul McCartney, and weighed 20 pounds less than Justina. Consequently, when they made love, Bill was always on top, and his face fell against her sternum plate. He couldn't reach her face, so they couldn't kiss very easily while in the throes of passion. Technology was going to fix that, once they were fitted for android partners. The new line of androids had a mimic switch, where when you flipped it, the Android's movements would mimic your partner's; so that when you were having sex with your android, you were really sharing a sexual experience with your partner, and vice-versa.

Justina looked at Bill, across the kitchen table, wine glass in hand. They had just finished a late dinner, and the twins were in bed. "Bill" she asked, "Tell me about the new androids. I haven't asked much about them because I don't want you to have to talk shop after you come home from work; but now that we're going to have our own, I think I need to understand how they work, and what to expect."

Bill returned her gaze with a tired smile. "They're a lot different from the one your father had when you were growing up, I imagine. I think he had one of the 30th century generation of androids, before electronic mind reading software was developed."

Bill didn't mention it, but he was also thinking about how nowadays, you were custom-fitted to your android partner, so that every proportion of your height and weight would match your opposite sex android partner's.

Justina slightly winced. "All I knew is that my mother hated it at first. I think she almost divorced Dad over the way he used to stare at that beautiful android body.—But she did get used to that, knowing it was just a machine; and I'm pretty sure there's not much more that would have kept him from having affairs, with women's bodies all looking 39 forever, once they reach that age."

"Justina, I would never have an affair on you; even if I couldn't have an android woman. I know how much that would hurt and betray you. I love you so deeply, that I could never forgive myself for doing anything that might make you leave me."

Justina felt a warm flush. She loved to hear Bill talk this way to her, and it just made her love him all the more. She smiled; "I know you're going to be more attracted your new android woman; but when you flip the switch, it's going to be me you're having sex with, and I can't wait to kiss you passionately while we are making love; I've been dreaming about it!"

"I know; it's probably going to be amazing!"

"Okay, now we're getting side-tracked, "Justina said flatly. "Just tell me what it's like to have one around, and how they can serve you. I think Dad's was only programmed to do laundry and have sex with him." She paused, "I used to hate the way her body parts had seams between them, like Frankenstein. It was kind of creepy."

Bill laughed; "don't worry, they look and feel utterly human now. They have a seamless body design; and they've perfected simulated biology. The new models have a respiratory system and a pulmonary system, just like people."

Justina showed curious concern. "They have warm blood pumping through their synthetic veins? What happens if they cut themselves—am I going to have to deal with a bloody mess?"

Bill answered quickly, "Actually, their blood is water with translucent chemical additives. The only stain they can leave is a water stain. If they bleed, you just shut them down and bandage them up. The monthly service charge we'll pay covers 24 hour repair service. It's one of the pluses of buying from U.S. Android. They pride themselves on quick response time."

Justina felt comforted, and the conversation was getting interesting. "I hear they feel like a real human being; their skin, their muscles, their body temperature, their touch?"

Bill nodded and she continued, "—But they have no senses, and they can't think; how do they avoid walking into a wall? How do they know to find a chair, to sit down?"

Bill showed off his knowledge. "They piggyback off the mind of their owner; his wireless connection will connect uniquely to yours; your brain retrofit hardware.—Except when you flip the mimic switch, in which case, he will connect uniquely to mine. Our DNA-based frequencies will be the only two he will be able to pick up-well, unless he's a networking android, but they're a lot more expensive, and they require special licensing. I don't think we'll ever want one of those."

A wave of distress came over Justina. "That's scary to think about; does that mean a networked android could piggyback off of someone in the room to see where they are going, while at the same time being partially controlled off another person's mind?"

Bill sensed that Justina knew more about androids than he had figured. She must have been talking to some of her friends about the subject more recently. Still, he didn't break stride. "That's where psychic boundaries come into play. A network android is pre-programmed to respond only in specific areas with each member of the network. For example, a business man or woman network android might be piggybacking off the brain retrofit system of a secretary occupying the same office, who would coordinate all of the androids motor skills, except for electronically psychic writing and typing commands which might be coming from a connection with the C.E.O.'s brain retrofit system. Of course, the android's verbal response could only be triggered by various word strings delivered at a specific vocal frequency; in this case, that of the secretary. Voice frequencies are like fingerprints. They are unique to each person."

Bill paused, while he tried to think how he could sum this up, and get back to the discussion about their particular androids that would be living with them in the near future. Finally, he said, "Network androids are more of a thing of the future; they really haven't caught on yet. They're way too expensive for most individuals, and company C.E.O.'s don't want them most of the time, because they're way too expensive, and too confusing to understand, in terms of their programming and operation. Anyway, we were talking about our androids; let's get back to that subject."

Justina rolled her eyes. She had started to get nervous about it again, "We've talked enough about androids for tonight. We still have about 4 months to talk about it before you complete the apprentice program, don't we?"

Bill shook his head affirmatively. "Yeah and it usually takes two weeks, after you select which body model you want, for the custom programming of an android to be completed, before delivery." Bill felt another little rise of excitement, as he remembered being informed, at the apprentice's meeting that day, that U.S. android now had over 10,000 models to choose from. There were probably over 100 beautiful android women his size in stock, to pick from.

Boston was just a speck on the globe. Bill and Justina's families were "strewn across the universe," so to speak. Bill's two 5th grandfathers were both nearing retirement, and two of his 10th grandfathers were still alive. Tenth grandfather—that's what you call your father's father's father's father's father's father's father's father's father's father's father. You kind of had to be brain retrofit to understand that concept; but with everybody living 500 years, that's how many relatives a young adult has. Bill and Justina had over 1,000 blood relatives between them.

Most of Bill and Justina's relatives still lived on earth, albeit in over 40 countries; but there were at least a few dozen of their relatives who lived on the nearby group of man-made planets-hence the expression, "strewn around the universe." It was a phrase you used mostly at family gatherings. Bill and Justina had never even met half of their relatives, and there were some they were likely to never meet, unless they were to visit man-made planets they didn't think they ever wanted to go to.

Bill and Justina dreamed that it might be cool to travel to planet CAP, (for capitalism) someday, where the laws and societal structure favored entrepreneurs. Some of the coolest inventions were coming out of that planet these days.

It might even be fun to visit planet S, (for socialism,) or planet COM, (for communism,) and much, much later in life, Bill and Justina thought they might want to visit planet REC, (for recreation,) a retirement community where you have to be over age 200 to get in. There are no businesses there, to speak of, except for stores and hotels, and companies related to home-building. It's all leisure activities, although it's a very active planet. The entire planet is filled with sports-related and game and hobby related activities you can take part in. Vacation resort companies have also filled the planet with resort activities and hotel accommodations. There is a huge concentration of manufactured goods ranging from sporting equipment, to advanced computer game systems of all sizes and types, and a whole host of hobby and avocation-related goods are sold and rented there. It's a huge cost-effective profit center for many worldwide manufacturers, which was the financial basis, making the creation of the planet possible. Single-family, and multi-unit housing also proliferates, but that's about all that exists there; well that, and media centers where you can get access to literally millions of books and movies, mostly all converted to 3D in this day and age, and translated to all different languages, and available in several different types of media formats as well.

However, Bill and Justina thought, who would ever want to go to planet DOM, (for domination,) where there's no sense of morality and everybody there is just trying to screw each other over?—And who would ever want to go to planet LIB (for libertarianism,) where they have that ridiculous society modeled after the wild ideas of Ayn Rand. Just the thought of landing at the Alan Greenspan Spaceport, named after the man whoalmost caused a worldwide financial collapse, in pre-historic times around the year 2000; that thought would put off most people.

But the most hated planet? That's planet P. It's where exiled sex offenders are sent. The united federation of planets voted to outlaw all androids modeled after children, and confiscated all of them; and when dozens of manufacturers of them threatened a class action lawsuit, it led to a solution where a small outpost planet was created, and all of the confiscated androids where shipped there. No other planet would allow their existence.

Anyone who landed there could never leave; that was unanimously voted in. Prisoners exiled there would be clothed, fed and housed in a prison-like environment, but once they had served their sentences, they could live out in the local community and even own a child android, if that's how they chose to live their life. Bill and Justina had no idea if any of their relatives lived there, because even if they did, no one in the family would want to admit it. In their wedding vows, Bill and Justina vowed never to speak of the planet, and that they would do all in their power to stamp out sex before age 18. This was a standard practice at most weddings nowadays.

Chapter Two

Four and a half-year old Alyssa tugged at her Mother's dress. She was the first to see Justina's sister, Barbara enter the baggage carousel area. "Look Mommy, it's Aunt Babs!" Alyssa ran through the small crowd of passengers waiting for the carousel to start moving. "Aunt Babs, Aunt Babs!!!" She exclaimed as she ran. She gave her aunt a great big hug. Tommy stayed with his mother. He was pretty sure his sister Alyssa would lead his Aunt back to where they were standing. Justina hadn't moved because she didn't want to forfeit her spot at the conveyor belt. The suitcases were now coming out, and she spied their bright red ones. The kid's suitcases were large because they were staying with their aunt for two weeks of their summer vacation. Without too much difficulty, Justina pulled them off the belt, and slid them onto the hand-cart, as Alyssa approached with Justina's sister, Barbara in tow.

Tommy now ran up and hugged her. "Hi, Aunt Babs!" he exclaimed, roused from his bored, tired state. He had fallen asleep on the plane ride from Boston's Logan airport. They chattered excitedly as they made their way through the San Francisco airport back to Barbara's car. "Aunt Babs, do you really have a pool at your new house?"

"Yes, Tommy; and you and Alyssa can go swimming as soon as we get there!" Babs had confirmed that their wishes would come true, and the twins jumped up and down with excitement. "Teresa, Caitlin and Melanie can't wait to see you!"

Barbara and Nick's triplets Teresa, Caitlin and Melanie were almost three years older, but more recently, the age difference didn't seem to matter. The cousins were already famous friends. The hardest part of their visits was getting them all to fall asleep at night. They laid awake talking and giggling together for hours usually, before Babs often had to raise her voice a bit finally, in order to get them to calm down. The next several days would be no exception.

By the time Justina left, the following Thursday morning, leaving her kids with her sister to take care of while she and Bill had a break, the kids had swam in the pool several times, watched movies together in the big screen theatre room sprawled on the sofas. They had gone shopping at the mall, and Nick had taken them on a boat ride in the San Francisco bay. Alyssa and Tommy were having a great time.

Nick and Barbara had moved into their new house six months earlier. Nick had owned a roofing company for 9 years now. He was running 5 crews, employing over 40 workers, and he was making money, hand over fist. They had bought a half-million dollar house in San Mateo, with all of the latest amenities. Nick's grandfather was a mid-level executive for U.S. Android out of San Francisco, and had given them "his and her" androids for a wedding present 8 years ago; so what better environment, for the twins to get used to having android servants in the house. It was perfect!

On the drive back to San Francisco airport, Barbara and Justina were alone in the car. Justina broke the silence. "Are you sure you're okay with having Alyssa and Tommy for this long? I mean, I hate to impose on you for such a large favor."

Barbara shook her head. "Nonsense; it will be nice to <u>have</u> them; and we're happy to help you and Bill out." "Thanks," Justina said with gratitude, "At our initial interview for the android fitting, they told us we'd need time to adjust, when they were first delivered; and they recommended that if we had close relatives whom the kids could stay with for a couple of weeks, it would be easier on us all, and we might adjust better to the new androids that will be living with us."

They continued to talk as intimately as close sisters do, for the remainder of the drive to the airport.

Half-an-hour later they kissed each other's cheeks and hugged at the gate. Justina looked uneasy as she spoke. "It's hard for me to leave Alyssa and Tommy so far away from home, for such a long time."

Barbara smiled back, as only an older sister could smile, "It's only an hour shuttle flight to Boston; you could come any day if you miss them." She paused; "I know, it's a five hundred dollar round trip, when you book it with less than 2 weeks' notice; and on yours and Bill's salaries, that probably won't happen-but they'll be fine, and so will you! Now, go try out those new androids with your husband!"

Android technology—it had become such a huge factor in the improved quality of life, for people of the last several generations. Just like man's earliest sophisticated invention of the automobile, at first they were expensive and problematic. But as time went by, they ironed out the wrinkles, through improving technology. As it was with cars, androids became more sophisticated, and they became better and more comfortable servants responding to human commands.

But unlike the limited physical relationship of man to machine of the 20th century, where you stepped on the gas pedal, and the car responded by accelerating, with android technology came the development of what was referred to as C.S.A. "Computerized Synthetic Awareness" technology. In the middle of the 24th century, scientists and doctors working together had developed a way to link human psychic thought with electronic memory and data processing function. Shortly thereafter came the first models of androids with psychic translator boxes.

Brain retrofit technology was in its youth at the time, but many people who could afford it had computer chips installed under their scalp on the top of their cranium, and memory signals were transmitted wirelessly to a dedicated file on the internet, set up specifically for each person.

Synthetic memory awareness technology also made it possible for data from the internet to be converted to psychic information, through non-specific feeling prompts that made you feel as though some knowledge you had access to would be helpful to call to consciousness at the moment, but you had to search yourself to figure out exactly what it was.—And of course, what it was, was information which your mind had stored on the internet, which could now be brought to your awareness.

Roughly 130 years later, further technological developments made it possible to add into the mix, factual information from a master website which we all had access to, much of which we had quite possibly never even learned, but it was information which was made available to you via your internal memory retrieval system, in addition to the information and memories stored in your subconscious, now mostly stored in your online memory file.

For most people, retrieving information from this huge online databank felt distinctly different because it was new information that had never entered your mind before. So, in the hierarchy of your thinking processes, scientist-doctors discovered it was subordinate in grabbing your attention.

As refinements were made subsequently, over a number of years following this initial discovery, software developments made it so that you could effectively turn on or off at will, your ability to take in this synthetically induced new information, the more intelligent of us being able to call any piece of information, from a much more vast pool of knowledge, into consciousness through the process of willingly searching yourself to bring it to your awareness.

Later, further developments also enabled you to commit to memory, any new information that had entered your consciousness via this huge online database. At that point, this information, now stored in your online memory file, could be even more easily recalled when necessary or most helpful.

Early on after these developments, it was discovered that the more intelligent of us who were fitted with brain retrofit hardware of this type, just naturally over time, extracted all of the memories from their brain, as they could now be converted into electronic data stored outside the brain, within their internet memory file.

Scientist-doctors also discovered that once some of the memories stored within a person's brain were extracted, the plasticity of the brain made it possible for newly dormant brain tissue to become used for the expansion of remaining brain functions; and as necessity is the mother of invention, this turned out to be mainly expanding our capacity to become more fully aware consciously, of more and more at once.

Android computerized brain technology made use of all of these developments. Perhaps, the greatest advances were as a result of the evolution of "psychic awareness conversion," where what a person was aware of at the moment could become instantly transferred and translated into C.S.A., or computerized synthetic awareness; which could be used to electronically direct the vocal and motor functions of an android.

Computer scientists began programming "Android brains" to detect and process signals of their owner's awareness into physical and vocal responses of the android. At this point, in the 31st century, android technology has advanced to the point where androids function pretty fully as extensions of their owner's awareness.

It was a typical day at U.S. Android in Boston, except that Bill had been summoned to the district manager's office while the hallway just outside it bustled with activity and chatter. Bill sat quietly, yet somewhat distracted.

The assistant with a headset on looked up from her desk, "Mr. Symms?—Mr. Posthauer will see you now." John Posthauer had been the head of the Massachusetts division of U.S Android in Boston for decades. He was fairly pleasant, quite sophisticated, and he tended to be pretty direct, especially to apprentices.

—But Bill had shown much promise, and Mr. Posthauer had taken a bit of a liking to the bright young man who had not only digested the technical aspects of android technology, but had also made some interesting marketing suggestions from time to time as well.

"Bill? Come in, have a seat," He gestured with a business-like smile. "So; you've graduated the apprentice program, and now you're a bonafide member of the marketing team!" He said with a congratulatory smile. "I'm going to give you a private office, and you'll be working with Jim Nakamine's group; you, Jim Lowe, Tom Birch, Russ Schmidt, Barry, Kathleen and Norma. Your first project will be the internet advertising campaign; but we can talk about that when you come back from vacation. Jim tells me you're taking delivery of your units tomorrow."

"Yes <u>sir</u>!" Bill could hardly hide his excitement, "we're scheduled for delivery at Eleven O'clock-I can't wait!"

Posthauer checked their preparedness, "Does Justina understand how her android is going to work; and how yours and hers will be linked?—I mean what's she's <u>supposed</u> to know, at least?"

"Yes sir; she downloaded last year's android operating manual off of the company internet site; she's called it all to her awareness, and she seems to have quite a thorough understanding of the material. We've talked a lot about it as well."

Posthauer nodded, "That's good; have you explained the overload safety functions to her?"

By law, Androids were fitted with function interrupters which would kick in under certain circumstances. The overload circuit breakers were for anger, aggression, fear, contempt, joy and general emotional overload. It ensured that an android would shut down before taking destructive or out of control action. It was important for android owners to know this in order to allay their possible fears, that theirs or their partner's android might cause them harm.

"Yes; she understands completely," Bill reassured. "Justina and I feel ready, and we are both looking forward to having the new androids in our lives. I told her to get ready for a whole new standard of living!"

Posthauer winked at Bill; they both knew there was more to it than Justina knew about. They stood up and shook hands, as Posthauer inserted a parting comment, "Improving people's standards of living is our business!—Enjoy; and we'll see you back here, two weeks from Monday. "Bill was exhilarated and relieved at the same time, that Posthauer hadn't made any comments or inquired into the personal aspects of the attractiveness of his selected android, or about sexuality. Bill felt it showed class that he was above this, and had high respect for his employee's privacy.

On his drive home, Bill felt grateful that his work week was ending on Thursday afternoon, instead of Friday. He would miss the end of the week traffic. Justina would arrive home from taking the twins to her sister's earlier that afternoon, and they had dinner reservations at "The Captain's table" on Rowe's wharf, to celebrate Bill's promotion. Bill was finally making the grade, after years of schooling and hard work.

He had the new android pair in the car with him as he drove home. He was more than a little nervous about what Justina's reaction would be when she discovered what he was keeping a secret from her these many months. When he got home, he found his apprehension was justified.

At first, he thought it seemed to be going okay during the introductions, but suddenly and unexpectedly her mood changed drastically. He tried to explain, but it was of no use.

"You lied to me!" Justina's eyes were full of anger and disbelief. "Stop saying you had to; you lied to me!"

Bill thought he might be ready for this moment, but he realized now that he wasn't at all. He had never seen Justina this angry; he was sufficiently paralyzed with fear.

Both androids were standing perfectly still. Shayna-1 was staring where she had last looked at Bill, and Adam-1 was staring where he had last looked at Justina. Both Androids had shut down on overload. Adam had gone off on anger overload, and Shayna had gone off on fear overload. Shayna had approached Justina and introduced herself saying, "I'm your husband's android, Shayna-1; how do you do?"—That's all it took. Justina had gone ballistic!

Even though the level of shock and anger on Justina's face was surprising, Bill maintained a slightly nervous smile, as though he had just played a practical joke on her; but this was no joke! Registering Bill's apparent amusement of sorts, she looked at him in bewilderment, as though she didn't even know the man she was married to. "You told me they only respond vocally to word strings spoken by their owner, and they don't talk to anyone but their owner . . . and you said they'd have mimic switches, and there's no switches at all!—not even a switch to shut them off!"

She finally stopped ranting, and was saying something Bill could respond to. He didn't waste any time answering her bewilderment. "They're a brand new line!—It's still a secret!! Look, I didn't want to do this at first but they talked me into it. "They convinced me that you'd never agree to be a guinea pig if you knew—that's what they told all eight of us young married apprentices in the marketing group. We were all in the same boat; we had to agree to do it their way, or we couldn't take part in the program! Look, if it makes you feel any better, we all decided to do it; the men and Kathleen! They convinced us that it's safe; and none of us wanted to miss the opportunity to be among the first owners of this incredible new generation of Androids. They're like people!—But they're still just extensions of us—we'll just be getting to know additional and different sides of each other. The scientist-doctors say we'll just fall deeper in love from getting to know each other better. It's based on the oldest adage of good people who fall in love with each other, "to know you is to love you!"—And they don't need mimic switches anymore; they mimic us whenever we both desire it strongly enough. As I said, they're both extensions of our conscious will; or at least their actions are."

Bill stopped babbling long enough to let this initial information sink in. He had remembered what was recommended for him to initially say, and he had delivered it pretty much word for word. Now he would wait for her to respond, just as it was suggested in the training classes; however long the silence would be before she spoke.—Then he would be on his own. The idea was to start the control group off on the right foot; but the company really wanted to learn how people would naturally respond to the new product, after they understood the most important new features. If there were going to be any last minute problems they could fix, they wanted to know about it before they released the new line of androids into the general public.

Bill turned to look at the two new androids while he left Justina alone with her thoughts, for what seemed like an eternity. He was studying Adam-1's features when the android suddenly came alive again. He approached Bill and extended his hand, "I'm your wife's android, Adam-1; how do you do?"

Bill wasn't going to shake the hand of a machine! He realized that the joke was on him. He turned to Justina, who was smiling, and she asked "are these things really safe?—and are we really going to find this enjoyable?" Bill figured maybe she was talking about the sex.

Bill shrugged. "I don't know, why don't we find out?!"

Justina put her hand to her mouth, "look, he's walking toward me, what should I do?!" Adam now stood in front of Justina.

Bill knew the right answer to that, "I don't know; he runs by your desires; you'd know better than I!" Justina now remembered that her android Adam would do whatever she wanted him to. Shayna stood still and gave Bill a sexy look, as he approached her and stood in front of her, looking her up and down. She was utterly beautiful. He reached out and touched her bare arm up near her shoulder. It felt warm and human, and she had the kind of creamy white skin he loved on a woman. He took the liberty to stare openly at her ample round breasts.

Just then Shayna spoke, "if there was anyone else in the room right now your behavior would be inappropriate." (Justina was, as a joke, speaking to him through the voice of Shayna.)

Slightly embarrassed, Bill looked up at Justina who again was smiling at him, "I suppose, the more she turns you on, the more I'm going to feel your passion!"

Bill nodded, relieved and impressed; "Now you've got the idea!"

Shayna gave Bill another sexy smile. "Let's kiss."

Bill looked up at Justina again, and her sly smile gave him the go ahead he needed. He gazed into Shayna's beautiful eyes, and kissed her warm, full lips. Justina suddenly sighed.

He touched her cheek with affection and wonder.

Justina sighed again, "That feels incredible!—You've never touched me like that before!"

Bill looked suddenly over at Justina, realizing what was happening. It was just like they said; the automatic mimicking had kicked in, because they had both desired it enough. "Let's go into the bedroom, whaddaya say?"

Justina smiled and held out her hand, and as they walked down the hall to the bedroom hand in hand, Bill wondered what Justina was thinking. He knew what <u>he</u> was thinking; how glad he was that they had bought that king size bed last month, in preparation for this!

Suddenly it dawned on him, wait a minute, Adam was standing two feet away from Justina while he was kissing Shayna.—So that's what Dr. Pfifer meant when he told the control group, at the last lecture, that there was a surprise related to the new mimic features. He had said, "Don't worry, I'm sure none of you will be upset by it; and you'll be receiving the written supplement about it, I think by the next time we meet, after your vacations. It was a last-minute new development added just before production. There wasn't time to get the explanation into the manual." It was a parting comment.

You see in the previous versions of androids with the mimicking function, she could only feel how he was touching his android when her android was touching her in the same place, at the same time.—But Justina had just felt Bill's touch through the medium of his touching his android! The explanation for this, is that at the eleventh hour before production of the new line of android prototypes, a group of leading engineers had convinced the team of scientist-doctors in charge of the project, that it would be even better if you could also be psychologically stimulated, a bit like a phantom leg in an amputee for instance, when someone else was touching the android who was psychically connected to you!

It was an idea they were going to try to develop, and add to the next generation of androids, but a brilliant young scientist-doctor working on the team had made a breakthrough discovery the very next month, which allowed them to add the feature into the prototype androids being newly manufactured. So now, you could get double stimulation, when your mate was touching their android which was psychically connected to you, while you were being mimic-touched by your android which was psychically connected to your mate! However, Bill realized that he and Justina really were guinea pigs, because there's no way the scientist-doctors could know how potentially distracting this would be, if you were trying to read, or concentrate on something else, while your horny mate was ravaging the android psychically connected to you! He made a snap decision not to bring up this subject to Justina before they had a chance to feel the effects of making love using their new androids. He didn't want to let anything get in the way of this moment he had been waiting for!

It was early the next morning and the sunrise was beautiful, Bill thought, as he stretched his sore body. A slight breeze was blowing as he and Justina sat out on the deck sipping coffee, listening to the birds singing their morning songs to each other in the trees. Justina's long blonde hair was slightly disheveled, but Bill loved looking at her pretty face as her hair waved in the breeze. He knew this unusually good feeling had something to do with the new androids, and certainly he was feeling the contentment of having experienced the intimacy of an intense sexual experience with a woman you were so in love with, whom you knew was probably feeling the same way, while you were gazing at each other in the aftermath, the following morning.—But even so, this was a level of contentment and satisfaction he had never felt before, and he had a really good feeling about he and Justina's future lives with the addition of these new androids. He could only guess that Justina was feeling this way too. He spoke, feeling the effects of a slight hangover, "I guess it's a good thing for the overload switches!"

Justina stretched her sore body as she smiled back at Bill. "Yeah, otherwise we might have never stopped!"

Realizing they had been alone for 10 minutes on the deck, having left the androids lying quietly in bed when they went to the kitchen to make coffee, she said, "they can't move if you're not in the room with them, can they?"

Bill kind of knew what she was thinking, "Nope—they're programmed not even to stand unless you're in the same room with them; I guess, just so you can get away from them as long as you want; you know, to avoid the ball-and-chain effect."

Justina gave Bill a sly smile, "I thought you said there would be an adjustment period; I feel adjusted already!—No, but seriously, what's supposed to be the adjustment difficulty with these new models?"

"Well, the sexual hangover, for one thing; but I noticed that both of our androids went off on overload at the same time; we couldn't have both worn out at the same time, could we?"

Justina thought for a second, "No, your fatigue must have shut them both down somehow; I remember feeling I could have gone on a little longer."

"Yeah, but it's probably a good thing; aren't you feeling kind of tired this morning?"

"Oh, I'm wrecked!" Justina affirmed, "But I've never felt so good!" She and Bill had spent the afternoon having sex with the androids the day before, and Justina was so tired that Shayna-1 had to make dinner while they collapsed into chairs at the kitchen table.

After dinner, they had watched a movie in bed, until Bill suddenly got curious, which started another sex-fest, but this time it consisted of touching their androids every different kind of way imaginable, giving each other a wide variety of different kinds of physical and psychic sexual stimulus, until they fell asleep, exhausted, around eleven o'clock.

They had both slept soundly, but woke early at first light, feeling sore, and feeling the stress and excitement of having the prototype androids now in their lives.

The next few weeks seemed to go by quickly, but not so quickly that they didn't leave a lasting memory for Bill and Justina, of how their lives together had been changed, possibly forever. It seemed to be a decidedly improved quality of life for both of them.

At first, their androids spoke to their owners, Bill and Justina, from time to time, but neither Bill nor Justina had said a word back to either android; and why would they? Talking to your android would be a little like talking to a ventriloquist's doll, when your partner who was controlling what the android was saying was right next to you in the room.

—And of course, talking to your partner's android, whom your thoughts controlled, was like mental masturbation of sorts; and again, what was the point of that, when you could talk to your partner instead? Besides, it seemed like a good way to develop a split personality! Neither of them wanted to get closer to this possibility.

At first, Bill and Justina had spent a lot of time together, but as the week wore on, they spent more and more time apart. Often, they would take their android partner out with them into the world, when they were shopping or doing errands. That was one of the surprising new features of this new generation of synthetic people. When both androids were alone in a room, neither one could function on their own; but if either Bill or Justina were in the room with them, both androids could function, making use of Bill or Justina's visual perceptions to guide them.

With their existing wireless internet connections, all four of them were constantly connected whenever Bill and Justina were with their androids together; but in an ingenious way; it was undesirable for anyone else to be able to know your thoughts, or read your mind; so it was made difficult and expensive, as well as illegal to integrate with anyone else's brain hardware or software via the Internet. Only the androids could be aware of each other's thoughts, and so be an extension of the integrated thoughts of each owner.

It was widely believed that people were meant to be autonomous individuals, and should not be psychically connected in a direct sense. This is why these laws and safeguards were put into effect.

But the situation with these new androids was different, because the connection was somewhat abstract, or indirect. With this new arrangement, when you were with your android, which is psychically connected to your partner, your partner wasn't conscious of the thoughts and feelings exchanged between you and your android, or even the vocal or physical expressions of the android, unless your partner voluntarily chose to concentrate on this brain activity occurring inside their mind.

Remember, concerning android technology, that the only way you are psychically connected to the android that your thoughts are controlling, is when you feel a slightly queasy feeling, which is a nonspecific stress telling you that something is bugging you, but you have to willingly search your mind in order to become aware of anything more than that.

If you are busy with other thoughts, you can choose to ignore the slightly queasy feeling. However, on the other side of that, just like looking at a beautiful sunset while listening to a good song; you are aware of, and potentially enjoying the pleasurable effects of whatever experiences you are able to be cognizant of on any level, to the extent which you have the ability to multi-task within your mind.

So with the help of these new androids, one person can effectively control two bodies, and have two separate relationships with your partner, including separately distinct conversations and physical interactions, going on at the same time! Isn't this multi-tasking at its best?!

—But now add the dimension that in addition, you're now able to have a relationship with a very attractive android partner, where mentally every exchange is just getting to know a different side of your partner better; and every romantic or sexual exchange you are having with the android is producing additional often rewarding thoughts and feelings within your partner, while you are enjoying yourself intensely as well! It's a good life in the thirty-first century; a long life and a good life!

CHAPTER THREE

"SUBORDINATE INITIATIVE"—THE SCIENTIST-DOCTORS WHO were at the forefront of the new generation of android servants they were developing, knew that this was the key to success in their new project. They realized very early on, once they had mastered split-brain function within an android, that there were potential power issues.

With "his and her" androids, clearly the owner of the android had to be in full control over the behavior and actions of their android. The whole idea of having an android in the first place, was in order to have a slave servant of sorts; so there was a problem to be solved.

If, for example, The husband's slave servant android woman was mainly powered functionally by a psychic connection to the wife's mind; and if the husband was trying to get the android woman to do something that was against the wife's will, it was almost sure to cause overwhelming difficulty, if we allow the android to comply with this kind of a demand.

That didn't turn out to be such a problem, because in early experimentation, it was discovered that the android would go off on overload in a case like this, as opposed to complying with the demand; but we couldn't be having these androids suddenly becoming non-functional without warning all the time!

As a solution, the android's electronic brain was programmed to detect sufficient stress levels, and issue a verbal overload warning message. In the previous example of the husband demanding his android servant woman, controlled by his wife, to do something against the wife's will, the new prototypes responded by saying, for example, "Your current demand is causing an anger overload."

When the husband hears his android's overload warning, he has to realize that if he doesn't rescind the demand, or inquire immediately what the thoughts are, causing the wife's upset on the issue, the android will go off on overload, before responding subordinately to the demand of the owner, in this case the husband, like usual.

The word string the owner would have to speak to his android when receiving the android's overload warning was simply, "What's the trouble?" This would program the android's electronic brain to search the mind of its controller, in this case the wife, for the pertinent thoughts behind the wife's upset at the idea of the android doing what the husband was demanding.

The breakthrough development allowing for this android function was the successful programming of an android brain to search the mind controlling it, for awareness. As a result of this advance, the android was now able to call the subconscious thoughts of the controlling person, to consciousness. It meant that an android had now achieved a sense of consciousness, which is about as human as you can get!

So in terms of subordinate initiative, in the above example, the wife's desires and initiatives would generally be subordinate to the commands the husband might give to his female android, as long as these demands were not overly disturbing to the wife; yet in no case would the female android in this example be able to be used by the wife, to try to command the husband.

Instead, at worst, as far as the husband was concerned, his female android might go off on overload if he was too insistent that the android do something against the wife's will; and of course, vice-versa concerning the wife with her android man.

Because each android has a synthetic form of consciousness, being able to search the unconscious mind of the person who's mind is controlling it, it is, in a sense, a separate person in itself, often expressing different thoughts and feelings than the person controlling it is consciously thinking, feeling and expressing at the very same time. Therefore, it is a manifestation of a split personality, which has been created purposely within that controlling person, for the purposes of multi-tasking, or if you will, being in two places at the same time.

Recapping, a "his and hers" android is a synthetic person who can serve you, reason with you, or at worst shut down until the controlling person becomes aware of the problem and restores the android to service; but your android will never try to command you, or demand anything of you. What an ideal companion, right?

—But then an idea for even further usefulness occurred to the scientist-doctors. It was based on an aspect of potential that they called the "Chinese wall" effect. It might function, they thought, like banks with an investment arm, and a savings and lending arm.

Back in the twentieth century, the Glass-Stiegel act was created to make it illegal for the bank's two operations to become intermingled. A bank's investment arm was kept from taking the savings deposits of its customers, for example, to use in the investment arm's activities of buying investments, because if the investments went belly up, then the customers' deposits were lost, and customers couldn't then draw out their deposits when they wanted the cash back.

The act separated the savings from the investment activities, by having two separate and distinct pools of money, even though they were both owned by the same bank.

It was mentioned earlier that at this point, it is currently illegal for two people to connect their minds directly through the internet, which is however, connected to each person's retrofit hardware and software; but the new androids effectively create a Chinese wall of sorts, because now you have two entities, an android with a separate consciousness, as distinct from the human being that android is psychically connected to, who has his or her own separate consciousness; yet both of these conscious entities, the android and its owner, are tapping into the same pool of subconscious information and thought processes, if you will.

This being the case, it's more or less of a Chinese wall situation if the two "his and hers" androids relate to each other either through their internet connections, or verbally to each other in the presence of one or both parties of the couple they serve. This is so because the thoughts of the husband's consciousness are still unknown to the wife's consciousness. It is also true that the thoughts in the wife's consciousness are still unknown to the husband's consciousness.

By the way, I should mention that a version of "his and his" androids, and "hers and hers" androids were also available for gay couples.

With this in mind, let's review the possible types of communication which could occur in the lives of the controlling couple. Via verbal communication, the couple could communicate, human consciousness to human consciousness; and potentially any combination of the androids and the two human partners could verbally communicate, human consciousness to synthetic android consciousness.

In addition, the two androids could now also talk to one another, if at least one person of the married couple is also present; and another facet of the communications possibilities is that the thoughts in the subconscious minds of each controlling partner in the couple could be collectively made known to the synthetic consciousness of either or both androids.

Finally, the woman could verbally communicate with the woman android she controls, thus relating two different conscious sides of the same person to one another, and vice versa concerning conversations between the man and the man android.

It's quite possible that this all may work to the great benefit of the couple, or theoretically, at worst it could cause them to split up eventually, or potentially it could even cause psychological damage perhaps, to one or both of them. This is mainly why US Android wanted to try a prototype experiment before releasing "hi and hers" androids to the general public.

Potential psychological damage to the android's owners was the big potential problem which in the greatest sense renders Bill and Justina guinea pigs, being the new owners of "his and hers" androids.

Of course, another question is how this might affect their children.

CHAPTER FOUR

ON THE EVE OF the tenth day after Bill and Justina had taken delivery of their "His and hers" android pair, the four of them were all sitting in the living room as Bill had planned. This was the point it was suggested, in Bill's training classes, that he reveal all of the different types of communication possibilities which could potentially go on between them, to Justina, as the uneducated partner in the test group couple.

According to the recommendations of US android, both parties of couples with children had to have achieved an adequate understanding of the way the androids function in their lives, before their children were introduced to the androids.

Three of the couples, within the group of eight in the prototype testing group were in the position that only one person of the couple were employed by US android, and the other partner was not. Barry and Kathleen were both working for US android, were married, and they had the advantage that they had both received full training, and had been briefed on every aspect of the prototype androids' operation and characteristics.

Justina was still a "Babe in the woods" compared to Kathleen, in this respect, although she was very bright, and had adapted wonderfully, showing much tolerance and flexibility in taking part in the prototype experiment. She was, after all, a scientist teacher with a doctorate degree.

Still, Justina would be returning to San Mateo to pick up the kids and bring them home from her sister's on Friday, and bill was more than a little anxious about this.

They had finished a delicious dinner which Shayna-1 had fixed. They had discovered that Shayna-1 was a much better cook than Adam-1, and Bill knew this was so because Shayna-1 had full access to Justina's knowledge about cooking, which was rather extensive compared to Bill's knowledge of cooking. He barely knew how to boil an egg. He had eaten out most of the time before he and Justina had started living together.

Adam-1 had only limited access to Justina's cooking knowledge because beyond being capable of using Justina's visual perception to guide his physical movements when Bill wasn't in the same room with him, Adam-1's only psychic connection to Justina's mind was through his electronic brain connection with Shayna-1, who was powered by Justina's thoughts.

Bill had been informed during the training classes, that given the way the android's brains were programmed, the only way Adam-1 could become aware of thoughts and information in Justina's mind, was in communicating verbally, android consciousness to android consciousness, or nonverbally, through their internet connection, android to android.

Adam-1, for example, could only become aware of what Shayna-1's synthetic consciousness was aware of at any moment. He did not have the ability to search the subconscious mind of Justina, like Shayna-1 could.

If Shayna-1 was using her synthetic consciousness to perform functions or activities demanded of her by Bill, who was her owner, and at the same time Adam-1 was either electronically or verbally asking Shayna-1 for information to assist him in cooking a meal which Justina had asked Adam-1 to cook, Shayna-1's ability to multi-task was limited, and she would use the greater part of her synthetic consciousness to serve Bill, rather than pay attention to anything Adam-1 was asking of her.

This means that Adam-1 might only have part of the information he would need to do a good job of cooking a meal, for example. So this was the final aspect of hierarchy to be understood by Justina, and Bill would now try to explain it to her in a way that made sense.

Bill now gazed over at Justina, who appeared contented and comfortable, the two of them relaxing after a big dinner, complete with appetizers and desert. "Sweetie, I want you to understand something about the way we will be relating to one another, now that we have these new androids. It's what they call "Subordinate initiative" at the training sessions. I'm going to have Adam-1 give you the explanation, so that nobody will go off on overload!" Bill was kind of joking with this comment; but at the same time he was realizing that he had learned a new concept from having the androids, which was that it would probably be a further improvement in their standard of living if he tried to show more respect and concern for how what he might say to her at any time, would potentially affect Justina, in terms of emotional impact. It could only be good always to try and lessen that impact.

Adam-1 had the edge over Bill, in communicating to Justina, in that he had a direct connection to Shayna-1, who was powered by Justina's thoughts, so this could guide him in determining what to say and what not to say, in trying to make a point Bill was trying to get across to Justina.

On cue, Adam-1 turned to Justina to speak, "I guess I should begin by telling you that I am aware of how much Bill loves you, and of course so are you because he tells you and shows you in many ways,—But even though I am just another part of Bill, I am as different to you as I am different from him, given the fact that I have a separate consciousness from his.

You've openly told Bill that you are quite honestly more turned on sexually to my android body than to his; and he's okay with that; in fact he's happy for you in this respect. Bill only hopes that you are as okay with, and as happy for him, that he is more turned on sexually by Shayna-1's body than yours."

Justina looked over at Bill with a little anxiety, and then turned back to face Adam-1, "This is a little weird, listening to you speak to me this way; it really drives home the point that you are a lot more than a slave servant to me.—But to answer your question, yes, I am okay with Bill loving Shayna-1's body as much as I love yours, and I too am happy for him in this respect; that he can now enjoy more intense pleasure from being with the most beautiful woman he could have his pick of, even though she's an android." Justina turned briefly to Bill, "Don't ever think it's okay to touch any other woman but her!" she said very emphatically.

She turned back to Adam-1, "Okay, you can continue now." Adam-1 smiled at her a little like Bill would have, but his facial features were so different from Bill's, that if she didn't know he was just a different side of Bill, she wouldn't think the two were related in any way at all.

Adam-1 continued speaking, "Because Bill and I are different, in that for example we could both say something different to you at the same time, and in some ways I am capable of communicating almost as deeply with you as he is; and of course the same is true between Bill and Shayna-1; but Bill thinks we should be referred to as Adam and Shayna, and drop the "one."

Justina smiled slightly, "Okay Adam; I thought you had something more important to tell me though."

"Of course," Adam got on to the more important topic, "Bill is just using me like power steering at this moment, because it's easier to avoid saying something upsetting to you if I say it for him, using Shayna's guidance. Bill wanted me to help you to understand the power structure of our servant initiatives; me and Shayna, that is. Bill wanted me to assure you that Shayna would never help Bill do anything that would be very upsetting to you, or that you wouldn't approve of. Shayna is programmed to serve Bill in every other way, but she is utterly incapable of doing anything against you; in fact she will go off on overload before doing so.

Justina nodded, "Okay; that's nice to know."

Adam continued, "And by the same token, I am incapable of doing anything you might demand of me which is sufficiently disturbing to, or against the will of Bill. You haven't made any of these kinds of demands on me yet; but if you did, I am programmed to give you what's called a verbal overload warning.

Adam paused, and then smiled as an idea came over him. He decide to entertain Justina a bit, while delivering these serious messages. It could only help, and after all, it was a manifestation of the affectionate, fun-loving side of Bill which he hoped Adam would show to her every chance he got. "For example," he said, "If you were to command me to kiss a man on the lips, I would say, "Your current command is causing a disgust overload."

Justina was amused, and hip to his kidding, just as he suspected she would be. "There's no such thing as a disgust overload, is there?" Adam shook his head no, and with a smile, she continued, "Let's see, there's anger, aggression, fear, hate, contempt, fatigue, disappointment, joy, and sadness overload . . . do you mean that if it was anything more nonspecific, or if it was a mixture of these, you'd tell me that what I was asking of you was causing you to go off on general emotional overload?"

"Exactly," Adam pointed at her as he realized she understood the idea he was trying to get across very well. "So when I give you an overload warning, you have to either rescind the command, or say, "What's the trouble," and you have to do this pretty much right away, if you want to ensure that I won't go off on overload."

Justina seemed to understand, so he continued, "By saying "What's the trouble," in response to my overload warning, it will initialize my programming to search Bill's mind for the specific thoughts behind his troubled feelings about what you are asking me to do. Do you follow me?"

"Yes, I think I do," Justina nodded, "You want me to understand how and when you and Shayna can most effectively communicate directly between you, and you also want me to understand who is subordinate to who, under the different possible circumstances we will be finding ourselves in, from day to day."

Bill interrupted, "That was exactly the point of this conversation, dear. You grasped it all, and you pass the test with flying colors!" he smiled warmly.

Friday came all too quickly, and Justina flew back to San Mateo to visit with Barbara and Nick, and of course to pick up the twins. She had left Adam lying dormant on the bed; but Bill would take advantage of his time to be alone with the beautiful Shayna.

He did really appreciate the fact that he could still be with Justina, through his interaction with Shayna, even when Justina was three thousand miles away visiting with her sister; but Bill also realized that he was falling in love with Shayna on a level like she was just like another beautiful woman, whom his wife was sanctioning him to have an ongoing affair with, strangely enough.

It's funny that although Shayna was supposed to be the slave servant, Bill enjoyed sexually pleasuring her so much and so often that Shayna had to give Bill fatigue overload warnings several times that weekend while Justina was away. Still, he was saving himself for them to resume their quadruple sexual relations once Justina returned.

Bill was glad their bedroom was one hundred percent soundproof, so he could comply with the laws stipulating isolation, sexually speaking, from any children who might be in the house. Not only was it considered best for children to have no idea of any sexual relations or activity at this point in their lives, but the laws were such that if a minor under the age of eighteen gave a statement to the police, or testified in court that they had seen or even heard adult sexual activity in progress, any participant in that sexual act seen or heard, would have to serve a minimum of one year of incarceration, and engage in continual sexual reform treatment during that period.

The laws had significantly reduced the incidence of minors in any way being exposed to sexuality, before age eighteen.

Bill made a mental note that he should not forget that, whenever he and Justina and the androids were in front of Tommy and Alyssa.

If he was in the same room with Adam, or even if Justina was with Adam, so that he was active, Bill's mental note might well have been picked up by Adam, who could then transfer it to Shayna, who could commit it to Justina's memory, as Shayna shared Justina's subconscious mind with her. As you can imagine, there is great leverage to having "his and hers" androids in the thirty-first century.

Chapter Five

Barbara had no trouble picking up Justina at the other end of the flight. As they were pulling away from the arrivals curb at the US Air terminal within San Francisco Airport, Barbara carried on a conversation with Justina while paying close attention to the frenetic traffic whizzing all around them. "it's a lot easier picking you up here curbside, than parking in the parking garage and walking all the way to the baggage terminal; but are you sure your carry-on has enough clothes and everything, to carry you through the weekend?"

"I'll make do," Justina replied confidently, "How were the twins last week?—I'm sorry I didn't Skype you, but you wouldn't believe what Bill and I have been going through with our new androids; wait 'till I tell you about it . . ."

"Yeah, I figured as much; that's why I didn't Skype you either . . . The sex was that good, huh?"

It was more than just the sex, believe me!—You have to keep this between you and Nick; don't even tell the triplets, but our new androids? They're experimental prototypes. Bill and I are part of a control group trying out this new generation of US Android models; Barbara, you wouldn't believe it, they are so advanced, and so different from yours and Nick's androids; I don't even know where to begin, to tell you."

"You're kidding!—US Android has come out with the new model? Nick's grandfather told us on the QT that they were working on a new generation of androids, but I wasn't sure if he wasn't just playing with us; you know how he sometimes plays practical jokes. He and his new wife visited us last month, over Memorial Day weekend."

They stayed with you?—They live only an hour away, in San Rafael; and I wouldn't think Nick would invite them for a visit, because he would be too upset that Fred wasn't still with his mother, whom he had divorced."

"Well, you're right; it is only sixty miles from our house to San Rafael, but there would have been a lot of holiday traffic, for one thing, if they drove up and back in one day; and besides, Nick's mother was having an affair at the same time as his father was; they both remarried after the divorce. Nick got over that years ago."

Justina conceded, "I suppose you're right; they didn't have "his and hers" androids to keep them together like we do. Fred always said he wouldn't have androids in the house; he had enough of them, working for US Android."

"Did you know that Fred left US Android a few years ago? Now he works for a Japanese android company; he mostly markets Asian models to wealthy guys who are into that sort of thing. Nick's grandfather was furious when Fred decided to leave US Android; but what could he do?—So tell me about the new androids; what's different about them? Do they have four arms or something?" Barbara joked.

"No, but between us, Bill and I have four heads now!"

"What?! What do you mean?" Barbara looked bewildered.

"Each of the new androids has a synthetic consciousness; which is connected to me and Bill through our brain retrofit hardware; you know, through the internet. We share our subconscious minds with them!"

"Wow!—Fred was telling us they were working on that, last time we saw he and his wife on Memorial day, but we were getting drunk on banana daiquiris; I thought he was just kidding!"

"Nope; it's no joke; now mine and Bill's subconscious minds are connected through a Chinese wall arrangement within the androids.

"What does that mean?" Barbara looked curious and puzzled, "I thought it was illegal for two people to connect their minds through the Internet. Why would you want to do that anyway—do you want Bill to know your every thought?!"

"Well, it's kind of complicated," Justina tried to explain, "We're connected, but we're not. Bill says it's all perfectly legal. Get this; Bill had my android explain it to me!"

"What's this Chinese wall thing?"

"Well, for instance, Shayna is Bill's android partner, but she's connected to me, and she has access to my subconscious thoughts and memories. Adam is connected to Bill in the same way, and Adam and Shayna are connected through the internet too; so they can share thoughts that come to their synthetic consciousness through our subconscious mind connections. Mine and Bill's thoughts and memories are passed between us through the medium of Adam and Shayna; it's neat how it works."

"That is truly amazing!" Barbara said, realizing the impact of what Justina was telling her, "So when Bill is with Shayna, he is having a relationship with another side of you, I get it."

"Yeah, and when I am conscious that Bill is touching Shayna, I can actually feel the sensation in my body, of where and how Bill is touching her, so like when Bill is caressing her breast, I can feel it like he's caressing mine; and Bill can feel it when I touch Adam too; so we can have an intimate exchange through the android bodies; it's an amazing feeling, because Bill and I can both be having sexual relations with our perfect-bodied android servants, and be having a sexual exchange of sorts with each other at the same time!"

Barbara was in awe, "That's incredible!—That must do wonders for your sex life—How much better is it; having sex, I mean?"

"Barbara, all I can say is, it's incredible! Because my android? Adam, that is, he's the most handsome, hunky guy you could imagine; and he's quite large, I mean you know, down there . . ." Justina had a devilish smile as she recalled the multiple orgasms, and the wonderful feelings she had experienced while Adam had ravished her.

Barbara smiled back, "I get the picture!—But if they can read your mind and then talk about it, isn't that a problem?"

"Yeah, it's a bit of a two-edged sword; but they are subordinate to Bill and I; Adam follows my commands as a priority, and Shayna follows Bill's commands as a priority. I ordered my android, Adam, not to give out any information retrieved from my online memory file to anyone without my permission, including Bill; and Bill has ordered Shayna not to divulge any secrets to me either; so it's not going to be a problem."

"This all sounds so unbelievable; isn't it blowing your mind?!"

"Why do you think I haven't Skyped you in the last two weeks! Normally, I would have Skyped several times, just to talk to Tommy and Alyssa."

"Don't worry about that; the twins have been having a ball with Teresa, Kaitlin and Melanie. They've been so busy, they've hardly mentioned your names. They've been hanging out together all day, and like yesterday, I took them all to the water park, while Nick was at work."

"It was so good of you to watch them for us these past two weeks; I don't know how I can ever thank you." Justina was being all too serious.

"Just give me Adam for the weekend!" Barbara joked.

Back at the house, the children greeted Justina and Barbara with much exuberance. Tommy and Alyssa really seemed to have all but forgotten their parents, but seeing Justina triggered their remembrance of their great love and attachment to their mother. Justina was more reserved in appearance, but she was just as relieved and excited to be re-united with them as well.

"Mommy, Mommy, Mommy!" Alyssa chanted, "We missed you Mommy!"

"Tommy was right behind, yelling Mommy, Mommy too. He was truly excited to see Justina. The time at his aunt and uncle's had been good for him. Justina could see that the time he spent with his carefree, fun loving cousins had helped to draw him out more. He seemed happier than usual.

After dinner, the five kids went off to the big screen theatre room to watch a new animated cartoon movie that Barbara had downloaded for them earlier that afternoon.

This left Barbara, Nick, and Justina to sip wine and chat in the dining room. Barbara filled Nick in on the scoop about Justina and Bill's new androids, with Justina chiming in to clarify the details, which Barbara had picked up pretty well on their trip back from the airport. Eventually, Nick expressed the same concerns that Barbara had started to talk about, before the end of their brief trip home had interrupted their conversation.

Justina was getting a little tired, but she couldn't leave them hanging, now that she had told them enough that they just needed to hear the rest; so she continued answering Nick and Barbara's questions, and filling them in on all she had learned about the androids; disclosing some of their interaction with Adam and Shayna.

Nick finally asked, "Does Shayna know what you're thinking, so she could tell Bill if he asks?"

"Nope; she has no idea what's come to my awareness, what I'm concentrating on, or what I am consciously thinking; that's the beauty of it. She only taps into the pool of my greater knowledge; the information and memories which are stored in my online memory; and she can't do anything which is against my will, or so I'm told. So far, I'd say I believe it."

Nick continued, "But she can draw out the underlying thoughts in your subconscious, and use them to guide herself acting in your best interest, as she does things for Bill like you might, if you were available, and with him instead . . ." Nick was catching on. The conversation continued on for a while, before they joined their children in the theatre room, to finish watching the movie with them. The movie was pretty clever and entertaining, providing some comic relief that was much appreciated, after the long, stressful day.

Having slept well and spent the morning together as a family, first sitting around the breakfast table eating fresh fruit and melon balls, sausage and eggs, cooked to order by Tina-7, and served by Johnny-5, Nick had shut the two androids off while Barbara got the kids in their swimsuits.

"Why don't we go out onto the deck," Nick suggested to Justina, "It's nice out today, and that way we can watch the children while they play in the pool."

"Okay," Justina was in a mild, agreeable mood, "I'd like to see what you've done with the yard out back anyway. From here, I can see that you've planted a few trees, and you sure have a lot of flowers out there!"

"That's Barbara's department. She takes Johnny-5 out there and spends hours turning over the beds, planting shrubs and flowers she buys, like every other Sunday when I'm home to watch the girls. She loves working in the garden, and Johnny-5 does the heavy work . . ."

"Johnny-5!" Justina laughed, "That's such a funny name!— That's the name of the robot in that children's movie from the twentieth century, isn't it?"

"Yes, exactly; the movie's called "Short Circuit." He's the smart robot. Our Johnny-5 is actually registered as John-5372; but when we first got him, Barbara was doing crossword puzzles, and he had all the answers; so she nicknamed him Johnny-5 and it stuck. The girls like it too. The first time they saw the movie, they were all pointing to the screen and saying, "Johnny-5, Johnny-5!"

Justina thought back, "That movie came out in the late nineteen hundreds. It was probably such a great big hit because artificial intelligence was just a pipe dream back then. If they could only see us now; androids as real as human beings with a sense of consciousness . . ."

"Yeah, speaking of that," Nick said in a more serious tone, "What are you going to tell Tommy and Alyssa about Adam and Shayna?"

Just then, the kids came bounding through the living room, laughing and giggling as they made their way to the pool. Nick noticed how cute the girls looked in their new one-piece bathing suits, which Barbara had bought them at the mall earlier in the week. He opened the door as they ran through, out onto the back deck, and then down the stairs to the pool.

Barbara entered the room behind them, coffee cup in hand. Nick filled her in, "Justina and I were just talking about going out onto the back deck; she was admiring your flowers."

Barbara smiled, a little pride in her eyes. Nick continued, "I was just asking what she and Bill are planning to tell Tommy and Alyssa about the new androids."

Justina answered as she followed Nick and Barbara out onto the deck, "Actually, Bill thinks we should play it down. Their friends' parents have androids, and they're used to your two; Bill says they're probably too young to notice the difference."

"Yeah, you're probably right," Barbara commented, "They seem to take ours for granted; maybe they won't notice anything different about Adam and Shayna."

Sunday night, Barbara took Justina, Tommy and Alyssa to the airport for their trip home. After saying goodbye to the twins, Barbara kissed Justina goodbye, wishing her good luck. The flight back east was uneventful. By the time Justina got the kids home, they were both fast asleep in the car, and Bill came out to carry Alyssa in to bed, as Justina had carried Tommy in.

The following morning, Tommy awoke first, and he encountered his mother sitting and talking with Shayna in the kitchen. Hearing an unfamiliar voice, Alyssa too had awoken and came into the kitchen to find Shayna with her mom.

Bill had left earlier for work, leaving the twins and Justina with Shayna for the day, to get acquainted. During the course of the day, they had played Monopoly, spent a few hours at the park, Skyped Justina's sister Barbara, and the twins had talked back and forth with their cousins. Shayna had fixed a baked chicken dinner; and after they ate, they watched a movie together on the couch in the living room.

It was close to bed-time, and Bill still hadn't arrived home from work, but Justina knew that sometimes traffic was especially bad coming home from work on Monday evenings during rush hours.

Shayna and Adam were inactive in the master bedroom, and Justina sat on the sofa with Alyssa while Tommy assembled a puzzle on the carpet in front of them.

"Mommy?" Alyssa asked, "How come you don't use a number at the end when you talk to her; everybody else does when they talk to their andoids . . ."

"Androids," Justina corrected, "I don't know, I guess they don't need us to; why, does that bother you?"

Tommy looked up from his puzzle, "I think it's cool!"

"Yeah, it's cool!" Alyssa echoed, "It's like she's a real person; she doesn't even have switches like Tina-7 and Johnny-5 . . . Mommy? Where is the other one? How come we haven't got to meet him? What's his name?"

"Adam," Justina replied, smiling to herself as she remembered his handsome face, "Daddy and I thought we'd spend the day today with Shayna, and then we can spend time with Adam tomorrow."

Tommy was busy with his puzzle and didn't respond. Alyssa was placated, "Okay . . . Mommy? Will Shayna come out tomorrow too? I like Shayna."

"Me too," Tommy chimed in," It's fun having androids!"

"Well, if you like," Justina replied with a little delight and relief, "We can visit with both of them tomorrow."

"Goody!" Alyssa exclaimed, as she and Tommy clapped their hands and wiggled around, "Mommy? Shayna is just like you; she even says some of the same things you do; like "Eat your badayda."

Justina smiled; it was a phrase her grandfather used when she was a child. Justina was not big on vegetables back then. Her grandfather told her it was the way Irish immigrants spoke when the country was very young, in the old days. He had said it to her a few times while she was staring across the table with a puzzled look on her face, until she looked down at the remaining item on her plate—"Oh, I get it; eat your potato." The kids had heard it from her last year, along with the explanation.

Justina told a little white lie in response, "It's just the way she was programmed; Daddy and I programmed her to say that." She wondered how long it would be before she and Bill could explain that these androids were really just her Mommy and Daddy inside. It seemed like it would be a really long time, and she didn't like having to lie; but she knew that sometimes you kind of had to, with children. It was one of her least favorite things about parenting; but Justina was resolved to do whatever it took to raise their children the best way possible; of this she felt pretty certain.

Bill finally came home a little after eight-thirty, and Justina noticed right away that he looked unusually tired and stressed out. Tommy and Alyssa had been in bed for half-an-hour, and were probably fast asleep, Justina figured.

"Sweetie, I'm sorry I'm so late," Bill lamented, "I had no idea I would be when I called you at four-thirty, but just after we hung up, John Posthauer called me into his office, and I've been there ever since. John said we could talk about it as long as it took; you won't believe the offer he made."

Justina was concerned, listening to him and eyeing his frazzled condition, "Whatever were you talking with him about for like, three hours? You've never stayed this late at work before . . ."

"I know; but what they told me is incredible; it took that long for them to explain it to me, and answer all my questions. I'm still in a daze!—Here's the scoop; our androids? They're not just "his and hers" androids; well they are now; but they're actually set up to serve a whole family of four!—And they want that family to be ours!"

"What do you mean? Shayna has been serving our family all day; she played with the kids at the park, she made dinner for us, she played Monopoly with us, and she found a good movie online, that the twins loved . . ."

"That's great sweetie!" Bill said with enthusiasm, "I'm glad things are working out that well so far; but what I'm talking about is different; they're designed specifically for a family with a boy and a girl, to be connected to them the same way we are; they're programmed to have two owners each!"

Justina was taken completely by surprise, "They want to hook up our children to these androids?! No way! Forget it!"

"I know it sounds crazy, but just hear me out. If you don't want to do it, I'll understand; but you've got to hear what they told me about it; and they've made us an unbelievable offer. I just spent three hours talking to John and the head scientist-doctor on the design team. Will you at least listen to what they said?" Bills eyes were pleading desperately.

Justina had already decided it was completely out of the question, but out of curiosity and her great love for Bill, she delayed her utter refusal and instead replied, "Alright Bill, tell me, what did they say?"

"Okay, first, they're making an unbelievable offer; you've got to hear this to believe it; but the main thing is, they've half-convinced me that this is the best thing we could do for our children. The parenting support and educational catalyst aspects are of a whole new dimension. Androids have been used in experimental education workshops successfully for years now; and there's been some experimental use of android companions for babysitting at day care centers; you know, hooking them up to a child's brain retrofit hardware for a few hours at a time. They've been very successful programs, and in many cases, the children involved have excelled in their classes at school, and in developing more and better friendships. I've been reading reports and research results this afternoon."

Justina's curiosity was building, "What's this offer they made?"

"Well, let me explain first; you'll see why. You see, they want to use a few people involved in the project, who understand about the features and technical aspects. That's where I come in; that, and I'm on the marketing team, and they want somebody young, with a fairly strong background in marketing, and John Posthauer thinks I'm the man!"

Justina was growing impatient, "What are you leading up to? Get to the point!"

"Okay; I'm almost finished; well they know you have a doctorate in education with a science background, and we have boy and girl twins, which the scientist-doctors say might have the greatest potential for success, and marketing potential as well.—So this is it; if we agree to participate, and we spend ten hours a week giving feedback and talking about our experiences, for the next ten years, they say they will give us a billion dollars of retirement income over the rest of our lives; a billion dollars! Can you believe it? We can retire at age thirty three!"

Justina was beginning to see why Bill was so stressed. This was all so wild! "That's crazy!—Why would they offer that much?"

"That's the thing," Bill had wondered the same thing, "John told me that the potential market for this is huge; he says they could sell for a hundred thousand a pair, and there's over a hundred million families in the US alone, that could probably afford them!"

"Oh, I see . . ." Justina did the math, "That's like, ten trillion in sales, huh?"

"Anyway; he's invited us to talk to the key people on the development team this Friday. He just wants us to think about it—that's all he's asking; what do you think we should do?"

Justina shook her head in overwhelming disbelief, "Well, we've got a few days to think about it; why don't you see how much information you can dig up on how it's supposed to effect the kids, because that's the bottom line. If there's any chance it could hurt Tommy or Alyssa, there's no way we could even consider this. We'd also have to be able to back out at any time."

"That's one of the things that John assured me," Bill answered her quickly, "Not only could we back out immediately any time, but we'd still get paid a large sum of money. He said we'd get five million if we just tried it for a week!—I guess they have to offer a lot in order to get anyone to try this . . . but he says all their research points to the fact that it's safe; it's the unanimous opinion of the government panel that approved the production of the prototypes."

"Yeah, with ten trillion in sales in the U.S. alone at stake, who's to say that government panel wasn't paid off or something."

I don't know," said Bill, "I kind of doubt that they'd all be willing to risk their careers and reputations on this. I heard the committee hired dozens of independent scientist-doctors, psychiatrists and other experts to study the project thoroughly, and submit objective reports for the committee's review over the last six months."

"Yeah, still it's not their children's lives that are at stake."

Bill nodded, "I guess that's why they're offering so much money."

Justina gazed upon Bill with adoring eyes. She had been waiting and wondering and worrying about him for the last few hours, after being away from him for the weekend.

She wrapped her arms around him, "I love you so much," she said sincerely, "You are the nicest person I know," she confessed to him as they embraced. Bill felt so grateful for her in his life; and so relieved that she had been able to share the huge burden of this stressful news, and related offer. He was speechless at the overwhelming amount of love and adoration he sensed Justina had for him. He just held her quietly as he sat on the sofa with her, feeling like the luckiest man on earth.

Exhausted, they slept soundly, pressing up against each other in the middle of the king size bed, with Adam and Shayna on either side of them. Waking up at one point, Bill could feel a slight difference in the way Shayna's synthetic skin felt, compared to Justina pressing up against him on his other side, but Shayna's voluptuous curves and matching body size seemed to make up for that.

Asleep, Justina cuddled Adam instinctively, cluing Bill in that his large, hunky body size, matching hers more closely, was more desirable to her than his. He started to feel jealous, but then a warm, wonderful feeling came over him as he drifted off to sleep again, aware that somewhere deep inside of him, Justina's warm, rapturous love was for just another side of him being communicated to him through Adam's contact with her body.

The dynamic of Adam's company the next day, in the presence of Tommy and Alyssa, was different. There was no physical touching between them, yet Justina felt in touch psychologically with a part of Bill she was familiar with. It didn't dawn on her until halfway through the day, that recently she had been too consumed with the physical aspects of Adam, to fully sense the psychic connection she had to Bill whenever she was with Adam. She realized with delight that she didn't have to miss Bill so much today, while she spent the day alone with the twins and the two androids.

Feeling confident that Adam and Shayna had functioned flawlessly in public, she took the five of them miniature golfing, after Shayna had fixed grilled cheese sandwiches for lunch.

They had just finished the fourth hole when Justina realized she had a minor problem to deal with. "Mommy?" Alyssa asked sheepishly, "Adam and Shayna are way better than we are; how come they're getting theirs in the hole all the time?"

Justina addressed Tommy and Alyssa together, "Don't you two worry about how anyone else is doing; just do the best you can, and try to have fun; you'll get better at this after we play more." Her response had constituted instinctively good motherly advice for the children, but she had also been kind of surprised herself. Adam and Shayna were putting like experts, scoring below par on every hole so far.

Just then, another young mother walked by, following her three kids to the next hole, "Your friends are really good at this!" she complimented.

Tommy was quick to respond, "They're androids."

The woman laughed, as she looked up at Justina, "That's pretty funny!"

When she had passed, Alyssa turned to her mother, "Mommy? Why did she say it was funny?"

Justina surely understood; Adam and Shayna looked utterly human, they spoke and acted utterly human, and they had no android switches. "Nothing dear; you and Tommy go to the next hole; see it over there, with the number five on the sign?—I have to talk with Adam and Shayna for a minute; we'll catch up to you."

Justina walked back to Adam, and quietly whispered to him, "Listen, can you try to play more like the kids? You're both playing too good!—How can you play that well anyway? Bill and I can't putt like that!"

Adam answered for he and Shayna, "When you announced we were going to play miniature golf, I downloaded a golf tutorial; and then I informed Shayna of the web address."

"Oh, I see," Justina's curiosity was resolved, "Well, please observe how the rest of us are playing, and try not to do any better than us on the scoring."

Adam and Shayna nodded almost simultaneously. Adam gestured for Justina to lead them to the next hole, and they caught up with Alyssa and Tommy and continued, dumbing down a bit.

That night, after the twins were asleep, Bill led Adam and Shayna into the bedroom, and left them there so they would shut down while he talked with Justina in the living room. "How did it go with the twins, and Adam and Shayna?" Bill asked.

"Things went just fine, for the most part," Justina answered, "Alyssa really likes Adam; she was quieter than usual around him; I think she finds him very handsome; I can tell by the way she looks at him. She's a little like me; she knows he's not a real person, but still . . ."

"You said things went fine for the most part; what did you mean by saying that; what happened?"

Justina told bill about their encounter with the young mother at the miniature golf course. "What are we going to do if one of the kids has a play date over here?—I mean, it's going to become pretty obvious in short order, that Adam and Shayna are not like normal androids, isn't it?"

Bill thought for a moment, "Well, we'll have to play it by ear I suppose. We can just say that they are new. Actually, it sounds, from your experience at mini-golf, like everyone is mostly going to assume they are just people; that may be our greatest blessing in disguise."

Justina sighed, "I don't know, Bill; maybe we just need to take them back—unless we decide by some slim chance, to hook them up to the twins for a week; how much did you say we could earn for doing that; five million?"

"Yeah; I know, it sounds pretty tempting, doesn't it?"

"Oh, I don't know," Justina had second thoughts, "How much does lifetime therapy cost if it screws up their thinking processes?"

Bill smiled slightly at the joke, "I emailed you sixteen reports today; eleven of them were independent test results on the specific effects of android integration with children through their brain retrofit systems; mostly preschool, but Tommy and Alyssa aren't much older. The other five reports I sent you are mostly safety-related government reports from members of the committee I was telling you about; but within them are the findings of the panel of different experts consulted on the project."

"I know; I saw the folder already; and I've read through one of the reports on possible risks involved for the children. I don't really understand a lot of the jargon," Justina admitted.

"Somewhere in that folder is a glossary of terms which John thought you might find helpful; why don't you try looking at that tomorrow?"

Justina sighed again, "I just can't believe I am seriously considering this . . ."

Bill nodded in acknowledgement, "I know; me too . . . I just didn't think we should pass up this opportunity without at least giving it a closer look. We still have until Thursday to decide if we want to take the next step, and go to that meeting on Friday."

"What would we do with the kids on Friday, if we go?"

"John said we could bring them with us, and leave them in the company's day care center for a couple of hours while we talk. Actually, John's assistant also offered to take them out to a museum or something . . ."

"Well, let's see what I find in those reports tomorrow; meanwhile, see what you can find out on your end."

Bill and Justina read reports and conducted their own research over the Internet during the next two days. Although the billion dollar carrot undoubtedly influenced their objectivity, neither Bill nor Justina stumbled on any information which would preclude them from going forward with the proposed meeting. Consequently, they found themselves in front of a well-dressed group of experts seated around the conference room table on Friday at one o'clock.

The presentation by the head scientist-doctor on the design team was very impressive, and it started an hour-long question and answer session between the couple and the various supporting specialists; which included the head psychiatrist, an independent child psychologist, an android computer hardware design specialist, a computer software design engineer, the head of advertising, and the regional head of accounting for US Android. All except for the child psychologist were, of course, US Android senior staff members.

Toward the end of the meeting, John Posthauer, who had remained unusually silent, finally keyed in on Justina, knowing she was the real "Mother bear" of the twins, so to speak. "Justina, do you think you have a reasonable understanding of the way you would all be connected together with the androids, if you were to go ahead with this?"

Justina answered with little hesitation, "Well, let me see if I can recap what I've learned so far about the double ownership aspects; I want to make sure I understand how this would affect all of us. Correct me if I'm wrong, but I think what you are saying is that Tommy would be psychically connected to Adam, the way Bill is; and Alyssa would be psychically connected to Shayna the same way I am.—But their connections would mainly be for the purposes of establishing a servant, slash educator relationship between Alyssa and Shayna, and between Tommy and Adam.—And Bill and I would monitor all of the interaction between the androids and the children through our own links between us and Adam and Shayna, right?"

"Precisely!" Posthauer acknowledged, "And your children's' command priority would always be subordinate to yours and Bill's."

Justina kept going, "and the androids could see through the eyes of the children as well as mine and Bill's, so that would mean they would remain fully functional as long as anyone in the family was with them."

Posthauer picked up on an opportunity to explain further, "Yes, and either Adam or Shayna could babysit using the knowledge and judgment within you and Bill; indeed you and Bill would still be in charge while Adam and Shayna act in your absence."

Justina formed a new question, "—And I'll sense what's happening between Alyssa and Shayna; and Bill will sense what is happening between Adam and Tommy?"

"The slightest trouble," Posthauer answered, "Even while you and Bill are asleep, would wake you up like an alarm clock." Posthauer felt this was proceeding well.

Justina continued, "—And along with serving Tommy, Adam would augment Tommy's education?—And in the same way, this would happen between Shayna and Alyssa?"

"That's right!" Posthauer closed in on the initial objective of the meeting, "—And you and Bill would be responsible for twelve speaking engagements each year, and you two would come in for a two hour session twice a week in the evening, to work with staff and give us feedback; and ten years of this schedule would net you a billion dollars!"

"So if we're still interested," Justina picked up, "We would meet again here next Wednesday?"

"Right," Posthauer answered evenly.

They hit the highway heading out of the city at around three-thirty, well ahead of the worst Friday afternoon traffic. Alyssa called up to Justina from the back seat, "Mommy? Tommy made a funny joke at the museum of ancient history . . ."

John Posthauer's assistant had taken Tommy and Alyssa to lunch, and then to two adjacent museums downtown, while Bill and Justina's meeting with the staff was going on.

Justina looked back and saw Alyssa's amused expression, "Did you have a good time with Carolyn this afternoon?"

"Yes," Alyssa answered, "Mommy? We were looking at old signs at the museum?—And there was one from when you used to have to stop at a booth and pay a toll? Well it was a big sign that said, "Slow down, get ticket one mile ahead." Tommy said they should have another sign that said, "Speed up, get another ticket a few miles down the road!"

As they laughed, Alyssa pointed out the window, "Mommy? What does that sign mean?"

Justina looked, and Alyssa had been pointing to an electronic billboard which said in big letters, "Detox from E-Tox." She looked over at Bill, and they cracked a smile at each other over the cleverness of the ad. She thought how best to respond, and she finally said, "It's about being intoxicated."

"What's intoxitated," Alyssa asked.

"Intoxicated," Justina corrected, "You know, like when people drink too much."

"Oh, you mean like great-grandpa did on Christmas? He was really silly; he was drunk, wasn't he?" Tommy asked.

"Yes, he sure was!" Justina confirmed. She realized she had successfully avoided an issue that Tommy and Alyssa would have to deal with when they got older, of whether they would drink or do drugs.

A few seconds of silence went by before she turned to Bill, and said in a low serious tone, "You don't suppose that might be a problem with this project, do you?"

"What's a problem, Mommy?" Alyssa had unexpectedly overheard. Bill glanced quickly at Justina, and quietly said, "Later, Hun."

"Later what?" Alyssa probed further.

Justina called back to her, "Nothing Alyssa; it doesn't concern you."

Okay; Mommy? Can I play with your jewelry when we get home?" Kids could be so obedient and flexible.

Alyssa Skyped her neighborhood friend Carol as soon as they got home, after Justina let her paw through her jewelry box, "Look Carol! I'm wearing Mommy's necklace! She said we could play with her jewelry; can you come over?"

Tommy went next door to play with his friend Jack, who had gotten a PlayStation 3100 for his birthday the week before. Alyssa and Carol took Justina's costume jewelry box into Alyssa's room; which left Justina and Bill to talk out on the deck, in the late afternoon sun.

They both sat comfortably, sipping on their glasses of wine. "Ah, this is the good life," Bill said in a pleasant mood, "A good cigar, a glass of wine, a little E-Tox: it's nice to be home early, while the sun is still shining."

"Yeah, about the E-Tox," Justina picked back up on their earlier conversation in the car, "The company can't find out you're connected, can they?"

"Well, they can randomly test me, but I've never heard of them doing that unless an employee has an obvious problem. No, it's company policy that they don't monitor your personal internet account, unless there's reason to suspect you're involved with anything illegal.—And even if you do get busted for E-Tox, it's just a $500 dollar fine; there's so many people doing it these days."

E-Tox had been around for hundreds of years. It hadn't been clamped down on by the authorities to much of an extent at first, because it had basically ended the physical deterioration inherent in active drug addiction. It had also pretty much put an end to pushers and drug cartels, and the growth and production of almost all varieties of illegal drugs.

The effects of those drugs were now instead achieved via electronic signals, psychically affecting you through the medium of your brain retrofit system, connected to the Internet.

It was technically illegal in the US as in other countries, to have an E-Tox account, but if you knew the right computer tech, they could hook you up with an E-Tox account as long as you continued to pay for the amount of signal you used.

As with the package stores of old, purveyors of this type of intoxicant were allowed to function unhindered, as long as they weren't selling to minors. The only users who got in trouble with the law were those who were getting obviously intoxicated in ways affecting their critical performance, like safe driving, or otherwise controlling yourself in public. You typically didn't run into much of a problem with doing E-Tox as long as you were only using small amounts, so that it was only mildly affecting you, and also provided you didn't have any trouble with the law.

However, as with drugs, you could use too much and become overly intoxicated, and you could definitely become psychologically addicted in ways that could ruin your life. There were really two schools of thought along these lines.

One was that if you had problems with excessive intoxication, it indicated that you needed psychological counseling and/or other help to deal with this problem, which could in many ways help you to learn how to use in ways which minimized your troubles to within a manageable level, while affording you some continued benefits from reasonably mild levels of intoxication.

Then, if this therapy was unsuccessful in helping you to limit your E-Tox intake effectively, or if you otherwise didn't want to take any risks, you could simply abstain and live straight, from that point forward.

The other school of thought was that if you ran into problems with intoxication, this indicated that you have a disease of the mind, and the only known way of managing your life, if you have this disease, is to completely abstain from all intoxicants. This was not considered to be a cure, by any means, but it was to be a way of life, one day at a time.

Naturally, there were two rival ideas concerning intoxication; one that held mild and manageable levels of intoxication to be a catalyst to achievement, and healthy fulfillment, and the other which held that intoxicants are a hindrance to naturally healthy development, and a barrier to otherwise fairly trouble-free living.

There had been enough E-Tox-related trouble within society, that the legislators took the conservative view that, whereas all people could potentially live straight, not everybody could live without having significant problems while using E-Tox. This was largely responsible for the current laws making E-Tox illegal.

However, Bill and Justina were in the camp that saw benefits to milder levels of intoxication; and Bill particularly believed E-Tox could be used successfully as a catalyst to human development, as well as a boost to your standard of living, related to your level of enjoyment and fulfillment. It helped him to think in more complex ways than he could when he was straight, it helped him to concentrate longer and harder on possible ways of solving some of his more difficult problems, and it helped him get in touch with and process information he could draw together, coming to new realizations and other helpful conclusions. He didn't see why a great many of us should have to "put on their handicaps," so to speak, just because some others, a minority at that, as far as he knew, could not seem to make constructive use of E-Tox.

—But when he had gotten into debates about it with people who took the other view, they had sometimes suggested that he was in the minority in his thinking, and there seemed to be very little hard proof that anyone could fall back on, beyond the fact that those going to support group meetings for living straight seemed to be in a pretty serious minority, compared to all of those in a given city or town.

Anyway, just like prohibition in the early 1900's, there were enough people enjoying the effects of E-Tox, that enforcement of the law was only really emphasized in situations where offenders were causing sufficient harm.

Though there were potential dangers and disadvantages associated with E-Tox use, Bill believed the potential benefits and positive effects far outweighed them, at least in his case; so he chose to maintain an E-Tox account, which he tapped into throughout the day, maintaining a level of E-Tox effects while he carried out most of his daily activities. He acknowledged that he was an E-Tox addict, but he chose this lifestyle and he valued it.

Justina preferred the natural intoxication of wine and booze to E-Tox, and alcohol was her drug of choice, but she was aware of Bill's E-Tox use, and his views on the subject, and she supported him, just as he supported her continual enjoyment of wine and other spirits at times. As far as she was concerned, she didn't know what made Bill the wonderful way he was, but he seemed like such a good man, and a nice man, so she was behind him in just about everything he wanted to do. This reciprocity had also made for a strong bond in the relationship.

As far as Justina's intoxication, she drank in the evenings mostly, up to that point, and she got a bit too tipsy some of the time, but Bill didn't criticize her or complain, like some of her friends' husbands. She thought that Bill was exceptionally nice, that instead of giving her trouble about what she wanted to do in this respect, he picked up the slack, in terms of effectively parenting the twins when she was too intoxicated to perform well as a parent herself; and Bill otherwise held down the matters of the household, whenever Justina became somewhat incapacitated from drinking too much. Bill never became incapacitated himself; he was always in control of his faculties.

They loved each other, supported each other, complimented each other, and effectively covered for each other in every necessary way. The year she was pregnant with the twins, Justina had quit drinking, having been able to do this out of a strong sense of motherly responsibility. However, after the twins were born, she had resumed having a few glasses of wine, or a few drinks with Bill in the evenings.

Bill loved Justina very much, and they had enjoyed many good years together. Husbands and wives' online E-account statements were made available to each other by law. In fact, a copy of Bill's

E-Tox statement was emailed to Justina every month so of course, Justina knew about about Bill's illegal E-Tox account, and she condoned its existence, as well as his use. In his mind, Bill would live with whatever drinking problems might arise for Justina, and try to help her to the best of his ability gladly, in exchange for her blind faith in him and his beliefs, about the positive effects of using E-Tox. Because of all of these factors, plus the fact that they respected and admired each other, and greatly enjoyed each other's company, Bill and Justina had a very tight relationship. Bill had gone over most of these basic points with Justina in the past, and they really had no secrets from each other in this respect; but just the same, he had recapitulated, as they sat out on the deck together.

Savoring the moment with Bill while taking a sip of wine, Justina felt a sense of having been placated by Bill's explanation on the subject. She mostly agreed with his perspective on the E-Tox issue, in connection with their possible participation in the family-android protocol testing project, "So you don't plan to bring it up if they don't; is that what you are saying?"

"Yeah; I don't think it will be much of an object. I mean, they do want to test how these androids will work out in a natural family setting, right?—There would be plenty of other couples using E-Tox, who might buy these androids, obviously. Hey, it's a billion dollar offer; I'm not going to say anything that might screw things up; I mean, assuming we decide to go through with it, that is."

"You know," Justina said after a few seconds, "I was thinking about that, and I was wondering how much it would actually cost the company to fund that payout."

"Yeah, I was thinking about that too; probably not much more than a hundred million, assuming they were going to pay us $2 million a year, after the ten years was up, and let the balance grow at a rate of like 8 percent a year, conservatively." Bill was just venturing a guess.

"—And what happens if US android goes out of business?" Justina asked, "What guarantee would we have that we'd see more than a fraction of that billion, say if we live for the next 500 years, which is current life expectancy?"

Bill nodded, "You're probably right; we'll have to look into that more; but let's not look a gift horse in the mouth!"

"How many couples are doing this?"

"I think a hundred or so, nationwide; why do you ask?"

"I don't know; I was just curious. I was thinking about the company's total outlay; but then again, if they have a hundred couples touring the world giving talks about the virtues of family-android ownership every month, as you say, the gross sales potential is astounding!"

"This is true; maybe there's some room to negotiate a flat fee; say two hundred million, that we could invest ourselves over the next five hundred years."

They sat quietly in the late afternoon sun for a few more minutes, before Justina got up, "I'm, 'gonna go check on Alyssa and Carol; I told them that they could play with my costume jewelry; I just want to make sure they're not making a mess."

Wednesday afternoon, Bill and Justina were again in the conference room at US Android, talking with the same group of company representatives. They talked for over two hours, and by this time, most of their concerns had been addressed to their satisfaction, concerning how the androids would be jointly connected to them and the twins. It was beginning to look somewhat conceivable that they might be willing to get involved, from the standpoint of safety, feasibility and potential child-rearing benefits.

Justina was first to broach the money issues again, "Okay, so say we decide to go ahead with this arrangement; what kind of pay would we receive initially, and how would the pension payment work?"

Justina expected he would offer like $2 million a year for 500 years, but Posthauer had the unpleasant task of explaining it wouldn't work that way.

"Justina, I hate to break this to you, but we've had further thoughts about the way we might go forward with this, and we've decided that we can't make any payments to you initially. You see, the press will eat us alive if they find out we're paying a billion dollars per couple to try this out. They'll make it out to be the most dangerous idea; when you and I know it isn't. We've done our research, and we have all kinds of assurances that this will almost definitely work out to everyone's great benefit; especially the educational and developmental benefits for the children involved.—But for obvious reasons, we're going to ask you to sign a gag agreement on the billion. As far as paying you during the testing period, the company's advertising division has convinced us not to do that, because again the press would destroy us, in terms of ruining the effectiveness of our advertising efforts. "Sure," they'll say, "Give a family enough money, and they'll not only live more comfortably, but they will say anything US Android wants them to say, about how things are working out; and they'll avoid talking about any problems if there are any!"

Bill sat silently, because he already knew about all of this. He had purposely avoided telling Justina however, because he didn't want to say anything that might completely turn her off to the idea. He was counseled to let upper management explain, and he would let Justina try to negotiate a financial deal which would make it worth her while.

"Wait a minute!" she started out, "You mean to tell me that you can't pay us a dime for ten years?!"

Posthauer continued to unfold the company's reasoning for this decision, "I know this is hard to hear, but there's another reason; we want to see how families manage, continuing in their normal work routines while paying for the expenditure of purchasing the android pair, with a somewhat conservative income."

Justina got that bewildered look which Bill had seen the night he first talked to her about the whole idea; and he began to worry that the whole thing might be unraveling for them right before his very eyes, as she totally lost all composure, "You want us to make monthly payments on our androids?! Bill said they were a gift, as part of his signing bonus!" She looked over to Bill with wild eyes, "Bill, do you know about this? What's going on?!"

"Okay, now calm down Justina," Posthauer said, maintaining control, "Just let me explain everything. This has all just come about because of pressure from the advertising arm of our company. Bill will still get the entire $100,000 signing bonus, in cash though. We want to be able to tell the public that the initial owners of our new family-android line have paid for them out of their normal earnings, through our financing arrangements. We want the public to see that they can afford this new development—In short, Justina, we're offering you a lot of money to participate, but you're going to have to wait, to receive it."

"I see," Justina said as the wheels turned, "I guess I can see why you're trying to set it up this way . . . but Bill and I were thinking; what if we go through the ten year project, and US android goes out of business at some point; what assurances can you give us that we'll actually see the money we're being promised?"

"We've thought about that too," Posthauer responded, "That's why we're offering a lump sum payment option. I'll let Dan here, explain it; he's our regional vice president of accounting."

"Thanks, John," Dan picked up the conversation on cue, "Yes, in lieu of receiving payments out of the company pension fund, we would be willing to offer a lump sum payment of an amount initially needed to ensure a $2 million dollar a year payout over 500 years. Assuming a five percent compounded rate of return on the seed capital, this comes to a hundred and twenty-two million."

"A tenth?!" Justina countered, "I want half."

"We realize we made a mistake in the way we presented this offer initially; but we wanted it to sound as attractive as possible to prospective participants. The truth is, though, that the company has to commit to this payout for a hundred participants; we'd be parking a lump sum in an escrow account, on the signing of the agreement, at which point the money would be out of our hands. If everybody takes this lump sum payout option, that's over twelve billion we have to lay out, in cash!"

Justina shook her head; she wasn't buying any big corporate bullshit, "Listen, you run your numbers any way you want; Bill and I figured you'd make trillions of dollars, if this project has any success. I know you have a projected budget to stay within, and I'm willing to come down a bit; but we could all suffer damages, and we might not even be able to work, if something goes wrong. I've got to know that I can provide for my babies in case something like that happens; even though the whole damned staff has assured us it won't. We want two-hundred million put in escrow; we're going to need at least that, or we're walking out right now!"

Bill had been given the ultimatum by Justina the previous night, and he had agreed to let Justina set the financial terms and conditions, and give her the last word, as far as actually going ahead or walking away.

Dan didn't bat an eyelash, "I can't go that high; I've only been authorized to go up to a hundred and fifty million, by the president of the company himself; you sign the contracts right now, and I'll have the money in escrow for you by the end of the week."

Justina realized that as one of a hundred couples, she probably wasn't going to get any more than this out of the company, and it wasn't enough to support the family for the rest of their lives if something went terribly wrong; but weighing the probabilities, she realized that if it was well-invested, they could quite possibly turn the money into two billion or more in the next 500 years, and that was an amazing amount of money to contemplate having. She nodded her approval.

Little did Bill and Justina know, that a copy of their signed contract would be emailed to every company office in the country, as the first acceptance of these sought-after arrangements; setting a precedent which 99 other couples would follow suit on, for the $122 million dollar flat fee offer.

As soon as Justina nodded in agreement however, Posthauer leaned over to the intercom and pressed the talk button, "Carolyn?—One hundred and fifty million; and bring the contracts in right away, as soon as they are printed." Everything else was completed. She was just waiting for the amount to plug in, before printing.

The contracts they were presented with were twenty-seven pages of legalize, but Bill and Justina had hired a lawyer to sit in with them on this final meeting. The lawyer spent another hour with them, explaining the contract provisions, and letting them know what they were signing.

The basic terms were that Bill and Justina were to come in to the office for interviews and progress reports on Monday and Thursday evenings from 6:30 to 8:30 pm; and they had to agree to get on an airplane every first Saturday of the month (Friday nights when traveling overseas), upon which they would travel to a designated city, attend a briefing, and be the featured speakers at a Saturday afternoon seminar from 3pm to 5pm, returning home on a flight scheduled to arrive in Boston no later than 10pm on Sunday night.

Psychic connections between the family and the two androids, as specified, were to be maintained continuously over the course of the ten-year period, unless they filed a notarized program cancellation form, signed by both Bill and Justina, in which case US Android service techs would come out to the house and disconnect everybody, and bring in the two androids. If this option was elected, the escrow account would be closed, and Bill and Justina would instead receive payment of five million for the first complete week of continuous family connection to the androids, and ten thousand per week, for every week in addition to the first week of connection after that. That meant that if they elected to cancel out before the end of the ten-year term, the most they could earn was about ten million, as opposed to a hundred and fifty million, if they remained connected, and fulfilled the requirements of the agreement.

Bill and Justina would even earn interest on the amount placed in escrow, which at current rates could grow to become upwards of two hundred and forty million by the time they received the lump sum payment at the end of the ten-year term.

Justina had talked herself into it, but all she could think of on the ride home, in shocking silence, was the devastating risk that if things went horribly wrong, the twins could be screwed up for life; and if they didn't stay connected for at least a week, they might not even get any money for this! It was a hellatious gamble, but both she and Bill had spent weeks of hard effort, with as much objectivity as they could muster, before coming to the conclusion that the probabilities seemed to be in their favor.

Bill finally broke the silence, "Sweetie, I know you're nervous; I'm a bit nervous too, but I think we quite possibly just made the best decision of our lives."

"I sure hope so," Justina said with a sigh.

There wasn't much to worry about after all; that's what Bill and Justina were both thinking after the end of the first week of being connected, as a family, to Adam and Shayna.—At least, that's what they said to each other, sitting on the deck the following Friday night.

Justina had just checked, and Alyssa and Tommy were both in bed asleep. So were Adam and Shayna; or at least they were inactive;

an android doesn't sleep, of course. Bill and Justina had moved the computer and Skype terminal into the mostly unused dining room, freeing up their home office off the main hallway to be converted into a bedroom for Adam and Shayna.

All week, they had put the two androids to bed in their new bedroom, when Tommy and Alyssa had gone to bed around 8pm, in their own bedrooms down the hall. With no one around them, Adam and Shayna went inactive for the night every night that week. Bill and Justina had decided this was the safest way to start out.

They had only had sex, with the androids' assistance, once that week. Neither Tommy nor Alyssa, who were playing with friends out of the house at the time, showed any signs of in any way being aware of the encounter. Bill and Justina had both made subtle inquiries to Tommy and Alyssa, separately during the hours that followed.

So, the "Chines walls" were working apparently quite well. Tommy and Justina were being served well by Adam, and Alyssa and Bill were being served well by Shayna.

Bill was always the boss of Shayna, with Alyssa's demands being subordinate to Bill's at any moment; and in the same fashion, Justina was always the boss of Adam, with Tommy's demands remaining subordinate to Justina's.

Things seemed under control, and were working out well so far. Justina and Bill embraced, standing at the railing, on the deck. Justina sighed, "I'm glad things are working out well so far . . ."

"Yeah," Bill responded, "—And we've already made at least five million, as of four o'clock!" They both smiled in satisfaction.

CHAPTER SIX

WHAT MAKES HUMAN RELATIONSHIPS such a potentially beautiful thing, it seems, is when two people who have befriended one another, having developed a similar point of view on many subjects, they can help each other, because, for example, maybe one of them has a great undeveloped capacity, and the other has a smaller capacity which they have perhaps learned how to develop pretty fully. Working together, they can teach each other, and nurture any undeveloped potential in either one of them.

Bill and Justina were a prime example of this complimentary type of relationship. Bill had a pretty good understanding of the psychology behind human emotional development, and he knew that optimized development along these lines gives you a strong will, and a heightened sense of energy, greatly augmenting your ability to utilize all of your potential; and Justina was exceedingly bright, but until she met Bill, she had overwhelming emotional issues blocking the development of some of her intellectual potential. Justina had been helped significantly over the course of their time together, which had helped her achieve getting her doctorate, and present herself in a formidable way which landed her such a great job. Bill had also helped Justina to negotiate some of the day-to-day problems that arose with students, other teachers, and the principal over the years; taking her from an overly emotional response, to giving her the ability to work things out more rationally.

Many of us might believe that two lovers who are grounded in conventional understanding, and who also share many of the same beliefs, are the epitome of social development; yet it's pretty clear to others of us that what people conventionally believe and understand is in some cases just plain untrue. As this story contends, we can only improve ourselves by abandoning this falseness, and embracing the ever-elusive truth.

One critical example of this might be concerning religion. The further we look back into the past, in recorded history, the more widely and strongly people embraced a conception that we are watched over and guided by one or more external Gods; or some of us did not have this conception, but perhaps we feared that if it were true, and we didn't heed the messages supposedly sent to us by God or Gods, as delivered by self-proclaimed prophets, or ministers, or in holy books, we may suffer wrath and punishment.

Perhaps in an effort to disguise this threat, one of the main religious messages created for us is that if we do listen to and heed the messages of the prophets, ministers and holy books, we will be granted eternal life; or life beyond death. I suppose this constitutes a carrot instead of a threat.

—But Gods or no Gods, religious messages spoken and written by man over the ages have greatly helped us to gain individual and collective understanding of the most healthy, constructive and developmental ideas and concepts we might embrace for our own good.

The only truth we can all be certain of, with regard to religious faith, is that there is either an external God or gods, or there isn't; and only one of these can be true; and in an absolute sense, it is literally impossible to know with complete certainty which is true. We can only feel more or less certain. Yet quite obviously, each of us truly believes one way or the other. Perhaps some of us may change our mind about this over the course of a lifetime.

As it relates to our story, way back in the twenty-first century, when worldwide popular consensus began to be used for the creation of laws we all are to live by, it became clear, as a voted on issue, that the majority of us believed it was those who were absolutely convinced that at least one external God existed, these seemed to be the ones who were causing trouble and mass destruction and death; particularly premature death by murder in wars.

Different countries and terrorist groups which were run based on the perceived certainty of their leaders' religious beliefs, were in conflict with the beliefs and perceptions of most of the rest of us; and of course, conflict ensued because these religious leaders wanted world order in accordance with their particular beliefs and understanding.

There seemed to be no way to contain these people's destructive behavior as they walked among us, and that's when necessity became the mother of invention once again, and the first man-made planet was created, to exile these people to.

People who openly declared their absolute faith in the existence of at least one God who presided over us, were arrested and exiled to planet R, which stood for religion, in an effort to protect mankind from self-annihilation.

The result was that people all over the world saw that the power of law and government for the people by the people, through consensus voting, was so great, that no smaller collective group of people have ever risen up to challenge it in any significant way ever since; and the world has been without war for over eight hundred years because of this development.

Curiously, there had turned out to be a very small percentage of us who actually had real conviction about having any sense of a presence in our world beyond ourselves and others, so the number of people who were exiled in this manner was very small, as was the first man-made planet.

At the time this was happening, a committee of worldwide representatives was convened to extract all of the worldly words of wisdom from the various Bibles and other religious books, compiling it into a new publication called "The Good Book."

The book was put together by an elected worldwide committee of prominent business-women, doctors, scientists and ministers, overseen by another large committee of psychologists. The goal was to consolidate knowledge about our infinitely wiser subconscious minds, which we were advised to develop increasing conscious contact with, through means collectively voted as the most useful concepts and ideas that an individual could embrace, for healthy development.

Ministers who, by law, could no longer preach the absolute existence of God, then talked about the possibility that God exists, but in any event, how we could use the concept of God to view our subconscious thinking processes, and the information and memories we store there, of which we can only be consciously aware of a fraction of this knowledge at any time. It has been suggested that the collective wisdom of all of our subconscious minds is possibly as powerful as a God.

Among other messages, The Good Book suggests that the most healthy and developmental use we can make of our conscious awareness is to seek to get in touch with the most important aspects of our inner intelligence, and communicate it to each other when appropriate in our daily lives.

Of course, without the overbearing insistence of the existence of an external God, our pervasive emphasis on the fear of God and the Devil, and self-denial for future gain, has somewhat dissipated within the fiber of society, and our sense of morality is evolving to become more internally based.

Yet, our societal conception of an external God has been strongly held throughout eternity, and there is still a significant percentage of us who either have some sense of the existence of an external God, or fear that there may be one, and are therefore holding on to the ideas and teachings of the Bible or other religious literature, to guide their thoughts and behavior by.

Regardless of these internalized beliefs, a person maintains an outward appearance, or a veneer he or she presents to the world around them, and then of course in addition, there is the background of their nature and experiences which have basically formed much of who they are inside.

Current 31st century laws concerning the connection of brain retrofit systems between any two people, protect individuals from having to reveal themselves to each other in detail, allowing us to keep certain secrets if we wish, as we strategically think it is in our best interest. Some people use this license more than others. Before we go further with our story, let's view Bill and Justina in this respect, especially in light of evolving changes in religious trends.

As far back as Bill could remember, he never really had much of a sense of the possibility that an external God exists, except at occasional times when things just seemed too unlikely to be coincidental, but that was once in a blue moon, and certainly never before he had heard several people contend the existence of a God. Even as a very young and impressionable child, he had never really bought the concept some people were trying to feed him.

He did, however, get the message loud and clear that there are authorities in people's lives, and you effectively had to at least act as though you agree with their judgments, and accept and conform with their wishes, and their imposed limitations on the spectrum of possible behaviors you might allow yourself.

—But in spite of this, he also believed he owed it to himself to try and experience as much positive excitement and joy as he had opportunities to pursue, provided it didn't appear to him that he was causing any significant harm to others in the process. It was never Bill's nature to step on anyone's toes to get what he wanted.

With this outlook in mind, Bill behaved pretty acceptably and agreeably with others and his parents, who were his main authorities, except where it came to sexual sharing.

For example, Bill realized very early on that it was exciting and intriguing to see his sister naked, and she seemed to enjoy a level of excitement from having sex-play with him as well. Consequently, they had a good deal of sex-play whenever they could secretly get away with it, at times, in their early years of growing up together.

After a few years of this, Bill sort of graduated to having regular sex-play with another girl around the same age instead. When his sexual appetite in this respect was being satisfied by her, more or less, he hardly ever had sex-play again with his sister.

Later, he also enjoyed sex-play with a few of his relatives too, and he never felt immoral, or that he was doing anything significantly wrong. He certainly wasn't doing anything that wasn't a hundred percent consensual.

He was even coerced fairly regularly during his early teenage years, into sexually pleasuring a couple of friends when he really didn't want to, whom he didn't feel any sexual excitement or attraction to. He did it because they were insistent, and ultimately he didn't mind pleasing a friend in this way; it didn't cost him much, emotionally speaking or otherwise, in his estimation.—Well at a few points, the unwanted insistence was more than a nuisance, though. Still, it didn't give him any sense that he was being significantly damaged, emotionally or sexually. It was just a part of his life at the moment, which he had to get used to. There was never any doubt in his mind that if anybody's sexual advances or demands on him were uncomfortable enough, or particularly unpleasant, he could stop this kind of activity from happening.

When Bill met Justina, he got his first taste of her feelings of jealousy and possessiveness; and he realized that if he wanted a long-term relationship, he would at least have to feign exclusivity.

Later, while freely moving about the city during graduate school, he discovered places he could see a woman naked, and feel her up; although the guys always kept their clothes on, and this activity only lasted a few minutes at a time with each girl you paid a few bucks to see.

Then, the authorities clamped down and closed all of these places, and this activity wasn't available any more for Bill. These experiences were the only part of Bill's sex life that he didn't disclose to Justina. She was otherwise aware of the full scope of Bill's sexual experiences and development.

Since then, the only sexual experience Bill had outside of his marriage with Justina was that he fell prey to a one-night stand with a friend's girlfriend. Somehow, Justina had sensed something, and Bill had confessed, pretty much immediately afterward. She got extremely upset with Bill, and she wouldn't even talk to him for several days. It had almost ruined their relationship, which, of course, was very special and important to Bill; so he pledged to Justina, and resolved in his own mind, that he would stay faithful indefinitely, to the extent he could muster the self-control.—And the more he thought about it, the more he believed he could probably stay pretty well satisfied with one good sexual partner.

As far as Justina's inner beliefs and sexual orientation, she could afford to tell Bill everything, and keep no secrets, because there was nothing in her past which would drive Bill away.

Bill knew that she believed in God, pretty much without question, although she didn't necessarily believe everything printed in the Bible. She had her own independent sense of what God thought was okay for her to think and do, which in many ways matched Bill's inner sense of morality, explaining some of why they got along so well.

When Justina was a young girl, an older boy in the neighborhood used to meet her at a tree-house nearby, and he would give her candy to look at her and play with her sexually. Later, she had a couple of boyfriends before she met Bill, but Bill took her to a whole new dimension sexually, which was astoundingly pleasurable for her;

Bill was much more experienced with pleasuring women, than her earlier boyfriends were.

Justina was still a virgin when she married Bill, but one night, a few months after their marriage, she ran into her first boyfriend at a teacher's conference in Boston, and Justina invited him up to her hotel room for a drink. It was just a stray wild night, but they had been close once, and he was horny for her, and she was no longer a virgin, so she consented to having sex.

She told Bill about it the next day in tears, and he had forgiven her, knowing how she could get when she drank, sometimes. They had decided they weren't going to have children right away, and the tiny gold valves Bill had had installed in his vas deferens were turned off; so when Justina started having morning sickness, and tested positive for pregnancy a couple of months later, they both knew it wasn't Bill's child.

To be supportive, Bill told Justina that he didn't care if he ever had kids of his own at that point, and he would just be happy to raise whom they later discovered were her twins, with Justina; who had really wanted babies in the worst way, she had admitted to him. Thus, Tommy and Alyssa had been born almost five years ago.

Of course, this had been the reason why Bill had so easily agreed to let Justina negotiate the terms of any agreement they might sign to participate in the prototype family-android program.

Along with the issues of E-Tox and Justina's drinking, Bill had purposely avoided disclosing to US Android that the twins weren't his children. He didn't want anything to get in the way of his chances to become a billionaire in ten years, certainly; but he also believed in his company, which had been around for several centuries, on the cutting edge of android technology; and as part of the marketing team, he had studied much about the aspects of development built into this new generation of androids being released. Then too, in the previous weeks, Bill and Justina had learned of the purported safety and tremendous potential as a catalyst to effective child-rearing and education, inherent in connecting to the new family-android line.

To Bill and Justina's relief, their lawyer had explained to them that there were no conditions to the contract they were signing, besides continuous connection and minimum requirements, in terms of the time commitments and the scope of their participation over the ten year period, in order to receive full payment.

Their lawyer advised them that although Bill could technically lose his job for his E-Tox use, at worst; unless they couldn't keep up with their payments on the androids, or failed to fulfill their minimum requirements, which were basically showing up a few times a week and making minimal efforts, there was nothing the company could do to cancel the contract, or withhold final payment at the end of the ten years.

US Android's legal department had, of course advised management that they might want to include some conditions, but after some consideration they elected not to, as they were looking for guinea pigs of any type that were a couple charged with the responsibility of raising the children they were connecting the androids to with them; so ultimately, this was the only item of preliminary investigation.

The more important aspect of the company's selection qualifications for the couples to be involved was a more subjective evaluation of what they thought a particular marketing employee's capability was to sell the new product at seminars, assuming the androids were working out reasonably well for them.

Chapter Seven

It was the following Tuesday night after the androids had been connected to the family. It was a little after 6:30, and Bill and Justina sat across the table from Barry and Kathleen in the conference room at US Android's Boston office. They chatted comfortably, as Barry, Kathleen and Bill worked together daily. The two couples had also been out to dinner together several times in the past year, so they knew each other pretty well socially as well.

Jim Nakamine walked in and took his place at the head of the table. He turned to Justina, who was sitting closest to him, and extended his hand, "Justina, hi, I'm Jim Nakamine; I think we've met at the company annual parties . . ."

Justina shook his hand and nodded, "Of course, how are you Jim?"

"I'm doing well, thank you. I wanted to welcome you to our little group; I suppose Bill has told you that I'm head of the marketing group which Bill and Kathleen and Barry are a part of. We are the marketing arm for the Massachusetts division of US Android. Our group is in charge of marketing this new line of family-androids, and I'll be the one working with the four of you on the required reporting, interviewing and speaking engagements which you have agreed to, as part of your contract with us. There will be other staff members involved, but I will be working directly with you and coordinating the effort."

Justina looked into his sincere eyes as he spoke. He was a young, handsome Japanese man with jet black hair, nicely styled. He seemed mild-mannered and thoughtful, behind his pleasant, professional manner.

Jim then turned to the rest of the group and got right down to business, "I wanted to share with you some ideas we've been discussing amongst the senior staff members, and get your feedback; we all have to work together on this; it's important to me that we are all heard, and that we're all as comfortable as possible with each other as we work together."

He paused while everybody gave an approving smile, and then he continued, "Of course, our most important considerations center around how each member of your family is doing, as far as their interactions, and the effects of your contact, individually and collectively, with your android pair. Our staff psychologists and scientist-doctors will be working closely with you on these issues. In fact, Karen Anderson, our head psychologist, and Paulina Mann, the scientist doctor that is the head of the design team, will both be joining us shortly; but first, I wanted to tell you about what the senior marketing staff came up with at today's meeting. This is just an idea; let me know what you think."

Jim looked at them excitedly, but with some anxiety as he spoke, after a short pause, "We've had several good people working on this, and this is kind of a conglomeration of all of their thoughts and ideas."

He turned his gaze to Bill and continued, "Bill, as I'm sure you know, Barry and Kathleen have agreed to be publicly known as participants in the project. Their children attend a private school, so we figure they won't be bothered as much by the other students and the press, in that private setting; especially since we have the school's cooperation; but you and Justina and your children could remain as anonymous participants. This is the main idea we discussed today. You see, we'd like to do a seminar marketing program right here in Boston during the business day. At the same time, we want to accomplish a few other objectives. First, since we will be marketing to businesswomen and men, we wanted to show people that your android can even be an effective worker alongside of you at the workplace, in that they are so realistically human, as well as sophisticated, and reliable. Of course, you have to be in the same room with your android in order for them to do the work; but here is the team's idea: Bill, you could be an audience member at the seminars, while Adam-1 speaks for you on stage. No one would know who's android he was; we would just tell the audience that he was being psychically controlled by someone in the room—What do you think?"

Bill nodded, "Sounds alright to <u>me</u>."

Jim kept going, "But there's more; we want to protect your family, especially your kids, from media attention, and keep them from being singled out in school; because then, in the final analysis, we'll have more realistic test results as well. What we propose is that, so he can't lead the press to you, we keep Adam-1 here in the building for a while. It would mean that he wouldn't be living at home with you, but on the good side, Bill, you could go home early every day, and spend more alone time with Justina while Shayna watches Tommy and Alyssa, for example. What do you think?"

Justina spoke first, "It's alright with me, if it's alright with you, Bill."

"How about the monthly speaking engagements?" Bill asked Jim.

"We'd waive those, while we were doing the weekly seminars."

Barry spoke up, "Boy, I'd take that deal! I'd like to be home when Justin and Andy get home from school, and to have more time alone with Kathleen!"

Kathleen added, "I wish we could be "incognito" too, but it will also be cool to be a local celebrity; and we're being paid more to be highly visible participants; so we make out pretty well too."

Justina turned to Jim, "Does this mean that Kathleen and Barry will be doing the traveling seminars on the first weekend of the month by themselves?"

"For a while," Jim responded, "If everyone's okay with this arrangement."

Just then, there was a knock on the conference room door, and an attractive middle-aged woman stuck her head in the room, "Jim, are we too early?"

"Oh, no Karen," Jim waved her in, "Your timing is perfect; come in, both of you."

The two women entered and joined the five of them at the table, "Justina," Jim introduced, "This is Doctor Karen Anderson, our head psychologist, and Paulina Mann, the head scientist-doctor on the design team."

Justina nodded at both of them, "It's very nice to meet you."

The balance of the two-hour session was spent talking about the family dynamics of being psychically connected to their android pairs. Unlike Bill and Justina, Barry and Kathleen slept with their androids, Holly-1 and Mark-1, every night, but many of Barry and Kathleen's experiences were similar otherwise.

The meeting ended promptly at 8:30, and Bill and Justina had made the drive home, and were heading down their street about a half-an-hour later. A familiar car passed them a block before they pulled into the driveway, "That was Chuck!" Justina said with a note of disgust, "He probably just brought the twins back; I've told him so many times that he has to get them back by eight o'clock; he knows that's their bedtime, and they have to get up for school in the morning; he's such a jerk!"

Bill shook his head silently in response. Tommy and Alyssa's real father didn't seem all that bad to him, but Justina had some serious resentments against Chuck.

"I'm so sorry I ever told him the twins were his," Justina lamented, "Although I do have to admit, we did make two beautiful children together. Alyssa and Tommy are <u>so</u> precious!"

"Yes, they sure are," Bill agreed, "They're both wonderful children."

"He couldn't just see them when it was convenient for us, help out with the expense of their brain retrofit systems, and offer a reasonable amount of child support; he had to fight for joint custody. Lucky for us that his stupid money is so important to him that we got him to back off on the joint custody issue, and we got him down to two short visits a week in exchange for cutting the child support payments to a quarter of what the court would have probably mandated otherwise."

"Yeah, he may be a bit of a jerk," Bill added, "But at least he agreed to switch to taking the twins on Monday and Thursday nights, while we are at our meetings."

Justina chuckled, "Yeah, if he knew Tommy and Alyssa were hooked up to androids, he'd have a fit!"

"Not to worry," Bill mused, "They can't tell him what they don't even know themselves!"

"Knowing him," Justina pointed up, "When he eventually finds out, he'll try to sue us for half the money we get out of US Android."

Bill nodded, "Yeah, I suppose we'll have to tell the twins eventually, but if everything works as well as it's supposed to, it'll mainly be to explain how they are doing so much better than their friends; and we can explain to them at that point, that if they tell him, as the father of our minor children, he might be able to take us back to court, to force our disconnection, in which case we'd lose our $200 million—wow! We were so busy thinking about everything else, we completely missed thinking about that possibility!"

"Believe me," Justina said with confidence, "If he doesn't think it's hurting the twins, he'd much rather us stay connected for the ten years, and instead vie for a cut of the action."

"Yeah, I suppose you're right," Bill realized, "If anything went wrong, we'd want to disconnect anyway; Tommy and Alyssa are more important than even a fortune, to us too, of course."

Feeling a little more relieved, having talked through their realizations about their vulnerability to Chuck, Bill and Justina entered the house to find Tommy, Alyssa and Shayna in the living room. It was the twins' second day back at school that day.

The twins had been telling Shayna about the movie they had just seen with their father. Although she had engaged in friendly conversation with them briefly, Shayna also knew it was late, so she was just announcing to them, "Okay you two, it's time to get ready for bed . . . Oh look! It's your Mom and Bill!"

"Hi Mommy!" Alyssa ran up and gave Justina a big hug.

"Hey guys," Justina answered unexcitedly because she was still upset that Chuck had brought them home so late, "Okay now, go get ready for bed like Shayna told you; I'll come and kiss you good night once you're in bed."

Bill went to the kitchen and opened a bottle of wine, and poured two glasses. Justina followed, and she threw her arms around Bill and kissed him before picking up her wine glass and taking the first sip.

Later that night, while Bill and Justina were lying in bed watching TV, winding down to go to sleep, Alyssa appeared in the doorway of their bedroom, "Mommy? Can I sleep with you tonight?" she asked sweetly.

Justina hesitated for a moment, then responded, "Okay sweetheart."

Alyssa walked around the king size bed, and crawled in, cuddling with Bill, as she had many nights in the past couple of years. She fell asleep shortly, and not too long after, Bill and Justina turned off the lamps on the night tables on either side of the bed, and clicked off the TV, and fell asleep too.

Later in the night, Bill awoke as always, and carried Alyssa, mostly asleep, back to her bed, laid her down and covered her with her blanket, kissed her on the forehead, and made his way back to bed.

As it was Bill's habit, he stopped in the kitchen to pour himself a glass of milk first, which settled his stomach and helped him fall back asleep.

The next morning, Bill brought Adam to work with him, where he would be left in the lab, inactive for the night whenever Bill went home for the day. Every Monday, Wednesday and Friday, some of the marketing staff, along with Bill and Adam, would put on a luncheon seminar from twelve to two, in the ballroom at the Hyatt downtown, sometimes for different corporate clients, and sometimes just for the general public. As planned, Bill would sit with other marketing staff at the US Android table, a round table sitting eight, like all of the other tables in the room. No one knew it was his mind that was running Adam.

The family-android prototype experiment would remain a secret to the public, but any of these people at the seminars could order a pair of "his and hers" androids, or even just a single android of the new line. Again, it was their risk as to whether they wanted to take a chance on the unproven new line of androids being released by US Android.

Little did the crowd know that Adam-1 was really a "family-android" whose owners were going to receive a couple hundred million dollars just for trying him out!

After each seminar, the staff and Adam would travel together in a van, back to the US Android building, and Bill would usually head home by 3pm, after leaving Adam in the lab for the night. No one would be the wiser.

Chapter Eight

It was the night after Thanksgiving weekend. Leaving Shayna at home, the family had traveled to Stamford, Connecticut, to Justina's parents' house for Thanksgiving. Justina's two sisters were there with their families, along with their grandfathers and their wives, and her great grandfather on her mother's side, who had just turned 120.

Bill's sister, Amy, had also arrived with her partner Tessa, whom she had recently married. They had been living together for a few years, but they really wanted to adopt a child since they obviously couldn't have one together, so they got married and began their search, just months earlier.

The house was of ample size, having six bedrooms, and a large dining room that would seat twenty people, around a large dining room table. Houses had to be large to accommodate extended family, as people lived to nearly five hundred years of age in many cases.

Bill and Justina and the twins had gotten home fairly late on Sunday night, after the final dinner party of the weekend. They had carried Tommy and Alyssa, both fast asleep, to their beds.

They retired to the deck, even though it was a bit cold that night, and they had to keep their jackets on. Justina was reflecting on the weekend as they clanked their wine glasses in a toast to being alone together, "I wonder what it would be like to be gay . . ." she mused.

Bill smiled as he picked up her vibes, "I don't know, do you think you would be open about it?—Or would you probably try to make it look like you were heterosexual, and have a discreet relationship outside of your marriage or something?" he inquired, trying to get a better sense of what bothered her about gayness.

"That's a good question," Justina replied as she nodded her head up and down a few times, "It doesn't seem awkward for Amy and Tess to be among us at our family gatherings, but they just don't seem to realize that many of us wouldn't have gay relations, probably mostly because we wouldn't want to be looked down upon by the vast majority of people around us who aren't gay."

"That may be true," Bill countered, "But I've experienced gay sex, not by choice, mind you; my cousin more or less forced it on me.—But even though I consider myself quite heterosexual, I actually came to enjoy the experience of pleasuring someone of my own sex, and I came to realize that a healthy human being just naturally enjoys sexual experiences with probably a variety of others of either the same or opposite sex, in different circumstances. I think many of us just choose to limit ourselves to one gender or another. Of course, our life experiences and the amount of pleasure we got from our earlier sexual contact would influence that greatly, it would seem."

Justina washed her hands of the idea. She grimaced, and ended conversation on the topic, "I don't know; I don't understand it, being openly gay; but speaking of sex, are you in the mood?" she asked with a smile.

It had been "Back to the routine" the next day, and Bill and Justina were fairly tired by the time they got home from work. Still, they went to the park together, leaving Shayna to look after the twins while they enjoyed the late afternoon sun.

Shayna made dinner for the family when Bill and Justina returned from the park, after which they all watched TV together in the living room until it was the twins' bedtime.

A little later, Bill and Justina were in their bedroom winding down and getting ready for bed themselves when Alyssa strode in and asked once again if she could crawl into bed with them.

"No, Alyssa," Justina replied unexpectedly, "You go and sleep in your own bed tonight. I don't want you to come in here and sleep with us anymore; you're getting too old for that." Alyssa froze for a second, "Go on," Justina continued, "Bill will tuck you in, in a few minutes."

Alyssa frowned a bit, but obediently left. Justina turned to Bill, "Would you mind putting her to bed? I'm tired."

"Sure." Bill climbed out of bed and followed Alyssa down the hall to her bedroom. She hopped into bed, and Bill climbed in beside her, and they snuggled like they always did, for a few minutes; after which he kissed her on the forehead and made his way back to bed next to Justina.

As bill climbed back into bed, Justina followed up on the subject, "It was fine for a while, but I just don't think it's healthy for her to sleep with us every night, at this stage of her life. I think she's old enough now that she should sleep in her own bed."

Bill was kind of going to miss her warm, snuggly little body lying next to him, but he, like Alyssa, accepted and agreed casually with Justina's motherly judgment, nodding and responding, "Uh-huh."

Later that night, when Bill awoke, as he customarily did at least a few times almost every night, he suddenly remembered he had Shayna now to snuggle with. Justina had always told him, starting years before, that she wanted to be left alone while she slept, and she always slept three feet away, on the other side of the bed these days; so Bill made his way down the hall to Shayna's bed. It was a single bed, but she became active when he entered the room, and moved over to make room for Bill as he climbed in beside her.

He laid with her, feeling her warm, wonderful sexy body pressed up against him for an hour or so, before he got up and went back to bed in the master bedroom. Justina continued to sleep through the night, as she always did, except to get up briefly to go to the bathroom sometimes.

This was the beginning of a routine that would continue for the next several years. Sometimes, Bill would be horny and have sex with Shayna.

Seminars with the anonymously owned Adam-1 generated much interest, and led to a small stream of steady sales of androids to those who were adventurous enough to make themselves guinea pigs to their own experiments with the new generation of androids.

However, there was a general nationwide caution against the potentially disastrous consequences, or at least the possible troublesome side effects associated with becoming connected to one of the new type of androids, and most states banned ownership or connection to this new generation of androids before the end of the federally-recommended test period of five years. At that point a formal review was to be conducted by a government committee, with the results published via the Internet, to the public.

During the five-year test period, Massachusetts, California and Nevada turned out to be the only three states where residents could legally own the new generation of androids.

Because it was a controversial issue, the Massachusetts division of US Android decided to send Barry and Kathleen overseas only, to conduct seminars in countries where there were no restrictions on ownership of "his and hers" androids in place. So, one weekend a month, Barry and Kathleen got to see the world together.

Five years went by, and there were very few problems reported by the participants in the family-android test program; so US Android started advertising the new line of "family-androids" now available to the public.

When the issue was put out to vote, the public consensus aired on the conservative side, and again, only Massachusetts, California and Nevada citizens voted to allow people to legally own them.

The rest of the states went with the government committee's recommendation that they be tested for another five years, just to make sure all the bugs were ironed out before they could be endorsed by the committee, and made widely available to the general public.

Still, there were a fair number of people who were pretty comfortable that there was little risk at this point, and didn't want to wait another five years. In fact, some families moved to the states where it was legal to own "family-androids" and probably a lot of those couples were mainly thinking about how their kids might excel in their learning, and otherwise benefit from being connected to family-androids with them.

Bill and Justina's family was to remain anonymous during the balance of the ten-year test period, which meant that Adam-1 was to continue to remain inactive in the lab at the US Android building when Bill left for home every afternoon, and on weekends.—But they would put Adam to further good use.

The senior marketing staff continued to come up with further ideas, and one of them was that Bill would run the retail sales operations for the Boston outlet of US Android, with the store located on the street level of the corporate office building; the same building, of course, that Adam was confined to, except on Monday,

Wednesday and Friday afternoons when they would do the seminars in the ballroom at the Hyatt.

The idea was to be able to announce at the end of the ten-year test period, that Bill and the android he controlled, had together successfully run the company's retail sales operations and tutoring studios in Boston, available to the general public.

The next idea of the marketing staff was that since the retail sales operations consisted of an 8 person sales and administrative store staff, and a 30 person private teaching staff, who gave weekly tutoring sessions to several hundred community members connected to the new androids, mostly children actually, the supervision of the overall operations should be split.

It was unanimously voted by the staff committee that the directorship position for the tutoring studios be offered to Justina. After all, not only was she Bill's wife, and hooked up as an active participant in the Family-android prototype test program, but her third grade senior high school biology class had been winners of the state-wide science class competition, receiving the "Class Project Government Grant," the last two years in a row! Justina was obviously very good at teaching and working with children.

The private tutoring offered by the US Android retail arm in Boston catered mostly to children connected to family-androids, whose parents wanted their children to also learn how to make the most effective use of their android servants, to help them excel at educational and emotional development.

Justina would hire and manage, evaluate, and in some cases let go of less effective and less popular tutors employed by the studios. The tutoring lessons, half-hour or hour-long private sessions, conducted one on one with a tutor, the student and their android servant, were taught between the hours of 3pm and 9pm weekdays, and 9 to 5 on Saturdays. Justina's oversight was not a full-time position. In fact, it fit in perfectly for a public school teacher for whom the school day ended at 3pm.

Justina accepted the position in order to support Bill's success, to be with him more, and because she knew she would be a very appropriate and effective coordinator of tutoring operations, which were a valued community service as well.

She came down to the store and worked at her desk in the lesson studio office after school on weekdays, and on Saturdays sometimes.

Bill was appointed director of retail sales operations for the store; but as head of operations, he also had responsibility for payroll and accounting for the tutoring operation, as part of the retail outlet's business activities.

Android sales had been fairly robust for the store historically, but now that the whole country was well aware of the quite newsworthy new android line, which if successful, would quite possibly turn the android sales business on its ear at the end of the five year test period. The new line of androids was so superior that most people would wait for the government okay at the end of the second five-year testing period, and buy a new android then, instead of buying last year's models; so business fell way off, as far as android sales.

Yet, Bill was charged with the responsibility of competently managing the retail sales operation as profitably as possible. This was coupled with the equally important responsibility of managing the continual operation of the tutoring studios, which in turn would help the general public in the local area have more success at making optimal use of the new line of family-androids.

So, even though android sales were down, and therefore profitability, the operation had to sustain itself, including paying operating expenses which would become more difficult to pay for out of gross profits.

At this point it was determined that Bill was to lay off all other store staff, and he and Adam were to single-handedly make all of the store's business decisions, and fulfill all necessary duties including the challenge of maintaining a level of profitability going forward.

This included hiring and managing of apprentices, completing store inventory, the handling of special orders, orders for android repair parts and accessories for stock, payroll for the 40-person combined staff, accounts payable, accounts receivable, book-keeping and tax-related accounting, advertising, vendor relations, repairs, cleaning and store maintenance.

Another aspect of support was the ordering and stocking of educational software to assist tutors with their teaching efforts; and also stocking of android brain hardware and software, as well.

Because of the reduced income related to decreased sales, the store could no longer afford to hire extra staff and outside assistance, like a part-time book-keeper, or a payroll service, etc . . . —Bill and Adam had to do everything themselves instead.

There were several aspects of financial strain on the operation, even so. The store had to stock at least a few other brands of androids, so there would be at least some selection of brand names to pick from, like there was at most other android stores.

Android manufacturers supplying stores however, had minimum order requirements, in order for a store to remain an authorized dealer for each brand, and these companies' outside sales reps were always calling with special promotional offers, specials and quantity discounts on different items. They made it attractive and tempting to try and stretch the store stock spending budget beyond reasonable levels.

The employer-paid portion of Social Security taxes on 40 staff members was onerous. Internet search listings and display ads were expensive, yet if you wanted the same visibility as other android stores in the area, you had to also stretch your advertising budget.

Teachers and customers expected the store to stock a reasonable variety of hardware and software to support tutoring operations.

The store had a network of computer terminals with shared software programs for retail operations and printing of sales receipts, lesson contracts and lesson scheduling, a message log which had to be tended to, credit card charge processing arrangements and internet access facility; and the multiple user software licensing annual fees were also pretty expensive.

That, and the computer equipment wore out early due to heavy use, needing to be replaced almost every other year. This required installation, repair, and system maintenance provided by an outside computer specialist firm, which was also expensive.

Then, the tutoring operation had its own share of overhead expenses. It ran independent advertising campaigns for private lesson sign-ups for two semesters of lessons coinciding with the semesters of the public schools, and a summer session separately. The studios paid rent separately for the teaching studio space. There were other studio maintenance costs, like cleaning and painting of the studios periodically, and worn carpeting replacement, plumbing and electrical repairs; the list of ongoing expenses went on and on.

Consequently, with an inability to pay for all of this out of dwindling store profits, Bill arranged for ever-increasing lines of credit, secured by US Android's equity in their building in downtown Boston, where all of these operations took place.

Bill worked pretty hard, but the operation really required a very popular, extremely socially adept community icon to be at the helm of store operations, in order to create and maintain community visibility, and ultimately to generate enough sales to support business costs, and improve profitability.

Bill knew he didn't fit the bill, but he was at least able to maintain the continued operation of the entity as they had inherited operations, without showing outward signs of the overwhelming financial strain which the business was under. It would be newsworthy, and bad news at that, if US Android's test program wasn't even popular enough to support itself.

Bill and Justina's financial difficulties were exacerbated by a tutoring staff insurrection caused mainly by Justina, during their first year of managing the operation. Bill thought it had something to do with Justina's drinking problem, but she was quite unreserved and uninhibited in dealing with the existing tutoring staff when they first took over. Some of the staff had long-standing positions, and large followings, in terms of being highly recommended and popular, having dozens of loyal students.

A few of these popular teachers "ruled the roost" as it were, and this rubbed Justina the wrong way. She had her own conception of how tutoring operations should run, in every aspect, from prospective tutor qualifications, to determining which week would be vacation for tutors and students each semester, and cancellation and refund policy; and of course, which tutor would be assigned to work with each student, depending on different factors. There were lots of bad vibes between Justina and the teaching staff over these issues.

There were clashes between Justina and the long-standing staff members at times, and some strained things happened, like one time, Justina came into the store one day after school, and a self-important tutor was having a late lunch, sitting in Justina's chair, with her feet on the desk. When she saw Justina come in, she looked up and said,

"I hope you don't think I'm going to get up; I'm comfortable here, and I'm going to finish my lunch!" Imagine saying that to your boss while sitting at his desk!

The clash got worse, until unexpectedly a group of tutors, inspired by a few of the troublemakers, broke off and started their own tutoring studio across town. They took a third of the students with them, and most of the lesson profits, to boot.

Justina proved herself afterward, hiring a new group of teachers in replacement, and slowly regenerated the lost business; but it took years, and her attitude and behavior continued to be a turn-off to several staff members. Her drinking problem was getting worse, but Bill still covered for her in every way he could, and he refrained from confronting her, partly because he didn't want to be confronted about his E-Tox use.

Finally however, the five year test period was about up, and a government agency was reviewing reports generated from interviewing the participants willing to take part in the study, which numbered in the thousands of families nationwide. Lots of families had decided that the risks were worth it, to get involved with family-androids. Each year, more and more families were coming forward with good results, and word had spread pretty quickly, although the majority of families opted to wait until the government study was complete, after the five year test period, to look into getting family-androids.

Tommy and Alyssa were now in the fall of their first year in college, at age ten. John Posthauer was putting pressure on Bill and Justina to tell the twins they were connected to Adam and Shayna, and there was very little standing in the way of this, they thought, other than the fear of Chuck finding out and taking aggressive legal action.

Still, Bill and Justina didn't have much concern about letting the twins know they were connected, because they were developing beautifully in every way, and it was obvious that this was at least partially due to the fact they were connected to family-androids.

Alyssa in particular had really hit the cover off the ball, so to speak. Both she and Tommy had become very popular among their classmates at school, but Alyssa had been elected class president in her junior and senior year in high school. She had also gotten straight A's in the top-level classes, continually throughout her schooling, and she scored extremely high on her college entrance exams.

She had also scored high on several advanced placement tests which she had recently taken, and the result was that she had landed a full science scholarship at Johns Hopkins.

Alyssa had even secured a government grant for research on an aspect of psychic thought conversion into electronic data, by submitting a paper she had written on the subject, along with the application her professor had helped her fill out and submit the previous month.

Tommy hadn't done quite as well in school, having gotten some B's and C's in some of his courses; but he seemed to want to work on his own, without much reliance on Shayna's help. His grades had improved in high school, and he had been accepted at Boston University, where he was also just finishing up his first semester.

Bill and Justina had informed Tommy and Alyssa about their family involvement in the new android test program, as planned, after thanksgiving dinner. Alyssa and Tommy were quite surprised to hear that they were connected psychically to the androids, for they had no sense of this. Then, it dawned on them that their parents had kept this from them for five years! That was really shocking and bewildering.

It was at that point that Bill and Justina had explained the multiple reasons why they felt they couldn't be open with Tommy and Alyssa before then: Worry that the shock of knowing might cause distress which they wouldn't feel otherwise, worry that the other kids at school might alienate themselves from associating normally with them, worry that if the press found out, the family might be subject to negative public scrutiny, worry that if Chuck found out, he'd take legal action to have them disconnected from the androids before any potential bad effects might develop, and finally, worry that they might blow their chances to stick it out for ten years in order to earn over $200 million in cash at the end of the tunnel.

After quite some discussion that night, Alyssa and Tommy were somewhat more calmed, and they began to understand what was still at stake, unless they were fully cooperative, and also very careful of who they might, and might not want to share anything about this with, including their father.

Bill and Justina had strategically picked that moment to tell Tommy and Alyssa, because it was the first time they would all be together since August, when both of them went to live in the dorms, on campus at college.

It had also been arranged that interviews with the twins, for the purposes of the government agency review, were scheduled for that weekend, while Tommy and Alyssa were on holiday. Once informed, the twins went to their interviews on Saturday morning, and, as agreed, they didn't tell Chuck anything about it.

The family all agreed that they would wait to let Chuck in on the family secret until over winter break, which was less than a month away, giving them a reasonable amount of time to figure out how best to break it to him. After all, there were still five years to go, if they wanted to receive the $200 million, and the twins would be his minor children during that entire time. They had to be artful, as Chuck was both conservative and somewhat emotionally volatile. Still, Alyssa and Tommy couldn't fathom keeping it from him.

They each returned to school the following Sunday night, where they talked back and forth on Skype, about the predicament they had found themselves in.

Chapter Nine

WINTER BREAK WAS TO start for Alyssa on Friday, December 18th, and for Tommy it would start on the following Wednesday. The time was upon them to figure out how to tell Chuck about their connection to Shayna and Adam.

Bill and Justina had decided that the safest way to do so was to offer chuck $10 million of the money, in exchange for his continued support, if they stayed connected until the ten years was up.

To be on the safe side, they had their lawyer draw up a legal agreement which offered ten million each, to chuck, Tommy and Alyssa, contingent on their staying connected to Adam and Shayna for the remaining five years of their contract with US Android. They would present the agreement for his signature when they told Chuck.

Bill and Justina had figured that although Chuck would initially be quite shocked and disturbed to discover what had gone on secretly behind his back, he would ultimately be encouraged that the twins were doing well in every visible aspect, especially Alyssa, who was beginning to emerge as a real genius.

That, and the financial carrot, they thought, would probably incline Chuck to support their continuance with the family-android test project.

It was Thursday night, December 17th around 7pm, and Alyssa had decided to Skype Tommy from her computer terminal in her dorm room one last time before leaving for winter break.

When she reached him, and he had shooed his roommate out of the dorm room, she brought up the issue, "You know, I go home tomorrow for the holidays, and I don't know when your school lets out, but you're in Boston anyway, so you're close to home if you want to come home for the weekend . . ."

"I have my last mid-term next Tuesday," Tommy informed her.

"So if you don't come home this weekend, when will you be coming home?—Some time next week, I assume . . ." Alyssa waited for Tommy to respond.

"Yeah, probably Tuesday night; I've got basketball practice this weekend."

"Oh yeah, right," Alyssa remembered, "How are you doing on the team these days; is coach Lane still putting you in more often?"

"I've started, the last two games," Tommy answered with some degree of modesty at first. Then he couldn't resist the temptation to boast, "I scored twelve points in the last game we played."

"That's great! Mom Skyped me, she says she was hoping to have us all including Dad, for dinner on Sunday; I guess I'll have to tell her we have to wait until a week from Sunday, when you'll be home. She'll probably be a bit disappointed; I think she wants to get it over with."

"You mean telling Dad about the family-android project?"

"Duh!" Alyssa gave Tommy a sarcastic grin, "What else would I mean?"

They continued talking for about twenty minutes. Tommy and Alyssa had always been close, and their closeness had continued throughout their schooling. Even in pre-school, they had sat next to each other. One time, they memorized a long song together, and performed it for the class, with the parents watching. Their memorization was very impressive, and it was also a testament to their close kinship. They had many of the same friends throughout grammar school, and junior high.

When they entered high school however, the school system's policy was to split up twins and put them in different classrooms, but this didn't change the fact that they still shared many of the same friends. It did, however, start to give them a sense of independence, which was probably healthy.

Alyssa was always very mature for her age, and as socially adept as she was flexible. Being more developed emotionally, in some ways, than Tommy, she hooked up with a boy her age and had a relationship going with him during her sophomore year, but as often is the case with first relationships, it didn't last. He wasn't on enough of the same level of maturity, and ultimately he didn't conform to her wishes, as far as behaving as she would like.

Since they broke up, Alyssa had been too preoccupied with her schoolwork and her social circle of popular girls, to get into another relationship. Alyssa was always talking about issues like clothing and popular bands and concerts, and various other items of popular gossip; and she was very independently active.

Throughout high school though, Tommy had stayed quite interactive with Alyssa, having many friends and acquaintances in common. He was very supportive and helpful with Alyssa's campaigning for class president, convincing many popular classmates that Alyssa would be the best choice to represent their interests, and to organize the coolest activities, class trips and dances, etc . . .

Tommy was attracted to some girls in his grade, but he liked to hang out with his guy friends, and he was a little more aloof socially, with the opposite sex. He was perfectly happy without getting into any relationships in high school. He was more of a jock, playing soccer and basketball on the varsity teams.

Part of what made Tommy and Alyssa so popular was the fact that Bill supplied them with all the accoutrements; he took Tommy and Alyssa to the mall regularly to buy in-fashion clothes, carted them around to their friends' houses, and paid for their movie downloads and song downloads from I-tunes. He bought them new computers whenever the next upgrade was available, and he set up a ten screen Skype station for them, which was installed in the converted dining room. After all, moving the office to the dining room only took up eight feet on one end of the twenty-two foot room.

Tommy and Alyssa really had fun talking to ten friends at once on Skype, together and separately. It was even more fun when they had friends over, and went on Skype. All in all, they really had a pretty good upbringing in many ways.

Justina maintained good relations with the twins as well, but her drinking problem got worse over time, and she tended to stay home after getting home from US Android for the day. When she and Bill started running the store, she was often too tired at the end of the day, to interact much with the twins at night; which was fine with Alyssa and Tommy. They had homework and busy social lives.

Justina got into the routine of going to bed around 10pm, falling asleep from being somewhat intoxicated usually. She had told Bill, shortly after Adam had moved to US Android, that she missed having their four-way sexual encounters, but she said she was willing to sacrifice that if he was, and they made a pact to only have sex with each other, during the ten year test period, just for safety's sake.

After all, they realized that after they received the $200 million, they would still have upwards of 470 years to have sex together with the androids!

The following week flew by quickly for Bill, and before he knew it, it was Sunday afternoon, and he was greeting Chuck at the door, to join them for dinner, as he had accepted Justina's invitation earlier in the week.

It was the first time Chuck had seen Alyssa since the Sunday after Thanksgiving. He had since seen Tommy at his basketball games a couple of times, but he really hadn't spent much time with Tommy after the games, so this was the first time he had gotten to spend any appreciable time with Tommy and Alyssa.

After exchanging greetings, Justina served everybody drinks in the living room while dinner cooked. "Well Tommy," Chuck said, "I guess I'll see you at least, at your games this winter, when I can get there. Alyssa, I don't suppose I'll get to see you much next semester, though."

Chuck eyed Alyssa more carefully, "That's a nice dress; where did you get it?"

Alyssa smiled modestly, "Bill got it for me at the Gap yesterday. I really like it a lot!"

"It's a nice print," Chuck complimented, "It almost looks like Laura Ashley."

"Yeah, some styles never go out of fashion," Bill added.

Chuck looked around, "Where's Shayna?" he asked.

"She's in her room," Justina answered, "I thought I'd cook for us myself today."

"I smell rosemary," Chuck said with a smile.

"We're having rack of lamb; I got it on sale yesterday."

"Yeah, Mom bought enough to feed an army!" Alyssa added.

Justina blushed slightly, "I love to buy things on sale; what can I say?—At five dollars a pound, I bought them out, and half-way filled the freezer!" She laughed proudly.

"Well, it's good to see you two," Chuck said, looking back and forth at Tommy and Alyssa, "You both look great!"

Bill saw a gleam of pride in Chuck's eyes for his two wonderful children, which reminded him, "Oh yeah, did you hear about Alyssa's grant?"

Chuck nodded as he glanced over at Bill, "I heard about that; Alyssa Skyped me when she first heard the news." He turned to Alyssa, "Congratulations!—Tell me more about it; you said it had to do with psychic conversion?"

Alyssa summarized the events, "Well, my professor said he was working on a theory; the school had built him a research lab. Anyway, I started asking him some questions about it after class one day, and he gave me some of the papers he wrote. All I did was read through them, and make a few comments; but he said I thought of some things that he had never put together, so he asked me to be on his research team!"

"That's great!" Chuck said enthusiastically, "Then you said you wrote a paper yourself?"

"Albert asked me to sum up an explanation of what I had realized from reading his papers, so I explained it step by step in a paper I wrote for his review. The next thing I knew, he was handing me the grant application. He said that the experiment which I had suggested we might try, would probably require some expensive equipment which was beyond his budget for the year, and he used my paper and my name to apply for further funding."

"That's really good! He used your paper to apply?"

Alyssa smiled proudly, "Yes, that, and a short explanation he wrote to go with it, got us the grant!"

"That's really great!—How much is it for?"

"Half-a-million!—Can you believe it?"

Chuck showed genuine surprise at the significant chunk of money at hand, "Wow! When do they fund it?"

Alyssa smiled with excitement, "They've already sent us the purchase order number! We put an order in to Texas Instruments just last week; we should have the new equipment next month!"

Justina had gone back into the kitchen while they were talking. She burst in through the swinging door from the kitchen into the dining room, calling out to the rest of the family in the living room, "Dinner's ready; why don't we sit down . . . Bill, would you open a bottle of wine?—The glasses are on the table."

Justina was very much at home commanding the action, despite her deference to Bill at times. She had always sort of worn the pants of the household. Bill didn't really mind at all, the fact that Justina had strong leadership qualities. He admired and respected this, as he didn't possess much in the way of these qualities himself.

Bill did, however, have a kind of quiet strength, and it was he who uttered the first words about what they had to explain to Chuck, still sitting at the dinner table sipping wine, after finishing the scrumptious dinner Justina had fixed them, "Chuck, there's something we've been planning to tell you, concerning the twins, and also us," he motioned to Justina and himself, "—And it may be a bit of a surprise to you that we've kept from telling you this for such a long time, but we have some strategic reasons why we've kept this a secret from you. We've been involved in a program at US Android for quite some time now. As you know, a new generation of "Family-androids" that US Android had developed was released into the public recently."

Chuck nodded, "Yes, a few people I know actually have them; but isn't there a several year test period before most other states will release them into the general public?"

"Exactly," Bill continued, "Well, this might come as a bit of a shock to you, but they actually developed the new strain of family-androids about five years ago, and our family has been a participant in a prototype testing project."

"But doesn't that take two androids?" Chuck asked, "I thought you just had the one; Shayna."

"Well, almost no one is aware of this, but, we have a second one; you may have heard of him; he's actually famous in downtown Boston; Adam-1."

Chuck looked puzzled, "The one that's been involved at the seminars at the Hyatt?"

"The one and the same," Bill answered, "He's actually controlled by me."

"Bill, this <u>is</u> a surprise," Chuck choked back, getting increasingly worked up, "But what does that have to do with Tommy and Alyssa?"

Bill swallowed hard, "Well, they've actually been connected to Adam and Shayna too. Remember, this is a family-android project . . ."

"They have!? How come nobody talked to me about this!?" Chuck became somewhat indignant, "Justina!? What's going on?"

Bill put up a hand to stop Justina from answering, as he continued the explanation, "Chuck, there were several reasons. The first is that we had to sign what US Android referred to as a gag order, or an agreement to keep it confidential. The second is that in order to avoid being the subject of controversy in the news, and because we were advised not to under the circumstances, we didn't tell the children either . . ."

"You connected them to androids and you didn't tell them!?" Chuck turned to Tommy and Alyssa, "Didn't you realize you were connected?"

Tommy answered for the two of them, "Alyssa and I talked about it, and now that we think back, something did feel a bit different to us when Adam and Shayna were here at the beginning, but we both thought it was just the effects of having androids."

Chuck was thinking back, "I don't remember a male android; how long ago was this?"

"Five years ago, Dad," Tommy answered.

"Well, it's just lucky that nothing really bad happened to you; but this was very dangerous, and irresponsible!"

Bill fielded the comment, "I know what you're thinking, and it <u>was</u> a risk, but Justina and I <u>researched</u> this, and we met many times with the design team, and child psychologists, and we read related studies, and we went into this with our eyes open."

"It was still very experimental, and I'm very upset that I wasn't even consulted!—Are Tommy and Alyssa still connected to these two androids?"

"Well, that's what we wanted to talk to you about Chuck," Bill kept jumping in, in order to take the heat off of Justina, "What we do from here on somewhat involves you, as the twins' father; but under the contract we signed, we get paid a substantial sum if we stay connected for another five years."

Chuck frowned, "Five more years! That's ridiculous!—Just how much are they offering?" Chuck's veneer was beginning to crack.

Justina now smiled as Bill answered, "Enough that we can offer you ten million dollars!—If we can stay connected until then."

Chuck tried to choke back his surprise and delight, "Wow! Ten Million!?—I still say you're very lucky that Tommy and Alyssa don't appear to have been hurt by doing this." He hesitated while he thought for a few seconds, and then he asked somewhat slyly, "What would you want me to do for this money, should I take you up on this offer?"

Justina spoke for the first time, "All we need is for you to support our efforts, and be there for Tommy and Alyssa."

"—And keep quiet about the money they're offering us," Bill added, "We've drawn up an agreement we were hoping you would sign."

Justina took the lead again, "The thing is, we need you to sign it tonight while you're here, in order to ensure your silence, if you are willing to support us; otherwise, we will be violating our gag agreement, and we'll have to drop out of the program. That would mean we couldn't offer you any money."

"Huh—I see!," Chuck said, coming up to speed.

They talked on for almost two hours, answering Chuck's questions and explaining how the parents' connections to the androids were different from the children's.

Chuck kept going on about how he couldn't sign anything his lawyer hadn't seen first. However, after reading through the one page document written in pretty clear, plain English, Chuck was finally persuaded to sign it, considering his alternative.

When he finally left, after talking with Tommy and Alyssa alone together in the living room for a few minutes, Justina hugged Bill as they watched Chuck's tail lights disappear.

"See?" Justina remarked, "I told you he'd go for the money!"

Chapter Ten

THE FOLLOWING MONDAY NIGHT, Bill and Justina entered the conference room on the first floor of the US Android building at 6:30 as usual, only to find John Posthauer sitting at the head of the table. He motioned to them as he spoke, "Bill? Justina? Come on in; have a seat; Barry and Kathleen will be in, in a minute. We were all having dinner at Rudy's across the street. How are things going at the store?"

"Eh; they're going okay," Bill said a little grimly, "Nobody wants to do inventory with me this weekend, and we only have a little over a week until year-end, to do it.—That, and I'm trying to figure out how to squeeze out some year-end bonuses; maybe we'll have more sales next week . . ."

Justina rolled her eyes, "Yeah, that, and some of the tutors have been complaining, because a few of their students aren't showing up. School vacation doesn't start until the end of the week, but some of the parents have already taken their families on holiday, skiing, or visiting family or whatever; and they haven't bothered to call to let us know; so the tutors are sitting in their rooms for hours at a time, waiting for the next student. They're a little bored and frustrated."

"That's too bad, "Posthauer frowned; then he perked up a bit, "It sounds like you two will be happier when the holidays are over!"

Bill nodded, "Yeah, anyway, I'm surprised to see you here with us tonight; what's the occasion?"

"Well, something's come up; I'll wait to tell you about it until we're all here. Jim's rounding up Karen and Paulina—Oh, here they are; ladies, come in."

Jim followed, and Barry and Kathleen came in a few seconds later. Bill wondered why the head scientist-doctor and the head psychologist were called in.

Posthauer began the meeting, "Good; I'm glad you're all here. Last month, Donald Thompson, the head of the family-android evaluation committee, contacted Thomas Perry, the President at our home office in Newport Beach. As you know, the committee began receiving the five year evaluation reports in October, and it wasn't long before a problem was evident. What Mr. Thompson told Mr. Perry was that it became evident during some of last month's interviews with the children, that there were some instances of sexual memories being experienced by the children connected to family-androids involved in the project."

Justina was appalled, "How is that possible?!—They were adamant about assuring us that both parents would receive a distress alarm, and an android would shut down before anything like that could happen!"

"Yes, and the software worked just fine in many cases, but what they discovered is that if the parent controlling the android in question was intoxicated beyond a point, they couldn't sense the alarm. Even this wouldn't be a problem normally, because one android would send a message to the other, who would shut it down; but when the other parent's desire was stronger than their sense of morality and legal concern, it didn't always work."

Justina was following the explanation, "So you're saying, androids were committing what is legally considered sexual assault on the children they were supposed to be serving?"

Posthauer nodded, "In some cases, I'm afraid so . . ."

Jim Nakamine jumped in, "But only in three percent of the reports from the interviews completed so far."

Kathleen interjected, "But that's in addition to the parents with family-androids who were arrested for sexual assault reported by other means, right?"

"Yes." Posthauer answered, "That's correct; there were twenty-seven cases of arrest for sexual assault by family-android owners in the past five years, which were reported by the other parent, or the children themselves, directly to the authorities; but, of course, this is a much lower percentage than the sexual assault arrests in the general public. After all, there are over forty-three-thousand people nationwide who own family-androids we produced," Posthauer defended, "That's much less than one in a thousand!"

Jim finished answering Kathleen's question, "But you're right; that three percent is different. You see, in addition to the interviews "one-on-one" with children, they each filled out an anonymous questionnaire, and this is where they discovered that a few of the children who hadn't reported it otherwise to parents and authorities, disclosed that there had been some sexual bleedthrough memories they were aware of, stemming from sexual activity between the adult owners and one of their family-androids. Remember, this is three out of a hundred . . ."

In many cases, it was when the wife was intoxicated and passed out, and the husband would have sex with his android, and memories of the sexually pleasurable feelings would accidentally end up in the daughter's online memory file; at least this is what the committee is contending. As Justina alluded to earlier, this would send a strong distress alarm to the mother theoretically, so she would become consciously aware that these memories were being perceived by the daughter. Also, in a few cases, it was discovered that subconsciously, the father was directing the android he controlled, to touch the daughter in ways which he might find sexually gratifying; so it was only in cases where the husband's sense of morality, fear of legal consequences, or of emotional and physical damage to the daughter, when none of these could stop his overwhelming sexual desire, this was the only case where something like this could happen. You see, we didn't have a sufficient safeguard for this level of mental illness."

Bill shook his head in disbelief, "Then there's no way they can approve family-androids for the market, is there?"

Posthauer spoke up, "Well, that's what this meeting is about; one, to let you know about this problem a few days before the news articles and reports hit the street, so you can brace yourselves; but the reason we didn't say anything sooner, is because the design team got right on this last month, and I just received word that a new module has been developed, which we have termed a "parental control interface module," which apparently corrects the problem; excuse the pun.—It's supposedly a foolproof way to ensure that this will never happen again, because it will store and inject the other parent's values and inclinations relating to sexual activity between the android and either child, or any child connected to it for that matter, to act as a controller in the case one of the parents isn't able to control his sexual appetite, or is too intoxicated to act responsibly themselves."

Kathleen brought up a question, "Wait; if they knew about this a month ago, why hasn't this been all over the news?"

"Well, we can thank Thomas Perry for that," Posthauer answered, "He convinced Don Thompson, the head of the government evaluation committee, that the new family-androids were such an important advancement to mankind otherwise, and he assured Don that our scientist-doctors were certain they could develop a fix for this; and he got them to keep the information classified until we could announce the remedy along with the problem."

"Wait!" Barry objected, "What about the lawsuits meanwhile?"

"There's going to be so many lawsuits over this," Posthauer answered as he shook his head, "Our legal team will be busy for years!"

Kathleen put her hand to her forehead, and gazed in bewilderment, "So what are we going to do now?"

"Good question Kathleen, " Posthauer said, speaking more encouragingly, "We've been working with the government on this in the last few weeks, and here's what we've worked out: First, we're going to announce a massive recall," Posthauer turned to the head scientist-doctor, "Paulina, do you want to talk about that for us?"

"Yes, thank you John; the parental control interface module plugs into a USB port, which are standard in the computer brains of all of our family-androids. The modification can be completed as easily as we can plug it in; but this new parental control module must be programmed by both parents. Therefore, each parent will have to come in to any of the fifty-two US Android facilities that have a lab, and transfer their values and inclinations as electronically converted data, into the module. This can be achieved through a process discovered by Albert Freudenthal; known foremost for his work on psychic conversion. His discoveries have now made it possible to probe a person's mind for answers to specific questions, and convert the psychic data in response, into electronic data we can load into this module.

Bill looked at Justina, "That's who our daughter Alyssa works with!" he said with some incredulity.

"Yeah!" Justina added, "She probably helped to design this new device!"

"Well if she did," Posthauer interrupted, "it would be classified information. Paulina, do you want to tell us anything more?"

"Yes John, I just wanted to add that in the future, this can be done at the same time you are being fitted for a new android, but for all of the recalls, I'm afraid each owner will have to come in to our labs."

Bill started to do the math, "You said there's forty-three-thousand sets of family-androids out there?—in the three states where it is legal to own family-androids?"

"Yes. I know what you're thinking," Paulina picked up, "But there are only about eleven thousand here in Massachusetts, and we have twenty-two labs statewide, altogether; that's about five hundred android pairs to be repaired per location; although the distribution isn't that even; we'll have over eight hundred families to service here in Boston, for example."

"Sixteen hundred parents and sixteen hundred androids!?" Bill was panicked.

"Well it only takes half an hour per couple to load the modules, and they can be installed in the androids pretty much right away afterwards. If we get a good transfer system going between the lab and the repair staff, we should be able to complete the modifications in about ten weeks."

"I guess that's not so bad," Justina said optimistically, "But what about the test program and the marketing plans?"

"The committee came down hard on us," Posthauer said seriously, "They're extending the evaluation period another five years."

Jim Nakamine now took control of the meeting, as he and Posthauer had planned earlier, "So basically we're going to keep on doing just what we have been doing. We anticipate at least some improvement in sales, because the committee's five year evaluation is showing some very favorable results in most aspects; even though the sexual assault problem will undoubtedly hurt us considerably."

The room was silent for a good twenty seconds as they all processed all that had been disclosed, "Well, we've been doing this for five years," Bill finally said wearily, "I guess we can do it for another five; Justina? What do you think?" Bill turned to Posthauer, "I assume our ten year contract is still good?"

"It is," Posthauer said steadily with confidence.

Barry turned to Kathleen, "I'm in if you're in."

Posthauer looked over at Karen, “You’ve been sitting here pretty quietly through all of this—Is there anything you wanted to add?”

“No John, I just wanted to sit in on the meeting, and note everybody’s reactions. If there was more of a problem, I might have said something, but I think everything went off reasonably well, considering the severity of the situation. One thing I did want to add, was that it also happened between the woman android and the son, in some instances. Jim just used the male android—daughter example for illustration.”

They continued to talk about the feedback US Android had received so far, from the government’s family android evaluation committee, for the balance of the two hour session.

Walking out of the building together afterward, the two couples, Barry and Kathleen, and Bill and Justina, shared their relief and optimism that despite the sexual problem, the government committee’s research seemed to show very encouraging results so far, about the positive effect of families being connected to the new family-android pairs over the past five years.

The next morning, Bill came in to work earlier than usual, as he had woken up early, feeling distressed; and he realized he had to speak to Posthauer right away, about the situation with the store.

When he got to Posthauer’s office an hour later, he greeted Posthauer’s assistant, “Hi Sarah; is he in?”

“You’re in luck,” she answered, “He was scheduled for a presentation from an artificial tissue manufacturer, but the reps from New York Skin and Muscle got delayed in traffic. I just got a call that they’ll be a half-hour late.” She leaned into the intercom speaker, “John? Can you see Bill Symms? He’s here and he wants to speak with you. Just so you’ll know, Sean Douglass from New York Skin just called, and they won’t be here for about forty-five minutes; they got held up in traffic.”

After a slight delay, John responded, “Sure; send him in.”

Bill walked into John’s office with a small stack of paper in his hands, “Hi John; do you have a few minutes?”

“Sure, what do you have there?” John pointed to the papers.

"Here, this is my projection spreadsheet, and this is the general ledger summary report I just printed, showing the sales figures and expenses for the last quarter."

"Okay," John looked harried, "I don't have time to look at them now; can you tell me what they say?"

"Well, the projection shows a budget shortfall of over $300,000 for the next twelve months; and the general ledger report shows that we owe $298,000 on our line of credit now, and we're showing a loss again for the quarter. I need roughly twenty-thousand to make the last payroll of the year next week, and pay the payroll taxes, and we won't take in any more sales revenue to speak of probably, until the first week of January, when we start to receive payments for next year's tutoring sessions."

Posthauer thumbed through the papers quickly, with a concerned look on his face, "How much is your limit on the line of credit?"

"Three hundred thousand." Bill said flatly.

"Well, why do you think you're having so much trouble?"

Bill sighed, "We just don't have the sales to support these expenses."

"Well, couldn't you spend less on goods? Look at the amount of money you spent on androids for stock!"

Bill got defensive, "But John, the store has been a Yamaha dealer for the last fifty plus years, and they tell us we have to buy at least twenty androids with our fall dating order in order to remain an authorized Yamaha dealer; that's almost three hundred thousand right there . . . and we've been carrying that new Chinese line, Eastman; they're really popular these days because they're decent, and cheap; but even they have a fifteen android minimum fall dating order."

"Fall dating," John shook his head, "What's that again?"

"Well, that's an order they work with you to place in January, which gets delivered right away, and you have until the fall to pay for it; you do it in monthly payments, and there's no interest, as long as it's paid off by October."

"I see," John acknowledged, "But didn't you tell me that last year, you only sold thirty US Android models, other than the, what was it, forty-two pairs of family-androids the store sold?"

"That's right; besides the family-android sales, we sold a total of forty-four of the older style androids."

John shook his head, "So besides the thirty older US Android models you sold, you sold fourteen of the thirty-five androids you bought for stock last year?"

"Yes; in fact it's been like that for the last few years, really. We're running out of room in the store room. We have over seventy unsold androids in there," Bill reported glumly.

"Jesus!" John exclaimed, "That's over a million dollars of androids, at cost, isn't it?" After Bill nodded back, John continued, "Can't you sell some of them to other android stores?"

"Yeah, but they only pay pennies on the dollar for older models. We'd have to take a huge loss to sell them off."

"Won't Yamaha or Eastman take them back?" Posthauer asked.

"The thing is, some of those androids are over five years old. They might take back last year's models, but most of them are older."

"Well that's ridiculous!" John retorted, "Those big companies can't smother their dealers with excess inventory like that!"

"I've already talked to them about it; I told Yamaha and Eastman we didn't have any more money in our line of credit, and we can only order a small amount on fall dating this year," Bill informed Posthauer.

"What did they say?" John asked in anticipation.

"They've both cleared the way to cut our orders way back."

"Oh good!" John was pleased that Bill seemed to be managing the situation, at least to some extent.

"I talked to Justina about the payroll shortfall, and she's willing to lend us the money out of her inheritance from her ninth great grandfather, who died last year; but I wanted you to know how challenging things are, running the store under the circumstances. I was hoping to come back to work in the marketing department, and let someone else run the store, once the family-androids were approved by the government committee after the five years, but since that's not going to happen for another five years now, I think I'm going to need some help from you, if I'm going to continue to run the store operations in a way the government committee is going to look favorably upon, as far as mine and Adam's effectiveness, when they do their next evaluation."

"You just keep hanging in there Bill," Posthauer reassured, "I know things have been tough, but sales of family-androids should pick up, after the committee's five year results get published on the Internet next month. I think this sexual problem is fairly small, in comparison to all of the other good results they'll be talking about in that report, when it comes out."

Bill nodded, "I hope so, John; we keep liquidating fifteen to twenty thousand at a time, of Justina's mutual fund holdings, to pay off our personal credit card balances we're running up, because even with Justina's teaching income, we're not making enough income from the store to meet our personal expenses."

"I see . . ." John said with a hurt look on his face, "I'm afraid I'm in a bit of a pickle myself; upper management is putting a lot of pressure on me to avoid subsidizing you. They want our android-assisted sales operation not to look bad on the books. Do you think you could manage on your own resources for a while, until sales hopefully pick up?"

"I don't know; I'll talk to Justina about it; but she's pretty upset that we are going through her inheritance pretty rapidly, which is sort of her security blanket, if you know what I mean—It's difficult when you have kids—I mean we don't have any other guarantees as far as a fall back, in case this project causes us damages . . ."

CHAPTER ELEVEN

MONEY, MONEY, MONEY! IT'S always such an issue. It does however, make the world go 'round. In the old days, it was wars and crooked politics, causing financial collapse of different sorts, which was responsible for huge government deficits, leading to greater burdens on the tax-paying people.

Then, it was smooth sailing for a while, once Internet voting and popular consensus government decision-making caught on worldwide. The uncontrollable troublemakers were banished to Planet R, the religious outpost. However, on the good side, with the banishment of those who believed in the definite existence of God, war ceased to exist on earth.

There were also no more corrupt political decisions to cause financial destruction, now that all political decisions were voted on by the masses. The worldwide government budget became balanced.—But our next financial hurdle was population control, which was dealt with by creating more man-made planets.

Those with an inclination to get away from the melting pot chose to emigrate to one of the different planets which were created. By the beginning of the thirty-first century, there were seven man-made planets, created at a total cost of over $400 trillion. The planets themselves generate some tax revenue to pay for this, but the primary source of tax revenue to pay down this global deficit is from the inhabitants of the earth; who also benefit most by the relief from the hardship of vast overpopulation.

With people living over five hundred years in some cases, there are often over twenty generations of living relatives in any given family. As you can imagine, inheritance problems were prolific. Much of the inheritance passed on by older generations ended up in the pockets of the lawyers representing the inheriting relatives, who would then pay inheritance taxes on the remaining amounts that would trickle down to them.

When the issue came to be voted on in recent years, the public elected that all inheritance go directly to reduce the deficit, in lieu of abolishing personal income taxes, except for Social Security taxes. So, instead of a bunch of tax attorneys getting rich, we were paying down the deficit, so the burden of this won't be passed on to future generations.

Luckily for Justina, her ninth grandfather, or in other words twenty-one generations back, died at the age of 421, shortly before this law was passed, and she and her two sisters inherited over $500,000 each, after inheritance taxes were paid.

Although her mutual fund holdings had earned over $350,000 in investment income over the past ten years of her marriage to Bill, the liquidations to pay the family's credit card balances, and to pay capital gains taxes on the liquidated amounts, coupled with taxes on investment income, paid by further liquidation of these funds, had left Justina with less than $450,000 in current mutual fund holdings. Now she was to liquidate another $40,000 to pay off the family's current credit card balances, and half of that was to be a loan to the store, to meet its year-end expenses.

She was not happy that her inheritance was dwindling under the weight of these ongoing expenses; but she loved Bill, and supported and believed in him, and she knew he was working hard to fulfill all of the responsibilities necessary in order to make the store run smoothly. She also knew it would be more than a feather in their cap, if they could manage operations successfully with Adam-1's help for the duration of the test period. It would be further evidence that family-androids are good for society.

Regarding income taxes, it should also be mentioned that although there is currently no income tax for individuals, investment income and capital gains are still taxed. These proceeds go to pay for government operations and infrastructure; and some of these taxes also get appropriated to pay for government costs on the man-made planets.

The seven man-made planets existing as of the year 3061 were planet CAP (for capitalism), planet COM (for communism), planet REC (for retired individuals only), planet LIB (for libertarian) as well as the much larger Earth-2, which was created in the twenty-fifth century, and Earth-3 which was created in the thirtieth century, and of course, planet P, a prison outpost planet, which was created to exile sex offenders to, segregating them from the rest of us, while they were enrolled in a variety of rehabilitation programs.

It was possible for some of these criminals to prove their rehabilitation, and to re-enter society as a citizen in the general public on planet P, but the consensus vote on all three earth planets was to keep these people segregated for life on the prison outpost planet, as there was no known way of removing their inclinations to become sexually involved with children.

Then too, the manufacturers of child androids were pretty upset that laws were put into place to round up all child androids, sold and unsold, confiscating billions of dollars of them worldwide; and there needed to be a place to remove these androids to, and the owners of these androids needed to be compensated somehow for losing these assets.

It was voted that the world government would buy up all the child androids from their owners for half of the original sale price, for those who could produce receipts; or owners who could not produce receipts would receive a flat fee of $8,000 for turning in their child android to their local android store. This was a vast expense the government paid out in order to round up and remove all child androids from service, but it was voted into law that it was illegal to own a child android on the three earths.

The confiscated child androids were then transported to the prison outpost planet, where a colony of child android manufacturers and those who wished to own a child android could relocate to. However, you could not move to any other planet from that point on, once you moved into this community on the prison outpost planet. As you can imagine, not many people lived there, as a percentage of the overall population of the universe, as of the thirty-first century.

The prison outpost planet was the second man-made planet, and it was pretty small, as was planet religion.

As far as the two other man-made planets which were general extensions of earth, earth-2 consisted of a huge chunk cut and blasted out of Mars, and towed back to near earth, where it was put into gravitational orbit, and it was to stave off overpopulation for upwards of five hundred years; however, it filled up in about half that time, and thus, earth-3 began in the planning stages.

Earth-3 was nearly twice the size of earth-2, and it was cut and blasted out of Saturn. It took over twenty years to tow it back to near earth and start it on its gravitational orbit, but it is still mostly uninhabited. Consequently, the world government is giving out parcels of land to those who choose to relocate. Bill's father relocated to earth-3, and lives in a newer community in a very clement area, with four golf courses nearby, and shopping centers within a few miles of his house.

He now works as a consultant to the local government in his area, to finance municipal projects, such as sports stadiums, dams, schools, bridges, solar energy projects, etc . . .

Having a successful career in investments, the state where Paul and his wife Lauren now lives, pays Paul a consulting fee to put together financing for these projects, as the land develops to accommodate Earth's increasing population overflow.

Chapter Twelve

Bill arrived home at around five on Friday afternoon, to find Justina sitting on the sofa, watching the news, "Hi Bill, you should watch this; it's a report about US Android."

"What is it saying?" Bill asked.

"Well, the news is scandalizing the sexual assault charges in connection with the family-androids in the study, and it's taking a toll on the reports of the otherwise positive results over the five year period."

"Yeah, sales are down this month, with all this bad press; someone should report the percentage of adults in the general public that end up molesting children; I'll bet it's a significantly higher percentage than the instances of bleedthrough sexual memories experienced by children as a result of their connection to family-androids."

"Yeah, well they're also raising some doubt as to whether the new parental control module will ensure that absolutely no sexuality is exchanged between family-androids and the children they are connected to."

"Oh that's great," Bill said sarcastically, "Now they're going to hurt our sales even more."

"A lot of people are being conservative about this issue, but there will be those who aren't as concerned; maybe sales will pick up after this blows over somewhat," Justina placated Bill.

"I had a long talk with John today about the future of the store. He was saying US Android is audited annually; and he doesn't want it on the books that the parent company is subsidizing the store; and he's asking if we will personally lend the store money for the next five years, to keep operations going, if sales don't pick up. He wants the operation to at least appear to support itself."

"I don't know Bill; this is all such a big gamble; first we gamble on how connecting the twins to our family-androids might adversely affect them, and we gamble that we'll be able to stay connected for ten years; and now, John Posthauer is asking us to gamble my inheritance money away too, in order to hold this unprofitable store open for another five years!"

"I know, I know; but just think about how this may quite possibly turn out; we may well end up with well over $200 million! So what if we go through a third of a million making that happen!?"

"Yeah, well no one else has to put up their life savings in order to make this money, they just have to stay connected. We have to stay connected, work our asses off, and probably go through a half-a-million of my inheritance; how is that fair?!"

"Justina, we're still lucky compared with most folks; I mean, who makes two hundred million in ten years?"

"Yeah, that's true, but it just irks me," Justina let on to Bill.

Bill wasn't fazed. He kept pointing up the other side of the coin, "Well, we're getting $5,000 in commission for each android pair we sell as a result of the seminars at the Hyatt; that could amount to $200,000 a year, right there," Bill argued.

Justina persisted too, "What difference does it make if we have to give it all back in loans to the store, which may even never get paid back to us?!"

"Justina," Bill said in exasperation, "I know this has all gotten pretty hairy, but let's just go with it. Assuming this all works out, we could retire in five years if we want," he suggested, "Just as soon as we've completed our connection to the androids for the ten year period."

"Yeah, I suppose you're right," Justina sighed, getting over some of her resentment, "We can try to hang in there, and make things work for another five years, like we've done for the last five; maybe sales will pick up, like you say, after this bad press blows over."

"That's the spirit!" Bill pulled her close and gave her a great big hug and a kiss, "We can do this; and we're going to be rich!"

The next several months went by slowly, as android sales didn't pick up much. Finally, in the first week of June, at their Monday night meeting, John Posthauer joined them to discuss another idea the marketing group had.

"Bill, Justina," he said encouragingly, "We want to draw more people to the seminars, and we thought of an idea of how we can do that; it's something we could try for the next few months. We figured that if we lower the price of family-android pairs to the store, maybe we could offer a free set of androids each month, in a raffle. We were thinking that we might charge fifty dollars a ticket. We could structure it so the tickets would only be sold to people who showed up and sat through a seminar, and the ticket sale proceeds would go to the store, offsetting the cost of your additional outlay somewhat; what do you think?"

Bill spoke first, "That would probably cost twenty thousand a month! How could we possibly make that up?"

"Well," Posthauer answered, "If the extra people attending the seminars resulted in the sale of even one more pair of family-androids per month, that's about a thirty-thousand dollar gross profit for the store, isn't that right?"

Justina interrupted, "—And you think this would draw out more people to the seminars?"

"We'd like to try. We thought this over, and we could offer to wholesale the raffled off family-android pair to the store at a price of twenty-thousand; that's a ten thousand dollar discount off the normal wholesale cost to you; what do you think?"

"I don't know," Bill said tentatively, "I suppose we could try it, and see how it works; Justina, what do you think? Could we use some of your inheritance money to fund this initiative?"

"Twenty thousand a month?"

"Well, we would be taking in some of the cost in raffle ticket sales, right John?"

"Yes; let's say we sold two-hundred raffle tickets per month, or an average of fifty per seminar each week; that would generate ten-thousand, which would all filter in to the store."

Justina gave in, "I don't know; I suppose we could try it for a few months and see how well it works . . ."

"Okay then," Posthauer said, "We'll make announcements at the seminars, and online on our website starting next week. How soon do you think you could come up with the twenty-thousand for the first pair?"

Bill jumped in, "I can usually liquidate Justina's mutual fund holdings within a week or so; I'll call first thing in the morning and get the process underway; is that alright with you Justina?"

Bill half-expected Justina to put up some resistance, or at least make some sarcastic comment, but she just nodded her head quietly, in agreement.

Over the next several months, Bill and Justina about broke even on the initiative, but it did raise interest and sales a little bit. Besides selling an extra android pair about every two months, it was also putting four more android pairs into service each month as well.

The trouble was, the store kept having to pay increased expenses to keep the doors open, and the money they were liquidating wasn't getting paid back to Justina's mutual fund account. Instead, they were taking an extra sixty thousand a year in salary draw, but this was quickly spent in paying for living expenses and paying tuition and housing for Alyssa and Tommy's college education.

By the end of that year, Justina's mutual fund account had dwindled another hundred thousand, and they had only recovered sixty thousand of that in extra salary. At that rate, they were losing eighty thousand a year on the store.

One night in December, Bill came out of the dining room, where he had been working in their home office, with spreadsheets showing this outcome, "Dear?" Bill dropped gingerly, "The store continues to lose money, and there doesn't seem to be anything I can do about it. At this rate, we will run out of funds in your mutual fund account at least a year before we hit the ten year mark."

"Jesus, Bill!" Justina exclaimed hotly, "You've got to do something to lower the store's expenses; if we run out of money, this whole venture will fall apart!"

"Well," Bill offered, "We could stop paying the teachers as employees, and start paying them as independent contractors; that would save us about forty-thousand in social security contributions . . . What do you think; could you talk the teachers into working for us as independent contractors?"

"That's a good idea! They can do their <u>own</u> taxes! We don't need to keep making Social Security contributions for them. Come to think of it, it would probably cost them less than it costs us, to pay their own Social Security taxes out of income, due to the business write-off's they would probably be able to report on their <u>own</u> tax returns! I don't imagine that very many, if any of them, would quit; most of them have too many students to just walk away from working for us."

"If some of them do, you can find other teachers to take their place, can't you?"

Justina nodded in agreement, "I could fill a couple of spots if we happen to lose a couple of teachers over this; but I don't think we will. I'll write a memo tomorrow, and put it in the teachers' boxes. Then, hopefully, they will be prepared for when we cut them a different paycheck next week."

Bill found other ways to reduce expenses, like cutting way back on making orders for stock, of teachers' requests for software.

A year-end inventory was completed in early January, showing lots of software the teachers had asked the store to carry, which wasn't being sold. Some of it was returned, and some of it was offered at sale prices, and displayed where students would see it as they went in for their tutoring sessions. An Internet offering of old model androids was auctioned off on E-bay, and roughly a third of the original cost was recovered, allowing the store a tax write-off on the other two thirds. This was useful because, of course, businesses still had to pay income taxes, even though individual income taxes had been abolished.

New android sales did pick up a bit more toward year-end, and Justina didn't have to liquidate any more of her mutual fund account from October on, so that saved $60,000. They were making it work, by hook or by crook.

CHAPTER THIRTEEN

TIME PASSED BY, AND as it turned out, one year before the ten year period would be up, Bill and Justina found themselves on the eve of grave trouble. Justina's drinking problem had gotten worse and worse. She had still managed to go down to the store every day during the week, and oversee the Tutoring operations, but her moody behavior had alienated the teaching staff so much that once again, a group of them had broken off and started their own competing tutoring operation across town. This time, they took more than half of the students with them.

Even though Justina scrambled to hire seven new tutors within a month, the tutoring operation became quite unprofitable with such a reduction in the number of students enrolled in the tutoring program.

Justina was drinking throughout the day, and she commonly passed out around nine o'clock, which left Bill up by himself until past midnight, when he finally fell asleep. He took solace in the fact that Shayna was there to be with him. He had sex with Shayna a few nights a week in her bed, while Justina slept. He was getting along okay, other than the fact the store had grown increasingly unprofitable, despite his best efforts. However, he had only one more year to hang in there until they would receive the $200 million dollar lump sum payment from US Android.

Justina's mutual fund account had dwindled to a little under fifty thousand dollars. New android sales had dropped off recently, after reports that it would only be another year before the government review of the results of having a pair of family-androids. People were waiting for this to occur before they would consider purchasing them. The number of people commonly showing up for seminars at the Hyatt dropped off to less than a dozen per lunchtime session, which wasn't worth the cost of putting on the seminars any more.

John Posthauer had pulled the plug on the seminar marketing program a few months earlier, but Adam was still working with Bill at the store, and this was of great assistance to Bill, who had laid off even all but two part time store staff members, making his job that much more difficult; but he was forced to run a skeleton crew staff in order to save money. The store was no longer able to generate enough revenue to pay for staff, so the number of store staff had slowly been reduced to two besides Bill and Adam.

Then one night, Justina hit three parked cars on the way home from going to visit Tommy, who was now living in an apartment in downtown Boston. She kept going, and got home, but someone had seen her car, and called the Police.

Two Police cars ended up in Justina and Bill's driveway, and Justina was called out of the house, "Ma'am, I'm Officer Joe Brown. I am going to perform a sobriety test; I need you to pay close attention, and only do what I ask you when I ask; is that clear?"

"Yes," Justina said in a drunken drawl. She was in shock at having been caught, and under scrutiny. "Do you know who I am?" She drawled on, "I am a prize-winning science teacher at Natick High School, and I run the tutoring operation at US Android."

"Ma'am, I don't care who you are or what you do," the officer responded, "All I care is whether you pass the sobriety test; have you been drinking tonight?"

"A little bit, earlier."

"Well I'm going to beam this laser-line here onto the road, and I want you to walk it, only when I instruct you to start. Don't do anything before I ask you to, alright?" the officer commanded her. He pulled the trigger on his laser gun, and a straight line about 8 feet long appeared on the road in front of them.

Justina immediately started to walk the line. Bill stood by, an onlooker. He wanted to tell her to wait until the officer asked her to walk the line, but he felt it was a futile thing to say, because she obviously wasn't going to pass the sobriety test in the shape she was in. She stumbled way off the line.

"Okay, I'm placing you under arrest. Do you know you hit three parked cars on your way home tonight?"

Justina didn't answer; she was in shock as the officer put her in handcuffs, and loaded her into the back seat of his cruiser. They took off as Bill watched in shock himself. He was somewhat high on E-Tox, but as usual, he was in full control of his faculties. An officer had remained behind, and he addressed Bill in the driveway, "Are you alright?"

"Yes, I'm fine," Bill answered.

"You're fine!?—Your wife just got hauled in on drunken driving charges, and you're fine?"

"Well no; I mean I understand what happened just now, and there isn't anything I can do; will I be able to pick her up from the station later?"

"In an hour or two," the officer answered, "We have to book her, and give her a breathalyzer test to determine her blood alcohol level; and we'll have to interrogate her after she sobers up a bit; it may be a couple of hours."

Bill nodded, "I understand; will you call me when I can come and pick her up?"

"Why don't you give me your number, and I'll pass it on to the arresting officer at the station."

It was almost eleven o'clock when Bill finally picked up Justina from the Natick Police station. She had blown into the breathalyzer, which showed her blood alcohol level at .23 percent, when she had first arrived at the station, but they tested her again two hours later, and her blood alcohol level had dropped to under .10; they couldn't let her go into the public until the level had dropped to below the legal limit.

"How are you doing?" Bill asked her as they walked to the car.

"I feel pretty lousy," she confessed.

"I'm sorry," Bill said with sincerity.

"I just want to go home and go to sleep."

"Yeah, it's getting late." Not much was said on the way home. When they got home about ten minutes later, Justina ducked into the bathroom and had a snort out of a bottle she had hidden under the sink, in the vanity cabinet. She went to bed and fell asleep pretty quickly. Bill climbed in bed down the hall with Shayna and just held her. Her warm body felt good as always. After an hour or so, he left Shayna and crawled into bed next to Justina.

The next morning, Justina was up early. Bill had stayed in bed until past ten, and Justina came in to wake him, "Bill?—I need to talk to you," she said in a soft, sincere, sober voice, "I've been thinking about it, and I want to stop drinking; but I don't know what to do; can you help me? Where do I go?"

Bill rubbed the sleep from his eyes. Justina's response to the incident of the night before was not a big surprise, but it was a pleasant surprise, and he felt called upon to help Justina take the first step in getting sober, "I'll call the hospital; they'll know where to bring you, to detox."

Justina started crying, "I've made such a mess of my life," she sobbed.

"Don't worry; we'll get you some help," Bill said encouragingly.

Bill took Justina to a detox facility across town, for a one week detox period, and then she went to a rehab from there, for a thirty day inpatient program. Bill visited her on weekends, as she slowly regained her strength and composure.

Finally, five weeks later she returned home, to live a newly sober lifestyle. When Bill had gone to pick her up from rehab, they had met with Robin Turner, the head of the rehab about the fact that Bill still was resigned to use E-Tox, and drink some beer and wine, even though Justina needed to stay sober.

Surprisingly, Robin hadn't said this would never work; she had an open mind to the idea that maybe the marriage would still work, with one partner sober, and the other one still using substances and E-Tox.

They left the rehab, encouraged that things might work out alright for them from this point on, now that Justina was sober.

—And things were alright for about a month, until one night, Justina finally let Bill know how she was feeling about the arrangement, "Bill, it really bothers me that you duck into Tommy's room several times a night, to drink wine and beer; I can smell it on you, and that's not good for my sobriety. Then, your eyes are glassy all the time; I know that you are doing a lot of E-Tox. I see your Internet statement every month."

Bill got defensive, "I'm not doing any more E-Tox than usual; I've done about the same amount for the last several years!"

"Bill, I can't go on living this way; you've got to stop doing E-Tox and drinking; don't you see what it's doing to you? Why do you think the store isn't running well? You can't make good decisions while you are under the influence, don't you see?!"

Bill tried desperately to stick up for himself, under her extreme scrutiny, "Justina; the store is doing poorly because the business is a setup for failure, given the lopsidedness of the expenses. You <u>know</u> we are just trying to keep the doors open until the ten year test period is up!"

"I don't <u>believe</u> that!" Justina said indignantly, "I think your ineffectiveness at running the store is due, in large part, to your E-Tox use and your drinking, just like I am realizing that my ineffectiveness at running the tutoring operation was largely due to my drinking."

This theme became the status quo for the next several months; Bill trying to defend his style of living, and Justina attacking him in every way she could, to try and get him to stop drinking and doing E-Tox.

There were no more child rearing issues, as Tommy was working for US Steel, and living by himself in an apartment in Boston; and Alyssa had finished graduate school at Johns

Hopkins, and was working for Doctor Albert Freudenthal, doing research on mind teleportation. Freudenthal had developed a theory that a person's thoughts and feelings could be transported to an android body, thus giving you a new body to occupy, if only temporarily. Alyssa was the one who had actually given the seed idea to him, and she was the prodigy on his team who had made the most headway in bringing this from theory into practice. She had been given her own laboratory of computer equipment, and she preferred to work alone a lot of the time. She had taken an apartment near the lab, in downtown Philadelphia, where Doctor Freudenthal also kept his own research facility. The two worked closely together, Skyping each other a few times a week. Freudenthal would come to visit Alyssa at least a couple of times a month, to track her progress. As she was very busy in her research, Alyssa only made it home for a weekend once every few months, but she kept in touch will Bill and Justina by Skype almost every week.

Barry and Kathleen kept in close touch with Bill and Justina; they met every Monday night, and Thursday night in the conference room with Jim Nakamine for two hours, comparing notes on how things were working out, being connected to their android pairs.

In order to stay sober, Justina started going to Intoxicants Anonymous meetings locally as soon as she came out of rehab. Early on, she ran into Karen, the head psychologist of US Android at a meeting, and Karen let on that she too had had problems with drinking, and was getting sober in the program. The two of them got to know each other more and more as the months went by.

Finally, about seven months before the ten year family-android test period was up, Karen came to Justina one night after a meeting, and gave her some very bad news, "Justina, I need to tell you about what we just discovered. Barbara Flynn, who is in charge of psychological testing at our Boston division of US Android, had a meeting with Kathleen about a week ago. Kathleen had caught Holly-1, their female android, coming out of their son Andy's room one Saturday morning, so she knew they were sleeping together. Karen came to see me, and I sent her to Barbara, who took a new approach. She got government permission to search Andy's Internet memory file; something which previously has never been approved, due to privacy issues; but Kathleen had concerns about possible sexual interaction between Holly-1 and Andy, who is still a minor. Anyway, when Barbara searched Andy's Internet memory file, she discovered that not only were Holly-1 and Andy having sex together regularly, but she also found there was some bleedthrough of memories of sexual experiences between Kathleen and Daniel-1, Barry and Kathleen's male android. Barbara had to report this to the authorities; and this is <u>very</u> upsetting, but Kathleen is now up on charges of sexual assault with a minor, because her sexual encounters were responsible for the bleedthrough to Andy's memory.—But here's the most troubling thing regarding your own connections; Barbara also searched the Internet memory files of the other children involved in the family-android test project, and it turns out that there was also some memory bleedthrough between Alyssa and Shayna-1; memories apparently of Shayna's sexual encounters with Bill."

Justina was mortified, "But how is that possible?! Bill and I have had a pact, that we wouldn't even have any sex with our androids until the test period was over?!"

Karen shook her head, "Well, apparently Bill has been having sex with Shayna regularly, and Alyssa has been sensing aspects of the sexual interaction. You should also be aware that Bill will be brought up on charges of sexual assault because of this."

Justina wasn't listening; she was getting more and more angry about the fact that Bill had violated their pact, and was having sex with Shayna, "Bill with his E-Tox and drinking!" she said hotly, "He deserves to get arrested for what he did! This has corrupted Alyssa, I'm sure; how long has this been going on?!"

"Apparently all during the test period," Karen answered evenly.

"Nine years?! I can't believe he has done this to her!"

"Well, I should point up that this is actually the fault of a Chinese wall software malfunction. If it had worked as the design team had planned, none of this would have happened," Barbara educated.

"I don't care!" Justina responded, "We knew not to trust this wouldn't happen; Bill deliberately violated our pact, which we made <u>specifically</u> to ensure that something like this wouldn't happen!"

Justina went home immediately, to confront Bill. When she got home, she found Bill locked in Tommy's room, having a glass of wine. She knocked on the door furiously, "Bill?! Come out here; I want to talk to you, right away!"

Bill put down his wine glass and opened the door, "What is it?" he asked, bracing himself for what sounded like bad news, from Justina's angry words.

"You've been having sex with Shayna all along, haven't you?!" she lit into him.

"But baby; you were drunk and passed out all those nights, during the whole time we've been connected; what was I supposed to do? Shayna was right there in the next room, warm and willing . . ."

"Well, you're in big trouble now; a woman named Barbara Flynn, of the psychological testing team at US Android, got government sanction to gain access to Alyssa's memory files on the Internet, and apparently, Alyssa has been aware of the sexual interaction between you and Shayna for the past nine years!"

"How did that happen?! The Chinese wall software was supposed to prevent anything like that from happening!"

"Well it happened, and now you're going to be arrested for sexual assault."

"Wait! All I did was to have sex with Shayna, my android, which is perfectly legal. This constitutes sexual assault on Alyssa?! That's crazy!"

"You may think so, but all I know is that Alyssa experienced sexual memories for over nine years!" Justina paused for a moment while the wheels were turning in her mind; then she delivered her ultimatum, "This may seem a little rash," she said almost sheepishly at first, "But I want you out of this house immediately!"

"Baby?! Calm down; you can't mean that," Bill said weakly.

"I do mean it! I want you to pack your bags and leave tonight!"

Bill stood there in the hallway, looking at Justina in shock for several seconds; then he finally said, "Alright, if that's what you want . . ."

Justina had been so vehement on the intoxication issue; now she was even more vehement on the technicality that legally it is considered sexual assault, to be the parent who is responsible for the sexual activity with his android which caused the bleedthrough memories occurring to a child connected to a family-android.

It seemed pretty certain to Bill that this was the end of his relationship with Justina, if this was how she felt about the sexual activity he had been having with Shayna.

Still, he had yet to consult a lawyer; maybe these charges could be fought; and maybe Justina would even forgive him, at least eventually. He couldn't be sure of anything yet.

Bill packed two suitcases and took his laptop. Shayna was still inactive, in her bed, when Bill left. The questions were going through his mind, what happens to our connections to the family-androids? Will Justina divorce me? How could she blow getting the two hundred million after nine years of working for it? He would have to wait for these answers.

Bill drove to the Americas Inn in Natick and checked in around nine. He had brought a half a case of wine which was in Tommy's room, locked in a closet, and he had also brought two six-packs of beer as well, which were in the small refrigerator he had put in Tommy's room. There was nothing left in the house for Justina to drink. Bill was upset, but he didn't want Justina to drink over this mess; that wouldn't help any.

He decided he needed a little boost, however, and he booted up his laptop and went to the E-Tox site, ordering a little more than his usual amount. As soon as the order was in, he instantly felt better, as the feeling of intoxication washed over him. He opened a beer and sat back against the headboard of the bed, to watch TV and calm down a little, after all of the excitement.

He found a movie and began to watch, but just then, his cell phone rang. He answered it, and there was Justina's face on the Skype screen, "I was worried about you;" she said with weakness and genuine concern, "I wasn't sure what you would do; are you alright?" she asked somewhat sympathetically.

"No, I'm not al<u>right</u>!" Bill responded with gentle indignation, "But I'm not going to do anything rash, if that's what you mean."

"You could go into the detox facility that you took me to . . ."

"No, I'm not going to give up E-Tox or booze," Bill said flatly.

There was a pause, "Where are you?" Justina asked.

"I'm at a hotel nearby; I just checked in."

"Bill?" Justina had obviously thought through her next statement, and had found no other alternative, "I want you to know that I will <u>always</u> love you," she said warmly and sincerely, "But I don't want you to contact me, ever again," she said with a tone of firm finality.

"But what about our connections to the androids, and the two hundred million?" Bill asked adeptly, considering his shock.

Justina had worked this out too, "I won't put in a termination notice, if you won't; and we can stay connected, but I don't want to see you ever again."

"If that's what you want . . ." Bill said hesitatingly.

There were a few more seconds of silence; then Justina made her final comment, "Bye, Bill; take care of yourself."—She hung up.

The next morning, the phone rang and woke Bill up, "Hello?" he said groggily.

"Is this William Symms?"

"Yes it is," Bill answered, waking up a little.

"This is detective Peter Nesbit, at the Natick Police Station; did you know there's a warrant out for your arrest?"

"No; I didn't know that."

"It was put out two days ago; we need you to come and turn yourself in, otherwise we have to come out and arrest you and bring you in, in handcuffs; you don't want us to have to do that, do you?"

"No, sir; how soon do I have to come in?"

"Why don't you come in later this morning."

"What time?" Bill asked anxiously.

"Any time later this morning; we'll be waiting for you."

Bill hung up and went immediately to his laptop, and pulled up his E-Tox account. He cancelled his supply for the day. Next, he called in to work. The store manager answered, "US Android store; this is Bob, can I help you?"

"Hi Bob, it's me; how are things going so far today?"

"Oh, hi Bill; Everything's pretty quiet so far; Phil from Yamaha called, he said he's got some specials on software this month; he's wondering if we need anything."

"Well, no, we can't afford to buy anything more this month; you can call him back and tell him; listen, this is all pretty crazy, but I'm being arrested; apparently, there was some bleedthrough memories of sexual activity between me and my android Shayna, which registered in my stepdaughter Alyssa's online memory file, and I'm being blamed."

"You're being blamed? How come?"

"Because the memories Alyssa is experiencing are of sexual contact between me and Shayna; it's a long story, but listen, I have to go in to the Police station this morning, so you'll be on your own; is Jim in?"

"Yes, he's here."

"Good; I should be in this afternoon I imagine, if I can get my mother to post bail. I'll call you when I can shake loose; will you two be alright until then?"

"Yes, don't worry about us, we'll be fine; I'll wait to hear from you."

Next, Bill called his mother, "Hi, Mom?"

"Hi Bill, How are you? I haven't heard from you in a while; is everything alright?"

"Well no, actually I'm being arrested this morning. You see, there was some bleedthrough of some of my sexual thoughts, and acts that went on between me and Shayna, which ended up in Alyssa's online memory file, and now I'm being brought up on charges of sexual assault, because of this."

"Oh, Bill!" she pleaded seriously, "I worried that something like this might happen, when you told me you were all connected to the androids. What have you done?"

"Well frankly, I don't see what I did wrong here; this doesn't make any sense to me, there was never any sexual contact between me and Alyssa; this is an indirect charge; all I did was to have sex with Shayna sometimes at night, but since Alyssa is also psychically connected to Shayna, and she apparently has some memories of our experiences, this is considered sexual assault of a minor."

"Have you been arrested?"

"I just got a call from the sergeant at the police station saying there is a warrant out for my arrest; I'm going in to the Police station this morning; I was wondering if you could bail me out later today?"

Almost without pause, she quickly stated emphatically, "Of course I'll put up bail! When should I come?"

"I don't know; I'll have to call you from the station."

"Alright; I'm sorry you've got yourself into trouble over this; have you called your father?"

"No, not yet; I guess I'll Skype him now."

She sighed as she paused briefly, considering the sad ramifications of the situation for Bill, "Alright; I'll be on the other end of the phone; you just call me with the particulars."

Bill hung up and Skyped his father, "Hi, Dad?"

"Hi Bill, it's good to hear your voice; how is everything?"

"Not so good Dad; I'm being arrested this morning; I just got a call from a detective at the Natick Police station; apparently there's a warrant out for my arrest."

"Oh?" Bill's father said with mild surprise, "What are you being arrested for?"

"Well, US Android tapped into Alyssa's Internet memory account and discovered that she has been having sexual memories, which she has been picking up from Shayna, and they're saying I'm responsible."

"Is what you are saying, that you have been having sex with Shayna, and Alyssa has somehow become aware of these interactions, and your sexual thoughts and feelings?"

"Exactly."

"I know you told me a couple of months ago that you all have been connected to your two androids; how long has this been going on?"

"Nine years," Bill answered flatly.

"Jesus Bill, why did you ever agree to go into this test program in the first place? You knew it was highly experimental . . ."

"Dad, there was a lot of money at stake, and they reassured us that they had done a lot of research; these problems were all supposed to be headed off at the pass."

"Well, you've certainly got yourself into some serious trouble . . . Okay, I want you to call my lawyer and get his recommendation for a specialized lawyer to handle this case. Let me get you his number . . ."

"Okay Dad, I'll Skype him right now."

"His name is David Greenberg, and his number is area code 2032-2458-38769, have you got that?"

Bill saw the trouble and disappointment on his father's face on the Skype screen in his cell phone, "Dad, I'm sorry; I hope I can get some help, and fight this . . ."

"I sure hope so; otherwise you'll probably go to prison for this, and we wouldn't want that . . ."

When Bill finished up his call to his father, he dialed David Hellman's office. A pleasant sounding professional woman's voice greeted him, "Dewey, Franklin and Greenberg; good morning, can I help you? This is Jennifer . . ."

Bill came out of the daze which her soothing voice had put him in, "Oh, good morning; this is Bill Symms, is Mister Greenberg in?"

"Yes, I believe he is; may I tell him what this is regarding?"

"Yes, well my father is a personal friend of Dave's, and he suggested I speak to him about getting a recommendation. Unfortunately, I've gotten into some legal trouble . . ."

"Of course; I should have recognized the last name; you're Paul Symms' son?"

"Yes, that's right," Bill confirmed.

"Let me tell Mister Greenberg you are on the line; would you like me to turn on our Skype screen?"

"Yes, that would be great . . ." Bill said cordially.

With little delay, a handsome middle aged man's face appeared on Bill's Skype screen, "Hi, Bill, is it?" Bill nodded and he continued, "Dave Greenberg; what can I do for you?"

"Hi Dave, my father gave me your number, and said that you may be able to recommend a good lawyer to represent me. I've been arrested in an unusual situation where my stepdaughter and I were psychically connected to my female android, and due to a "Chinese wall" software malfunction, my stepdaughter developed an awareness of sexual activity going on between me and this android woman, including some of my sexual thoughts and feelings at the time; and because of this I have been arrested for sexual assault."

Greenberg took in what Bill was explaining to him, "I see; so you and your wife connected the family to a pair of family-androids?"

"Yes, exactly . . ." Bill replied, almost a little surprised that Greenberg knew this would be the only set of circumstances where this particular type of problem situation could develop.

"Well, let me see; why don't you give John Flanders a call; he gets involved with sexual assault cases, particularly where family members are arrested. John has an excellent record; he is a fine attorney, I've known him for years. I don't know if he will have availability to take on your case, but you'd be lucky to have him represent you."

"Does he take on high profile cases usually? Is that what you're saying?" Bill asked skeptically.

"Well, yes, I suppose he often does; but as I say, he is as good a lawyer as you could find, for a case like yours, in my opinion. Whether he will have the availability to take you on as a client is another thing; but that would be a good place for you to start."

Bill nodded his approval, "Okay, well thank you for the referral; do you have a number for him?"

Within minutes, Bill was looking at another middle aged man with a well-groomed beard, on his Skype screen; after having spoken briefly with his receptionist about the nature of his situation. He felt a bit uneasy about talking about such a personal situation with other than a highly specialized lawyer at first, but he realized that John Flanders' assistant was undoubtedly part of a confidentially structured inter-office network of communication, and if he was going to be well-represented, he would have to become comfortable with his lawyer's other staff members understanding various aspects of his situation. Indeed, he may not even get to talk to Mr. Flanders without first making John aware of his predicament through the medium of his assistant. Bill knew that John Flanders was a busy guy.

He waited on the line for another thirty seconds before a competent sounding man came on the line, "John Flanders . . ."

"Hi, John?—This is Bill Symms, I was referred to you by Dave Greenberg; I assume your assistant has already informed you, I'm being arrested this morning for fourth degree sexual assault, and this involves our family-android situation. My wife and I, and my two stepchildren, are all connected to the android pair, and my stepdaughter has been experiencing bleedthrough sexual memories, of which I am being held responsible for; Dave Greenberg says this might be something you can help me with. Have you had other cases of this nature?"

John was quite well up to speed, "Yes, in fact I'm working on a similar case right now; a woman reported her husband because her young daughter came to her and said she remembered her father touching their female android sexually in her dreams. The woman is suing US Android, and her husband was arrested a few months ago. I'm in talks with the prosecutor on it right now; as a matter of fact, I just came from court."

"Well, I'm due to turn myself in at the Police station later this morning."

"Okay; don't say anything; let them book you and read you your arrest report, and you'll have an opportunity to call someone to bail you out when they are through; do you have someone who will post bail?"

"Yes; my mother said she'll post bail for me."

"Good; do you have a job?"

"Yes; I'm working for US Android; that's how I got mixed up in this in the first place; we're part of a ten year test program for the new family-androids."

"Have you ever been arrested before?"

"No; this is my first time."

"—And you're how old?"

"I'm thirty-two."

"Good; it's a first offense, this is a grey area; maybe we can get you off without any jail time. Listen, on a first offense of this type, the bail shouldn't be any higher than Five thousand. Your mother should be able to get a bail bondsman to put up that amount with a five hundred dollar fee."

"Okay; when could I come in to see you?—Some time in the next few days I hope . . ."

"Let me look on my calendar; let's see, why don't you come in Friday morning at nine-thirty."

"Do I need to bring anything?"

"No; I'll get a copy of the Police report, and we'll go from there."

Bill got to the Police station a little before eleven. He was booked, read his rights, and given one phone call. He called his mother and gave her the bad news; his bail was set at fifty thousand!

Then, he was put into a jail cell, where he sat waiting for the bail bondsman and his mother to arrive at the Police station. Almost two hours went by before the sergeant finally came to open the cell and let him out. Thankfully, at least he didn't have to share the cell with anyone.

He walked up to his mother, who was sitting in the lobby, "Hi Bill; I'm sorry it took so long, but we had to call a different bondsman; the one I initially called didn't go up that high; he only went to ten-thousand."

"Yeah, I can't believe the bail was set so high; it's not like I'm a flight risk, or anything."

"Well, they take this sort of thing very seriously. There was an article in the Boston Globe about you, and it was published online as well. Let's just say it doesn't exactly cast you in a good light. Why don't you come back to my house, and I'll let you see it."

"Okay; I'll follow you back to your place, but then I've got to go in to the store . . ."

"Bill's mother gave him a discerning look, "You may not want to go back to the store after you see the article; customers may get angry with you."

Just then, Bill's phone rang. It was John Posthauer, "Hi John, what's up?"

"Bill, I saw the article in the Globe about you, and it's bad press for us, you know. I'm afraid I'm going to have to ask you to leave the store's employ effective immediately, I'm sorry Bill . . ."

"But John! This was a problem that wouldn't have happened if the Chinese wall software was working properly; something went wrong with it; the bleedthrough was really US Android's fault!"

"That may be true, but my hands are tied; I received a call from the President of the company himself. He says we can't afford to have anyone charged with sexual assault under our employ. We're going to have to suspend you until the case is over."

"But John! That could take months, or even longer; that's what my lawyer just told me . . ."

"I'm sorry Bill; we're going to need you to turn in your keys; can you come in this afternoon?"

Bill called his father, to give him an update of what was happening. "Hi Dad; I just called to tell you that Mom freed me on bail, and she had to put up five thousand dollars; my bail was fifty thousand! Can you believe it?"

"Well, I'm not surprised; these sexual assault cases are very high profile these days."

"—And I got suspended from work until the case is over; can you believe that?!"

"Oh Christ; do you have any savings?"

"Well, I have a retirement account with about fifty thousand in it; I suppose I can borrow from that."

"Good; I'll send you some money until you can manage to get a hold of some of those funds; can you roll over your pension funds into an IRA?"

"I don't know Dad, I'll try."

"Did you call the lawyer that Dave Greenberg recommended?"

"Yes; and I have an appointment Friday morning at nine-thirty."

"Well I'm going to come to that meeting with you; I want to get first-hand information, and see what we can do to help you."

"Dad, that's not necessary . . ."

"Bill, I really think you need my help; I have some experience with the legal system, and I want to be there to support you in every way I can."

Bill felt the dual stress of really not wanting his father to assert his point of view and his old-fashioned understanding about how, conventionally, to proceed; while at the same time sensing his father's desperate need to exert every possible effort in his power to fight the seemingly unstoppable momentum toward his demise from any standing within the community, at the rate things were going. He felt overwhelmingly moved to yield to his father, in the final analysis, "Alright; if you insist; the meeting is at nine-thirty at John Flanders' office. You can come to the hotel here, and we'll go together."

"I'll catch a flight tomorrow, and I'll be there Friday morning; what hotel are you staying at?"

"I'm at the Americas Inn, in Natick."

"Well, why don't you try to relax; I'm going to wire five thousand dollars to your account, so you'll have some money, Do you have a check, so I can get the bank routing number, and your checking account number?"

At four o'clock, Bill went to the bank and drew out five hundred dollars of the money his father had wired. He also transferred two hundred dollars to his E-Tox account. When he returned to the hotel, he booted his laptop and went to the site, and ordered his usual amount. Feeling the wave of intoxication coming over him, he got his bathing suit on and went down to the Jacuzzi for a long soak. He took a Styrofoam cup of wine with him. The sign said there was no alcohol allowed in the pool area, but he didn't care; he thought his chances of anyone taking notice of this was pretty remote.

There was nobody at the Jacuzzi when he arrived, and he sat on the bench seat, moving slowly back and forth in front of the jets, soothing his back. He felt a pleasant contentment as he soaked for almost an hour. A couple arrived with their young daughter, and joined him in the Jacuzzi. The sign said no one under the age of sixteen was allowed in the Jacuzzi, but they didn't heed the directive. The young girl swam around in the Jacuzzi, back and forth from parent to parent. Bill watched the interaction between them, remembering how he and Justina used to swim with Tommy and Alyssa when they were young.

A plain-looking middle aged woman came down to the pool area and sat in the sauna while they soaked in the Jacuzzi. Since the sauna was heated up, Bill walked in and had a seat after he got out of the Jacuzzi. Waves of warmth wafted over his relaxed body for another half an hour, before he returned to his room.

He cracked open a Heineken and fired up his computer. He went to an adult website, and enjoyed some triple X action for an hour or so before dinner. It was great how E-Tox and alcohol took his mind off his troubles for the time being, and he had forgotten how exciting it was to look at good porn.

Around seven o'clock, Bill got dressed, got into his car, and drove to a steakhouse nearby. He ordered a gin and tonic, and a T-bone steak, with a twice-baked potato, for dinner. He was going to eat at the bar, so he sat there on a bar stool, sipping his drink and waiting for his dinner to be served.

The bartender was an attractive young woman around twenty-five or so, he guessed. The bar was full, and a few other patrons were eating dinner at the bar too. He struck up a conversation with the older man sitting next to him, "It's nice to have a pretty, young barmaid, isn't it?"

She heard the comment and smiled over at them while mixing a drink, "I haven't seen you before; are you from around here?" she asked, directing her glance to Bill.

"I'm from across town, but my wife threw me out; so I'm staying at the Americas Inn." Bill spoke freely, mildly high on E-Tox and feeling the effects of the booze kick in.

"I come from Maine," the man sitting next to him disclosed, "And I got divorced years ago, so I don't have to worry about getting kicked out any more; but my wife got the house, and all I can afford is a crummy apartment these days!"

"What brings you down here?" the barmaid asked the man, out of curiosity.

"My son-in-law has some work for me; soundproofing. He's got three projects, and he could use the help. My daughter's pregnant, and they're already saddled with twins, so I'll be doing some babysitting too."

"Soundproofing?" Bill asked, "You mean master bedrooms?"

"Yeah, for families getting androids; and for parents who want to make sure they don't get arrested for sex charges, in case the kids see or hear anything sexual going on between their parents."

"Yeah, well if they're getting family-androids, it may not help," Bill said nonchalantly, "All the soundproofing in the world won't save you from being arrested for bleedthrough sexual memories registering in the online memory file of the child."

"What's that?" the barmaid asked.

"Bleedthrough?" Bill responded, "That's when your wife and kids are hooked up to family-androids, and you share sexual experiences with your android, and your son or daughter becomes aware of the activity and/or your sexual thoughts, because they are psychically connected to the same android."

"That hardly seems fair, someone getting arrested for that; it's an android malfunction, isn't it?" the barmaid continued to banter with Bill.

"How do you know about family-androids?" Bill questioned her.

"My father used to work for US Android, before he got laid off; production of the new generation slowed down several months ago; and they say it's due to the trouble with family-android electronic brain malfunction; it's been in the news and everything."

"Yeah, well I'm one of the casualties," Bill spouted, "My android malfunctioned and I'm being arrested, as though it was my fault!"

"You can't trust them androids," the man on the bar stool next to Bill interjected, "You're better off stayin' away from them altogether."

Bill realized he was struck with a dilemma; he believed in his company, and in the safe and formidable operation of the new androids in their lives up until now, in every other respect. He felt like only he could see that maybe there was perhaps no really significant problem with the androids; his kids seemed to be doing just fine.

Possibly it was really more a problem with the laws surrounding sexual exchange.

"One thing's for sure," the barmaid added, "It's a big scandal, and it seems a lot of people are getting arrested for sexual assault because of these new androids."

"Well, it's really only about three percent of the people who own family-androids; but besides the arrest, the worst thing is that my wife has ended our relationship over this; she doesn't want me to contact her any more, she said."

"Sounds pretty serious . . ." the man next to Bill commented, "By the way, I'm Tom; Tom Piper."

"Bill Symms," Bill shot back, "So how come you aren't at your daughter's house; don't they have room for you?"

"Yeah, but they're away on vacation this week; they'll be back on Friday, so I'm staying at the Ramada."

"Oh yeah? What are they charging you for a room?" Bill asked.

"One-Sixty; but I've got a coupon, so I get a break on that price." Tom said happily.

"Yeah, that's about what I'm paying at the Americas Inn, but they have a sauna and a Jacuzzi, so it's worth it," Bill sipped his gin and tonic.

"That's pretty steep," Tom said as he took a bite of his steak, "Are you going to find an apartment?"

Bill shrugged, "Yeah, I guess I'm going to have to; I've got to conserve my cash; my lawyer says it could be at least several months before he can work out some kind of a deal with the prosecutor."

The waitress placed Bill's dinner in front of him, "Crushed pepper?" she asked routinely.

"Sure, a little . . . It's busy around here tonight."

"It's not too bad; you should see it on a Saturday night; there's hardly room to walk."

"It's a nice atmosphere in here. The décor is out of the twentieth century it looks like."

"The late nineteen hundreds actually, People still wore ten gallon hats, and ate aged beef."

"And is this steak aged beef?"

"Well no, it's a lot better for you than aged beef of the nineteen hundreds; they grow the beef in a lab; no more slaughtering of cows, of course; no cholesterol, no fat; it's all synthetic, and highly nutritional, for that matter." She held the pepper grinder over his plate, and began to grind, "Say when . . ."

Bill waited a few seconds before stopping her, "Okay that's good."

Bill talked with Tom while he ate his dinner. He continued to flirt with the barmaid. He ordered another gin and tonic before ordering a tall cup of coffee to sober up a bit before the drive back to the hotel.

Once back, he stood at the front desk until the clerk came from the back room, "Do you have android service here?"

She smiled at him, "What time did you want company?"

"Oh, in about half an hour; will that work?"

"I think so; I'll call when they're on the way up; what room are you in, did you say?"

"Room two-o-two," Bill answered after thinking for a second.

"Returning to his room, he cracked a beer and started watching porn, to get into the mood. He thought of how Justina would have disapproved of him having sex with an android other than Shayna, but he quickly put it out of his mind, remembering how Justina had told him things between the two of them were over, and she never wanted to talk to him, ever again.

Half-an-hour later, he opened his door for the android and her female controller, "Hi, come on in," he greeted.

"Hello, I'm Rose, and this is Audrey 24, I'll sit in a chair in the corner here while you two frolic."

It was a little awkward having a strange woman watching as he took off Audrey's clothes and started caressing her. Rose started to squirm a bit as she was feeling what Bill was doing to Audrey, "For another hundred bucks, I'll join in and make it a threesome," Rose offered seductively from the corner."

"No thanks," Bill answered her immediately, "I don't want to take a chance on getting a disease or something, no offense; but Audrey's all the woman I need tonight; she's quite beautiful, you know."

"Thanks," Audrey said as she bent down to kiss Bill sensually on the lips.

"Oh, you are a good kisser," Bill remarked as he slid his hands over her sexy body.

Bill lost himself in sexual rapture for the next hour with Audrey. Then Rose spoke up, "Your time's up, unless you want to pay for another hour."

Bill grimaced, "No, that's alright, I think I'm sufficiently satisfied."

"How long will you be staying with us?" Rose asked.

"Oh, a few days I guess; it depends on how long it takes me to find an apartment."

"Well, we'll be here if you want us to visit you again; just ask for Audrey at the front desk."

"I may take you up on that; she's really very good at this."

"I'll take that as a compliment," Rose said in her seductive voice, as she put on a bit of a devilish grin.

Friday morning fell, and Bill's father knocked on the door at eight-thirty as planned. Hi Dad! It's sure good to see you . . ." Bill smiled warmly at his father as he opened the door a little further to let him in, "How was your trip?"

"Well, these rocket powered jets are hard on you; the G force when they take off is hard on an old man's heart."

"Dad! You're not an old man; you're only forty-seven!"

"Yeah, I'm just kidding; the flight was a bit long, but it was uneventful, if that's what you mean."

"Are you hungry? Let's get breakfast, you want to? There's a diner on the way to John's office."

"Sure, we can talk about the case a bit before we get there."

"I hope John's got some ideas; because otherwise, it looks like I'm pretty screwed. I looked up similar cases on the internet yesterday, and most of the time it seems like men in my situation are not only sent to prison, but they are exiled to Planet P."

"Yes, well I've discovered the same thing, researching it on my end. It looks like you may have gotten yourself into some real trouble here."

"Yeah, well it's a first offense, and it seems like US Android is mainly to blame . . ."

"Tell me Bill, I know you've had some experience with E-Tox in the past; were you high on E-Tox when you were laying with Shayna?"

Bill hesitated before answering, "Well yeah, I've had an E-Tox account all along."

"And have you been drinking too?"

"Yeah, but I don't drink that much really."

"Oh Bill;" Paul shook his head, "This won't play well with the authorities . . ." Then he brightened a bit, "But on the other hand, if we claim you have a substance abuse problem, maybe it will be a mitigating factor."

"Do you think so?" Bill asked hopefully, "I'll tell you something else; Justina has had a bad drinking problem for the last several years; do you think the judge may take that into account?"

"Was she drunk when you were laying with Shayna?"

"In most cases; she would often pass out at night, in fact she passed out almost every night that I eventually went in and visited Shayna in her room; that's why I visited Shayna in the middle of the night, in the first place; Justina was almost never available to me after like ten o'clock."

"Well I don't know much about the way these android connections are looked at in court; it could be that this would be a mitigating factor as well."

They continued to talk as they drove to the diner and had breakfast together. They arrived at John's office at nine-twenty, and they were ushered into the conference room to wait for John to get off the phone and join them.

"I'm sorry you've had to wait so long," John said as he entered the room fifteen minutes later."

"John, this my father," Bill introduced.

"Paul Symms," Bill's father said as he extended a hand.

"Nice to meet you both; I was just Skyping with a client who's up on similar charges. His wife is asking for a divorce, and she's planning on taking everything . . ."

"Can she do that?" Bill's father asked with incredulity, "I thought that in a divorce, Massachusetts law gives half of the combined assets to each partner."

"Yes, well she's claiming that she'll have her daughter sue for anything my client might get in the divorce settlement."

Bill spoke up, "Is this all over some bleedthrough sexual activity, like me?"

"Well no," John responded, "He was actually going farther, and having sex with his stepdaughter too, so it's a little different."

"Well in my case, I was cuddling and having sex with my android, and my stepdaughter registered memories of this in her internet memory file."

"I did look up a few similar cases, and it doesn't seem to matter," John said grimly, "It's still considered sexual assault in the fourth degree, and it's usually punishable in the same way."

"How is that possible?!" Bill's father exclaimed, "This is a case where it's really the responsibility of the android manufacturer for a software malfunction; I can hardly believe this should come down solely on Bill . . ."

John continued, "Well, you'd think that it would be the case that the android company, did you say it was US Android?" Bill nodded and John continued, "You'd think that they would be at least partially responsible, but the way the law looks at it, you made the decision to connect your family to the androids, and you took the risk, so they consider you responsible, since the activity your stepdaughter had the memories of involved you. I'd have to look at your contract with US Android, but in most cases, it says in the contract that you are taking full responsibility, and they usually claim that at the time the contracts were signed, you had been warned that something of this nature could go wrong."

"That's ridiculous!" Bill's father interrupted, "Bill was part of a test group, as an employee of US Android. They should take some responsibility for this . . ."

"Well actually, there have been a few cases against US Android where the company has been sued successfully, but it is usually the victim that gets the money, and US Android is held harmless, in terms of any legal charges against the company; their legal department has gone to great lengths to make sure it doesn't fall on them if something goes wrong."

"But this <u>does</u> fall on the company!" Bill's father objected, "I'm sure that Bill would have never touched Alyssa sexually, or otherwise, in any way that might disturb her . . ."

"Paul," John answered, "If there's any way we can pin it on them, we'll try to make US Android the culprit; I was just stating the case law to date. Let's get the facts from Bill, and I'll see what I can do."

"Well, we've all been connected to the androids for about nine years now, and normally, my wife would have sensed the bleedthrough and put a stop to it, but she has had a serious drinking problem until very recently, she just stopped drinking . . ."

"Shayna is the android?" John interrupted to ask.

"Yes, and Alyssa is my stepdaughter," Bill added.

"I'm sorry, but I haven't been able to get the Police report yet," John admitted a little sheepishly, "I should be getting it today at some point."

Paul spoke up, "John, Bill has been on drugs for the entire time this has happened, he has an E-Tox account, and he has also been drinking regularly; can we plead that he has a substance abuse problem? Will that help?"

"It may be a mitigating factor, if he is able to stop all use of E-Tox, and all other substances, and produce clean urine tests from this point on, up until the trial, assuming we eventually go to trial."

Bill looked forlorned suddenly, "I'll have to stop doing E-Tox?"

John looked into Bill's eyes compassionately, "I'm afraid so; the Police will be granted access to your internet account, and they'll see you've been using. If we're going to use this in your defense, you'll have to terminate your E-Tox account; not to mention there could be further charges against you for having the account."

"Are you saying I may be busted for E-Tox as well now?" Bill asked.

"Well, if we can show that you have stopped, I may be able to get those charges dropped," John counseled.

Paul interrupted, "Do you think you can stay clean for the duration of the time it takes to resolve these charges?"

"Yes," Bill answered immediately, "I'll cancel my E-Tox account right away."

"—And you'll stop drinking as well?" Paul added, looking for further confirmation.

"Yeah, I can do that," Bill said sadly.

"Good," John said, "I'll try to talk with the prosecutor next week; I don't know how soon they'll assign a prosecutor to your case, but usually it's done pretty much right away."

"Will it be a man or a woman?" Paul asked.

"It will be a woman; they only assign women prosecutors to these cases," John responded.

"Well <u>that's</u> not good," Paul vented, "A woman prosecutor is going to be biased against a man to some extent, isn't she?"

"Yes, I'm afraid so; that usually is the case," John answered, "—And it also usually makes it more difficult to work things out for the better for someone in your position. Most of the time, these cases are settled through plea bargaining; but that will mean pleading guilty, or at least not contesting the charges."

Bill's face showed that he didn't like hearing what he was hearing. John saw his expression and continued more optimistically, "But we do have some mitigating factors here. It seems we can surely document that there was a software malfunction, there were no sexual acts between you and Alyssa, your wife was somewhat incapacitated to fulfill her responsibilities as Alyssa's mother, and we can claim that your judgment was impaired by your own substance use, and hopefully, we will be able to produce evidence that you've stopped using all intoxicants. So as I say, I'll have an opportunity to talk with the prosecutor next week most likely, and I'll let you know what her initial reaction is."

Bill dropped his father off at the Ramada after the meeting, and made his way back to his own hotel room at the Americas Inn. As he collapsed on the bed, his heart was heavy, as he really didn't want to have to give up E-Tox and drinking. He booted up his computer, and ordered an unusually high dose of E-Tox for a last hurrah. He savored the feeling which he would no longer be able to enjoy, at least, probably for quite some time now, as he felt the wonderful buzz kick in. After a few more minutes of relaxing, he got into his bathing suit, to enjoy the Jacuzzi, the pool and the sauna while stoned, for one last time.

He still had a half a case of good cabernet, which he realized he would now have to give away, or otherwise dispose of, but first he would enjoy one more bottle. He also cracked a beer, and had a few slugs before heading downstairs. He stopped at the front desk, to schedule a last fling on E-Tox with Audrey.

No one was in the pool area when he arrived; he had the place to himself. He was sitting in the Jacuzzi for about fifteen minutes when an attractive young mother came in with her two kids. The kids swam in the pool while she got into the Jacuzzi.

"Hi," Bill greeted casually as she sat down on the bench opposite him and began enjoying the jets.

"Hi," she returned, "I guess we have the place to ourselves this morning."

"Yeah, I guess everybody else is working."

"I would be working too, but my boss is away, and I can't find a babysitter," she disclosed.

"Where do you work?" Bill asked, making conversation.

"I'm the assistant to the president at Blackwater; it's an investment firm."

"Oh, my father used to be in the investment business; he worked for Templeton."

"That's our competition," she shot back, "We run a similar product; it's a fund that mainly invests pension funds in the global market."

"Oh, do you invest in any operations on the new planets?"

"Well, certainly not in any businesses on planet P," she said as she smiled, "We don't want our name to be associated with any businesses there; but we do have investments in some municipal bonds on Earth-3, and we have some equity investments in businesses on Earth-2, in our hedge fund."

"Earth-3, huh?—That's where my father is living; in fact he works for the government, setting up financing for municipal projects. It's a bit of a pioneering effort, but he's making progress with it."

"Is that right? We may be an investor on one of his projects. We just bought bonds on a bridge project that's recently gotten underway, I know."

"It's a small world;" Bill pulled out an old cliché, "Actually, I guess I shouldn't say that any more, now that we've got three worlds."

"They are small worlds in some ways," she said, "The government bonds in all three are linked to the same index now."

"Oh?—Does Blackwater own shares in the index fund?"

"Yes, we use it to hedge our bets on Earth-3; it's such a new venture that we couldn't comfortably hold as many investments there without it."

"I guess that makes sense," Bill acknowledged.

She looked curiously now at Bill, "What type of work do you do, if I may ask?"

"I work for US Android; I'm in the marketing department."

"So you are in on selling family-androids, and his and hers androids?"

"That's right!" Bill was pleased that she knew something about his line of work, "It's been a hard sell; we've been waiting for government approval. We're about one year away from it, but there's problems."

"I'll say; I read about the big sex assault scandal."

Bill didn't want to get into it, so he just smiled, "Well I've got some time off, so I'm going to try not to think about it; they've actually developed a fix for the problem; we'll see what's going to happen once all of those androids come in for recall . . ." Bill's thoughts swirled around in his mind for a few moments, before he turned his gaze back to her, "How about you? How much time off do you have, before you have to go back?"

"I've got until next Wednesday, but we'll be checking out tomorrow; we're just getting away for an overnight. The kids wanted to swim in the pool, and I wanted to relax in the Jacuzzi, and take a sauna."

"Yeah, I just turned the sauna on a few minutes ago; it ought to be warmed up pretty soon. Is your husband going to join you later?"

"No, I'm divorced; it's just me and the kids now."

"Oh, how long ago did you get divorced?"

"Let's see, it's been about a year now."

"Do you have custody of your children?"

"No, we have joint custody, but the kids are normally with me all week; he has them on the weekends twice a month, and he takes them out for dinner sometimes during the week. Then I get to go out to the gym!" She said with a smile.

"Every week?"

"Yes, unless he's traveling on business, which is only about once a month."

"How old are your kids?"

"Nancy is eleven, and Shawn is turning seven next month."

"Your daughter is big, for eleven."

"Yes, and she's beginning to date now; she'll be going to college soon."

"Does she have a steady boyfriend?"

"She's dating a couple of different guys; she's not ready to go steady yet."

"Smart girl; she should take her time; she's got her whole life ahead of her."

She glanced over her shoulder to check on her kids, "Shawn, stay in the shallow end; it's too dangerous for you to follow your sister into the deep end." She turned back to Bill, "He's taking swimming lessons this summer, but he still doesn't know how to swim very well."

"I didn't learn to swim until I was nine myself," Bill commented.

"My mother put me in a swim class when I was five, but I really didn't know how to swim very well until I was about Shawn's age; I was a slow learner." There was an awkward pause in the conversation before Bill thought to ask her, "Well, do you want to join me in the sauna? I think it's probably getting hot by now."

"Sure, I'm April, by the way . . ."

"Bill; nice to meet you."

They talked in the sauna for another twenty minutes or so, before Bill headed back to his room. He had to prepare himself for Audrey's visit.

The maid had come in and cleaned the room and made his bed by the time he returned. He showered, and then went to an online porn site, to put himself in the mood before Audrey and Rose came around.

This time, Bill paid for the second hour and really let loose with Audrey. Rose sat patiently in the corner until Bill finally finished.

After they left, Bill called his friend Gary, and told him about his arrest and the situation with Justina and US Android. "Gary, I don't understand why Justina is acting so extreme about this; I never raped Alyssa, I never performed sexual acts on her, and I never asked her to perform any sexual acts on me. That is what I would consider to be sexual assault. All I ever did was cuddle with her. I had all the great sex with Shayna, when I wasn't having it with Justina . . ." Bill continued to purge himself of the stresses of his troubling issues for several minutes.

Gary listened with empathy, and consoled his long-time friend while they had a long, mutually gratifying conversation.

Gary invited Bill for a visit, and they made plans for Bill to come down to Alabama for a long weekend the following week. They both agreed it would be good for Bill to get away and forget about his troubles for a while. There was nothing else he could do, for the moment; he would just have to wait for John to prepare his defense.

Chapter Fourteen

Alyssa awoke to the sound of the rain beating on the roof above her. She had enjoyed sleeping in after having worked long hours, intensely the previous night, and really all during the preceding week, on her new project with Albert.

They had landed a rather sizable government grant, by presenting Alyssa's graduate school thesis. Building on some of Albert Freudenthal's foundational ideas, she had contended that based on the results of their most recent collaborative experiments, where isolated memories were able to be wirelessly transferred and stored, in a computer which was designed with the capability to recall these memories and process them, thus representing artificial intelligence; Alyssa had stated that because of this advancement, theoretically, she should be able to convert the psychic content of a person's mind into electronic signals and data; and then, using the latest android technology, beam their presence into an android body, almost like a temporary brain transplant.

The validation she had received, in being awarded the grant, after the scientific advancement committee reviewed her proposal for further experimentation along these lines, proved to be very exhilarating for her.

However, on a much more disturbing note, two weeks earlier Alyssa was informed she had been technically sexually assaulted, according to current laws. She was further distressed by the fact that, earlier that week, she had been subpoenaed to testify under hypnosis in the trial against Bill, should Bill's lawyer recommend going to trial and fight the charges, as opposed to taking a plea deal.

Alyssa tried to put it out of her mind; she couldn't fathom testifying against her own parent who had raised her, and she didn't really feel sexually violated, to any extent that she was moved to come forward of her own initiative and report it to anyone.

She sat down at her Skype terminal after a breakfast of oatmeal and coffee, and noticed that Tommy had left a message for her to call him. She hit the return Skype button and waited for Tommy to answer.

"Hi Tommy."

"Hi Alyssa, I'm glad you called. I haven't been able to reach you for over a week; what's happening?"

"Oh, I've been working in the lab with Albert on our grant project rather intensely; we got onto something and we wanted to keep working while the ideas were still fresh in our minds."

"The mind teleporting project I assume . . ."

"Yes, we just ordered some more equipment, and a few of the new generation of androids to experiment with. We're going to try to transfer thoughts from Albert's assistant to the electronic brain of an android next month, if we can ascertain that our theories are correct; but we have a lot of work ahead of us."

"You look tired; are you alright?"

"Yes, I'm fine; I just woke up, and I've been recovering from the long hours we spent last week in the lab."

"What's going on with the sexual assault case against Bill?" Tommy probed, "Have you had any more contact with US Android?"

"No, but I went to see the psychiatrist they recommended me to a week ago Friday, and he told me some interesting facts."

"Oh—What did he say?"

"He said that US Android considers me a genius, and he went on to tell me about a few other children taking part in the family-android test project; he said that the common thread among the genius children in the project was that they had received tender nurturing, psychologically speaking, and more broad exposure to adult ideas and concepts, including in a lot of cases, sensing a man's sexual desires for a female, or vice-versa. He's theorized that experiencing pleasant feelings of sexual stimulation augmented a sense of how wonderful it is to be alive, and this possibly exhilarated and inspired these genius children a lot more than children who did not have these experiences and senses."

"Wow! That's pretty amazing; did you tell Bill?"

"No, remember? I can't have any contact with Bill while these sexual assault charges are pending."

"That's right; that's a shame, because you and Bill have been pretty tight over the years."

"Yeah, but the head psychologist at US Android told me that I should be very upset about this having happened, because the experts say this kind of behavior between a stepfather and a minor stepdaughter can be very damaging. She put me under hypnosis, and she played back the recording of the session for me afterward, and I <u>was</u> a bit disturbed to remember the full magnitude of what I have been exposed to sexually, over the years; but up until then, I hadn't really had any real serious concerns or disturbances, related to it."

"That's interesting," Tommy commented.

Alyssa continued filling Tommy in, "I met with Mom and the prosecutor last Thursday, and they convinced me that I must speak up against what happened to me, in order to stop this kind of adult to minor sexual abuse from happening in the future."

"Really? It was that bad, huh?"

"They say Bill robbed me of my childhood."

"That sounds pretty serious; but you seem to have turned out pretty well, haven't you?"

"Yeah, I'm pretty torn; I appreciate what Bill has done for me over the years, but after being stoked up by Mom and the prosecutor, I'm feeling somewhat angry at him for potentially damaging me, and causing this scandal. The psychologist and the psychiatrist I saw both told me I may have trouble sustaining a romantic and sexual relationship, for the rest of my life."

"Well, I guess you've only had the one relationship, but that lasted a year or so, didn't it?"

"Yes, and I've kind of been married to my work these days; I haven't had time for a relationship; but I don't know what I'm up against for the future."

"Yeah, I guess not . . . Well do you want to get together this weekend? I could come up to Philadelphia on Friday, and stay the weekend . . ."

"That would be great!—I need someone to talk to more about this whole situation, and Albert and I are taking the weekend off anyway; we're just waiting for the new equipment to arrive."

"Fine, I should get there by around two, or three; maybe we could have a late lunch together . . ."

"Okay; we'll see you then; have a good rest of the week; I'll look forward to seeing you on Friday."

Alyssa hung up and went back to bed. Tommy's feedback, that she looked tired, had put Alyssa in touch with her own deep sense of exhaustion. She fell back asleep for several hours, before waking, a bit more refreshed.

Bill and his father arrived at John's office at three-thirty, and met with him in the conference room for a second time. John came into the conference room carrying a fairly thick folder containing the Police report, case law and his notes on his meeting with the prosecutor the preceding week, "Hi Bill, Paul; good to see you." He looked at Bill and asked somewhat compassionately, "How are you holding up? I know it's been a tough last couple of weeks, but I have some news to share with you about my meeting with Donna Smith; she's the prosecutor who's been assigned to your case."

Bill was a bit surprised, as he had figured that lawyers were all about getting down to business, "I'm fine, thank you," he answered calmly.

Paul spoke somewhat impatiently, "John, why don't you tell us what went on in your talks with Donna . . ."

John suddenly turned very businesslike, "Yes, I argued the point that this was US Android's screw-up, and I mentioned the substance abuse issue, but she's gotten a hold of the contract between you and US Android, and she's claiming that you were warned, and they have a valid disclaimer. Law also provides that since you were using E-Tox, it was technically illegal for you to enter into a binding legal agreement, but she does recognize that it is a mitigating factor that you were having substance abuse issues. She offered a plea deal of ten to forty years in a state prison here in Massachusetts, and she emphasized that there was more than enough evidence against you to convict you if we went to trial, whereby you might well be exiled to planet P, and as you know, that's permanent."

"I could get exiled to planet P over this?!" Bill gasped, "It was a computer malfunction!"

"This was just my first go around with Donna," John explained, "We have a court date for August tenth at ten o'clock. That's when I'll have a chance to talk with Donna and judge Thomas in chambers. We'll get his take on this; he has the final decision unless we go to trial, and he may be more sympathetic to your situation, in light of the circumstances."

"Well I should hope so, "Paul interjected, "At least the judge is a man!"

"Male influence may help," John responded in peer-like fashion.

"Let me ask you," Paul thought of an idea, "What if I talked to Justina? Isn't it true that what the minor victim's mother wants in terms of punishment, is a big factor in the outcome?"

"Yes it is true, Paul, that what the victim wants in terms of punishment is the main driving force behind the plea deal they'll ultimately be offering, but I don't think it's a good idea for you to be talking to Justina. It's been my experience in these cases that the mother is usually not inclined to back down on wanting the maximum sentence. Why don't you let me try and get to Justina through the means of negotiating with the prosecutor, and see if we can't emphasize that, if we did decide to go to trial, we would be making a strong case for the fact this all stems mainly from a computer-brain software malfunction, and emphasizing that Bill had no way of knowing, if he was significantly disturbing or corrupting Alyssa."

"That sounds like a good strategy," Bill commented, "Will you write a letter to Justina, to that effect?"

"Well no, that generally isn't done, but I can talk to Donna, and ask her to pass on that information."

"John," Paul interjected, "How about if I write a letter to Justina; can you ask Donna to pass a letter from me on to Justina?"

John hesitated for several seconds as he contemplated this idea. He finally cocked his head a bit, and responded, "I wouldn't advise that; but if you want to write a letter to the prosecutor, I don't see any harm which could come of that, as long as I can review the letter, and edit the content."

Paul nodded in approval, "Alright; I'll write up a draft and email it to you, and we'll go from there."

Bill put himself in the loop. "Why don't you send it to me first, Dad, and let me also have some input into this as well," he suggested.

"Alright; we'll work on it together, and then we'll email it to John when we're through." Paul added.

"Okay; I'm due in court in about twenty minutes," John announced, "So I have to get going, but I'll look for your email and give you my comments."

Bill dropped his father back at the Ramada and went back to his hotel. After searching for a little over a week, he had finally found a furnished apartment, which he would be moving into the following day. He had canceled his E-Tox account the week before, and he gave his wine away to April. They had exchanged Skype numbers, the morning she checked out, and they had told each other that they planned to keep in touch.

Bill imagined that he might Skype with her a few times, and after they got to know each other better, maybe ask her out for a date; but he had his doubts due to the fact that she had children. He remembered how John had cautioned him that the court may frown upon his entering into a relationship with a woman having children, while these charges were pending, and he didn't need any more complications. It also seemed somewhat likely that he might be going to jail in the not-too-distant future. All in all, he seemed pretty unsure of his future.

CHAPTER FIFTEEN

ANOTHER TWO MONTHS WENT by, as Bill's case was given two continuances, which meant John wasn't able to meet with the judge and the prosecutor both together yet, although he had talked with both of them separately. It was really due to the fact that the prosecutor hadn't yet made it to court, on the days Bill was scheduled to appear.

John had given the letter which the three of them, Bill, his father and John, had collectively wrote to Donna, and she had told John that she would pass on a copy to Justina.

John had given the feedback to Bill and his father, that during John's talks separately with Judge Thomas, the judge was quite a bit more sympathetic to Bill's plight than the prosecutor has been, but he had also said that there wasn't much he could do if the prosecutor kept pressing for jail time.

Today was Bill's third appearance in court, and he sat patiently on the bench, waiting for John to emerge from the judge's chambers. John was finally getting to talk with Judge Thomas and Donna Smith, in a three-way battle over Bill's fate.

Bill's father had taken an apartment in the local area himself, as John had told him, quite surprisingly, that it wasn't uncommon for these kinds of cases to take months, if not even a couple of years sometimes, to get resolved; even if the case never went to trial! He had stepped out of the courtroom to make a call to his wife, to counsel her on how to proceed with negotiations on the municipal bridge project he had been working on before he came back to Boston to help Bill, "Hi Lauren, how are you today?"

"Hi Paul; I'm okay, how is Bill's case going? Has Bill's lawyer talked to the judge and the prosecutor yet?"

"They're talking now; we should know something in the next half-an-hour or so; I'll keep you posted. Have you heard from Ned Spitzer on whether they're moving ahead with the bridge project this month?"

"I talked with his office an hour ago; his assistant said Ned would be Skyping you this afternoon, after his meeting with the zoning board; apparently there's an issue with homeowners signing a petition to block the project . . ."

"Really?—Why don't you call Tim Johnson and let him know. Maybe he could sit in on the meeting; when is it scheduled for, do you know?"

"One o'clock; I'll call Tim and tell him you'd like him to be there. I also got a call from Scott Donaldson on the Maximus Dam project. He wants to have a conference call with you and Ralph Steiner, who is the head of the committee, tomorrow at three o'clock; will you be available?"

"Sure; call him back and tell him I'll be waiting for his call. Can you overnight the file to me, so I can review my notes?"

"I could just send it electronically, if you'd like . . ."

"No, there's too much confidential information in that file; I wouldn't want other contractors to get their hands on the sealed bids of the other contractors who made bids, in case any of them have hired good hackers."

"Sure, I understand; I'll call Inter-Galactic Express for a pickup; if I get it to them before noon, it will get to you tomorrow morning."

"Thank you; how is everything else going?"

"Fine; the gardener is coming out this afternoon to do some weeding, and I'll have to tell him where to plant the new shrubs. I'm going to have him place them around the pool. You know, the shrubs we had out there got a fungus?—All but three of them have died."

"Alright; I'm sure you can handle it. Did they put in the new floor in the living room yesterday?"

"Yes, and it looks wonderful! They were here all day yesterday, but they finished up around four."

"That's good; how does it look?" Paul asked curiously.

"Oh! I have to tell you that the synthetic Albanian hardwood is absolutely magnificent! It has a very regal look. Wait 'till you see it . . ."

"Good; I'll look forward to seeing it when I get back; I'm planning to return for the weekend on Friday, assuming there is some resolution in Bill's case today; we're waiting for the prosecutor's final offer; then we have to decide whether we're going to trial or not."

"Well, I wish you luck; I love you!"

"Love you too; I'll be in touch . . ."

Paul went back into the courtroom and sat on the bench with Bill for another twenty minutes before John emerged from the judge's chambers and waved them over. When they made their way into the lobby, John gave them the news, "Well, Justina wasn't swayed by our letter; Donna is still pushing for ten to forty years on a plea deal; otherwise we go to trial next month."

Bill shook his head, looking grimly at John, and then at his father, "—And US Android is getting off Scott-free?"

"There is a class-action suit being put together against US Android, and it seems likely that there will be a sizable settlement, but there are no criminal charges being brought; US Android's legal team was very thorough in writing up the contracts in a way that protects them from legal action other than a civil suit."

"John, what are the chances we might win if we go to trial on this?" Paul asked hopefully.

"Well, as we've talked about, there are several mitigating factors," John responded, "There's probably an even chance Bill will walk away from this unscathed if we go to trial, but there's obviously no guarantees . . ."

"I don't know if I want to risk being exiled to planet P," Bill said skeptically.

"There is that risk; but the hour is now upon us where we have to announce which way we want to go. It's your decision; what do you want me to say?"

"Well, I don't want to go to prison for the next forty years, that's for sure," Bill responded, "Do you really think we have a pretty good chance of winning if we go to trial?"

"It depends a lot on the jury, but I think I could present a strong case that you did nothing wrong; you didn't have any sexual acts with your stepdaughter, all of your sexual exchanges were either with Justina, or with your android. There's really no precedent in these cases yet, but I could make the argument that it doesn't seem fair, that you should be exiled for this; maybe the jury would be sympathetic."

"Well if you think there is a good chance I could get off, I think I'd rather go to trial; what do you think, Dad?"

"John, what are the other mitigating factors, in your mind?" Paul asked.

"There's the fact that Justina was drunk and passed out while Alyssa was being exposed to this mild form of sexuality; and it would have normally fallen on Justina's shoulders to sense what was happening and put a stop to it; I could argue that US Android had no legal access to Alyssa's internet memory file, and perhaps because of the scope of the prototype testing project being undertaken they should have; there's the fact that you were leaned on heavily, to take part in this experiment, as a member of the marketing team at US Android at the time this new strain of androids was first manufactured; and there's the fact that you were not aware of any harm or damage, or the potential magnitude of family upset for Alyssa's fairly indirect exposure to some amount of sexual expression, or the severity of legal consequences in the case that something like this were to become public knowledge; we could argue that you were only behaving reasonably as a naturally motivated man might; and finally that you weren't aware of any significant wrongdoing on your part, pretty much during the entire time it was going on, isn't that right, Bill?"

Paul nodded, "It does seem like you have a pretty strong case to argue, John. What do you <u>think</u>; are you up to it?"

John answered right away, "Well as I say, there are no guarantees, but I'll fight hard for you every step of the way, if going to trial is the route you decide to take."

"Then let's go to trial," Bill said definitively.

John looked at Paul, for any objections, and seeing none, he turned back to Bill, "I'll tell them that we're proceeding to trial on this, and we can meet in my office early next week to discuss our strategy."

"John, do you think we could meet on Friday morning?" Paul asked, "I'm flying back on Friday afternoon, and I'd feel a lot better if I knew the basic strategy before I left."

John thought for a few seconds, "I guess I could fit you in; but it would have to be early; can you come in around eight-thirty?"

"Bill looked at his father, "Yes, I think that would be fine; that's alright with you Dad?"

"Friday morning at eight-thirty it is," Paul replied.

The three of them met on Friday as planned. John let them know he would be going after US Android, trying to poke holes in their disclaimer in the contract Bill and Justina had signed nine years back. He would try to establish that management had skipped over discussion on that clause, which appeared in fine print somewhere embedded in the middle of the contract.

Bill would try to make contact with the lawyer they had used to go over the contact with them at US Android's offices, to get his statement that it was not discussed, the fact that US Android would be held harmless, if anything went wrong and there were legal charges brought against Bill and or Justina during the term of their contract.

John would also contact the rehab Justina went to in order to stop drinking, to build further evidence against her, and he would try to introduce her as the main culprit, establishing the fact that she had evaded her responsibility to become aware of any sexual bleedthrough, or any other significant threats or disturbances her daughter might be experiencing, and to stop the sexual contact between Bill and Shayna immediately, in the case this was necessary.

These were the first steps they would take in order to build a case for Bill's defense. Bill and his father had left John's office, somewhat more confident than when they had arrived, developing some amount of optimism that they could put together a solid defense.

Paul got on his flight to return to Earth-3 that afternoon. He would arrive home the following morning. Bill was feeling a little lonely, so he Skyped April, "Hi April, do you remember me from the Americas Inn last month?"

"Sure, Bill, right?"

"Yeah; I didn't tell you before, but I am actually one of the parties involved in the sexual assault scandal at US Android.

Me and my wife signed up for a prototype program where we and our two children were connected to family-androids. In fact, we've been connected for over nine years now."

"Wow! That's a long time; I understand they just discovered there were unknown software malfunctions; was this happening during this entire time?—Exactly what happened?"

"Well, it's a long story, but basically when I had some sexual contact with my female counterpart android, there was bleedthrough to my stepdaughter's internet memory file; in other words she has memories, and other aspects of awareness, of the nature and magnitude of my sexual desires. The prosecutor contended to my lawyer, that my stepdaughter has been exposed to severely inappropriate sexual thoughts and behavior; and I'm to blame for this; they're charging me with sexual assault."

"Oh boy;—Are you going to fight it?"

"Yes, we go to trial next month; I was just at my lawyer's this morning, going over our strategy."

"Well I wish you luck; are you working meanwhile?"

"No, US Android has actually suspended me from working there, for the duration of the trial; even though I haven't really done anything wrong, as far as I can see; do you believe that?!"

"It sounds like you're having some hard luck these days."

"How's it going for you?"

"I'm doing alright; Nancy is away at summer camp, and Shawn is away with his friend's family this week; they rented a condo on the Jersey Shore for the week."

"Oh; so you have the house to yourself . . . Do you have any more vacation days, because now would be a good time to use them, wouldn't it?"

"I have three more days, and I'm taking Thursday, Friday and Monday off."

"Maybe we could go out for lunch on Thursday or Friday, what do you think?"

"I'm not doing anything on Friday afternoon . . ."

"Okay; I'm having dinner with my son Tommy on Friday, but I'm free for lunch; what do you say I pick you up at noon?"

"That would be fine; let me give you directions . . ."

Friday morning Bill slept in. The day before, he had again contacted Sid Rosenbaum, the lawyer who had accompanied and advised them at the time they originally signed the contracts with US android, beginning their participation in the ten year family-android protocol testing project. Sid had finished going over their contract with US Android, earlier in the week, and Bill had been able to secure a promise to get a statement from Sid to the effect that US Android didn't in fact make any mention of their disclaimer, that US Android would be held harmless if there was any kind of software problem while they were connected to Adam and Shayna, for the duration of the prototype test period. After he had finished the Skype call, he felt a little more at ease; which was part of the reason he had slept so well. He got ready and left his apartment for his date a little after eleven-thirty.

April looked hot when Bill went to pick her up at noon. She had on a pink dress with a green flowery print, and she wore her beautiful brown hair down. It rested on either side of her cleavage. Bill had to make an effort not to stare at her cleavage as he held the door open to let her out of the house.

"Hi April; you look stunning in that dress, although you looked great in your bathing suit at the Jacuzzi too!"

"Thank you," she said modestly, "I thought I would dress up since we are going to the Elephant Bar; it's a pretty classy place."

"Yes, I used to go there with Justina," he admitted, and then checked himself, "Oh, I shouldn't be talking about my ex-wife probably."

"No, I don't mind; you were married for how long?" she asked.

"Let's see, about fifteen years; we got married the year before Tommy and Alyssa were born."

"So the twins are fourteen then . . ."

"Yeah, they'll be fifteen in November."

They climbed into the car, "When does Nancy turn twelve?" Bill asked.

"She turns twelve in January; January twelfth, to be exact." Talking about it had made her acutely aware that, in some respects, time had flown by, "I can hardly believe she's that old; it seems like it was just yesterday that she was going to kindergarten."

"The years do pass by; when's Shawn going to turn eight?"

"Next month; he'll be going to the same school as Nancy this fall."

"Oh? I thought Nancy would be going to college this fall . . ."

"No, she actually stayed back a year, so she'll be a senior this year."

"Are you going to be able to afford to send her to college?"

"Yes; my ex-husband is supposed to pay for it, but he doesn't make enough money at his job, so I'll probably have to pitch in."

"I guess it's a good thing you have a steady job at Blackwater."

Yes, it sure is," April said with a note of relief.

There was an awkward pause while Bill decided how much he was going to say about his situation with the legal case against him. Looking into her beautiful brown eyes, he finally spoke, "I'm hoping to get off of these charges against me, when we go to trial next month, or shortly thereafter . . ."

"Well maybe we can come here to celebrate!" April offered optimistically.

"Yeah!" Bill said, getting into the mood, "I <u>sure</u> would look forward to <u>that</u>!"

"Is Justina going ahead with the divorce?"

"No, she withdrew her petition last month; she's waiting for the case against me to be over with. I guess she figures that if I lose, she'll have an easy time getting everything in the divorce."

"Oh, she's being ruthless, is she?"

"Yeah; let's talk about something else, I really don't want to talk about it . . ."

"Okay; so what are you doing with your time these days?"

"Well, I've been visiting with my friends on the weekends; I have a good friend Gary, who has had me down to Alabama twice since all of this broke out. He took me to New Orleans last month, and we're going sailing together next weekend."

"That should take your mind off things," April intuited, "What part of Alabama does he live in? I have relatives in Montgomery."

"He's in Fairhope; I think that's about a hundred and fifty miles north; he's right on the coast."

"I've been down there; that's on Mobile Bay . . ."

"Oh; how did you know; did you vacation there?"

"We stayed at a condo on the water once down there for a week; unbelievable seafood!" she remembered, reminded of the trip.

"Yeah, now that all the oil is tapped out from under the gulf, there's no more oil spills to ruin the fishing."

"Yes, the water is as clear as in the Bahamas."

"Yeah the new levy has been holding between the gulf and the Atlantic Ocean; it's amazing how clean the Gulf is now, all the way to Mexico."

"Yeah, I miss my sister; I should go down to visit her, maybe over Labor Day weekend . . ."

"So how long do you have until your kids come back?"

"They come back on Sunday night, why?"

"Oh, I just was thinking how much I miss the Jacuzzi and the sauna at the Americas Inn; are you interested in maybe going over there this afternoon for a while? They change the water in Jacuzzi every Thursday, for the weekend, so it should be nice and clean."

"Yeah, we could do that."

"Well, how about if after lunch we go back to your place, so you can get your bathing suit, and then we can stop off at my apartment so I could pick up a few things."

"That sounds fine."

They ate lunch leisurely and got back to April's around one-thirty. She threw a few things into an overnight bag while Bill waited in the car, and then they went to Bill's apartment.

They got to the Americas Inn at around two-thirty and checked into their room. Bill helped April out of her dress, and she had on a sexy bikini with a halter top underneath. To keep things comfortable, Bill had slipped into the bathroom, to change into his bathing suit. They made their way down to the pool area. As they were walking, Bill remembered his last visit to the Jacuzzi in an altered state of mind; he missed his E-Tox, but now he had April's company to enjoy instead; he'd be alright, he thought.

They sat in the Jacuzzi and had a sauna together for the next hour or so, and then they came back to the room. "I'm so relaxed right now," April said as she sat down on the edge of the bed. Her pretty face and her sexy body was a powerful aphrodisiac to Bill, who hadn't had any sexual contact for several weeks.

He sat on the bed next to her and took her in his arms and kissed her passionately. He had no feelings of guilt because John had told him that now that he was separated from Justina, he could get involved with another woman without any worries.

As it turned out, April was hungry for love too, as she hadn't been with anyone for months, herself. They made love rapturously, and afterwards they took a nap together, wrapped in each other's arms.

Chapter Sixteen

Alyssa slumped back into her chair, totally exhausted. Due to their excitement at being so close to seeing the results of the experiment, she had been working through the night with Albert, on the last finishing touches, before they would be ready to make their first attempts. Jim Flynn, Albert's assistant, was sitting in a chair in the lab booth, with wires attached to his scalp, ready to have his mind teleported into an android body in the next booth.

"Do you think we've thought of everything?" she asked Albert, who sipped his coffee, standing and looking into the two booths through the glass.

"I think we're ready," he said with confidence and tired excitement.

"Then let's turn on the signal generator and see if our theories were right," Alyssa said tiredly.

Albert walked over to the console and flipped the switch. The machine came on with a low hum as they watched for about thirty seconds. Then they eagerly made their way into the chamber with the android, only to find him smiling. "It worked!" he announced, "My mind is in this android body, and I seem to be able to control my body movements!"

Alyssa fainted, and Albert caught her under her arms before she fell. They had finally achieved mind teleportation, which they had been working on for the last three and a half years together.

"Alyssa!" Albert called to her as he flopped her into a chair just outside the booth. She came to with an embarrassed smile," Have we finally done it?" she asked weakly.

The android walked over to her desk and smiled at her, "Yes we have," he said proudly. "I'm Jim Flynn in every way but my body, and in fact, I'm feeling quite comfortable in this android body."

The news spread quickly; it was in all of the papers, and all over the internet, as the top story. The Boston Globe headline read, "Young prodigy Alyssa Symms, working with the famous Albert

Freudenthal develops the mental version of "Beam me up Scotty!" It is now possible to have your mind teleported into an android body!"

The next experiment was to beam Jim Flynn's mind to an android body in New York City, in Albert's lab there. The experiment was set to take place the following month, after the equipment was transported from Philadelphia and set up once again. It was a big undertaking, as the equipment necessary took up a 15 foot by 20 foot room at the lab in Philadelphia, and there was a lot of sensitive equipment indeed. Great care was taken as they dismantled and packed each piece of equipment for shipping.

Alyssa took the next several days off, but she could not fully relax because she knew the trial against Bill would begin the following week.

She was scheduled to go in for a hypnotic session that Wednesday, so the court could discover what she had remembered of Bill's sexual contact with Shayna, as well as the sexual thoughts of Bill's which had also registered in her online memory file. She was acutely aware that she was having mixed feelings about being the one to provide the chief evidence against Bill, whom she had always admired and adored.

Tommy was just arriving. He had taken a few days off from work to be with Alyssa through this difficult time. The doorbell rang, and Alyssa went to receive Tommy, "Hi Tommy, I'm glad you could come. How was your trip?"

"It was fine, except I got a bit of a late start, so I'm here a little later than I said I would be. Congratulations on your breakthrough with Albert; it's pretty amazing what you two have developed."

"Thank you; I was so overwhelmed that I fainted when I realized it was a success."

"Have you had lunch? I was thinking we could go out . . ."

"No, I haven't felt much like eating; I'm pretty upset about Bill's court case."

"I can imagine; you said you're meeting with the prosecutor later today?"

"Yes, she wants to review the details of the case with Mom and me."

Tommy went right to the heart of what he guessed would be the most disturbing thoughts Alyssa might be having, "I understand that if the prosecution wins the case, it's pretty much a given that Bill will be exiled to planet P . . ."

"Yes, and I really don't want that to happen, but Mom does; she is upset beyond words that this happened."

"Yeah, I know; I talked with her last night, and she's on the war path."

"What's your position on the situation?" Alyssa asked.

"I want Bill to get off of the charges; it doesn't seem to me that he is really guilty of any significant wrongdoing."

"Well, Mom and the head psychologist at US Android both said I may well have been pretty damaged emotionally by what I have experienced, and Bill should be punished."

"I don't know; how have you been damaged? You seem fine to me . . ."

"I know, and I feel fine, but I'm told I may have trouble maintaining a relationship with a man in the future, and it's true that I have not had any relations with a man in the past few years."

"Give it time; you're still young, sis, and the right man hasn't come along yet."

"Do you think so? I don't know whether to believe Paulina when she tells me I will have trouble."

"I doubt you will; is there any way you can back out of testifying against Bill, if you wanted to?"

"No, I don't think so, not at this point; I've given my commitment to Mom and Donna Smith."

"Well, let's talk about something else; I'm sure you've probably been thinking about nothing else for the last few days since you've been off work."

"You don't know the half of it; I haven't been able to sleep, and I've been plagued by thoughts of Bill being exiled to planet P . . ."

"It's really out of your hands at this point, isn't it?—Let's go out and get some lunch; you'll probably feel better if you get something in your stomach."

"Yes, I suppose you're right; where do you want to go?"

"We could go to the Pepper Mill; I'll buy you a mojito in the bar before lunch," Tommy offered, "You look like you could use a drink."

"Well, it is almost three; I suppose it's not too early to have a drink."

"That's the spirit! Come on, let's go before you change your mind.

It was the first Tuesday in September, and Bill had had a fitful Labor Day weekend. April had gone to visit her sister, so he had no outlet to stop thinking about the trial, which was beginning that day.

The judge entered the courtroom at a little after ten o'clock, and the proceedings began, "All rise," the bailiff announced, and everybody in the courtroom got to their feet.

"The prosecutor will read the charges against Mr. William Symms," the judge ordered.

"The charges are sexual assault in the fourth degree, and risk of injury to a minor. The victim is Alyssa Symms; the relationship to the defendant is that she is his stepdaughter," the prosecutor read.

The trial dragged on for weeks, as the defense tried to show that US Android was responsible for the bleedthrough memories of Bill's sexual thoughts, and the sexual activity that went on between Bill and Shayna.

The prosecutor argued that Bill and Justina had made a pact that they would have no sexual contact with Shayna and Adam for the duration of the ten year test period.

The defense then argued that Justina was passed out drunk every night, and Shayna was Bill's only outlet for sexual exchange. It was only natural and reasonable that he would have some sexual contact with her in the middle of the night.

The prosecutor argued back that Bill could have had sex with Justina earlier in the evenings in order to satisfy his sexual appetite; and Bill hid it from Justina that he was having sex with Shayna while she slept.

Ultimately, the jury threw in with the prosecution, and convicted Bill of both charges, and he was sentenced to exile to planet P, mercilessly.

Bill was taken into custody after the hearing, where he would wait in a state prison until enough prisoners who would be exiled to make a trip to planet P were gathered.

April came to visit him in jail, the following day, "Hi Bill; I'm sorry for the outcome of your trial; how are you feeling?"

"I'm still in shock; I can't believe they found me guilty."

"Do you have a cellmate?"

"Yeah, his name is Pat; he's in on charges that he had sex with a thirteen year old girl."

"How old is he?"

"He's twenty-nine."

"Is he going to be exiled to planet P with you?"

"Yeah; they say we'll be transported next month."

"I'm really sorry, Bill . . ."There was a long, uncomfortable pause in the conversation; then April finally broke the silence, "I'll write to you; will you be able to Skype?"

"Nope; and I'll have no one on the planet to visit me, so all I can do is write."

"That's too bad, but at least we'll be able to write back and forth . . . I'll miss you; are you getting enough sleep?"

"No; I haven't really been able to sleep well ever since I stopped using E-Tox. I was using an over-the-counter sleep aid, but they don't give out any sleep aids in prison; they don't really care if you sleep or not; I guess it's all part of the punishment."

"Well that's too bad," April said sympathetically, "Do you have a window?"

"Yeah; each cell has a six foot wide window, so there's plenty of light."

"How big is your cell?"

"It's about twelve by twenty, but it feels pretty small in comparison with the apartment I was living in; I had a twenty by twenty living room, a bedroom that was almost as big, and I had a back deck."

"Yes, I remember.—Well I guess you'll adapt; at least you have a cellmate to talk with."

"Yeah, he's a pretty nice guy; he just had a bad upbringing. His stepfather abused him as a child, and he got into cocaine at a young age; his stepfather was a bad influence."

April wasn't paying any attention to what Bill was saying, "Bill, I'm <u>so</u> sorry this has happened to you; it couldn't have happened to a nicer guy."

"Yeah, that's funny; that's what Justina used to say to me. She'd say, "You're the nicest person I know!" I guess that phrase is long gone . . .

Bill was transported to planet P the following month. He got to keep Pat as his cellmate. The cells were a little bigger, and they had a courtyard so they could get some sun, and the prisoners got to get out of their cells twice a day for two hours, where all of the prisoners congregated in a large common area the size of a football field.

The months went by, and before he knew it, Tommy wrote Bill a letter, informing him that the ten year test period was finally up, and that Justina had received a check from US Android in excess of $227 million, including the interest earned over the ten years, during which time the initially agreed upon $150 million had sat in escrow.

She had given Alyssa and Tommy each twenty-five million, so Tommy was flush. In his letter, Tommy had talked about coming to planet P to appeal Bill's decision, but Bill wrote back and told him not to, because he knew it meant he couldn't go back to earth, and he would have to live out his days on planet P; and he couldn't ask Tommy to do that.

Tommy wrote back and told Bill that he didn't care that he would be confined to the planet if he came to Bill's aid; and that he had heard there were cities where they both might live somewhat comfortably, assuming Tommy's efforts to get Bill out of prison.

He also informed Bill that a class action suit had been filed against US Android, and they were forced to liquidate their assets in order to pay off the settlement. It didn't really matter however, because they had been shut down anyway, from making any further developments in the area of family-android manufacturing, due to the sexual assault problem. They hadn't been able to come up with a consistently successful fix for that problem, in every case, so the government disallowed any further manufacturing of family-androids.

Alyssa and Doctor Freudenthal had however, developed their technology further, and it was now possible for people to have their minds beamed into androids on other planets. Beaming stations were being built all over the world, and people were lining up to go on vacations to the other man-made planets. Because of the distances involved, it was actually a lot less expensive than physically traveling to them anyway.

Tommy wrote again the following month, and informed Bill that his plans were solidifying, for him to come to planet P, and appeal Bill's case. Alyssa had also agreed to give Tommy the technological plans to effect mind-beaming transfers, so that he might try and get an android company on planet P to build a mind beaming station. There were no laws, yet, against beaming an exiled person's mind to another planet; and Tommy considered that if he was successful in appealing Bill's case, they may well be able beam their minds into androids on Earth, and still be able to visit family and friends.

Tommy's news lifted Bill's spirits, and he began to be more hopeful about his future. He began to fathom the possibility that he might be able to live freely within a local community, in a house here on planet P, which with all of his newfound riches, Tommy would certainly be able to buy for them. Bill had heard that there were small cities nearby, established partly to provide housing for the families of prison staff and those working in the community to provide services to the prison, from meals and medical care, to schooling and other educational training. These communities, of course, also housed former inmates who had completed their prison sentences, or who had otherwise gotten out of prison on probation, or parole.

Bill sat in his cell, reading the Boston paper, which Tommy had bought him a subscription to. Each issue usually came about a week late, but Bill enjoyed keeping up with current events. Laying on the top bunk, propped up on a pretty uncomfortable pillow, having finished reading an article, he called below to his cellmate, "Hey Pat, I just read an article on US Android, and they sold all of their technology to another android company in New York, who have started production of his and hers androids. The article says they are being bought up as fast as they are being manufactured. It doesn't surprise me; they are a pretty amazing advance."

"I wonder if they'll be produced here on planet P; it would be cool if they did, and they could come to prison here and give us conjugal visits!"

"I'd doubt it; we can't even Skype with our loved ones; they're never going to approve any type of conjugal visits."

"Yeah, you're probably right."

"But for years, up here, they've been making androids of the opposite sex that run off your thoughts, so you don't even need a partner in order to have an android of the opposite sex."

"Yeah, that's pretty cool, I guess; but isn't that a little like masturbation? I mean, what's the sense?"

"Yeah, maybe so, but a beautiful woman is a lot better than using your hand!" They both laughed at the thought.

"Yeah, I wonder what will eventually happen to relationships between a man and a woman?"

"I suppose they'll become less popular now that this new technology has been developed."

"Well maybe you'll own one once you get paroled; when did you say you were eligible for parole again?"

"Fifty years," Pat answered sadly.

"Yeah, well I'm up for probation after forty, but maybe Tommy will be able to appeal my case, and I'll get out next year!"

"Yeah, that really would be great; I'm rooting for you!"

Tommy arrived the following week, with his laptop and Bill's trial transcript. He visited Bill on Saturday, during the normal weekend visiting hours. There was only one other prisoner with Bill when he went down to the visiting room however, because he was the only one besides Bill who had someone who had actually moved to the planet in order to be with her lover. Most prisoners were there by themselves for life.

Bill sat across from Tommy and smiled as they greeted each other, "Tommy, I can't tell you how much I appreciate all you are doing for me, and I sure hope we're successful."

"I brought the appeal paperwork, and we plan to apply next week. I found a lawyer who has won several appeals, although he wasn't cheap; but whatever it costs, it's worth it if we can get you out of here."

"Did he say how long it takes before the case is heard?"

"Well, the appeal has to be granted, but in our case, he doesn't think that will be a problem, since I explained that you really are not responsible for any wrongdoing; I told him that this was just some bleedthrough memories which ended up in Alyssa's online memory file, as a result of an error in your android's software."

Bill was silent for a few seconds as he thought about the wording Tommy had used. After all, it wasn't just Alyssa's awareness of some of his sexual acts with Shayna, it was also her awareness of the degree and nature of his sexual appetite, that would undoubtedly come into play. He decided to let it go for now, and just find out a little more information, "What's this lawyer's name? Will he come and talk to me here?"

"His name is Phil Pierson, and yes, he lives about a half-hour away. He'll come and visit with you in the next couple of weeks. I have an appointment to see him next Tuesday."

"Well, you'll have to tell me what he says; I hear an appeal can take over a year, even if it's successful."

"Yeah, well they say it's faster here than it is on earth; the judicial system here is supposedly a lot more simple and streamlined."

"Yeah, the trouble is, even if an appeal is successful, once you get out, you're still confined to the planet . . ."

"That reminds me," Tommy said enthusiastically, "I have Alyssa's dissertation on mind teleportation, and a list of equipment needed. I have to do an Internet search for companies that produce androids here, and see if I can get one of them interested in creating a mind-beaming station."

"That would be great! Then we could get out of here and go back to Earth for a visit, or maybe visit Dad on Earth-3!"

"Well, you have to pay someone to look after your body at the beaming station, and it's usually not good to be away for more than a month at a time, as your body sits inactive."

"Still, a month visit to Earth or Earth-3 sounds awfully good to me right now!"

"There's a lot we have to accomplish before that can happen, but it is conceivable for the not-too-distant future."

"Gee, it's good to see you Tommy, you look great! How is Alyssa these days?"

"She's doing fine; she's writing a book on teleportation of the mind, for the layman to understand the principals behind how it works. She's got a few major publishers interested in it, and she isn't half done with it yet."

"Do you see your mother?"

"Well I've taken a gamble; I won't see her for quite some time probably, and if I do see her again, it will probably be in an android body, if we can effect teleportation from here."

"Is she still teaching?"

"Yes, she still teaches at Natick High School, even though she's a millionaire a couple of hundred times over."

"I guess she's going to keep busy doing work in her fields of interest, even if she doesn't need the income."

"She did buy a new house though, in a rich neighborhood across town."

"What about Adam and Shayna?"

"They got confiscated; the government gave Mom ten thousand dollars each for them."

"That's about a third of what they cost."

"Mom just wanted to get rid of them."

"Does she keep an android?"

"No, she doesn't want anything to do with them anymore."

"What do you suppose they'll do with all of those family-androids they confiscated?"

"The word is, they'll end up here on planet P. They will be reprogrammed to do manual labor, building roads and bridges and such, and they won't be connected to families with children anymore."

"It's a damned shame; I don't see what all the harm was that they had to do all that, shut down US Android and all."

"There are those who beg to differ."

"Alyssa is a byproduct of the family-android syndrome, and she's an out and out genius!"

"They say there's negative side effects."

"Well I don't see them in Alyssa, do you?"

"Frankly, no; but they say she may have trouble maintaining a relationship in the future."

"Has she been seeing anyone recently?"

"She has been dating a physicist from the lab she's been working in; he seems pretty nice, and everything seems to be going alright so far."

"That's nice; I'm happy for her. I sure hope she doesn't have any trouble maintaining a relationship."

"Yeah, me too."

"Where are you staying?"

"I'm staying at the Hampton Inn in Chilton; it's about twenty miles from here. It's pretty empty; there's hardly anyone else staying there; in fact, they tell me that there's only about forty-thousand people living in Chilton, although it's one of the bigger cities in the area. Most of the people living on the planet have houses in the suburbs."

"Yeah, I've heard there's a lot of developed area on the equator, where the weather is warm most of the year. It gets up to the mid-eighties there in the summer, and it rarely dips below sixty in the winter months." "You said there's an outdoor courtyard in the cell block; do you get to play sports?"

"Basketball; I play about twice a week; some of the guys are pretty good, so the games are pretty challenging. I'm not one of the high scorers, but I can dribble and pass it to those who can make their outside shots; at least I'm getting some exercise here."

"What do you do otherwise, when you are out of the cell?"

"We play cards and chess; I'm getting better at chess; I get lots of practice."

"Is everyone in there with you, in on sexual assault charges?"

"Yes, they keep us separated from the other prisoners; it keeps the fights down. Some of the guys that are in here on murder charges and stealing, who are from the local area, really hate sex offenders. They've had trouble mixing us with these prisoners in the past, so now they've segregated us."

"That's good; do you feel safe in here?"

"Yeah, most of the prisoners I hang out with have accepted their fate, and they just make the best of it."

"That's good; well, it looks like our time is about up, and I have to get back to the hotel. I have some work to do in order to be ready for my meeting with your lawyer on Tuesday morning. I'm writing down all the facts I can think of, surrounding your case."

“Well thank you, Tommy; it’s sure great to have you in my corner.”

“You take care of yourself; I’ll be back next weekend; I’ll probably come on Saturday, and I’ll give you an update on what I discuss with Phil Pierson.”

Chapter Seventeen

It was Monday morning at nine o'clock. Tommy sat behind his Skype screen on his laptop, waiting for the secretary to come back on. He had announced that he was "Tom Symms, brother of Alyssa Symms who invented mind teleportation recently,"—and that he wanted to talk to Ron Goldstein, the President of Atlas Android, about possibly using the technology.

"Ron Goldstein here," he greeted, "Are you really Alyssa Symms' brother?—The Alyssa Symms that invented mind teleportation?"

"Yes I am," Tommy answered evenly, "I was wondering if you would have any interest in developing mind teleportation here on planet P."

"I'm not sure we would have the capital to get involved; but I'd be happy to take a look at the specs; do you have them with you?"

"Yes; I brought my sister's thesis, and a list of equipment necessary in order to effect mind teleportation. Maybe you could find the capital to build a beaming station if you don't have it all yourself . . ."

"It sounds like a very interesting proposition; there's roughly twenty million people on this planet, and I'm sure many of them would want to take a trip to the rest of the world that they can't see otherwise. We all know that you can't leave, physically speaking, once you've moved here."

"That's why I was thinking it would be an especially great thing if we could introduce mind teleportation here."

"Why don't you come in later this week with what you have, and we'll take a look at it. You don't mind if our scientist-doctors here at Atlas Android have access to your material?"

"No, in fact that was what I was hoping you'd suggest. We'd need them to get involved if we were going to try and set it up."

"Where are you staying? Are you close by?"

"I'm staying at a Hampton Inn in Chilton. How far is Alderon from Chilton?"

"Oh, it's only an hour plane ride; you wouldn't want to drive it; it would take you about thirty-six hours!"

"Oh, you're quite a ways away then."

"Almost three thousand miles, to be exact; when would you be free to come down? We can put you up at the Alderon Hilton; it's a very nice hotel."

"I could come down on Wednesday; would that work for you?" Tommy asked with growing excitement.

"Let me check . . ." There was a pause, "Yes, I could see you at two o'clock."

"Fine, then I'll fly down Wednesday morning and rent a car from the airport; I'll call your assistant for directions."

"Very good; I'll see you Wednesday afternoon, I look forward to it."

Tommy hung up and Skyped Alyssa, "Hi sis; I just got off the phone with the president of a company called Atlas Android. He says they're interested in looking into setting up mind teleporting stations here, if he can raise the capital. I'm going to meet with him later in the week."

"Good, I'm glad; I miss you already, and you've only been gone for less than a week! Mom's all upset that you went to help Bill, and that you can't come back."

"Well, thanks to your invention, maybe I can come back to visit before too long."

"It will take months to set up the first beaming stations, if you can find a company to take on the project; and I don't know how I'm going to like you visiting in an android body anyway."

"Yeah, I know what you mean; it probably won't be the same as being there in person, but we'll cross that bridge when we come to it. For now, I'm just working on Bill's appeal, and possibly getting a mind beaming station developed here."

"Have you met with Bill's lawyer yet?"

"I meet with him tomorrow morning. He's got a good reputation here, so we'll see how it goes, but so far I'm optimistic."

"Mom thinks it's despicable that you're trying to get him off; she thinks Bill belongs in jail for life."

"I know; but I don't agree; I don't see what happened as any great fault on Bill's part, and I don't see why he should be even suffering imprisonment, much less 40 years of imprisonment and permanent banishment. For that matter, it will be forty years before he'd even be eligible for probation, unless this appeal is successful."

"I have mixed feelings about it myself; but I suppose time will tell what's in store for Bill. What's the area like? Are there houses available?"

"Yeah, I was surprised to discover that there are communities here just like on the earth.—But it was somewhat of a gamble to come here, because no one knows anything about this planet. You can't get information from any website about planet P, and nobody I talked to could tell me much about what I could expect to find here, in terms of living conditions."

"Do you suppose you'll buy a house, or do you think you'll just take an apartment?"

"I haven't really started looking into that yet. I guess I'll look into that after I've gotten the ball rolling with Bill's appeal, and once I've also gotten farther along with trying to get an android company to set up a beaming station. Maybe in a week or two, I'll start hunting for a place to live."

"How expensive are things there?"

"It seems my money will go a bit farther here than in Boston; my hotel costs about half of what I'd pay in downtown Boston, and the restaurants here are a good deal cheaper than back home too. I guess I'm about to find out how expensive airfare is here; I've got to fly about three thousand miles to my appointment with Atlas Android on Wednesday."

"You took all of your money with you, didn't you?"

"I have mom's check for twenty-five million in my wallet. I'm going to open an account and deposit it today."

"You'd better do it fast, before Mom stops payment on it or something."

"It's a cashier's check; she can't stop payment on it, but I will feel safer and more relieved once the funds become available to me. It may take at least a week for the funds to clear."

"Alright; if you need money before then, I could wire you some . . ."

"That won't be necessary; I have five thousand in traveler's checks; that should hold me over for a while."

"Oh Tommy; I miss you! I wish you didn't have to go off like you did . . ."

"I know, and I miss you too; I promise I'll Skype with you a couple of times a week; every night if you want . . ."

"I've started a new project with Albert; we're working on making further refinement in android technology. Now that we can effect mind teleportation, we need to make it so when you travel to an android body, you can feel everything you can when you're in your own body. Up until now, androids haven't really had to have a central nervous system."

"I see; you're going to make it so I can have a total human experience when I come to see you in my android body next year, or whenever?" he joked optimistically.

"Hopefully even sooner; I don't know if I can wait a whole year to see you and be with you again."

"Well, I'll see what I can do on my end."

Tommy arrived at Phil Pierson's office at nine on Tuesday morning. He handed Phil the transcripts of the trial against Bill which put him on planet P in prison. "Hi Phil, Tom Symms; here is the paperwork you asked for, on my stepfather's trial. The police report, the transcripts, the pre-sentence investigation, and his bio; was there anything else I'm missing?"

"I'll take a look; it sounds like you have everything though. Explain to me again, Bill, as an employee of US Android, took part in a prototype test program using family-androids, and this is where the legal trouble stemmed from?"

"Yes, we were all connected to two androids, Bill to Shayna-1; my mother, Bill's wife, to Adam-1, me to Adam-1 also, and my sister Alyssa to Shayna-1; everything seemed to work perfectly for years, until we found out that there were bleedthrough memories of sexual experiences between Bill and Shayna found in Alyssa's Internet memory file."

"And by bleedthrough, you mean the Chinese wall software malfunctioned, and Alyssa became aware of sexual experiences going on between Bill and Shayna . . ."

"That's right; and they labeled this as sexual assault in the fourth degree against Alyssa."

"That sounds ridiculous to me; it sounds like Bill got railroaded into prison over this. The laws are slightly more forgiving here on planet P, and I'm thinking that the judge may well grant an appeal in this case."

"That would be wonderful! How soon can you start the appeal process?"

"Let me do some preliminary groundwork this week, and we'll see if we can't file for the appeal next week."

"Okay; obviously, we can't call any witnesses besides myself; how does that work?"

"They'll use the witnesses' testimony in the transcripts. If need be, they may ask for a written statement from you or your family members, but as I say, they'll probably just review the transcripts."

"If they grant the appeal, will Bill be brought before a jury?"

"In all likelihood, yes; but the jury here is made up mostly of people who have been outcast by the system, so it is more likely to favor the defendant."

"This is all good news so far," Tommy reflected.

"Yes, your stepfather's case sounds like a good candidate for a successful appeal, at this point," Phil added.

"You'll contact me once you have gone over everything, won't you?"

"I'll let you know when we've submitted the paperwork for the appeal, probably next week."

"Very good then, I'll be in touch."

Wednesday morning, Tommy arrived at the Chilton Airport at eight-thirty, for a ten o'clock flight to Alderon. In the news shop, he picked up a copy of the local real estate paper, with color pictures of the houses listed for sale. He just wanted to get an idea of the price range, and what you got for your money.

He found that homes were selling in the range of about $95,000 to $3 million, with a lot of listings in the $200,000 range. Most of these were four bedroom houses in the suburban towns of Stafford, Knightsbridge, and Buxton. He had no idea how far away these towns were from the city of Chilton, but Tommy thought he wanted to stay as close as possible to the prison. He went back to the news shop and bought a map of the local area, just to check it out.

He found that Stafford was the closest suburban town to Chilton, so he made a mental note to check there first in his search for a home.

The Chilton paper he picked up didn't seem to have much news to report. There was an article about the prison workers' union which he found mildly interesting, since the union was losing a battle to raise the pension contributions for corrections officers, although there was a pay raise approved for overtime. He wondered if the CO's on Bill's block would begin working double shifts in order to get the benefit of the raise.

The article said that most of the money for prison workers was paid from funds made available by a grant from Earth, since the majority of the prisoners were convicted of crimes there, before being sentenced to exile on planet P.

Another article said that Chilton's business activities were steadily picking up, as flights from Earth had become less expensive over the past ten years.

He couldn't figure for the life of him why anyone would want to move to planet P, but apparently, taxes were lower, and the real estate prices were getting increasingly attractive. Still, you would be living on an outcast planet, and you would never be able to return to Earth, once you moved here.

He bought breakfast, and read the rest of his paper while waiting for the plane to board. He noticed a couple of attractive women walking through the airport, and he wondered if they were androids; their physical attributes seemed so perfect.

Tommy's flight was uneventful. He arrived at the Alderon Airport a little after noon, and headed for the rental car section. He sauntered up to the desk at Budget, "Hi, I wanted to rent a car for a couple of days, I'm not sure how long I'll be in town."

"Did you want to rent an electric model, or a hydrogen powered car?"

"What's the difference in price?" Tommy asked.

"The electric cars rent for sixty-eight dollars a day, or three hundred and twenty-five for the week. The hydrogen powered ones rent for a little more; they rent for eighty-eight dollars a day, or five-fifty for the week."

"Do you have convertibles?" Tommy asked out of curiosity.

"Not in the electric models, but we do have a Shelby Mustang convertible hydrogen powered car for ninety-eight dollars a day."

"Good, I'll take one of those. Can I rent it for a few days, and then if I decide to keep it for the week, can I convert to a weekly contract?"

"No, I would have to sign you up for the week now, in order to get the weekly rate."

"Fine, then I'll rent it for three days then."

"I'll need a license and a major credit card."

"Do you take American credit cards?"

"I'm afraid not; we need a planet P credit card."

Tommy left the rental car booth, and retrieved his luggage. He called for a taxi to take him downtown to his appointment. Having cashed one of his traveler's checks at the airport, he paid the one hundred dollar plus fare cost in cash and stepped out of the car at Atlas Android, at one-thirty. He grabbed a quick bite to eat, and arrived at Ron Goldstein's office a little before two.

The secretary was nibbling at lunch at her desk, as Tommy approached, "Hi, I'm here to see Ron Goldstein."

"Mr. Goldstein is in a meeting, but if you want to have a seat, I think he will be finished up shortly," the secretary said.

Tommy sat waiting in the outer office for about ten minutes, nervously leafing through the materials he would leave for Ron. Finally, two men came out of Ron's office and left. "Mr. Goldstein will see you now," the secretary announced.

Tommy entered a spacious corner office and stuck out his hand as Ron came from around his big desk to greet him, "Ron Goldstein," he said with a smile as they shook hands.

"Tom Symms," he responded.

"Sit down Tom; let's get a look at what you brought me. He reached out his hands, and Tommy gave the thick folder with Alyssa's dissertation and the specs for building a beaming station to Ron, "Here is everything; it's way beyond me, but Alyssa said she will make herself available to answer any questions while you make your evaluation."

"Very good; we may well have some questions for her. How many beaming stations have been set up on Earth, do you know?"

"I think there's a little over a hundred, mostly in metropolitan areas; there's four in New York, and they are busy as hell; everybody wants to try it out."

"Are there any overseas in other countries?"

"Let's see; there's one in England, there's one in Australia, and one in Japan, and there are two in India; and I think there are several in the planning stages. Before too long, I'd venture a guess they'll be in just about every country; oh, and there's one on Earth-3, and I think three on Earth-2."

"Well, that certainly sounds promising; are they able to beam people's minds into androids on Earth-2 and Earth-3?"

"Yes, it seems to work fine over long distances, so I'm sure it would work here too; although I understand it requires quite a bit of a power boost, to effect psychic teleportation over great distances."

"This sounds quite interesting; I'll have our scientist-doctors look into this right away. I've talked to someone at Accel Partners, that's the firm we have a relationship with for venture capital, and they are open to the possibility of backing this project, although I told them that I had no idea yet, of how much it might cost to set up a beaming station here in Alderon; this is the state capitol, in case you didn't know."

"Oh, that's good to know; is the planet P government located here?"

"Yes, our Federal government is in Clarion DC, which is a district in Alderon, about thirty miles from here."

"This all sounds hauntingly familiar," Tommy quipped.

"Yes, we are modeled very closely after the United States, in terms of our government structure."

Tommy got back to the subject at hand, "Would you need Federal approval to go ahead with this project, do you think?"

"Undoubtedly, but I know one of the legislators personally, so it may not take too long to get approval if we decide to go ahead with this."

"Good; I'll want to make visits to my family and friends, especially my sister, back on Earth eventually, so I hope this all works out!"

"Whyever did you come here anyway? You must have left a whole host of friends and family back on Earth."

"Well, actually you may have heard; are you familiar with a company called US Android?

Ron nodded, "I think I just recently read something about that company . . . family-android manufacturers, right?"

"Yes, well, my stepfather was a casualty of the failed family-android prototype testing project. You may have heard about some of the participants being arrested on charges of sexual assault, for bleedthrough memories which were found in the online memory files of some of the children taking part in the experiment.

"I did read about that; in some cases, the child registered memories of their parent's sexual thoughts and activity . . ."

"Yes, well in any case, we were connected to family-androids, and my sister apparently has memories of some sexual activities between my father and Shayna, his female android, stored in her online memory file; so he's here on planet P, in Chilton State Prison. I'm here to help appeal his case."

"That <u>is</u> ambitious of you; have you contacted a lawyer here yet?"

"Yes; we're using Phil Pierson in Chilton."

"Oh?—I haven't heard of him; does he have a record of successful appeals?"

"Yes, he's won a few cases, but he's never had a case involving bleedthrough sexual assault charges. As you may know, family-androids were a new experiment, so there's no precedent; but he feels positive about this; he thinks the appeal may well be granted under the circumstances."

"Well, I wish you luck; it doesn't sound like this was criminal behavior on your stepfather's part."

"That's what I thought, but apparently Alyssa may have problems in maintaining a relationship going forward, as a result of the lingering memories of these experiences, and the prosecutor, as well as my mother, wanted to punish Bill for this potential emotional damage."

"I see; well again, I wish you good luck. Will you be staying here in Alderon, or are you flying right back to Chilton?"

"I'm going to stick around for a few days; maybe I could facilitate contact between your staff and Alyssa. They may have questions only she can answer."

"Well I'm not sure we'll be ready to explore this fully right away, but I'll pass on the materials you brought. Meanwhile, would you like to take a tour of our facilities? We have several new models of personal androids, in case you may be interested."

"Thanks; I'd like that. I may actually be too young to buy a personal android yet; but it would be interesting to see what you have, for future purposes."

"Well you only have to be eighteen to own an android here on planet P; how old are you?"

"Oh really? I just turned eighteen in July, so I guess I'd qualify."

"Sure; also, here's a thought; if you might have interest in possibly coming to work for us, we may be able to offer you a position working in our marketing department; I could possibly set you up with an apprenticeship here, if you're interested in looking into it."

"I haven't really decided what I want to do, as far as work yet, but I may be interested. What would be the next step, if I did want to entertain the idea?"

"Well, I could set you up with an appointment to meet with Bob Adams; he heads up our marketing division; would you like that?"

"Can I meet with him in the next few days while I'm here?"

"I'm sure we could work out something; let me talk to him about it today. Why don't you give your Skype number to Sarah, my assistant, and we'll have someone call you to schedule a tour, and a meeting with the marketing department."

"Sure, that will be fine. Well thank you for your time, Ron; it was nice to meet you; I'll stay in touch."

Tommy made his way to the Bank of Alderon, which was just down the street from the offices of Atlas Android. There, he opened an account and deposited his check, and applied for a credit card. To his delight, he was told that not only was there a branch of the bank in Chilton, but that also his credit card application could be approved in as little as 24 hours.

He took a taxi to the Alderon Hilton and checked in. As soon as he unpacked, Tommy Skyped Alyssa to report to her on the results of his meeting with Ron Goldstein.

"Hi Alyssa, how's everything going back there?"

"Fine; how did your meeting go with Atlas Android?"

"That's what I'm calling to tell you about. I had a meeting with Ron Goldstein, he's the president, and he seemed very open to the possibility of developing a beaming station here on planet P. He's even talked with a venture capitalist already, about the idea; can you believe it? He hadn't even seen the materials I brought him today, and he already called a venture capital firm to get an idea of their level of possible interest in backing a project like this."

"That's pretty encouraging; what else did you learn about the company?"

"Well, they're a spin-off from a US corporation, Delta Android; but they were bought by a major investor in the stock market here, who saw their potential for growth and development in the android manufacturing business, both locally, and around the planet. They're using new technology which they recently bought from US Android, just as they were going down the tubes last year."

"Are they able to produce more life-like androids with this newer technology?"

"Ron claimed to, in our meeting. He offered me a tour of the manufacturing plant, and I guess I'll see more once I do that; maybe in the next few days. He also asked me if I might be interested in a marketing apprenticeship position, and he offered to set me up with a meeting, with the director of marketing; so it looks like I will be staying here in Alderon for the next several days. I think I'll rent a car for the week, tomorrow, assuming they approve my credit card application by then; it's a pain in the ass, the car rental places won't take a US credit card."

"You can't blame them; the US is like ten-thousand miles away."

"But with electronic links, I mean the bank I went to today said my $25 million would be good funds in less than a week; you'd think the car rental agencies could run credit card charges."

"Do they recognize your US citizenship?"

"Yes, for now; but since I can't leave the planet physically any more, I only have three months to change my citizenship, otherwise I'm subject to a fine, and even possible imprisonment."

"Oh, well I guess you'd better get that taken care of soon then; what else did you learn about Atlas Android; did this Ron fellow you met with tell you what the annual sales revenue is? I'm curious to know how much they do in android sales there."

"I think he said they move eight thousand units a year, but that's all over the planet, so it's pretty small compared to the world market on Earth."

"Well then maybe a beaming station or two will help bolster their sales . . ."

"Yeah; I imagine just about everyone on the planet would like to beam themselves anywhere else but here! After all, it is an outpost planet, made pretty much specifically for outcasts."

"Don't remind me; we know the P stands for pedophile; and it creeps me out to think you are stuck on a planet full of pedophiles; how do the people seem?"

"Well, the pedophiles are all in jail, except for the ones on parole and probation, so they're not all over the streets. The planet doesn't appear to be very populated, but the people I've met seem nice so far. I get the impression they are mostly guards and other employees working at prisons, as well as those working at companies that provide goods and services to the prisons. Other than that, there's probably the loved ones of exiled criminals; but they are not criminals themselves."

"How many prisons are there on planet P; do you know?"

"I haven't the foggiest idea, but you have to take into account that the planet houses prisoners from all over the Earth, so there's got to be a small percentage of the twelve billion people living there; and then there's prisoners from Earth-2 and Earth-3, and some of the other man-made planets as well, so there's probably millions of prisoners alone."

"Yes, but mainly pedophiles right?—So that narrows it down a little," Alyssa added.

"Also, apparently, some people move here to take advantage of the economic growth and development. It's like a developing nation here; you have to remember, Planet P has only been around for about forty years; and it's probably still in its developmental stages. There seems to be plenty of jobs available, although I think they are mainly blue collar; but I understand the population has just started to expand pretty exponentially in more recent years."

"How do you know so much about the planet? You just got there!"

"Well, actually, I arrived in the middle of the week, last week, and I couldn't visit with Bill until Saturday, so I did some research those first few days; I wanted learn as much as I could about the planet; and of course, I wanted to know what I had gotten myself into, as far as the outlook for my future here."

"Why don't you see if you can find out how many prisons, and how many prisoners are there currently; and what the overall population on the planet is. I'd be curious to know."

"Okay; that shouldn't be too difficult; anything else going on back there that I should know about?"

"Mom's started to date someone; he's the parent of one of Mom's students. He came in for a teacher conference and he asked her out after they got to know each other better, after a few parent-teacher conferences; I'll keep you posted."

"Well, I guess that's a positive development for her."

"Yes, it's been almost two years since she's dated anyone. I guess it took her a long time to get over Bill, even though she was very angry with him."

"Was? Is! She is still very angry with him; that's why she's so upset that you have gone to planet P to help Bill out."

"Yeah, I know, but I can't help but think Bill got the shaft in all of this; I mean he didn't really do what most people would consider as out and out sexual assault or anything."

"Well, we've been all through this; I've told you how it's been suggested that early exposure to aspects of adult sexuality can be damaging to a young girl like me as she is growing into adulthood."

"Yes, well we'll hope that you've come through it alright. Are you still seeing Alex, the physicist?"

"Yes, he took me out to dinner Saturday night, and we're getting together again this coming Saturday. I'm taking it slow, but he certainly seems interested in me, and I think he is handsome and kind; who knows where this will go?"

"It sounds good so far; well, I'll let you go, sis; I'm staying at the Hilton here in Alderon, and I've scheduled a massage, so I have to go down to the sports complex soon."

"Oh boy; aren't we spending some of Mom's money," Alyssa joked.

"It's not Mom's money anymore; it's mine!—And yeah, I'm splurging a little, but the plane ride here was long, and I'm a little achy, so I thought I'd treat myself."

"Well, enjoy; I'll talk to you again soon, I hope . . ."

Tommy showed up for his massage at 6pm as planned. It was no surprise that the massage was performed by an android who was very attractive. She had strong hands, and she worked her fingers into his sore back muscles for half an hour before he turned over. She massaged his face and arms and legs for the next half an hour. Then she made her offer to go with him back to his room.

"No thanks," he turned her down, "I'm kind of beat; I think I'll just have dinner and turn in early."

"Are you sure? I could come up and sleep with you and keep you warm . . ."

"And have the woman who controls you sitting in a chair, in a corner of the room the whole time? No thanks!"

Tommy had room service deliver a steak dinner to his room, and he watched a movie while eating, before turning off the TV and going to bed around nine.

He woke up early the next morning, having gotten a good night's sleep. He called Atlas Android, and Ron Goldstein's assistant Sarah informed him that they made an appointment for him to take a tour of the manufacturing operations at 11am that morning. Then, she had set him up with a meeting with the director of marketing, for an interview at two o'clock.

Even though Tommy hadn't slept as well as he thought he might, after the long, soothing massage he had received the day before, he noticed it was just 9am when he hung up, and rather than going back to bed, he got into his bathing suit and went down to soak in the Jacuzzi for a while before getting ready for his appointments.

The Jacuzzi was outside by the pool. It was a moderately warm, sunny day, and there was nobody else in the pool area when he arrived. Tommy thoroughly enjoyed the solitude of a long soak, as the pool area remained empty, except for the occasional android servant passing by while tidying up. The jets were good and hard, and they felt good as he positioned himself so that they blasted at his still-sore muscles. He felt totally relaxed by the time he was ready to go back to his room.

When he got there, the maid was just finishing up making his bed. She had cleaned the bathroom and vacuumed already, so he didn't have long to wait, to go back into his room, until she was done.

He decided to ask her a few questions about the city, "I just arrived yesterday, so I don't know my way around yet; can you tell me where I can find some clothing stores in the area?"

"Sure; there is a shopping center a few miles away, which has several clothing stores in it. You go down Eucalyptus Street about a mile, and turn right on Elm. The shopping center is about a mile up on the right."

"Thanks; how about a car rental place?"

"Well, most of them are at the airport, but that's fifteen minutes from here at least; I don't know of any right in the city, but if you go online, you may find something."

"Oh, and one other thing; can you tell me where I can find a Skype store? The Skype screen on my laptop is a little small; I wanted to get something bigger."

"I use Verizon; the nearest store is on Market Street downtown."

"That's the street my appointment is on, at Atlas Android."

"Well, you should have no trouble finding the Verizon store; it's about ten blocks away from the Atlas Android building. Are you getting an android? Is that why you have an appointment there?—I hope you don't mind my asking; I'm just curious . . ."

Tommy hesitated briefly before answering, thinking about how much he wanted to disclose about his business at Atlas Android, "Yes, I've been thinking about it," he finally said, deciding he would not mention anything about the real reasons for his meetings.

"Get a Melinda, or an Abby series. My friend's father works for Atlas Android, and he thinks they are the prettiest and the most well-programmed to suit a man's needs, if you know what I mean." She flashed a knowing grin.

"I'll keep that in mind," Tommy said cordially.

"Is there anything else I can do for you?"

"No, I think that's all I need to know for now. Thank you for your help."

The maid left, and Tommy's thoughts lingered on the idea of owning a female android. Still, he preferred to meet a real woman, but he wasn't at all sure if he was going to see any beautiful women he might be able to get to know, here on planet P. He decided to put it out of his mind for now.

The ringer on his Skype machine went off, signaling that he had a call coming in. He answered it, and sat staring into his mother's eyes for several seconds before speaking, "Hi Mom; how are you doing?"

"I'd be doing a lot better if you hadn't left us to go to that God-forsaken planet!"

"Mom; I'm sorry this is difficult for you, but I'm also carrying Alyssa's mind beaming research with me, and I'm trying to get an android company to build a beaming station here. I may be able to come back for a visit before too long, if I'm successful."

"Are you really working on an appeal for Bill?"

"Yes, I know it's not what you want, but I don't think he deserves to be locked up in prison for the rest of his life; he won't even be eligible for probation for forty years; that's an awful long time."

"Oh, please don't get me started, I'm so angry at him, and I get angrier and angrier every time I think about it; sometimes I could just scream! To think, he was having sex with that android every night while I slept, after we had a pact not to sleep with our androids until after the experiment."

"Mom! That's what guys do! If they get an android, they have sex with it; how can you blame him for doing what came natural to him; I mean, you can't expect him to be a saint . . ."

"So, stay there and help him, don't come home; just get him out of prison and you can both live there together for eternity, see if I care!"

"Mom! Don't be that way; I love you, and I want to see you again, soon, if it's possible. I've already met with one firm that may use Alyssa's plans, to create a beaming station here on planet P; I'm going back to talk with them more today."

"Fine, if you can arrange it; but if you get Bill out of prison, I will be so angry with you! He ruined Alyssa's childhood!"

"Mom; Alyssa is fine; she's dating that physicist at the lab where Alyssa and Albert have been developing the new technology, so that when you beam your mind into an android body, it will feel the same, living in that body, as living your own."

Justina suddenly changed her tone, "I know, she's told me quite a bit about it; it's fascinating! I'm so proud of her, she's such a genius!"

"Right, and she grew up with the support of our family, connected to an android who obviously helped her to achieve all she has . . ."

Justina cut Tommy off with an angry comment, "Well it's no thanks to that scoundrel Bill; she may never have a long-term relationship in her life because of him!"

"Alright, I'm not going to fight you on it; but let's just say we have a difference of opinion, and I don't think Alyssa is suffering a bad life from what is in her memory. I'm sorry, but as you know, I've decided to do what I can to help Bill."

"Tommy! I'm so mad at you for saying these things! I'm sorry, but I'm ending this call, goodbye!"

Tommy was left with his heart in his throat; he felt conflicted. On one hand he wanted to please his mother, and he felt guilty for trying to help Bill against her wishes; yet on the other hand, he felt indebted to Bill for being a good stepfather, and he didn't believe Bill should be punished, at least not so severely.

He felt keyed up, like he could use another massage, but there wasn't time before his eleven o'clock meeting at Atlas Android, so he calmed himself, got dressed, and took a taxi into the heart of the city. He had toast and coffee at a diner; he wasn't very hungry, but he needed something to settle his stomach a little before his meeting.

A little edgy, he showed up for his meeting ten minutes early, only to be greeted by a very pretty android woman at the front desk. "Good morning sir; how can I help you?" she said pleasantly with a big smile."

"I'd like to meet the woman who controls you!" he said instinctively.

"That would be me," a voice came from the other room, and then she appeared in the doorway, "I'm Kerry Arnold, and this is Abby, she's my android helper; she does a nice job at greeting customers, doesn't she?"

"She has your charm, I think," Tommy answered coyly.

"Are you here to look into getting an android today?" Kerry asked.

"Well, I'm actually here for a tour of the manufacturing arm of your company; it was set for 11am, I'm Tom Symms."

"Oh, Mr. Symms! I'm sorry, we're usually helping customers here; that's right, Mister Goldstein called down to us yesterday to ask us to give you a tour; we'd be happy to! Right this way . . . just a moment . . ." Kerry leaned into the intercom, "Pat? Will you and Stacey come out here and cover the front desk while I give a tour?"

The Skype screen lit up on her desk, and a middle aged woman who looked a little dumpy responded, "Yes, we'll be right out."

A minute later, they started their tour, "So Kerry; what is your position here?" Tommy asked as they walked down the hall towards the main factory area.

"I'm a programmer; I program androids to respond to their owner's needs. You see, the planning is all done up front; we do a profile on the prospective owner, and we customize the android's responses to that specific person's desires. Androids mainly do what you want them to anyway, but we find it helps satisfy the customer more if we customize, and if we tweak the response time and intensity, in accordance with the new owner's needs and desires."

"I see; you said "new owner's"—Does that mean you sometimes fit a used android for a new owner?"

"Yes, I've occasionally done that; but not usually."

Tommy nodded, "—And you double as a receptionist?"

"We all do; every manufacturing worker who has an android, that is. Thursday is my day to work the front desk with Abby, but I'm only on for the morning shift, and then I go back to programming, which is most of what I do, after lunch."

They walked through a double swinging door into a large open space. The pathway that went by the work stations was about five feet wide, and it was bordered by yellow lines. Kerry led the way,

"Don't go outside the yellow lines, for your safety, and also so as not to disturb the workers."

"Wow! This place is huge!" Tommy remarked.

"Yes, we need a lot of space; there are thirty-eight work stations housed here; and this is just the female android manufacturing area. The male androids are made in an almost identical fashion in another part of the building. These first three stations on the left are where we make the skeletons. You can see that in the first station, the raw bones are sandblasted so there are no burrs or rough edges. If there are any rough edges or sharp corners sticking out, they can eventually poke through the synthetic skin."

"It looks like there are three different sizes in these bins."

"Yes; we make four foot six inch, five-two and five-eight height models, depending on your preference."

Wow! There are a lot of bins with bones in them."

"Yes; there are eight bins for each size skeleton; one for arms and legs, one for backbones, one for ribs, one for skulls, one for hands, one for feet, one for fingers, and one for toes."

"How about the pelvis?"

"They are part of the backbone, as they are attached. If you will notice, the backbones and hips are already assembled when they reach us; the wiring for the electronic nerves is the most critical, so we use a company that manufactures these parts before they get here. It's the only thing we don't assemble here at the plant."

"I see; the shoulders and shoulder blades are attached too."

"Everything up to the head. Next is the assembly line for the limbs. At this station the arms and legs are attached using hinged pins."

"I see; they are drilled and screwed into the ends of the bones."

"Right; and next the hands are attached. The pins are much smaller, so we use titanium steel; we don't want the fingers to come loose or break at the joints."

"I see; wow! Look at all those bins for muscles!"

"Yes; we use three different sizes for each skeleton size; thin, medium size or standard, and heavy-set. The synthetic muscles come to us complete with tendons, which we attach by fusing them to the bones. The fusing process creates a burr where they are attached, so at this station, the burrs are ground down and smoothed out."

"Then, I see there is some wiring done at the next station."

"Yes; we use fiber-optic wiring, encased in soft plastic jackets, to wire the muscles up to where the brain will be connected. There are eight work stations for this; one for the arms, one for the legs, one for the feet, and one for the hands; one for the backbone, one for the neck, one for the shoulders, and one for the hips. Each skeleton is passed through all eight work stations before the skull is attached."

"Wow! That's remarkable; I never thought about all the steps necessary to make an android."

"It is pretty amazing, isn't it! Now down this corridor are the work stations for installing the skull, implanting the electronic brain, and connecting all of the fiber-optic nerves. This is the most critical part of the process. There are eleven work stations dedicated to this process alone."

"Wow! A lot has to happen before you put on the skin."

"It sure does! Next, we install the organs; an android only needs three; a synthetic heart, lungs, and a synthetic liver to keep the blood clean."

"Yeah, I guess an android doesn't need a stomach or a spleen or anything, it doesn't eat!"

Kerry smiled at his comment, and continued on, "These next two stations are where we install the lungs and the larynx, which the android uses to speak. It's modeled after the human larynx; and we can tighten or loosen the synthetic vocal chords, to raise or lower the pitch of the voice. We do that in the programming phase, after the android is fully assembled."

"That's fascinating! You can alter the pitch of the voice, to suit the owner . . ."

Kerry nodded, and then continued on to the next work station, "Well, "Then these next two stations are where we add the breasts and the vagina. We use shapes and sizes from the most popular online porn sites as a guide. Again, we have three sizes of breasts; small, medium and large."

"Do the vaginas have hair?"

"No, a female android doesn't have any hair except that on her head."

"What if you want pubic hair? Can it be added?"

"No, it's not part of the process, although I think there are android manufacturers, at least on Earth, who give you that option."

Kerry continued to lead them forward, "Here, you can see that the skin is in liquid form, and the body is immersed in this large vat; so when it dries, it is seamless. Then, in this last work station, the synthetic blood is added. It's basically water, with a few chemicals added."

"Wow! Thirty-eight work stations altogether, huh?"

"Yes; and then they go to the programming department. This is where the androids are programmed to respond in the manner according to the preferences and needs of the owner. As I say, we take a detailed profile of the prospective owner, and program the computer brain to respond accordingly."

"How many androids do you keep in stock?"

"We have over a hundred in the store room currently. About two thirds are women, as we find that there is more demand for them."

"How many androids do you sell per month, on average?"

"Oh I'd say we sell about thirty to fifty a month on average."

"And what is your sales price these days?"

"Our androids sell for Thirty-three thousand dollars plus tax. Why? Are you interested in buying one for yourself?"

"Well, we grew up with androids in the house, but I don't know whether I want one myself."

"I see you liked Abby; we have that model available in standard size. Would you like to see what we have in stock? I can take you to the store room . . ."

"Sure," Tommy said with piqued interest, "I'd be interested in seeing what you have."

"Okay; the stock room is on the next level; we could take the elevator."

They rode up to the second floor, and Kerry unlocked the door to the stock room. It was a surprisingly large room. Kerry continued in her friendly tone of voice, "I'll show you the female androids first; and then we can take a quick stroll down the aisles where the male androids are; here, let's go to the left."

The androids were standing, so you could see the height and the build, "They sure are pretty," Tommy remarked.

"If you see one you particularly like, we can stop and take a closer look."

They walked down three aisles with about twenty-five female androids standing, shoulder to shoulder, in each aisle. Tommy stopped to admire the ones he found the most attractive. Finally, he lingered by one that he found particularly sexy, "This one is a real doll!"

"That's our Becky series, but, of course, you can actually change her name to anything you would like . . ."

"That's very interesting; actually, I'm kind of partial to Becky; that's a nice name, and it seems to suit her."

"We can come back to her if you want, after we look at the male androids."

"Okay; let's go see the males."

They walked down the two aisles of men androids. When they were finished, Kerry summed up what they had seen, "So you can see that the male androids are a bit taller, they're all between four-eight and six feet tall."

"I noticed that all of the androids you have here on display are clothed."

"Yes; we sometimes have children walking through with their parents; and we think it's more decent anyway, to show them with their clothes on. If you'd like to see Becky with her clothes <u>off</u>, that can certainly be arranged too." Kerry said rather matter-of-factly.

"That's okay; I think I've seen enough for now; let's go back; I've got an appointment with someone in the marketing department at noon, and then I'm meeting again with Ron Goldstein at one, so I have a schedule to keep."

"That's fine; the marketing department is on this floor, so you haven't far to go. It's just down the hall to the right."

Tommy thanked Kerry and headed down the hall. He entered the marketing offices and found the receptionist seated at the desk in the outer office, "Hi, I'm Tom Symms. I have a one o'clock appointment, but it wasn't clear whether Paul Klein would be available to talk with me, or if I would be meeting with someone else."

"Why don't you have a seat; I'll see if Mr. Klein is in."

As Tommy sat, he picked up a "Modern Androids" magazine sitting on the end table, and found an article on the newest android features. He read that, with the new strain of androids now available, your android could be programmed with a separate personality, even though he or she would be connected psychically to you exclusively. It said that during the interview process, as owner, you would be asked to identify the personality characteristics which you find most pleasing, and many of these could be programmed into your android before delivery. Later, you could bring back your android for reprogramming, provided you are willing to pay a modest reprogramming fee of around five thousand dollars, on average.

Tommy considered again the possibility of owning Becky, with this new information in mind. As he was pondering the idea, the receptionist called to him, "Mr. Klein will see you now."

Paul Klein's office was the last one, at the end of the corridor. Tommy realized, of course, that he would have been likely to find the head of marketing occupying a spacious corner office. Paul Klien was sitting behind his desk, just ending a Skype call. Tommy waited briefly while Paul made a parting comment; then he hung up and turned to him, "Hi Tom; I'm Paul Klein; it's nice to meet you," he said in a casual, yet professional manner, "I understand you are the brother of Alyssa Symms; the recent inventor of mind beaming, is that right?"

"Yes; well, she was working in collaboration with Dr. Albert Freudenthal, but together they invented the process."

"Well, I'm thrilled to meet you, and very excited to hear that we are considering creating a beaming station here on planet P!" Paul's level of enthusiasm was contagious.

"Yes; that would be great, as I'd personally like to travel back to see my family, for one!"

"Ron Goldstein informed me that you may have interest in coming to work for us; do you have any experience in marketing or sales?"

"Well no, not really; my degree is in engineering, and I haven't started working yet, since I graduated a little over a year ago; you see, I have recently become independently wealthy; our family was part of a family-android experiment which took place over a ten year period, and we received a large lump sum payment at the end of this test period, some of which my mother has shared with us."

"Oh, and your father?" Paul spoke with an obvious curiosity, but he hesitated patiently, waiting for Tommy to clue him in. When Tommy still hadn't replied after a few moments, he issued a further prompt, "I assume your father was part of the experiment too; yet you only named your mother . . ."

"Well, he is actually my stepfather; and he is here on planet P in prison; that's actually why I'm here, to help him. I don't know how much you know about family-androids, since they are outlawed now, but we experienced what is known as "Bleed through" of the Chinese wall software installed in the android, and my stepfather was convicted of sexual assault of my sister, although he never really offended her to any degree, sexually."

"I see; then how is it possible that he was convicted of sexual assault?"

"Well, he actually took a plea deal; he didn't plead guilty to the charges. You see, he and Alyssa were both psychically connected to Shayna, his female android; and the Chinese wall software was supposed to protect him from this, but when he had sexual contact with Shayna, my sister Alyssa, who was also connected psychically to Shayna, registered memories of some of these experiences in her online memory file, which was discovered and reported to the government, when one of US Android's scientist-doctors had eventually become authorized to look into the online memory files of some of the children taking part in the experiment, toward the end of the test period. The same type of thing had happened to some of the other participants; but as you may be aware, the law places responsibility, for keeping the children from experiencing any exposure to adult sexuality, on the parent; so these unfortunate participants in the test project are being sentenced to exile here on planet P. I've hired a lawyer to try and appeal my stepfather's case, but at this point, we don't know what to expect, in terms of the results of an appeal."

"So now you're stuck on this planet for good . . ."

"Yes, unfortunately, but I'm trying to make the best of it; and as I say, if a mind beaming station is built here, I could possibly go back to Earth for a visit every so often."

"How does that work; the mind beaming? Can you experience physical touch?—I mean, you can't experience taste, because an android has no stomach, so they are not manufactured with taste buds . . ."

"Well actually, my sister is working on developing androids specifically designed for use in mind beaming, so that a person who's mind is beamed into an android body can experience just about every sense which they could while living in their <u>own</u> body. It's probably a ways off, but she and Dr. Freudenthal have been working on it."

"I guess you have a lot to hope for, for the future; a mind beaming station to be developed here on planet P, your sister's developments in android technology, a successful appeal for your stepfather . . ."

Tommy considered Paul's thoughtful realizations, "Yes, I suppose I do mainly have a lot of hopes at this point, and it's all going to take time, but I am somewhat optimistic at this point. So far, I haven't heard anything yet, which might bar any of these things from eventually coming to pass."

"Alright; I can see where you are coming from; meanwhile, would you have interest in possibly joining our marketing staff? I could put you in our apprenticeship program, and we could offer you at least a modest salary to start . . ."

Paul waited again, hopeful that he might have inclined Tommy to offer some positive comment; but when Tommy still hadn't responded several seconds later, made a further pitch, "Frankly, we could use someone with your prestige and contacts, to give us an edge on the competition . . ."

"I don't know," Tommy finally said, "I'd have to think about it, but I appreciate the offer. Could I get back to you on it, within a few weeks?"

"Sure; take your time; we wouldn't want you to rush your decision; we would want a firm commitment on your part, if you were going to join our staff."

"Can you tell me more about your marketing process, and its focus?" Tommy asked with feigned interest.

"Sure; let me walk you through our philosophy, and our various marketing strategies and advertising campaigns . . ."

They spent another half-hour together before Paul looked up at the clock, and stopped in his tracks, "I'm sorry, I didn't notice the time, but I have another meeting in about five minutes, so we'll have to cut it short at this point; but you can come back and we'll talk some more next week if you like."

"Thank you; I'll call your assistant to schedule an appointment." Paul walked him to the door and they shook hands.

Tommy still had an hour to kill before his appointment with Ron Goldstein, so he walked across the street to the bank. He found the bank officer he had spoken to the day before, sitting at his desk. He poked his head in the cubicle and was reminded of his name by the sign sitting on his desk, "Hi Curt, Tom Flynn; you took a credit card application from me yesterday, and I just thought I'd check to see if you've heard back yet about my approval . . ."

"Yes; Mr. Symms; come in, sit down; I'll go and check with that department for you; I'll be right back . . ."

As Curt walked off, Tommy noticed a pretty android teller talking to who was probably her controller. The woman was kind of frumpy looking, and probably was in her fifties, he guessed. He could see why she would only be the brains behind the pretty face that actually did the transactions with customers.

Curt came back about two minutes later, "Yes Mr. Symms; you were approved this morning. Here is your Visa card; your credit limit is fifty-thousand, but if you need more, we can probably arrange it on a collateralized basis."

"No, fifty-thousand should be plenty, thanks."

"Well if you'll just sign here, we can go to the automated teller machine and activate your card."

Tommy took a leisurely lunch, using his credit card to pay the charge, just to make sure it worked. He would go through with his plans to use it to rent a car later that afternoon, he thought.

"While he was sitting, sipping his lemonade, he suddenly spotted Kerry walking into the restaurant by herself. She was seated on the other side of the room, but she stood out as being the prettiest woman in the place, easily.

Tommy waited until he had finished his sandwich, and then he got up and crossed the large room, to see if she might be receptive to a visit. He approached her with a bright smile, "Hi Kerry; do you mind if I sit down?"

"No, not at all; please sit. How did your appointment with the marketing department go?"

"It was interesting; I met with Paul Klein, and he showed me the ropes a little."

"Oh; you met with the director of marketing, did you . . ."

"Yes; he offered me an apprenticeship."

"Just like that? What, do you have a degree in marketing or something?"

"No, it's a long story," Tommy said, so as not to make her aware of his background and the possible deal to build a beaming station, "But I have a connection . . ."

"What, do you have a relative that works here or something?"

"Well no, not exactly, but my sister may be working out a deal with senior management, to sell a new product."

"There's always something new being developed in the field of android technology, isn't there?"

"Yeah, I suppose that's true. Do you come here often for lunch?"

"No, it's too expensive for me; I usually order out from a take-out place across town; they deliver."

"And you eat in, at your office?"

"Yes; there's a lunch room. Atlas Android used to provide lunch, but they stopped due to dwindling profits. We used to sell hundreds of androids a month; but sales have slowed down a lot due to the fact that the planet is now pretty saturated with androids, at least for people who can afford them."

"No kidding?! I didn't realize that. Paul Klein didn't mention that at our meeting . . ."

"That's because he's embarking on a new strategy; to offer financing, so that lower income people can afford to purchase an android. The vast majority of people here on the planet are blue collar workers, earning about fifteen to thirty thousand a year. Paul thinks that if we could tap into that market, there could be huge potential profits, as there are over eleven million blue collar workers on this planet."

"Eleven million, huh? I didn't think the planet was that big . . ."

"Yeah, well there's over six million prisoners total on the planet, so, as you can imagine, there's also a lot of people working for the small businesses catering to the prisons. I think the overall population of the planet is about twenty-million; but that was as of a few years ago, so the population has probably grown a bit since then. The population here on planet P is actually growing pretty rapidly these days. There's quite a lot of new births each year, and not a lot of deaths, as you can imagine; since life expectancy is over ten times as long as this planet has been in existence!"

"Yes, I understand the planet is less than fifty years old, so I suppose there haven't been too many people that have died on planet P, to date."

"Yeah, I think less than a hundred."

"So I was wondering, are you involved with anyone currently? I noticed you don't wear a wedding ring, so you're probably not married . . ."

"I've actually had three men ask me to marry them, and I'm only eighteen; but I think they just wanted me for my looks; I don't think any of them took a real interest in me, as a person."

"Well, to be honest, I wanted to ask you out mainly because of your looks too, but I thought maybe we could also get to know each other a little better, over dinner sometime perhaps . . ."

"You're a pretty handsome young man yourself; do you mind if I ask how old you are?"

"I just turned eighteen myself; so what do you say; I'm in town for the next three days. I don't really know anyone here yet, and I kind of don't know what to do with myself; will you have dinner with me tomorrow night?"

Kerry thought for an awkward moment, before giving in, "Alright; do you have a car?"

"I'm going to rent one today, so I should have wheels. What time do you want me to pick you up?"

"How about eight o'clock? That will give me some time to wind down from work."

"Eight is fine; I look forward to it. Can you give me directions from the Hilton?"

Tommy was on time for his three o'clock appointment with Ron Goldstein. Ron's assistant, Sarah, ushered him right into Ron's office without a wait. He was reading something, but Tommy was too eager to wait for him to look up, "Hi Ron, how are you?"

"I'm just fine; and how are you this afternoon, Tom?" he asked with a smile.

"I'm good; I took the tour this morning, and I met with Paul Klein about two hours ago; I see you didn't waste any time getting me in to see folks here."

"Well I knew you were only going to be here for a few days, so I thought I'd set you up with appointments sooner rather than later. What do you think of our facilities?"

"I was fascinated! Kerry was very thorough in showing me around; I got to see the whole process. We toured the female android plant;—very interesting!"

"Good! I'm glad you enjoyed it; and how was your meeting with Paul Klein?"

"It was interesting, what he had to say; and he made me a job offer, but I told him I'd have to think about it."

"Well, you do that; we'd love to have you come to work for us."

"Thanks." Tommy had already moved on to the important topic he was most interested in, "Have you had any feedback from your scientist-doctor team on the beaming station?"

"I just got off the phone with Marissa Simons; she's our head scientist-doctor. I Skyped her because I knew you were coming in this afternoon. She's had a preliminary look at your sister's work, and she plans to have further discussion with your sister Alyssa, later this week. We have yet to put the financing together, but it seems very likely that we will be pursuing building a mind beaming station, assuming we can get the go-ahead from the Feds in Clarion DC, and the financing falls into place."

"That's great news!" Tommy exclaimed, a little embarrassed at his exuberance, afterward.

"Well, I thought I'd give you some good news, to go back to Chilton with. Hopefully, we can get you to come back to Alderon to stay . . ."

"I don't know; it's kind of far away from my stepfather. I was looking forward to visiting with him as often as possible while the appeal is going on."

"When are the visiting hours?" Ron asked.

"Saturday and Sunday mornings," Tommy replied.

"Well, you could catch the shuttle on the weekends; it's only an hour flight from here to Chilton . . ."

Yeah, I guess you're right; it gives me something to think about."

"I don't think we have your sister Alyssa's Skype number. Marissa wanted to contact her directly to have a discussion with her about the particulars of the equipment necessary in order to build a mind beaming station. Do you mind giving me the number?"

"Sure; I'd be happy to . . ."

"By the way, I heard from Kerry Atwood after your tour, and she said that the "Becky" model in the stock room caught your attention. We'd be happy to give her to you as a signing bonus, should you decide to come to work for us."

"Oh, that's very generous of you, and I might like to take a position with Atlas; it's just that I don't know how much time and energy it will be necessary for me to put into my stepfather's appeal case yet, and that takes precedence for me; but I will give it more thought, and get back to you next week perhaps."

"Next week would be fine; we'll await your decision. If you find you need some time to tackle matters of the appeal, I'm sure we could arrange to defer your starting date, if you decide you would like to come to work for us."

"Thanks; I'll keep that in mind."

"Well, Tom, I have a conference call coming in, and I really should prepare myself. I hate to cut our appointment short, but if there isn't anything else you need from me, I'll bid you farewell."

"Sure, that's fine; I'm very glad to hear that you are seriously considering building a mind beaming station; I'll tell Alyssa the good news; and please keep me informed of any more developments in that direction. I'll give you a call myself, next week, when I know more about my own situation."

"You do that; it's nice to see you; have a good trip back to Chilton."

Tommy took a taxi back to the airport to rent a car. He figured that would be as good a place as any to pick up the rental car, since he would be dropping it off there in a few days, when he went back to the airport, for his flight to Chilton.

He walked up to the Budget desk, and recognized the same man who had waited on him a few days earlier, when he had first arrived in Alderon. "Hi, do you still have that Shelby Mustang convertible hydrogen powered car for rent; you said it was ninety-eight dollars a day?"

"Let me check." The clerk looked it up on his computer, "Yes, we do; how long did you want to rent it for?"

"I'll be returning it on Friday; I think my flight is at noon."

"Well as I informed you earlier this week, we would need a credit card, and as we discussed, your U.S. credit card is not accepted here . . ."

Tommy waved his hand to stop the clerk, "I have since obtained a credit card here, so that won't be a problem."

"Oh, very good; can I have your license and your credit card then?"

"Sure; I hope it's not going to be a problem if my license is from Massachusetts."

"No, that isn't a problem, as long as it is current. You don't need a local license until you are a resident here, and then you have thirty days to get one at Motor Vehicles, in the town or city you move to. Do you have a residence address yet?"

"No, I'm staying at the Hilton in downtown Alderon."

"I see; well we'll need a Skype number we can contact you at . . . I assume you'll be needing insurance?"

Once the paperwork was done, Tommy picked up his car, and since it was sunny and seventy degrees out, he put down the top before heading for the airport exit. There was some traffic, but he got up to highway speed on the beltway back to Alderon. He arrived back at the Hilton a little after six, and parked his car in the parking garage.

Once back in his room, he Skyped Alyssa from his laptop, to give her the news, and report what had happened on his other appointments that day, "Hi Alyssa, how are you doing today?"

"Oh, I'm doing okay; it was a long day. Albert and I were working on taste buds, for the new series of androids we are creating, to house people who are mind-beamed into them. We're using an electronic neural transmitter, wired from the prototype android's tongue to his computer brain."

"Oh? How's that working?"

"It's a bit frustrating, but we're starting to have some success. How was your day? Did you have meetings at Atlas Android, or was that tomorrow?"

"No, it was today. I took a tour of their manufacturing operations. It was very interesting; I never realized all that goes into the android manufacturing process."

"Well, that's why they have to charge over thirty thousand dollars for one."

"Actually, I found out, the trade isn't so lucrative up here these days; they've pretty well saturated the market for androids, for people who can afford to pay cash for them. The company is shifting its marketing focus to blue collar workers. The marketing director I met with today told me that Atlas Android is planning to start offering financing over twenty years at a low interest rate, to entice lower-income workers to buy them."

"That's very interesting; I think here they'll only go as far as a six year loan, to buy an android."

"Well, apparently, something like two thirds of the people on the planet are blue collar workers, so they'll have something like ten million people to market to on a twenty year loan basis."

"That could be pretty profitable."

"Yeah, the company is after me to join their marketing staff, although I'd have to go through an apprenticeship program first. It takes a year, but they'll pay me a salary.—Not that I'll need it, but the more money I can earn, the more I can grow Mom's twenty-five million into a retirement nest egg."

"Yeah, you might as <u>well</u> work; you're probably going to be stuck there with nothing much else to do."

"Yes, but I may not want to start working until after the appeal; I don't know how long it will take, or how much I'll be needed."

"I don't know about up there, but I understand that an appeal here can take well over a year; sometimes two or three; you don't want to be out of work for that long, do you?"

"I don't know; I have to think more about it. I'm really waiting for Phil Pierson, Bill's lawyer, to tell me more about what's involved in the appeal process."

"When are you meeting with him next?"

"We're supposed to get together next week. I fly back to Chilton on Friday."

"What are you going to do in Alderon until then?"

"Oh, I thought I'd check out the real estate in the area; maybe drive out to the suburbs to see what the neighborhoods are like; and I have a dinner date for tomorrow night, with the gal who gave me the tour today."

"That's nice. Tell me about her. What's she like? Is she pretty?"

"Very . . . she also has a pretty android assistant who is, of course, psychically connected to her, whose name is Abby. She didn't come on the tour with us, but she may come along with us on our dinner date, I don't know."

"Oh; an android chaperone . . ."

"Very funny; no, I hope it will be just us two."

"Did you meet with Ron Goldstein again while you were there?"

"Yes, I had a quick meeting with Ron; he told me that everyone who he's talked to at the company about building a beaming station has responded positively, so far. You should expect a call from Marissa something or other; she's the head scientist-doctor at Atlas. She has some questions for you regarding the beaming station, I think it was on generating the signal strength you had specified, and I think she also wants to get more particulars on the equipment necessary, so I gave them your Skype number."

"That's fine; I'll look forward to hearing from her."

Tommy suddenly realized that he was very hungry, as he hadn't eaten anything all day, except for some toast in the morning. He decided to finish up the Skype call, "Well, I'm going to get myself a little snack, and have a cigar out on the balcony; and maybe take a little nap before going to pick Kerry up; so I'll sign off for now . . . I love you, Alyssa!"

"I love you too, Tommy!" she said with a parting smile, "You take care . . . I miss you!" she squeezed in before the screen went blank.

Chapter Eighteen

Tommy parked the Shelby Mustang, at the curb in front of Kerry's apartment building, at about eight o'clock as planned. He went to retrieve her for their date.

It was a modest building, and Tommy had to walk up three flights of stairs, as there was no elevator. This was obviously some of that blue collar housing that he read was prolific in the cities on planet P.

Kerry answered the door in her bathrobe, "Come on in; I'll just be another five minutes. I was Skyping with my sister, and I didn't notice the time."

"That's okay," Tommy said cordially, "I'm in no hurry." He came in and sat on the sofa next to Abby.

"Abby, why don't you show Tom some southern hospitality?"

Abby got up and came over to Tommy and sat on his lap. She wrapped her arms around his neck, and gave him a big kiss.

"Wow! She's very life-like . . . —I didn't know we were in the south . . ." Tommy said, a little confused.

"We're not!—She's just programmed to respond that way when I use those words," Kerry said as she applied makeup in the bathroom behind them. "A lot of our customers have never had contact with an android before when they come to look at purchasing one. I find it helps the men customers feel more positive about owning an android after she shows them some physical affection."

"Yeah, I guess that's a lot of the reason men buy a female android, for the romance and sex."

"Yes, well we try to show men that there are other features, of use to them as well. We try to impress upon them how much of a walking computer center an android woman can be, fully connected to everything online, from satellite navigational assistance and weather updates, to providing information on the latest technological advances. Then, of course, there are the day-to-day household benefits, like cooking and cleaning, and driving . . . Androids are very safe drivers. In fact, less than ten percent of all accidents are caused by android drivers, even though a lot of them may involve human drivers hitting an android driver; but the androids are rarely at fault."

Abby continued to stroke Tommy's hair and rub his chest while they talked. "Who taught her these moves?" Tommy asked.

"I worked pretty extensively with our senior programmers; she is mimicking my movements."

"I'd say you really know how to treat a man."

"Thanks; you can put the moves on her, but don't try to put the moves on me tonight; I'm not ready for sex or romance."

"Don't worry, I had no plans to try and put the moves on you tonight; I just wanted to have dinner with you."

"Oh? Are you sure you don't want to bring Abby along? She can sit with you and cuddle up to you . . ."

"That might feel a little weird when I'm trying to have conversation with you."

"Alright; we'll leave her home, but I'll let her keep you company while I get dressed."

"I thought an android couldn't be activated when you're not in the room with them . . ."

"Android technology keeps improving; the new models can run off of anyone in their presence who has brain retrofit hardware, which I assume you have."

"Yes, I've had it since I was five."

"She will use your sense of sight to continue functioning while I'm not in the room."

"Very interesting." Abby kissed him again, and he felt a surge of warmth. He called out to Kerry through the bedroom door, "I can see how these things can get addicting."

Kerry opened the bedroom door; she had put a dress on quickly, "I wanted to give you a taste of what Becky can do for you . . . You liked Becky particularly, didn't you?"

"Yeah, but I'd prefer the responses of a real woman."

"I see; well I guess I can understand that; but you'd probably be surprised at what an android woman can mimic, as far as romantic and sexual response."

"Yeah, still, I'd know it's not real, and I think it might creep me out."

"Suit yourself; I'm ready, shall we go?"

"Sure; where shall we go?" Tommy wanted her to see how flexible and non-controlling he could be.

"Well, Valley's is not too far from here, or there is a vegetarian place across town, if you'd prefer that . . ."

"I'm not crazy about vegetarian dishes, Valley's sounds fine to me . . ."

"Valley's it is then."

They walked down the three flights of stairs, and Tommy led the way to his car.

"Wow! Is this your car?"

"Yep, it's a rental."

"It's really snazzy, a convertible, huh?"

"Yeah, I put the top up, because I didn't want to blow your hair around."

"Nonsense! Are you kidding?!—I can brush it out when we get there; let's put the top down. I haven't ridden in a convertible since I was about ten!" she was getting a bit revved up, "My father used to have one."

Tommy hit the button on the dashboard, and the top went down, and folded out of the way, behind the back seat. "The weather's good for convertibles around here," Tommy remarked.

"Well it's a little cold in the winter to ride around in a convertible with the top down; it occasionally gets down into the thirties, but yeah, most of the year it's in the seventies and eighties."

"The thermometer on the dash says it's seventy-two." Kerry shook her head, and her long brown hair waved in the wind and tickled her face.

"This is fun!" she giggled, with a glowing smile, while brushing the hair off of her face.

Tommy used the valet parking service at the restaurant, handing the attendant a twenty as they walked toward the entrance. Kerry took a hairbrush out of her purse and straightened her hair. "This place was one of the very first restaurants built on the planet; so it's like, over thirty years old. You should like it, there's a wide selection on the menu."

They were seated by a window overlooking the river, "This is quite scenic," Tommy said, sipping his ice water.

"Isn't it, though?—It's on the outskirts of the city, so there's some nice trees, for a change. There's no trees in Alderon, to speak of, except for some small ones, planted on the tops of some of the buildings downtown."

Tommy smiled a bit, before changing the subject, "So, you said you were talking to your sister; is she older or younger?"

"I'm the baby in the family; my sister is eight years older than me. My parents were going to have boy and girl twins, but something went wrong with the fertility drugs, and it was just me."

"Well, judging by your looks, I'd say something went very right!"

"Thank you; my mother is very pretty, and I guess I got her looks; but she is thin, and my father is much broader, so I got the best of both of them."

"I'll say," Tommy remarked. Kerry had a perfect body, with plump breasts and a curvy behind, and she was almost as tall as him.

"You're pretty handsome yourself," Kerry complimented back.

"Thank you," Tommy said modestly, "Some people say I look just like my father, only a little taller and thinner."

"Do you have a good relationship with your real father?"

"Well, I haven't Skyped him since I've been here, but you remind me that I should contact him."

"He must be pretty upset that you came to live here."

"Yeah; nobody in my family took it well. My dad never liked my stepfather much, but he knows that I have a really tight relationship with Bill, and he agrees that Bill got the shaft in this whole situation, so I think he understands why I wanted to come to Bill's aid."

"Yes, but now that you're here, you can never go back."

"Well that's just the thing. I don't know if you heard, but on Earth, they've recently developed a way to beam your mind into an android body, and I actually brought the plans to build a beaming station here."

"That's amazing! You can actually have your mind transferred to an android body somewhere else?"

"Yep; and my sister actually developed it, with the assistance of a famous scientist she is working with, by the name of Albert Freudenthal."

"No kidding? They must be famous after developing that!"

"Yes, well Albert was pretty famous before they even met. The University he taught at built him a whole research facility on campus, where he was testing his general theories on psychic conversion. Alyssa was actually a student of his, which is how she met him.

"That's very interesting," Kerry said, as she listened intently.

"Yeah, well Albert gave her some of his papers to read, because she showed promise in his class as a student, and she actually provided him with much of the input he needed in order to develop a more solid foundation, in terms of validating the theories he had been inclined to believe were true."

"You said she was in college at the time; how old was she?"

Tommy squinted as he thought, "I believe she was only fourteen at the time."

"That's amazing!" Kerry whispered loudly.

"Yeah, well Alyssa's <u>Doctoral</u> thesis actually got them a sizeable government grant, which they worked off of for years, until they finally had this breakthrough.—And yes, she is a celebrity now. I think she's known all around the world."

Kerry was speechless for several seconds, as the wheels were turning, "So, have you contacted companies here, about building a mind beaming station?"

"Yes, well, that was originally the purpose of my contacting Atlas Android; and you could say I've gotten everybody's attention!—But that's how I happened to get the tour with you yesterday; and your marketing department has offered me a job too."

"That's great! So we may be working together . . ."

"Well, I haven't accepted the position yet, but I'm thinking seriously about it."

"Do you have any training or experience in marketing?"

"No, actually I have an engineering degree, but I may take Ron and Paul up on their offer to put me through an apprenticeship program."

"You say Paul; you mean Paul Klien?"

"Yes; I met with him the day I took the tour with you, remember?"

"Okay; yes I do remember, you had to cut our meeting short because you had another appointment . . ."

Tommy nodded and continued, "But anyway, I don't have any sales background. My stepfather <u>Bill</u> has a background in marketing. He worked for US Android."

"Oh; the company that went belly up last year?"

"Yes, you've heard of it?"

"It was on the news; we keep up on that sort of thing, being another android manufacturing company."

"But you've never heard about mind beaming?"

"No; that's news to me. We're kind of cut off from the rest of the world here in some ways."

"Well if Atlas Android decides to undertake this project, I'm sure it will be all over the news, all around the planet!"

Kerry thought about it for a few seconds, "I'd certainly like to travel to Earth, if a beaming station is built. Does it work that far?"

"Yes; there's a couple of beaming stations on Earth-3, and they've successfully beamed people back and forth from there."

"That's incredible! How expensive is it? Can people here afford to do it if it does become available?"

"It is pretty expensive to have your mind beamed long distances, but it must be somewhat affordable, because thousands of people are already doing it."

"Yeah, but it may only be wealthy people who sign up for it; you don't know how much it costs, huh?"

"I'll have to ask my sister; I'm sure <u>she</u> knows."

"Is she older than you?"

"We're twins."

"She's only eighteen, and she invented this?!"

"Yes, she was a child prodigy; a genius, if you will."

"So this Dr. Freudenthal; he was her teacher, in college?

"Yes, the college gave him a large grant to set up his research lab, in exchange for his agreeing to teach classes."

"And he singled her out . . ."

"Yes; Alyssa asked to see his research papers, and she helped him realize you could convert consciousness into transferable electronic files, not unlike the way we convert memories to electronic data and store it on the internet, for those with brain retrofit hardware."

"Oh, so you have to have brain retrofit hardware . . ."

"Yes, doesn't everyone these days?"

"Yes, that's true; that's how we can market androids to the middle class here; most people, even the lower-middle class, have brain retrofit hardware installed during their childhood; there's even Federal subsidy available for low income workers and their children, for this; so really, it has been made available to almost everyone on the planet."

"That's very interesting; yeah, I was wondering how they're going to market androids to low income people."

"So is she rich? Your sister?"

"She's probably not as wealthy as my mother. We were part of a test group of US Android's, we were all connected to family-androids; that's a pair of androids where the mother and the son are hooked up to the male android, and the father and the daughter are hooked up to the female android."

"Yeah, I heard about that; but they're outlawed now, aren't they? Family androids?"

"Yes, they were the undoing of US Android, for the same reason my stepfather is here in prison. Something went wrong with what they call the "Chinese wall" portion of the software, and they found what's called "bleedthrough sexual memories" in the online memory files of some of the children involved in the prototype testing program. It was as though they had experienced, on some level, the sexual acts between the parent and the android. Alyssa says she can't remember all that much, but it's proven that the memories are there in her online memory file; so Bill was convicted of sexual assault."

"So you're saying that your sister Alyssa was one of the children who had these bleedthrough sexual memories?—And your stepfather was convicted for sexual assault, and sentenced to prison here on planet P?"

"Yes, precisely," Tommy looked Kerry straight in the eye.

"Wow! How very <u>unfortunate</u> for him."

"Yes, he lost <u>everything</u>; my mother divorced him, he lost all of his assets, his career, and his freedom; for <u>good</u> unless we are successful in appealing his case."

"What do you mean, for good?—Does he have a life sentence?!"

Tommy shook his head, "Well no, he was given a suspended sentence; but that's after forty years . . ."

"He has to stay in prison for forty years?!" Kerry gasped.

"Unless I can help Bill appeal his <u>case</u> here."

"What does your lawyer think his chances are of getting Bill off?"

"He doesn't know yet; there aren't enough cases that there has been any precedent set yet, he says. He's talking with the judge and the prosecutor about it this week supposedly, and I have another meeting with him next Tuesday."

"Well good luck with that; so that's why you are only staying a few days here in Alderon?"

"Yes, exactly; and depending on what the lawyer says next week, I may or may not be back, at least for a while."

"I suppose you don't want me to spread this information around at work . . ."

"No, of <u>course</u> not; I wouldn't want anything to get in the way of Atlas Android deciding to go forward with plans to build a mind beaming station; and I'd appreciate it if you would keep it under your hat about my stepfather. When, and if, the company goes public with plans to build the mind beaming station, then it might be more okay with me if you want to divulge some of this information."

"Okay, I'll keep my mouth shut; I promise. Now, I could tell you about <u>me</u>, but I can <u>assure</u> you, it's not as exciting of a story as <u>your</u> background!"

Tommy smiled as he fielded the comment, "Let <u>me</u> be the judge of that; did you grow up in Alderon?"

"No, in Wilton; it's about fifty miles north. My father commuted to Alderon though; he worked for a company by the name of Deltoid muscle manufacturing. At that time, Deltoid had the contract to supply Atlas Android with synthetic muscle tissue; but they lost the contract to a larger company that moved here from Earth, I think about seven years ago."

"Does your father still work for Deltoid?"

"He got laid off last year due to the decreased demand these days for androids. He's looking for a job right now, but there doesn't seem to be very many openings in the industry.

He's thinking about changing careers, but he doesn't like the idea of going back to school, and he can't really afford it anyway, at this point."

"Yes; college is expensive these days. Does your mother work?"

"Yes, she's a nurse. They are basically living off of her income. Us kids are all grown, and on our own. I'm the youngest, and I moved out two years ago, after I graduated college. I got the job at Atlas right out of college. The school has a good placement program."

"You went to work right away as a programmer?"

"No, I had to go through a one year apprentice program, but I had the training, so it was pretty easy for me."

"So now that you are a programmer, do you meet with customers who have just bought an android?—Or do you just work from the interview sheets, and program the android accordingly?"

"Yes, I only work directly with the android to be programmed. There are other interview specialists who work with the customer, to get the information I will use."

"How long does it take to program an android these days, once you have the interview information?"

"It usually takes about half of a week; but with some customers it can take longer."

"That long, huh? I guess it's pretty intricate work . . ."

"It's a bit tedious, but I've done about fifty so far; it's pretty easy for me, it just takes time."

"Well, enough about work; tell me about your older sister; is she married?"

"Yeah, to her work," Kerry joked. "She runs a small catering business just outside of Clarion DC. It's in a little town called Rockland. She's got the in's with some local politicians, so she caters a lot of cocktail parties and fundraisers. She works seven days a week most weeks, and she never takes a vacation. I guess she must be making some pretty good money, but she continues to live in a small house, and she spends very little money. She says she's saving for an early retirement."

"She sounds ambitious."

"I guess she enjoys what she's doing."

"There are no <u>men</u> in her life?"

"She says she's too busy for a relationship, and she sees people getting divorced all around her, so she's kind of cynical about love relationships."

"It almost sounds like she's gay."

"No, she's not gay; that much I know. She's just had bad luck in relationships, and she hasn't had that many."

"Do you have any other brothers or sisters?"

Kerry nodded as she answered, "Yes, I have a brother who's twenty-nine. He's married, with two daughters; one's six and the older one is nine. He got married young; to his high school sweetheart."

"What does he do?"

"He's actually a corrections officer, at Chilton; and his wife just started working at Macy's, at the cosmetics counter last year, since the girls are in school; she works part time."

"So what's his name? He works at the prison in Chilton?"

"Yes, his name is Doug; he works on rotation; sometimes he's on days, sometimes nights; and occasionally he works the graveyard shift, but that's only a couple of months a year; mostly he's on days."

"I wonder if he knows Bill? What was your last name again?"

"Atwood, but it's a big prison. The chances of him being your stepfather's C.O. are pretty slim."

"What's a C.O.?" Tommy asked curiously.

"That's a corrections officer;—you've gotta start learning the jargon here, if you're going to live on this <u>prison-colony</u> of a planet!" Kerry said with a laugh. "-But like I was telling you, it's not likely that my brother would know your stepfather personally."

"Yeah, you're probably right; but that's an interesting coincidence. Does he live in Chilton?"

"Stafford; it's about fifteen miles outside Chilton."

"Oh, so he doesn't have that long of a commute."

"No; with traffic, it's about a half hour, in the morning."

"I'm thinking about coming to <u>work</u> at Atlas, and I'm looking into possibly buying a house here in the area; can you recommend a town or two that I might look first in?"

Kerry thought for a few seconds, "Well if you want to be close to downtown Alderon, I could recommend Fairhope; that's a nice community. There's a lake nearby, and there's some good shopping centers, and a movie theatre in town."

"Fairhope, huh? I'll have to put that on my list." Tommy smiled as he remembered his friend, Gary, "I have a friend who lives in Fairhope, Alabama, in the US, back on earth."

The comment didn't mean anything to Kerry; she kept on with her train of thought, "And there's Lincoln; that's a little north of Alderon, but it's pretty close to the Beltway, so it's not a bad commute, although the houses there are more expensive; I don't know how much you are looking to spend."

"I don't know either, but that gives me a couple of towns to look into; thanks," Tommy said with sincerity.

"I don't know if you've found a real estate agent to take you around yet, but if not, I can recommend Tony Romano with Thirty-Second Century; he's the one who found me the apartment I'm living in now. He's very professional, and he's been in the area now for about twenty years, so he knows the surrounding towns very well I think."

"You'll have to give me his Skype number."

They finished dinner around nine-thirty, and headed back to Kerry's apartment. Tommy walked her to her door and kissed her goodnight. As he did so, he held her close and embraced her, and felt her warmth. It was a kiss that made it seem to him like there were possibilities for the future with her. He could taste her cherry lip gloss as he drove back to the hotel.

The next morning, Tommy Skyped Tony Romano, and arranged to get together at two o'clock. Tony said he would look into the available housing in a few surrounding towns. He told Tommy that housing prices in the Fairhope area ranged from around two-hundred thousand to two million, and Tommy asked him to look in the two-to five hundred thousand range. He didn't think he wanted to spend more than three-hundred thousand, but he thought he'd at least take a look to see what luxury houses were like.

He went to the Alderon Mall downtown and bought some clothes and another suitcase to lug them back to Chilton. He had just enough time to make his noon massage, after which he took a quick shower and left for Tony's office around one-thirty. He arrived about ten minutes early, and was ushered into Tony's office.

Tommy approached the middle-aged man coming from around his desk, and stuck out a hand, "Hi, I'm Tom Symms."

"Hi; Tony Romano; nice to meet you," he said while giving Tommy a vigorous handshake, "Have a seat," Tony gestured, "I've found several houses for us to look at. You mentioned Fairhope, so I guess we can get started there, as there's a pretty good number of homes on the market in the two-hundred to five hundred thousand dollar price range in that area."

"Okay; shall we get started?" Tommy asked eagerly.

"Sure," Tony granted, to appear somewhat amenable, "We can take these printouts I made along with us, and we'll talk on the way . . ."

Fairhope was only about fifteen minutes outside Alderon, and shortly after getting off the highway at the first Fairhope exit, they pulled up in front of a small house in a housing tract where the houses were about twenty feet apart from each other.

"This is on the inexpensive side," Tony said as they opened the front door. "The yard is small, but there is a nice deck out back, with a hot tub sunken into it. The back yard is fenced in for privacy."

They walked through the house, which was all on one level. "This is only a two bedroom, huh?" Tommy remarked rhetorically, "Boy, you sure don't get too much for two hundred thousand," Tommy remarked.

"No, this is low the low end," Tony clarified, "This house is only going for one-seventy-nine, but it's kind of a bargain, pricewise, for the area; so I thought I'd show it to you first. Did you want to see something a little bigger?"

"Yes, definitely!" Tommy exclaimed mildly, to give Tony the feedback that they were way off base. Then he elaborated further, "Something with one or two more bedrooms possibly, and a back yard big enough for a pool, if I wanted to put one in."

"Okay, let's go over to Cherry Street; there's a nice three bedroom with a pool and a Jacuzzi, and it's a short drive to the downtown section."

Tommy was much more pleased with the second house they visited. It had a large living room, and a large office with a Skype station built in. There was a small pool in the back yard, with a Jacuzzi next to it, "This is more like it; how much does this one go for?"

"This one is more pricey; the owner is asking three-twenty-five, but he'll probably take a little less; it's been on the market for several months."

"This is nice, but I think I would like to find one that isn't in a housing tract. I want more privacy, and I'd like to have a bigger pool, if I was going to buy a house with a pool."

They looked at two more houses in Fairhope, before driving to Lincoln, where the houses were bigger, but it was fifteen miles further away from Alderon. When Tommy returned to the hotel, he Skyped Alyssa and told her about his travels, "Hi Alyssa; how is everything back in Philadelphia?"

"Not too good; there was a big storm, and the lab got water—damaged. The river nearby rose about six feet!"

"That's too bad; is this going to set you back in your work?"

"Yeah, we lost some equipment. Albert is out looking for another space at a higher elevation. We're probably going to have to move all our equipment, and it's going to set us back several weeks I think."

"How about your house? Did you get flooded there too?"

"Yes, I had a foot of water in the basement, but there wasn't much down there to get ruined."

"That's a lucky thing. Well, at least the weather here has been good. I went out looking at houses in the area today. I wanted to get some idea of what's available here, in case I move here and take that job at Atlas Android."

"What did you find? Anything decent?"

"Well, there was one nice house in a town called Fairhope that was particularly nice. There's a view of the lake, and the kitchen is quite nice; it's four bedrooms."

"Wow, that sounds pretty big!—How far is it from Alderon?"

"It's about twenty miles away; that's not too bad a commute, but it's going for over five-hundred-thousand."

"Well," Alyssa considered during a brief pause, "I guess that's affordable for you, if you want to spend that much. When are you going back to Chilton to see Bill's lawyer?"

"I go back tomorrow, and I have an appointment with Phil Pierson on Tuesday; so hopefully I'll know more by the next time I talk to you."

"Alright; well have a safe trip tomorrow."

"Okay; I'll Skype you on Monday afternoon, after I've met with Phil; bye sis."

Tommy's flight back to Chilton the next day was uneventful, and after renting a Grand Am hydrogen powered car at the airport, he drove downtown and checked back into the Hampton Inn at around three-thirty. He decided that the accommodations at the Hilton, where he had previously been staying, in Alderon, were much nicer, and he resolved to find a more luxurious hotel the next day. The Hampton Inn had no pool, and there were no services such as massages or room service. He had become spoiled, staying at the Alderon Hilton.

Saturday morning, Tommy visited Bill at the prison as planned, and he found Bill a little down when they first met.

Sensing this, Tommy addressed him more sympathetically, "Hi Bill, how are you holding up? You look a little down today; are they treating you alright here?"

"Well, we've been on lockdown all week. They come around three or four times a year, and search every cell looking for contraband. It makes for a long, hard week. They keep us in our cells for five days straight, and feed us through a little slot in the door.

"That sounds pretty frightful," Tommy said with empathy, "You'll have to excuse me, I'm not up to speed on all of this, but what exactly is "contraband?"

"Well, you know, knives or shanks, which are homemade knives people stab other inmates with, razor blades, drugs, child porn; stingers, made out of extension cords, which you use to heat up soup, or other foods; homemade pillows and such . . ."

"You can't have a pillow?" Tommy asked with some incredulity.

"Well, you can, but you have to buy it through the commissary; but that costs over twenty bucks, whereas you could buy one an inmate makes out of old clothes or T-shirts, for like three bucks."

Tommy became more curious, "How do people <u>get</u> child porn and drugs and stuff in here; how is that possible?!"

Bill smiled at Tommy's good question, "I think most of these things get smuggled in here by the C.O.'s, or guards, in case you don't know what a C.O. is . . ."

"Yeah, I already learned that one; corrections officer."

"Well anyway, I was telling you about our lockdown this week; my new cellmate is okay to talk to, but he has bad body odor. When we can't get out to shower, it gets really stinky in there."

"Oh man; I'm sorry for you Bill; did you get the books I sent you?"

"Yes, thank you; they're the only thing that's kept me sane all week. Adam's been writing a book, and he's hardly even been slowed down by the lockdown. He writes all day long, and then we watch TV at night. Thankfully, he <u>has</u> a TV. I was wondering, can you put some money in my commissary account? I'd like to get a TV too, and some snacks. I've been bumming snacks from Adam, and some of the shows he watches aren't too interesting to me, so I'd like to have my own TV."

"Sure; how much is a TV, do you know?"

"They go for about three hundred dollars."

"Fine; I'll put five hundred in your commissary account, and hopefully you'll be out before you've spent it all!"

"Yeah, wouldn't that be nice. You're going to see Phil Pierson this coming week?"

"Tuesday morning, first thing. I'm sure I'll have more news for you by next Saturday when I come to visit again."

"Yeah, I'd call you. But they won't let me call anyone other than a resident; so you'd have to move into a house or an apartment, and establish a permanent phone line. There's no Skype here; we're limited to talking on the phone for fifteen minutes a day."

"Well. Hopefully I'll be getting a place soon, but I haven't established where I want to live yet. You see, I've just come back from Alderon, about three-thousand miles from here. I found an android company that is looking into possibly building a mind beaming station here on planet P!"

"That would be great! Then, you could go back home and see Alyssa and your mother and father, and everyone."

"Yes, well it may take quite some time to set up. Apparently, they would have to get government approval, and I think most of the equipment necessary would have to be sent from Earth; and the android company would also need to secure financing in order to go ahead with this; but at least I've started the ball rolling."

"That's great, Tommy; I'm glad you're having success with it; I know you were worried about finding a company big enough, that they could afford to build a mind beaming station."

"Well actually, while I was there, this company called Atlas Android, who I approached about the beaming station idea, offered me a job in their marketing department; I'd be doing what you were doing at US Android, probably."

"But you said Alderon's Three-thousand miles away!"

"Yeah, and I know; that's one of the considerations; but I could still visit you on the weekends."

"Yeah, I suppose that's true; but it's a lot of trouble to come all that way; I might not see you for months at a time . . ."

"Nah, I'd come to visit you every few weeks; but you could also be <u>out</u> of here before too long; and I think it might be good to be close to this "Atlas Android," to help follow through on the beaming station building project, assuming they eventually decide to go ahead with it."

Bill didn't say anything, but Tommy could tell from his eyes that he was disappointed. "Bill, don't worry; I'm not going to make a decision right away. Let me talk to your lawyer next week, and find out what your chances are for the appeal, and his projected <u>time</u> table. I may well stay in this area, if it would be of more help in getting you out of here."

They spent the balance of the hour talking about Tommy's trip to Alderon; his stay at the Hilton, his tour of the android factory, the meetings with Ron Goldstein and the marketing director, the cool Shelby Mustang he rented, the houses he went to see in the suburbs of Alderon, and of course, his time spent with Kerry.

When it was time to go, they embraced over the table, "Well I'm glad the lockdown is over; hopefully this week will be a lot more bearable," Tommy said sincerely.

"Yeah, good luck in your meetings with Phil Pierson. I hope you have some good news to report, next time I see you."

Tommy went back to visit Bill on Sunday as well, but he had woken up not feeling well. He felt like he had a temperature, and he felt achy all over, and a little foggy on the brain. Still, he dragged himself up, not wanting to miss an opportunity to visit with Bill at every chance he had, while he was in Chilton. He took a hot shower, which made him feel a little better, and after getting dressed, he stopped at the diner down the street, to try and get something into his stomach.

After all of this, Tommy still wasn't feeling all that well, but he made his way to the prison just the same, and had a short visit with Bill. Afterward, he had returned to the hotel, and went back to bed.

He fell asleep quickly, and didn't wake up until early the next morning, having slept almost sixteen hours straight! He did feel a little better, though. He bathed and got dressed, and decided to drive downtown and see what different place he could find to have breakfast, besides the nearby diner.

The center of Chilton was pretty busy, Tommy thought, for 6:30 in the morning. On the sidewalks there were dozens of men in blue uniforms; interspersed with men and women in hospital scrubs, and women in white nurse's uniforms, as far as he could see in either direction.

This made more sense to him as he passed Mercy Hospital in the next block, however, he was curious to learn why all of these people were already out and about at this early hour.

He passed by the Marriott Towers, a little further down Main Street, noticing a "Restaurant Open" sign in the window; so he parked, where he could find a spot on the street, a few blocks further down, and he walked back to the restaurant.

A receptionist greeted him, "Good morning sir? Just one?"

"Huh?" Tommy grunted in his early morning fog, then he realized what was being asked, "Oh; yes, I'm by myself."

"Right this way, sir." Tommy was led to a table by the window, overlooking the street. The morning sun felt good on his face, as he had been holed up in a dark hotel room for quite some time.

He could hear the couple behind him talking, as he waited for his order of eggs benedict. "We'll have to remember not to come here at this hour, dear," the man was saying to the woman.

"Yes, the damned seven a.m. prison shift change, along with the nursing shift change at the hospital; you can't get service at this restaurant worth a damn!"

Tommy tuned out, as he remembered that Alyssa was an early bird, and he suddenly felt drawn to talk to her; so he took a chance, and dialed her Skype number. The phone rang several times. Finally,

Alyssa's sleepy face appeared on the screen. Her hair was mussed, "Oh, I'm sorry sis; I've woken you up . . ."

"No, it's alright," Alyssa soothed in a sleepy voice, "I had the alarm set to wake me up in five minutes anyway."

"Oh, okay . . ." Tommy was relieved to hear this; whether it was actually true or not.

"What's up?—You don't look too good; are you feeling okay?"

"Nah, I've come down with some kind of flu, or grip or something. I think I must have picked it up at the visiting room, at the prison."

"That's too bad, I'm sorry to hear that," Alyssa said sympathetically. "You never get sick," she continued, "It must be a pretty bad virus you've got going around up there . . ."

"Yeah, Bill told me there's a bad flu going around in there."

"Well, if you still aren't feeling well in another couple of days, you should probably go to a doctor."

"Thanks, but I need a sister now, not another mother!" Bill joked.

"Okay; I get the hint," Alyssa said with a sheepish smile, "You're taking care of yourself, though . . ."

"Yeah, I slept from like, one o'clock yesterday afternoon, until around five this morning!"

"Okay," she said, brightening, "Are you feeling better?"

"Yeah, I am feeling a little better; but I think I'm going to lay low another day, just to make sure. I hope I'll feel recovered by tomorrow morning, when I have to meet with Bill's lawyer."

"Oh that's tomorrow, huh?"

"Yeah, 9am."

"Alright, well rest up today; don't do anything I wouldn't do," she joked.

"What wouldn't you do?!" Tommy shot back at her with a laugh, emphasizing he knew she could be pretty unpredictable, "Bye sis . . ."

Chapter Nineteen

Tommy was up at the crack of dawn on Tuesday morning. He didn't sleep well the night before, as he was still getting over the lingerings of his illness, plus he also had anxiety about his meeting with Phil Pierson. He had decided to stay one more day at the Hampton Inn, until after he had met with Phil, hoping that what he had to say would dictate that he move closer to the action, surrounding Bill's case.

He waited until around seven a.m., so he wouldn't wake her, and then he Skyped Kerry, to try and catch her before she left for work, "Hi Kerry; am I catching you at a bad time?"

"Yeah, I'm just getting ready for work; you caught me before I put my makeup on," she said, with an uncomfortable look.

"You look beautiful to me; you don't <u>need</u> any makeup . . ."

"Thanks, but I feel naked without my makeup on."

"That's okay; I'd like to catch you when you <u>are</u> naked!"

"Very funny; what's up?"

"Oh. I woke up early; I have this meeting with Bill's lawyer this morning. I know I should be feeling optimistic, but for some reason I'm nervous."

"Don't be nervous; you said the case didn't involve your stepfather actually sexually assaulting your sister, didn't you?"

"Yes, but on Earth, they're funny about this bleedthrough stuff; I wonder if they'll be any more sympathetic here?"

"Yeah, some laws don't make much sense. I guess you've done the best that you can, to hire a good lawyer and hope for the best."

"Yes, I guess I am doing all I can."

"Listen I hate to cut it short, but I really have to go; Ron Goldstein wants to see me first thing this morning, and I don't want to be late. Can you Skype me this evening after work?"

"Sure; I'll do that." Tommy hung up, and started wondering what Ron Goldstein might be wanting to talk to Kerry about, so early in the morning. Maybe it had something to do with him.

Tommy sat fidgeting nervously in the outer office of the Pierson, Smith law offices. The secretary called over to him, "Mr. Pierson will see you now."

Tommy knew his way to Phil's office, and he found Phil at his computer, busily typing away, "Have a seat, Tom, I'll be right with you. I'm returning an email the judge sent me this morning on your stepfather's case."

Tommy sat quietly on the other side of Phil's desk, and waited for about two minutes, "Okay, there; I think that will get our message delivered in time before the ten o'clock court session."

"Did you file the petition last week?"

"Well . . . actually, I need to talk to you about that. I spoke last Wednesday in chambers with Judge Thompson; Joe Thompson; I've known him for years; anyway, he has had a few cases of this kind in the last year, and he says they haven't been willing to grant an appeal. The law clearly states that planet P must embrace all of the laws made on Earth, and accept the judgments of the court, in whatever district the sentence was imposed."

"That's terrible news! Is there anything we can do?"

"Yes; the judge told me that we'd be better off going for a sentence modification. He said it was almost certain that we could reduce the length of Bill's sentence, and there's even a possibility that he could be released on probation, and not have to serve any more time in prison."

"He'd be on probation as a sex offender?"

"If we're lucky; I can't guarantee we'd get that result."

"He'd never be able to get a decent job, as a sex offender, and he would have other restrictions, wouldn't he? Like not being able to travel out of state, and not being able to go to parks and malls . . ."

"Yes, well while all that is true, he would be a lot better off living in the community, outside of a jail cell."

"Yes, well that's for sure." Tommy sat with that thought for a few seconds, "What can I do to help you in preparing for a sentence modification hearing; anything?"

"There's actually very little you have to do; we'll use the transcripts from the trial on Earth. You could get letters from character witnesses on Bill's behalf, but otherwise, we just file the paperwork this week, and wait for the court date. I think we could get it on the docket for next month, if we get the paperwork in this week."

"I don't know who I could get for a character witness; maybe my sister would be willing; she's the victim, so that would be most helpful wouldn't it?"

"I'm not sure if that would be helpful or not; I'll have to consult the judge. I know on Earth, the court would frown on that. They would seek to avoid Bill's having contact with the victim under any circumstances, at least until the end of Bill's probation . . . Is there anyone from work, or friends of the family you could contact?"

"Well, US Android has gone out of business, so I probably can't get in contact with anyone Bill used to work with . . . —Although I think I <u>do</u> have a Skype number for Barry and Kathleen. <u>They</u> were associates of Bill's. I wonder if they would write a letter on his behalf."

"That's good;" Phil encouraged, "You try and dig up anyone who might write a letter attesting to Bill's good character, and I'll try and schedule the hearing as soon as possible."

"Is there a jury or a prosecutor involved? How does this work?" Tommy asked inquisitively.

"Well, the decision is entirely up to the judge, but there will be a prosecutor involved, and she will likely do some research into the background of the case; maybe use a contact in the Boston area to dig up the facts of the case; so if there's anything scandalous, it could be bad for us. Was Bill involved in any affairs, prostitution or child porn or anything?"

"No! Nothing of the sort; he worked at US Android by day, and he was at home at night. The only one he had sex with besides Mom was Shayna."

"That's his android . . ." Phil wanted to make sure.

"Right." Tommy confirmed.

"Well that's good; you dig up as many character witnesses as you can, and we'll be in touch . . ."

"Yes; Phil?—One other thing; is there any reason I shouldn't move to Alderon? I've been offered a job there, and I think I may want to settle in the area. Will it detract from the case if I were to do so?"

Phil thought briefly, then answering, "No, I can't imagine why . . . would you still be able to attend the hearings next month, or as soon as they can be scheduled?"

"Absolutely; in fact, if I couldn't be guaranteed I could get the time off from work, I would hold off on my start date until the proceedings are over."

"Do you have money to hold you over until then?"

"Yes; money won't be a problem; but time is. If there's any way we could get Bill out of jail sooner rather than later, I would be happy to pay you extra, if it might cost more."

"Well, I can't <u>bribe</u> anyone, if that's what you mean . . ."

"Of <u>course</u> not; I wasn't suggesting that; I just meant like if you want to hire a private investigator or something."

"I'll look over the transcripts again, but that may not be necessary. I believe your mother's drinking problem was well documented, and I think that is the key element we can focus on; her actions were very irresponsible for a mother of two; and in fact her lack of availability to Bill at night was also the main reason he had to seek sexual activity with his female android."

"Do you think that will bode well in court?"

"I think so; I'll have to look at the other cases that have come through Judge Thompson in the past year; I don't think there have been any similar cases before then."

"When should we meet again, Phil?"

"Why don't I Skype you when we have a court date, and we'll take it from there."

Tommy went back to the hotel, disappointed that they would not be able to appeal Bill's case. He realized he had suffered from wishful thinking again. He had sort of planned to get Bill off of his charges, and he had come ready to go to any lengths to make that happen.

Now, he was told there was nothing he could do but round up a few letters possibly. He knew that Bill was also very hopeful that the appeal might go through, and he would probably be crushed to find out that there was no chance for an appeal.

He knew that his challenge now was to keep Bill thinking in a positive direction about the sentence modification hearing they were planning on his behalf.

He realized that he could go online and find out all the information that was available about sex offenders on probation. He decided he would do so, and send it to Bill, to let him know what was possibly in store for him, and to prepare Bill for the next stage of what he should be focusing on, and hoping for.

He spent the next few hours surfing the web for information on sex offenders, writing down any useful bits of information as he went from website to website, collecting information.

He realized suddenly that he was way past check-out time, and resigned himself to stay another night at the Hampton Inn. He decided to look online for hotels in the area, to try and get an idea of what his options were.

That's when he found The Stafford Club for men. It was advertised as a sports complex with a hotel facility. Tommy missed his college days on the basketball team and the baseball team, and the ad said he could join a team, or that they would partner him up for tennis, racquetball, golf, or water sports.

He Skyped the hotel facility and made a reservation for the following day. He would stay there for the week, he thought. While online, Tommy also found an ad for the Android Café, and he decided to go there for a late lunch. The ad said you could select the android of your choice, who would dine with you and make conversation. He decided it would be a good first step in deciding if he wanted to own an android or not.

Tommy arrived at the Android Café a little after three, and found it pretty empty; but this was good news for him, because there were about two dozen android women and men in the waiting room, whom you could talk to in order to decide which partner you would like to have join you for your meal.

Tommy picked an attractive female out of the crowd, and approached her, "Are you available to have lunch with me?" he asked.

"Sure! I'm Joanne-165; you can just call me Joanne. Are you from out of town? I don't believe I've seen you here before."

"That's right; I'm from Earth; I've been on the planet for about a week."

Oh, well I can answer any questions you may have about the area; shopping centers, tourist attractions, mass transit, hotels, nightclubs and other things to do around the city . . . Should we sit down?"

"Oh, don't we need a waitress to seat us?"

"No, we can sit wherever you would like; the waitress will find us and take your order."

"Let's sit over by the window; follow me."

They walked across the large room and sat at a secluded table in the far corner, illuminated by the soft glow of a tinted window. "Are you just in the area for a visit, or are you considering becoming a resident?"

"I'm probably either going to live here, or in Alderon; I haven't decided yet."

"Alderon is the largest city on the planet; the current population is twenty-two million, eight-hundred and seventy-four."

"Is that so? What else do you know about Alderon?"

"It is twenty-nine-hundred and twenty-three miles from Chilton city limits; there are eight-hundred and seventeen stores, and twelve-hundred and thirty-six independent businesses in downtown Alderon; and the Global Capital is located there; in Clarion DC., which is a district of Alderon."

"When you say, "global," do you mean there is only one country on the planet?"

"Yes, there is one central government, and laws, of course, are determined by the citizens of the planet, as a single voting body."

"I see; well you do seem to know a lot; I've traveled there already, last week; and I looked at homes in the suburbs. What are homes selling for in Stafford?"

"You can own a one bedroom apartment for as little as eighty-three thousand dollars currently, and single family dwellings start at around one-hundred and twenty-thousand, and range into the millions; but most houses in this immediate area sell for under four hundred thousand."

"This is a little weird; I can't talk to you like person because you have no background or past to share with me; but let me at least, ask you some more questions, since you happen to be so informative."

"I can assure you that I am equipped to respond like a woman in just about every way, physically and mentally; but you can continue your line of questioning, if that is what you would prefer."

"I'm actually interested in finding out what you know about the Stafford Club. Do you have any information on that?"

"Yes, of course; the Stafford Club was founded twenty-two years ago; it was the first men's club in any of the Chilton suburbs. It was originally established as a sports complex, but in recent years, they have added a very upscale hotel facility, to cater to wealthy local residents who want to get away for a week or more on vacation. Some wealthy businessmen keep a room there on a yearly basis, and they entertain their out-of-town business guests there. There are several leagues you can join, from bowling to ice hockey, volleyball, football, baseball, soccer, basketball, and there are racquetball and tennis courts where you can sign up for an opponent if you don't already have someone to play with. Membership in the club has grown to a little over one-thousand currently, but the hotel usually has vacancies, because it is quite expensive to stay there. Is there anything else you would like to know about the club?"

"Yes; why is it only for men?"

"Well, Stafford started out as a penal colony for men who were paroled, or on probation, after serving prison sentences at Chilton State Prison. It is only since then that some of their families and loved ones have come to planet P to be with their spouse, partner or friend, or to raise a family. Now there's about twenty percent female population in Stafford, but it's still predominately a city of men. The club also has a large staff of female androids to cater to men's needs, if you know what I mean."

"I'm actually thinking about getting an android myself, but I prefer a real woman; no offense intended."

"Well, suit yourself, but other men have told me that they enjoy the experience of being with me just about as much as being with a real woman, and as you'll probably find out, real women are kind of scarce on this planet."

"I just don't know if I would enjoy a sexual experience with an android; I guess there's only one way to find out."

"There is a good android brothel downtown. I could tell you how to get there from here, if you wish."

Tommy cocked his head slightly as he spoke, "I don't know if I'm ready for that, but it's good to know."

"It's downtown on Market Street, about two blocks from the mall, in case you change your mind. It's called Ruby's."

"Well I've enjoyed talking with you; I think I'd rather eat my lunch alone, if you don't mind. I think it would be weird eating while you are just sitting there watching me."

"I understand. I'll just excuse myself; enjoy your lunch."

The evening went by slowly. Tommy Skyped Alyssa and they talked for a while; then he watched a movie on the small TV in his room and went to bed early.

Tuesday morning, Tommy packed up his suitcases and made his way over to the Stafford Club around ten o'clock. As he drove in, there was a golf course all around him, and it reminded him that he hadn't played golf in months. He had been so wrapped up in making his plans to move to planet P, and dealing with his family's objections to doing so, that he stopped playing any sports for a while. This would be a good opportunity to get back into it. He enjoyed playing golf and tennis, and he looked forward to getting into a basketball game if he could arrange it.

He found the hotel facility and checked in at the front desk, "Hi, I'm Tom Symms; I have a reservation I believe."

The pretty android woman behind the desk checked her computer, "Yes, welcome Mr. Symms; you'll be staying with us for the week?"

"Yes, that's correct."

"Would you like some help with your bags? I can call the bellhop, and he can show you to your room . . ."

"Yes, that would be fine . . . I think I'd like to play some golf today. How would I go about signing up to play?"

"You can visit the concierge; the desk is right across the lobby. They can help you with all of your sports plans for the week."

As Tommy might have figured, the bellhop was also an android. His looks were too perfect to be a hotel worker. He looked more like a movie star.

He showed Tommy to his room on the third floor. It overlooked the golf course, and he could see the tennis courts in the distance from his balcony as the bellhop put his suitcases on the stands in the corner. The room had a big screen TV, and a king size bed with lots of pillows, facing it. There was a large desk with a rolling arm chair. There was a three foot wide Skype screen on the desk. "Is that a docking station for my laptop?" Tommy asked.

"Yes sir; it has a standard port here," he pointed it out, "and the microphone is built in at the top of the screen."

There was a bar on the other side of the room. Tommy crossed the spacious room and opened the refrigerator, "I see this is stocked with plenty of snacks and drinks."

"Yes; we restock it daily, and what you consume is charged to your room bill."

"Yes, I figured as much."

"Is there anything else I can do for you sir?" the bellhop asked cordially.

"No, thank you; shall I give you a tip?"

"No, that won't be necessary." An android had no use for money.

After the bellhop left, Tommy scheduled a massage for five o'clock that afternoon, and he called down to the concierge desk to schedule his golf game. Then he got into his bathing suit and took the elevator down to the first level, where he found the pool and Jacuzzi. There were about a dozen other guests lounging and swimming, and sitting in the Jacuzzi. There were two pretty android servants taking orders and bringing drinks on small round trays. They were scantily clad, showing off their shapely bodies. It was a very pleasant scene. He enjoyed a swim in the warm pool, and a soak in the unusually hot Jacuzzi which relaxed him completely. This was living, he thought.

Tommy entered the pro shop at twelve-thirty, in time to rent a set of clubs for his one o'clock tee time. "Yes sir; can I help you?" The clerk looked like he could possibly be the golf pro at the course.

"Yes, I'm Tom Symms; I have a one o'clock tee time, and I'd like to rent a set of clubs; can you show me what you have?"

"Certainly sir; right this way." The clerk led him to a large room where there were dozens of sets of golf clubs, "Why don't you step up here and we'll get your swing speed; that will help us determine the right set of clubs for you."

"You really do go all out here; I'm impressed," Tommy said as he took the driver from the clerk and stepped up to the meter. He swung the club comfortably.

"You have a fast swing; I'd recommend a stiff shaft. I might recommend the Nickolas clubs. They're swing-weighted for extra distance."

"Is that so; well I'll try them if you're recommending them."

"I'll have them put on your cart. You'll be playing with an older gentleman who frequents the club; he's very good. His name is Peter Berne; he's right over there on the putting green, if you want to introduce yourself."

Yes, well I'll need some balls and tees, and a golf glove; oh, and a hat. Let me grab the putter before you take my bag."

Tommy enjoyed playing golf and tennis all week, and he even played basketball one afternoon. He was a bit sore and stiff on Saturday morning when he went to visit Bill, but it felt good to be getting back into shape.

He entered the visiting room, and Bill was already seated on the other side of the table. There was no one else in the room besides the C.O. sitting at his desk about twenty feet away, so they talked freely, "Hi Tommy, it's good to see you!"

"It's good to see you too. I've got mixed news to tell you. I met with Phil Pierson on Tuesday, and he had heard from the judge the preceding week. The bad news is that he told Phil that a successful appeal was unlikely. There have been two other cases similar to yours, where the family has brought forth an appeal, and they were turned down in both cases."

"Why? I thought you said the lawyer you consulted before you came to planet P told you that he thought it was somewhat likely that an appeal would work?"

"Yes, but he didn't know that under planet P law, they have to observe and uphold the decision of the court on Earth, as a rule. However, Phil said that we could go for a sentence modification; and under the circumstances you might get time served, and be released on probation."

"Man!" Bill cried out, with a deeply troubled look—I was hoping I could get off Scott-free, and not have to deal with the legal system . . ." He squirmed a bit as he thought more about the ramifications of what he was hearing, "Do you realize that Probation, for a sex offender, can be pretty onerous, even if I was to get time served?"

"Yes, but compared to sitting in jail for the next forty years, it would certainly be a lot better."

"Yeah, I guess I have to take what I can get . . ."

"Don't worry; I've looked into probation for a sex offender, and I understand it starts out with weekly visits to your probation officer, but over time, the visits become less frequent, as they get more comfortable with you. You would have to take sex offender treatment classes, but they are once a week, and you could be through with them in as little as eighteen months."

"Sex offender treatment classes?—But I didn't sexually offend anyone! What am I going to talk about in those classes?"

"Well I'm sure you can deal with it when the time comes; let's not get too far ahead of ourselves. First, we have to get you off on probation; that could take months, from what I understand. Phil has to apply for a sentence modification, and he says it takes a month or two to get a court date currently."

"Well . . ." Bill considered further, "I've been in jail for nine months now, so I guess I can hang in there for a few more months."

"That's the spirit! We're going to do everything we can to get you out of here on probation. Phil says we don't have to do anything yet, but if he thinks it would be helpful, we'll hire a private investigator on Earth, to get all the facts surrounding the case, and present mitigating factors."

"Well I appreciate everything you are doing for me here; I want you to know that."

"Sure; I also wanted to tell you that I'm going back to Alderon next week, to follow up on how things are progressing with Atlas android on the beaming station; and I'm thinking seriously about taking their job offer. It would be one way of staying on top of their plans and developments on the beaming station, and I told you I met a girl there who I might like to get to know better."

"Would you still come and visit me?"

"Sure! I can fly back here on the weekends. I've found a men's club with a nice hotel facility about twenty miles from here. It's a sports complex. I've played some golf this week, and they pair you up with a tennis partner and everything. It's a really a nice place to visit. I'd probably stay there most of the times I come here to Chilton."

"Well, if you think that's what you want to do . . ."

"I asked Phil if there was any reason I should stick around, and he told me there was really nothing I could do at this point; that we'd just have to wait.—So I'm going back to Alderon on Tuesday.—So this is probably the last time I will come and visit you on this trip, but I plan to be back again to visit you in in a few weeks, once I work out my next meeting to see Phil Pierson, so I'll see you then. Who knows, maybe I'll have more news about the beaming station by then . . ."

"Sure Tommy; you go and do what you think is best; I'll look forward to seeing you when you can fit in a visit."

"You know, it occurs to me that Alderon may be the best place for both of us, if I can get you out of here. I'm going to look into getting a house there. It's a lot like an American city, you'll see, or at least I hope you'll see in a few months."

Tommy finished out the week at the Stafford Club, and left on Tuesday morning for the Chilton Airport. He returned his rental car, and caught the 10am flight to Alderon, touching down a little after noon. He rented another Mustang convertible, a deep blue one this time, with a black synthetic leather top.

He pulled into the Alderon Hilton parking garage around one-thirty. He wheeled his bags into the hotel lobby and checked in, this time getting a room on the top floor. It was a penthouse suite. The clerk at the front desk told Tommy that it came complete with an android woman servant who stayed in the next room, and came when summoned, any time, day or night, to fulfill his every wish. After staying at the Stafford Club, Tommy was spoiled, so he tried to keep up the same level of service he was afforded there.

The luxury room at the Hilton turned out to be every bit as nice as the accommodations at the Stafford Club, only more modern.

A few minutes after he checked into his room, there was a knock on the door, "Hi, I'm Sally; I'll be serving you during your stay. Just call me on the intercom, and I will provide you with anything you need; anything," she emphasized as she gave him a provocative smile to drive home the point.

She was beautiful and shapely, with long blonde hair, but Tommy had no intention of having sex with her. However, he thought he may ask her to sleep next to him, with her warm, sexy body pressing up against him.

"That's good to know," Tommy answered her, "I'll call you later probably; maybe for a massage around bedtime."

Tommy unpacked his suitcases, and put his clothes away in the dressers. The suite had two dressers, as it was equipped to house a couple. He put his things in the bathroom, and noticed that it had a double sized tub, even a bday, and double sinks, with a long mirror, stretching over the length of the six foot long vanity. "Very elegant," he said to himself.

He set up his laptop on the desk, and plugged into the large Skype screen mounted to the wall behind it. First, he Skyped Ron Goldstein at Atlas Android, "Hi Ron; I'm back in Alderon; I just arrived; and I wanted to make an appointment with you to discuss the marketing position you offered me. I also wanted to check on your progress on the beaming station. Have there been any developments in the last week?"

"Yes, actually, we're in talks with Clarion Capital about possible financing. I'll tell you about it when we meet. Why don't you come in tomorrow at ten o'clock; will that work?"

"Yes, that would be fine; I'll see you then."

Next, Tommy Skyped the Thirty-Second Century Real estate office, and was connected with Tony Romano, "Hi Tony, it's Tom Symms. I was wondering, could we take another look at the house in Fairhope overlooking the lake? Is it still available?"

"Let me check my listings . . ." Tony pulled up his listings on his computer screen and scrolled down to the four bedroom house they had looked at in Fairhope, "Yes, I believe it still is. When would you like to see it? I could take you over there in the next couple of hours, or we can go tomorrow; what's your preference?"

"I can make it over to you, in as soon as an hour; why don't we go out and see it today?"

Fine; I could show you a couple of other houses in the area if you'd like. I have a new listing in Lincoln that's going for four-fifty, are you interested in seeing that?"

"No, I don't think so; Lincoln is a little far away; I want to stay closer to Alderon; I don't want to have to commute forty-five minutes in traffic every day to get to work, assuming I take the job I've been offered in downtown Alderon; but if you have anything that's three or four bedrooms, and not in a housing tract, I might like to see that."

"I'll look in the multiple listings database and see what I can find. It's two-thirty now, so I'll meet you here at my office at four-thirty?"

"Okay Tony, I'll see you then."

Tommy hung up and paced the floor. He didn't know what to do with himself for the next half hour, so he surfed on the internet under sports clubs, and found no entries. He looked under golf, and found that there were two golf courses outside the city, and as luck would have it, one of them was in Fairhope.

He surfed around a little more and found a cigar shop listed in downtown Alderon, so he decided to hit it on the way to Tony Romano's office. After a short nap, to help him get over the jet lag he was feeling, he unpacked his suitcases, and picked out a color-coordinated outfit, from the new clothes he had bought the week before.

Tommy got to the City Cigar store at a little before four, but he had some trouble finding a parking spot. He circled the block a few times, until he saw someone pull out, and he took the spot, about two blocks away from the store.

He had to hustle because he didn't want to be late for his three thirty meeting, but when he got inside, he was impressed. There was a large walk-in humidor, and the main showroom was filled with humidors and smaller cigar cabinets.

He headed for the walk-in humidor and checked it out in wonder. There were dozens of different brands of cigars. The sign overhead said they were all carcinogenic-free, so Tommy knew that there was no risk of getting cancer from smoking them.

A small man with a funny accent walked in behind him, "Can I be of help to you?" he asked, careful not to sound too obtrusive.

"Yes, I'm looking for some good cigars; can you recommend a few that are pretty mild, yet flavorful?"

The man picked out half a dozen cigars while, describing the types of synthetic tobacco and the wrappers they were made from, before Tommy stopped him, "That's enough for now; I'll come back later and maybe get a humidor from you, and then I'll get some more cigars to fill it up!" He said with a smile.

"Okay, you come back; we have good price on humidors; I pick out good cigars for you."

They walked to the register, and Tommy watched as he read the prices off each wrapper and entered them. "Okay, that will be one hundred and twenty-four eighty-six; just hundred and twenty good."

He was back on his way by twenty after four. Tony's office wasn't too far away. When he arrived, Tony was standing at the curb waiting for him. Tommy pulled up, "Shall we take my car? It's a rental with unlimited mileage, so it doesn't cost me anything extra . . ."

"Sure; we can go in your car. I've got the printouts with me. I found four other properties you might want to look at in Fairhope."

"Well, why don't you get in; you can tell me about them while we're driving."

Tony pitched him, about the four listings he had picked to look at, that here was one house which was going for seven hundred and forty-nine thousand, which Tommy said he had no interest in seeing, at that price. Tony had also informed him that the other three houses which listings he had dug up, actually were in housing tracts, even though the houses were pretty far away from each other; so Tommy declined to see any of them. They drove straight to the house which Tommy had liked most, the first time they went out together, and this time Tommy did a little more thorough inspection of the upstairs bedrooms.

There was a smaller deck off the master bedroom, which was a plus he hadn't noticed before, and two of the other three bedrooms had attached bathrooms. The bathroom in the master bedroom was elegant and spacious, with a double Jacuzzi tub.

The wood floors were freshly sanded and polyurethaned, and the walls were professionally painted to perfection. "The owner did a lot of work on this house after he moved out; that's why it is a little pricey," Tony justified, "-But come out back; there's something I want to show you; it's a little surprise."

They walked out into the back yard, and down the hill to the water's edge. Tony pointed to the left, behind some trees. "What's that?" Tommy asked.

"It's a boathouse. It holds up to a thirty foot long boat. The previous owner had the dock removed because it was rotted out, so from the house, it looks like there's nothing here at the water."

"Huh! I could build myself a dock and have a boat!"

"Yes you could; but as I told you last week, the owner is asking five-forty-nine. Can you afford that?"

"Yeah, that's a lot; what do you think he'd take possibly, if I were to make an offer?"

"Well, he might take five-ten, I don't know; I wouldn't offer any less than that."

"Okay; make him an offer at five-ten, and see what he says."

"I can Skype him right now if you'd like. My laptop's in my briefcase back at the car."

They walked up the long hill and around the side of the house to the driveway. Tony Skyped the owner directly, as it was his exclusive listing. "Yeah hi, Fred, I'm here at your property on Evergreen Street, with a buyer who likes the house; he would like to offer five-ten; whaddaya think, do we have a deal?"

"No, I can't let it go that cheaply; it's waterfront, and I just put sixty-three-thousand into restoring the floors and painting the house, inside and out. It's that new kind of paint; it's guaranteed for fifty years, well on the outside of the house anyway. I made sure that the guarantee is transferable, and I'll sign it over to you; but I won't take a penny less than five-thirty-five."

Tony looked over at Tommy, who grimaced and stood in silence for several seconds. The owner was not being very flexible, he thought; but on the other hand, it was a great house, in a pretty secluded location as well. Finally, he turned to Tony, and nodded his approval, “Okay, let’s go ahead with it.”

“Okay then, we have a deal!” Tony announced to both of them. “I’ll draw up the paperwork.” He turned to Bill, “Have you applied yet, for financing?”

Tommy grinned, “That won’t be necessary; I don’t <u>need</u> financing; I’ll pay cash. I can give you a check right now, if you’d like.”

“Wow! You must be loaded!”

Tommy grinned a little wider, “I do alright.”

“Well listen, if you want to take me back to the office, I’ll get working on the contract right away.”

“How soon do you think I can move in?” Tommy asked, with an eager tone.

“Well, if we don’t have to wait for financing to go through, I imagine we could go to closing, possibly as soon as next week. We might even be able to have you in there by the end of next week possibly, if everything goes smoothly.”

“Good; I’d like that.”

They headed back toward Tony’s office. About halfway there, Tony broke the silence, “So, do you have a family? I never asked you.”

“No, I’m not married.”

“Then what are you going to do with such a big house, if I may ask?”

“Well, I may get an android servant; that would take up one bedroom; and I’m hoping to have my father move in with me; hopefully he will be out on probation shortly; and I hope to get married in the next year or two, if I find the right girl.”

“Oh, do you want to have kids?”

“I was hoping to have boy and girl twins; that would fill up the other two bedrooms.”

“Those are some ambitious plans; I hope everything works out for you.”

Tommy dropped Tony off at the Thirty-Second Century office, and headed back to the Hilton. He stopped on the way to pick up a bottle of champagne. He almost never drank, but he hoped to invite Kerry over to celebrate, so he planned optimistically.

When he got back to his room, he Skyped Kerry. He figured she'd be home by now, as it was six o'clock. When Kerry answered, Tommy could see that she was in her bathrobe, "Hi Tom; where are you calling from? Are you still in Chilton?"

"No, I arrived back in Alderon this afternoon, and I actually just bought that house in Fairhope!—You know, the one that I had my *eye* on last week? I closed the deal with Tony Romano about an hour ago."

"Oh, that's great news! Are you excited?"

"Very!—I'm going in to Atlas tomorrow; I have another appointment with Ron Goldstein, and I plan to tell him that I've decided to take the job, and come to work for them in the marketing department."

"Oh; then we'll be *co-workers*!" she said with surprised delight, "so we *can* have lunch together!"

"Yes we can!—So I was wondering; do you want to come over tonight and have a glass of champagne to celebrate with me?"

"I don't know; I'm a little tired . . ." she said at first; and then she changed her mind, "-But I guess I could do that. Let me take a bath and relax a little. How about if I come over around eight-thirty?"

"That's fine; I'll be waiting for you.—You know how to get to the Alderon Hilton, don't you?"

"Yes, I know where it is; what room are you in?"

"I'm in room twelve-fourteen, on the top floor, in the penthouse."

"Oh, in the penthouse . . ." she said sarcastically, obviously impressed.

"Yeah, I figured, why not?—I might as well go in *style*!"

"Okay; well I'll see you in a bit . . ."

Tommy was even more excited now. He had bought a really cool house, and the girl of his dreams was now coming over to visit him. He made himself a cranberry and tonic and stepped out onto the patio to smoke a cigar. He had forgotten how good a good cigar tasted, and he savored the moment as he looked out over the city in the twilight.

After he was done with his smoke, he came in and Skyped Alyssa, "Hi sis; you're looking at the proud new owner of a house on a lake, about fifteen miles from where I plan to work."

"Wow! That's great! You really are making progress out there. How much did it cost?"

"Five-hundred-and thirty-five-thousand; but it's a four bedroom house, and I even have my own boathouse!"

"Four bedrooms, huh? Why did you buy such a big house?"

"Well, it's a long-term investment. I hope to raise a family there some day; but for now, I'm thinking of getting an android, and I'm hoping to have Bill come and live with me, if I can get him out of that prison."

"How did he take the news?—About the appeal?"

"Yeah, he was kind of upset that we won't be going for the appeal, but I explained that an appeal probably wouldn't be successful, and I told him about our new plan to try to get him out on probation."

"What does his lawyer say his chances are, of getting out right away?"

"Well, he said Bill would almost certainly get a reduced sentence, but he didn't say how many years he thought they might take off his sentence yet. He has to do some more research on similar case histories, and talk more with the judge and the prosecutor, to get a better idea . . ."

"Well, keep me posted. I've been talking to Marissa Simon; she's the head scientist-doctor at Atlas. She's called me three times in the last two days! I set her up with Trask Industries; they manufacture most of the equipment needed to set up a beaming station. They'll have to talk price, and arrange for transportation of the equipment to planet P. They're just trying to get some idea of the cost, so they can try and set up financing."

"That sounds like progress.—I'm going into Atlas in the morning, to meet again with Ron Goldstein; I think I'm going to take that marketing job they offered me. I need to do something to keep busy; and this way, I can keep an eye on developments with the beaming station."

"I guess it's good to be on the inside that way."

"How's Mom? Have you talked with her lately?"

"She misses you; she Skyped me yesterday. She met a new guy in the AA program, at a meeting she goes to regularly. She's been out with him three times already. He's single and he lives in an apartment in Natick. She says he used to play the field as a bachelor, for years, while he was drinking; but now that he's sober, he's looking for a long-term relationship."

"He never got married?"

"No, he's been a bit of a playboy."

"How old is he, do you know?"

"He's older than Mom; I think she said four years older."

"Well, tell her I was asking for her. I'll Skype her next week, after I've moved into my new place.—I don't know if I'm ready to talk to her just yet . . ."

"I know she's had trouble being civil with you; but she may well grow to accept what you've done, at least eventually. She loves you a lot, even though she's pretty angry with you at this point."

"How are things going with Albert? Have you come to any new developments recently?"

"Yes, we're a good ways along now; we've mastered taste, and we've developed an intestinal system which will allow for a daily bowel movement. Of course the food an android eats won't be digested, but at least it will be stored in the stomach and intestines for about twenty-four hours."

"That's great! I suppose I can look forward to tasting good food when I come to visit. What are you working on now?"

"We're working on sensation in the hands. It requires a lot more wiring from the fingers to the electronic brain, but of course, we're using fiber optics, so it won't take up much space."

"It sounds tedious. Well good luck with that; at this point, when do you think the new android prototypes might go into production?"

"Oh, we're at least several months from that; we still have to develop sexual sensation; that's probably going to be our most challenging task; but maybe we will be able to use the same receptors as for the hands; that might greatly reduce the amount of time it takes."

"Well who knows; maybe you'll have it finished and into production by the time we have a beaming station up here!"

"That would be nice for you; but quite honestly, it's probably going to be at least a couple of years before these androids become available."

"That long, huh?—Well take care; I'm having Kerry over for champagne in about an hour, so I'm going to take a bath and get ready."

"Oh? Since when do you drink champagne?"

"I just got a bottle to celebrate the purchase of my new house. I doubt I'll even finish one glass; we'll just use it to toast."

"Well, I'd be careful with that; you know that alcoholism is hereditary; I wouldn't want you to end up with a problem like Mom's."

"You worry too much sis; I'll be alright."

"Okay, I'll try not to worry; bye Tommy."

After a leisurely bath, Tommy sat down to watch the big screen TV for a while until Kerry arrived. He watched local news, which was of very little interest. Granite quarry stocks were up, as they had discovered a good deal of granite on the planet recently. Apparently, it was pretty cheap these days because everybody was using it in their kitchens and bathrooms, and the mining costs had been driven down, due to such a high volume of sales.

Lumber prices were falling, as forests planted fifty years back, with seedlings brought from Earth, had become somewhat fully grown, and were being harvested in droves around the planet.

There was a new program for computer voting being released, and all citizens were going to have to update by the next series of voting, beginning in about two months.

Other than that, there was a fire in an apartment complex on the outskirts of Alderon; nothing earth-shattering.

There was a knock on the door at around quarter to nine, and Tommy went to greet Kerry, "Hi!" Tommy exclaimed as he feasted his eyes on her, "Boy, don't you look beautiful! I like your hair like that." Kerry wore her hair down, curled nicely at the ends. She had on a pretty red dress with an unusual pattern that caught Tommy's eye.

"Thanks! I figured I'd get dressed up in case we went out to celebrate."

"I thought we could celebrate right here; I've got chilled champagne in the refrigerator, and I have an android servant here, who brought chocolate-covered strawberries, and some melon and fruit; how does that sound?"

Kerry entered the room and got an eyeful, "Wow! This place is great! The penthouse suite, huh? What did it cost you, if I may ask?"

"It was pretty expensive; over four hundred dollars a night; but I'll only be staying here for about a week, and after my stay at the Stafford Club, I'm pretty spoiled!"

"It was that nice, huh? Tell me about it."

"Okay; but first, let me pour us a glass of champagne, so we can make a toast to the successful purchase of my new home!"

"Alright!" Kerry echoed.

Tommy popped the cork on the champagne, and poured two fluted glasses for them. As Kerry surveyed the suite, she could see that the rooms were especially elegant, with expensive furniture, a large screen TV and a huge Skype screen, which Tommy's laptop was plugged into.

Tommy caught her gawking, "If you think this is nice, wait 'till I tell you about the Stafford Club; All of the walls in the hallways are raise panel, with really intricate, classy moldings; you know, old fashioned style, modeled after the ancient architecture of the nineteenth century or older." Kerry nodded as he continued, "The bedrooms were papered with real antique wallpaper, which they told me cost over a million dollars to buy and have shipped here from earth; can you believe it?!

"Wow!—That really is extravagant!"

Tommy thought further about his former accommodations at the Stafford Club, "Oh yeah, the bathroom was all granite, with expensive—looking ornate brass fixtures and towel bars." Tommy also informed her that the service was phenomenal; that it was an all android staff, who waited on you hand and foot. Tommy took the opportunity to brag a bit more, "They bring you drinks at poolside; oh, and the pool has a waterfall, and a rock garden on one end. It's absolutely magnificent!"

"And you said you played golf and tennis almost every day . . ."

Tommy nodded enthusiastically, "I really enjoyed it. It's too bad I couldn't find anything like it around here."

"Well, there's golf courses; and there's tennis courts on the other side of town that are pretty close by. I think there's some in Fairhope as well."

"Oh, good! I found the golf courses, surfing on the Internet this afternoon." He handed her a glass of champagne, "Shall we toast?"

"Yes; here's to a great new year in your new house!"

"Yes; you'll have to come see it after I move in."

"Okay! I'll have to think of a house-warming gift."

"It shouldn't be too hard," Tommy joked, "I don't have anything, at this point, except for two suitcases of clothes!"

"That's right! You'll have to buy furniture and appliances, and a new TV and everything; and a car!"

Yes, but it will be fun shopping for all that stuff.—Do you want to help me?—I might like some company when I'm picking out furniture, for example . . ."

Kerry smiled in agreement, "I suppose we could go out shopping together on the weekends . . ."

"I'm probably going to have to do alot of shopping in the next couple of weeks, but as far as you helping me, I'll catch you when I can. I'm thinking you could probably be of a lot of help; you would know the stores in the area."

"Yes, but I guess I should tell you . . ." Kerry looked at Tommy uneasily as she paused, "I'm kind of involved with another guy right now.—I told him about going out to dinner with you last week, and he got very jealous.—I've known him for over a year now, and he's asked me to marry him and everything . . ."

"Oh; I didn't know . . ."

"I told him no; I'm not ready to get married yet; I just turned eighteen, and I want to wait a couple of years; but he says he's pretty serious about me, and he said he doesn't want me to go out on any more dates with you . . ."

Tommy thought for a few seconds, during an awkward silence, "Does he know you're here tonight?" He finally asked.

"Yes, I Skyped him, and explained that you are new in town, and you wanted someone to celebrate with tonight, over getting a new house."

Tommy nodded silently, and Kerry explained further, "So I told him I'd spend the weekend with him, and that softened him up on my coming over to see you tonight."

"Well I'm kind of disappointed, to be honest with you; I was hoping we could get to know each other better;—but if you already have something going with this guy, what's his name?"

"Mike . . ."

"Well if you already have a good relationship with him, I don't want to try and come between you . . ."

There was another brief pause while Kerry considered Tommy's possible thoughts and feelings about what she was telling him, and then she thought to offer, "Don't get me wrong; I enjoy your company, and I really would like to get to know you better, as a <u>friend</u>; I'm sure we could at least have <u>lunch</u> together at work occasionally, assuming you come to work for Atlas."

"Yeah, sure!" Tommy pretended to be nonchalant, but inside he felt really disappointed, and Kerry could tell.

"Hey; don't look so deflated; you're really nice, and you're really cute! You shouldn't have any trouble meeting someone . . ."

Tommy gave her a look that might almost say "get real!" Then he softened his next comment, "Yeah, but on a planet with less than twenty percent women, competition is always going to be a problem . . ."

"I'll tell you what;" Kerry said in an encouraging manner, "I'll give you a chance to show me how much you want me, with a kiss." She smiled and let that sink in for a moment, and then she continued on with her line of thinking, "When he asked me, I told Mike I'd probably kiss you; and he probably thought I meant I would give you one kiss, at the end of the evening, while saying goodbye . . . — But I didn't actually say how <u>many</u> kisses and how long they might last. Would you like to kiss me?"

"<u>Oh</u> yeah . . ." Tommy leaned in and gave her a nice warm kiss, and then pulled back.

"That was <u>nice</u>," she said kind of dazed, "Kiss me again . . ." she said in a low, seductive voice. Then she smiled at her thought, "I want you to <u>keep</u> kissing me until there's a smile on your face!"

Tommy kissed her again and again, more and more passionately each time. It was an <u>incredibly</u> great feeling for him! They kissed for a good ten minutes. Finally, she sat up, "Okay, that's enough; if we do this any longer I'm going to have to spend the night with you here!"

"I wouldn't mind that . . ." Tommy answered softly, intrigued with the thought.

"Yes, but I wouldn't want to do that to Mike. I promised him tonight, that I'd have an exclusive relationship with him . . . but if I ever break up with him, I'll know where to get my kisses!"

"Yes, that was really nice; thank you Kerry; you saved the night from being a big let-down for me."

Kerry left around nine-thirty. It was a short but sweet visit that left Tommy in a fog of memory, of those kisses, and her sweet perfume. He still felt let down, but he also couldn't help thinking it was good to be alive; after that wonderful exchange.

There was a knock on the door. Tommy answered it, and it was Sally, "Hi, I just came to check on you. I noticed your friend left. Is there anything I can do for you? Are you ready for that massage perhaps?"

Sally's beauty was captivating. She had long, silky blonde hair, and she wore a pretty smile.

"Yeah, I'm a bit keyed up; I could go for a massage; why don't you come in."

"Actually, I'm 'gonna go next door and heat up a bottle of massage oil. Why don't you undress, and lay face down on the bed . . ." She saw the question that would probably be forming in his mind, and addressed the issue, "I have a key; I'll let myself in, in a few minutes."

"They give you a key to my room?" Tommy asked, a bit surprised.

"I'm only supposed to use it for emergencies, but no one will mind, in this case; that is, if you don't mind . . ."

Tommy didn't hesitate, "Sure, fine." Then he did pause for a few seconds, before adding, "Just don't ever come in without knocking."

Sally was gone for about ten minutes, after which she let herself in using her spare key, carrying with her a warm bottle of massage oil, which she set on the nightstand.

Tommy lay naked, face down, on the bed. Slowly, she eased onto the bed and straddled his back, and sat gently on his ass. She was wearing a mini-dress, and he could feel her warm inner thighs melting into his own. He was surprised that he was somewhat excited by this android; she felt warm and good.

She leaned over and grabbed the bottle off the nightstand and applied a coat of thick oil all over his back, and she began working her fingers into his tight back muscles methodically. She was good; besides pressing her fingers artfully into his sore, stiff muscles, she used her forearms and her elbows effectively, at points, sometimes leaning in and placing all of her weight, on one point on his back.

She kept on massaging him, for over an hour. It felt so good, and Tommy just laid there and felt more and more relaxed. Finally, she collapsed on his back; something an android woman had never done, while massaging him, before.

He could feel the warmth of her body, and her breath in his ear, and he was moved to ask her, "Will you stay, and sleep with me tonight?"

"Sure, I'd be happy to . . ." With that, she rolled off of him and stood up, pulling her dress off over her head; then removing her bra, and stepping out of her panties. Tommy, still lying face down, half-oblivious after the long massage, didn't even notice her pretty body, now completely naked. She crawled into bed beside him and cuddled up to him.

"She sure is a friendly android," he thought, "And she smells wonderful!" He fell asleep quickly, and slept soundly throughout the night.

Tommy awoke early the next morning, and Sally was cuddled all around him. Her body was so warm; it felt really divine. Her breathing was deep and even; she was sound asleep. "Wait! Androids don't sleep!" he thought to himself, "And is that pubic hair I feel rubbing up against my leg?!"

A few seconds later, he found himself quite relaxed again, as he regained his sense of the heavenly feeling of holding her close; while laying perfectly still, which he happily continued to do, so as not to wake her. It was almost half an hour before she finally woke up and realized where she was, "Oh, good morning!" She addressed him.

"Good morning; you're not an android, are you?"

She smiled, "I was wondering when you were going to figure that out."

"Who <u>are</u> you? Do you work for the hotel?"

Sally gave in, and decided to come clean, "No, I bribed the manager into letting me pose as the hotel's complimentary android assigned to you, as a guest staying in the penthouse. I got the idea once I saw you in the lobby, and overheard you making arrangements to rent this suite.—I actually know the manager; my company hosts conventions and has numerous out-of-town guests staying here, all throughout the year. That's how I was able to wangle posing as your android servant." Tommy, somewhat speechless, silently listened with interest as she continued, "My Company wanted me to approach you about getting the plans to build a mind beaming station." Tommy wondered, how could she possibly know about <u>that</u>?

She saw the confused look on his face, and offered, "My boss has a mole at Atlas Android, who found out you were working with them on the idea."

"You keep saying, "My company," who is your company?" Tommy asked, still somewhat bewildered.

"Centurion Android; we heard about your coming into town last week, with your sister's design for building a mind beaming station, so my boss assigned me to come and seek you out, and do what I could to lure you in to meet with him, along with the company's president . . . . —I don't know if I should be telling you all of this, but to be honest, ultimately, we were hoping to convince you to sell your plans to us, instead of Atlas . . ."

"I don't get it; why didn't you just approach me and ask?"

"Well, this was actually <u>my</u> idea, to pose as your android servant, in order to get to know you a little more intimately before talking about it; plus, you were cute!" she added with a smile, "But the company just wanted me to come and meet with you on the subject."

Tommy still looked a little puzzled, so Sally continued on, while she was on a roll and he was silent, "You see my boss, is also my husband; I'm married;—but he is much older, and he's not very appealing. I only married him mainly for his <u>money</u>, and I even <u>told</u> him so, but he still wanted to marry me, even knowing. He just asked that I be discreet if I'm going to have affairs."

"So you've decided you want to have an affair with me?"

'Yeah!—Well are you interested?"

Tommy was still mystified, "Wouldn't your husband have missed you when you didn't come home last night?"

"He's away on business; in fact he travels about half the time. He's the senior marketing rep for Centurion; he travels all over the planet, working mostly with our distributors."

"Well in that case, I'm glad you want to have an affair with me, because with your hairy little muff pressing up against my leg like that, you're making me really horny!"

"Oh, yeah?" she said coyly, "I've been squirming on your leg for the last five minutes; I'm glad you finally noticed."

He rolled her over, "Oh! You're blonde down there too!"

They hungrily made love for a good long time, both of them releasing weeks of pent up sexual energy. Afterward, they drew a hot bath and took turns washing each other's backs, dipping the washcloth in the warm water and squeezing it out and letting the warm water run down each other's backs.

When they had gotten dressed afterward, Tommy asked her, "Would you like to come shopping with me? I just bought a house, and I have to furnish it."

"I've got to go into work for a few hours, but my husband is away until Friday, and I'm yours for the next two nights; if you want me . . ." After a short pause, she added, "I don't think Sam will mind if I'm seen shopping with you, if that's what you want to do."

Tommy basked in her sexy beauty for a few seconds, "I see what you mean; well maybe we could do a little shopping and come back here."

"What about the beaming station?" Sally asked quickly, realizing she would have to report something back to her company, "Will you come in and meet with management about possibly giving us access to the plans?"

"I don't know; I'm pretty far along in my talks, at this point, and I think the folks at Atlas Android would be pretty upset if they didn't have an exclusive on this. They may have a lot more trouble in securing the financing for the project, if there was another company building one too."

"Well, would you at least come in talk to us? That's all I'm asking; one appointment . . ."

Tommy weighed her request, realizing that her tactics were especially persuasive, in the wake of their highly pleasurable all-night encounter, which had ended with a bang, literally! In light of their obvious infatuation with each other, he couldn't possibly have turned her down, "I suppose I could come in and talk about it; but it would have to be up to my sister Alyssa to decide, as far as having any involvement with Centurion. She and Dr. Albert Freudenthal have the rights to it. I can't promise anything . . ."

She cut him off, "One appointment; that's all I ask . . ."

"Okay; when were you thinking?"

"How about tomorrow? Would you be free at any point, like maybe in the afternoon?"

"I don't know," Tommy started thinking about his next day's schedule, and then interrupted himself, "But wait, I can't think about this now; I actually have an appointment at Atlas in about an hour. They've offered me a job, working in their marketing department."

"Okay, well I won't ask you to think of a time now," she said, respecting his need to focus on his immediate situation, "Why don't you think about it, and I could come back here, at, say, around five-thirty? We can spend the evening together; would you like that?"

"You could come, back here tonight?" Tommy jokingly stretched that word out, "I like the way you put that!" Then he turned more serious, seeing that Sally wasn't too amused, "Alright; Yes, I would love that!"

"Okay; I'll see you then; now I should really get dressed and go; I'm already late for work!" Sally grabbed her dress and her purse, and disappeared into the bathroom. Tommy also began to prepare himself, mentally and otherwise, for his meeting with Ron Goldstein.

Tommy felt conflicted as he drove into the heart of the city. Running down the source of his distress, in his mind, he realized that he was feeling weighed down with the stress of thinking about the competing offers which these two companies would undoubtedly make, each trying to nose out the other, as far as landing exclusive rights to build a beaming station. It was clear that bringing Centurion into the mix seemed to complicate matters.

He also realized that he had suddenly become more ambivalent about his previously solidified decision to go to work for Atlas Android, and as he was driving, he had a revelation, "Wait; maybe Centurion will make me a better job offer; I should be smart about this."

He arrived at Ron Goldstein's office, a few minutes after ten, and Sarah greeted him with a smile, "Mr. Goldstein has been waiting for you; let me tell him that you're here . . ." She looked down and noticed that Ron's line was lit up, "Oh, I guess he's still on the phone . . ."

Tommy sat in the outer office as Sarah waited for Ron to finish his call, before hailing him through the intercom, "Mr. Goldstein, Tom Symms is here to see you; should I send him in?"

"I need to Skype Dan Harrelson at Teledyne back briefly first, Sarah; can you ask him to wait a few minutes? Paul Klein is going to join us. Would you call down to Paul, and tell him we're ready for him?"

Tommy flipped through the annual report sitting on the coffee table in front of him while he waited. He discovered that Atlas Android had eighty-three employees at their Alderon facility. He studied a graph which showed new android sales had dropped off considerately, in the last few years.

He read the write-up in the annual report about how the company was starting a new marketing campaign to sell androids to men and women in lower income brackets, all over the planet; also explaining how the marketing department had completed studies showing a vast potential for expanded sales, assuming Atlas's marketing staff's current research efforts would also show that androids could be marketed effectively to these blue collar workers, and other types of lower-income workers. He read that the company was in talks with Clarion Capital to offer long range financing at below a seven percent interest rate, with a low down payment, perhaps starting at around three-hundred dollars.

Just then, Paul Klein entered the office and approached Tommy, "Hi Tom; nice to <u>see</u> you."

"Nice to see you too, Paul." They shook hands.

"Ron tells me that you are considering coming to work for us, is that right?"

"It's a good possibility; that's what I came in to talk to you about today."

Ron joined them in the outer office, "Hi Tom; I'm glad you came; I have some good news for you; why don't we adjourn to my office, and we can get started."

The three of them made their way into the spacious executive office, and sat around the large glass coffee table, in plush, comfortable chairs. As they did, Ron continued talking, "First, I want to tell you that Clarion Capital has agreed to finance the beaming station; with some conditions of course; but we could start the project as soon as next month, assuming we get approval from the government."

"That's great news, Ron!" Tommy said excitedly, "-Are you thinking of building it here at the plant, or is there not enough space available to house the project?"

"Yes; there is a vacant space on the third floor of this building. Assuming it is large enough, we plan to assemble a beaming station right here in the building," Ron said evenly.

"How have you left things with Alyssa and Dr. Freudenthal?" Tommy asked, probing further.

"We've sent contracts for them to sign, and we've asked them to expedite the process."

"That's good! These are all good steps."

"Wait 'till you hear what Paul has in mind.—Paul, why don't you inform Tom of your idea?"

"Sure;" Paul turned to Tommy, "We've been kicking around an idea, that I think you'll see, mainly involves you. Once the contracts to build the beaming station are signed, we thought we'd use you, to help us in our marketing campaign. We thought we'd ask you to go on television, and on the internet, as the brother of the inventor of the mind beaming station, and clue in the public on what's in store for them. We thought, that if your sister would agree to this, maybe we could offer the first one hundred customers signing up to try out mind beaming, a chance to meet with you here in our offices, while in a Skype session with Alyssa, allowing these customers a short interview with you both. What do you think?"

"Well, that's an idea; why don't you let me think about it, and I'll also talk to Alyssa, and see if she is willing."

Ron picked up the discussion, "We've talked it over with our bean counters, and we're prepared to offer you a salary of one hundred thousand a year, to come and join our marketing team, and help make a pitch to the public; what do you think of that idea?"

"That's quite a generous offer; it definitely gives me something to think about." Tommy replied, non-committedly, "I have some other considerations, though. For example, I've just bought a house in Fairhope, and I'd need some time to move in and furnish it; and as you both know, I'm working with a lawyer to try and get my stepfather out of prison; so it may actually be a couple of months before I'm ready to come to work."

"That's fine with us," Ron interjected, "Provided we could get you to sign an employment contract first; would you be willing to do that?"

Tommy thought carefully before responding. He wanted to sound somewhat inclined to take the position being offered, but he also strategically wanted to wait to commit, until after he had received a possible counter-offer from Centurion. He decided to try and buy himself some time. He collected his thoughts and spoke, "Why don't you give me a little time to work out exactly how long I'd need before coming to work. Could we meet again, maybe at the end of next week? I should know by then what my immediate plans are."

Ron pulled out his pocket computer and checked for an available time slot, "Okay; it looks like I have an opening in my schedule next Friday morning at ten-thirty. Why don't you come back then, and we'll take it from there."

After the meeting, Tommy headed straight back to the hotel, and Skyped Alyssa, "Hi sis, how are you doing?"

"Good! Me and Albert had a breakthrough discovery yesterday, and we may be done with sensation in the hands and fingers soon, because of it."

"Good! I have some new developments to report, on this end too, which I wanted to talk to you about. First, have you received contracts from Atlas Android, on buying the rights to build a beaming station?"

"Yes, we just got them this morning; why?"

"Because I've been approached by another android company, Centurion Android, and they apparently want to build a beaming station too. Has Atlas asked for an exclusive?"

"I don't know; I haven't had a chance to look at the paperwork they sent me yet."

"Well if they are, don't sign the contracts yet; I'm going to meet with Centurion probably tomorrow, and we'll see what they have to say. "-Is that alright?"

"You mean we might have two companies building beaming stations, you're thinking?"

"Exactly; if we can get them both to play ball."

"Well, the more the merrier, I suppose. Anything else happening?"

"Yes; I'm having an affair with a married woman . . ."

"You are?!" Alyssa seemed pretty surprised.

Tommy was unfazed, "She's actually the wife of the <u>marketing</u> director at Centurion. It's a long story, but she posed as my android servant, and I didn't realize she wasn't an android until after I slept with her."

"You're sleeping with androids?"

"Yeah, it's a funny story, but I decided to rent the penthouse suite at the Hilton here?—And it comes with a complimentary android servant; she stays in the next room, and you can call her in, any time you need her . . ."

"So you had sex with her, and slept with her?"

"I didn't have <u>sex</u> with her last night; that's not why I called her in; I just asked her to give me a massage, because she had offered earlier."

"I see; and how did you end up sleeping with her then?

"I thought I'd try asking her to sleep with me and keep me warm. I've heard that can be pretty pleasant."

"Well, that's true; I've slept with a few in the past, too."

"Then, when we woke up this morning, I discovered that she was just <u>posing</u> as an android servant hotel maid, and she was really stalking me to have an affair; apparently she doesn't sleep with her husband, it's a marriage of convenience."

"It sounds a bit fishy to <u>me</u>; what if the husband finds out that you <u>are</u> having an affair with her?"

"Apparently, he says she can <u>have</u> affairs, as long as she is discreet."

Alyssa shook her head, "Alright; it's your life; but be careful; I don't want to see you get <u>hurt</u>. She may love you and <u>leave</u> you . . ."

"I know; and I don't even know if this is just a ploy to get us to sell the rights to build a beaming station to Centurion; but I don't think so. I think she really digs me."

"Well; I'd rather see you get into a relationship with a <u>single woman</u>, but I guess you told me there is a shortage of women on the planet."

"I'm just rolling with the punches; I have to take what I can get!"

"Well, it doesn't sound like any way to start a family, if that's what you had in mind."

"I know; I haven't decided what to do about it; this just happened this morning. I'll have to figure it out."

"How did this Centurion Company find out about Atlas's plans to build a beaming station?"

"Well, Sally said they have a mole at Atlas."

"Huh, that's interesting; I guess they figure they <u>have</u> to have <u>some</u> effective way of keeping up with the competition."

"Yeah; I guess androids are big business here too. Well that's all for now; I'll keep you posted. Take care; I love you Alyssa . . ."

The day went by slowly for Tommy, but eventually five-thirty came, and Sally was right on time. Tommy answered the door, "Hi Sally, I've been <u>waiting</u> for you; how was your <u>day</u>?"

"It was good; how did your appointment go with Atlas?"

"Fine; they made me an interesting job offer, but I told them that I needed more time to consider it. I have an appointment to meet with them again next Friday."

"Oh good! I'm glad you left time to meet with us. We hope you will consider our <u>counter</u>-offer, for you to come to work for <u>us</u>."

"I talked with Alyssa, and she doesn't mind hearing you out. There may even be some possibility we could work with <u>both</u> companies, or at least that's what I'll be suggesting as one alternative. By the way, Atlas has already sent some contracts for her to sign; they may well want an exclusive agreement to put the beaming station into production;—but there may also be a way around that, I don't know."

"Well?—I went ahead and made an appointment for you, to come in at one o'clock tomorrow; is it possible for you to come in at that time?—Because if it's not . . ."

Tommy interrupted her, "Sure; I can make it then; will you be attending the meeting?"

"I'll be introducing you to our company president, and I'm sure there will be others at the meeting as well, but I don't think they want me at that meeting. I'm not one of the higher ups at the company. I work as an assistant to my husband."

"What's his name?—In case he is mentioned at the meeting tomorrow . . ."

"Sam Shapiro; but he won't be there; he's away until Friday."

"Yeah, that's right; you told me."

"So how about some loving?" Sally asked, with a slightly devilish smile, changing the subject, "I'm horny again. I've been thinking about you all day . . ."

"Ah I'm kind of worn out from this morning; how about if we do some shopping, and come back here later? I might be rejuvenated by then.—I Skyped the real estate agent this afternoon, and he said the seller will allow me to put things in the garage at the house, before the closing, since I'm paying cash; so I'm excited to start gathering things."

Sally considered Tommy's suggestion, in light of his being plum tuckered out, "I guess I can wait; what did you have in mind?"

"Well, the furniture stores are open late, and I Skyped an appliance store this afternoon, and found out they are open until nine."

Tommy and Sally went shopping until eight-thirty, and stopped at a restaurant on the way back to the hotel. When they came back, they got into the mood, and ended up making love until almost eleven, finally falling asleep in each other's arms.

Tommy woke up early again the next morning, and held Sally as she slept, for almost an hour, before she woke up. He loved holding her while she was sound asleep. As usual, her hair smelled heavenly, and her body felt warm and wonderful.

Finally she awoke around eight-thirty, "Good morning sleepyhead. I've been holding you for the last hour while you slept."

"I sleep really <u>well</u> with you," she intimated, "Normally I'm up by seven, but when I hug you like a teddy bear, I sleep really well."

"Speaking of Teddy Bears, I was curious, just how old <u>are</u> you?"

"Twenty-three," she said tentatively, "I know; I'm robbing the cradle.—What can I say?—I like younger <u>men</u>!"

"That's just <u>fine</u> with <u>me</u>!" Tommy said comfortably. He looked up at the clock, "What time do you have to be at work, by the way?"

Sally followed his eyes, over to the clock, "Oh, I should really get <u>going</u>. Sam is going to Skype me at ten o'clock, and I have some work to do before that, in order to have my report ready for him."

"Don't forget, I need directions to your offices before you go."

"Okay; our plant is really easy to find. You just take the beltway north, to the Prospect Street exit; it's exit twenty-two; and when you come down to the bottom of the off-ramp, you are looking at our building."

"That sounds easy enough; why don't I meet you at the front entrance at a-quarter-to-one?"

Sally got out of bed and got dressed quickly, and brushed her long blonde hair, as Tommy watched from the bed. After she left, he fell back asleep for another hour, clutching her pillow and enjoying her lovely scent.

When he finally got up, he was a little sore and stiff from the night's activities. So he went and sat in the Jacuzzi, and let the jets blast against his sore muscles for a while.

He showered and got dressed, and left the hotel a little after eleven. Tommy had decided to drive by a few car dealerships, which he found out were all next to each other, on Commerce Street, about a mile from the beltway entrance.

He had an hour to kill, so he just cruised through the dealership parking lots and took a gander at all the new models.

He saw one that he really liked the looks of, at a Lexus dealership; so he decided to park, and take a closer look.

"Hi there pard'ner!" a salesman greeted him before he reached the showroom, "What can I do you for?" He asked in a cool-sounding southern drawl, even though they were about ten-thousand miles from the southern US States, on earth.

"Oh, I was just out looking at cars;—I kinda' like that convertible over there; what kind of car is that?"

"That there's a hydrogen-powered Lexus sports coup. She may not be the fastest, but she's the most luxurious sports car on the market."

"Is the car female?" Tommy joked.

"Dat' der' car <u>talks</u> to ya; and she has a real sexah' voice too, if you ask me."

"What,—does it have android technology built in?"

"Yeah, she'll have a conversation with you if you want. It's powered by satellite signal, and the car's got an android brain for a computer. It's connected to a lahv' person, just like an android."

"Isn't that interesting!—But what if you don't want it to talk to you; can you shut it off?"

"Of course! Hit the button on the dash and she's gone. Then if you get into trouble or something, hit the button again and she'll come back online and help you."

"How much does one of those things cost?"

"That one there costs around eighty-grand, but she's fully loaded; four-hundred horsepower engine, six speed automatic transmission, power everything, three hundred watt stereo that plays every type of media available." The salesman was fully into his shpeel, so Tommy let him continue, "full leather interior; not <u>synthetic</u> leather, mind you; heated seats, mag rims and low profile tires that are guaranteed not to deflate; they're solid rubbah'. The suspension is extremelah' smooth in these cars; <u>real</u> responsive, yet verah' comferrable; you'll see; 'you wanna take 'er for a spin?"

"No, I don't have <u>time</u> right now, I have an appointment to get to, but I'll probably be back later.—Eighty-thousand's a little steep though; I can get a mustang fully loaded for about fifty-thousand . . ."

"This is <u>way</u> better than a Mustang. Wait 'till you see all the features on this car; come back later and I'll let'cha drahv' it. Bah' the way; I happen to notice you'was drahvin' a Mustang now . . ."

"Yeah, it's a rental car. I was thinking about maybe <u>buying</u> it. I have to find out how much the rental place would sell it to me for."

"Well don't bah' a rennul car! You don't know where it's been!" The salesman stopped himself, "Well, listen, I done' wanna to tell you what ta' do, but if you want a naahce luxury cah, you come back an' see me! Here at Lexus, we' got sev'ral nice models to choose from."

Tommy reached out a hand, to accept the salesman's business card, "Thanks, I'll probably be back later this afternoon."

The Centurion Android building was not anywhere near as large as the Atlas Android building; and Tommy began to wonder why, as he pulled up to it at twenty of one, and found a guest parking spot. He met Sally at the front entrance, and she walked him up to the president's office on the second level of the building. "Mr. Tillman?" she said, finding him in the outer office, "This is Tom Symms, whom you've been waiting to meet."

"Stan Tillman," He said as he shook hands with Tommy, "It's a pleasure to finally meet you. I've heard all sorts of things about you in the last couple of weeks."

"Yes, well, news travels fast around here, I understand."

"Well, the news you bring is fascinating; we're now able to beam our minds into an android, and live inside a completely different body!"

"Yes; it is pretty amazing, thanks to my sister and Dr. Freudenthal."

"Well Tom, we'd like to get in on this; we're prepared to build a beaming station, if you can get the plans to us."

"I know; Sally told me. The only thing is, Atlas Android has already sent contracts to my sister and Dr. Freudenthal to sign, and she called me back late this morning and told me that they want an exclusive."

"Has she signed the contract?—Because if not, we're prepared to make you a very generous offer to buy the plans."

"No, she hasn't acted yet. I told her you were interested, and she's decided to hold back until we explore this further."

"Good! We're prepared to offer five million for the plans, and we'll offer another twenty million to give us the exclusive."

"That is very generous." Tommy started to see that he was now rubbing elbows with high rollers; but he slowed things down and decided to play it cool, "I'll take it to my sister and see what she says."

"We'd also like to offer you a position with us. We'll pay you <u>twice</u> anything that Atlas might offer you, if you would be willing to work with our marketing department instead, and help us release a series of advertisements to the public, of course, using you as the <u>point</u> person."

"That would <u>also</u> be very generous, because they are offering me a hundred thousand a year to come to work for them in a similar capacity."

Stan didn't bat an eyelash, "Well then we'll offer you two hundred thousand . . ."

"Could I talk to your marketing director? I'd like to know what he has in mind specifically as a marketing campaign. Would it involve me traveling?"

"Yes; I'm sure it would involve some travel; we'd want you to spread the news around the planet about the upcoming availability of the beaming station; and we'd want a lot of people to be able to talk to you in person."

"I don't know that I'd like to do much traveling. I just bought a house in Fairhope, and I'd kind of like to stay local if I could."

"Maybe we could make it one week per month that you'd have to travel. Do you think you might be willing to travel one week per month?"

"I don't know; I'm in talks with Atlas, and I'm sure they'd be very disappointed to hear that I received another offer."

"I'd like you to talk with someone here whom you already know; maybe it will help you make up your mind." Stan leaned into the intercom, "Susan? Send her in . . ."

Kerry appeared in the doorway, "Hi Tom!"

"Kerry! What are you doing here?"

Stan spoke up, "She's the mole Sally was telling you about. She's the one who gave us the information about your coming into town."

Tommy was speechless, as Kerry continued, "They've offered me a position here as well. If you decide to come to work for Centurion, I'd come to work <u>with</u> you here; would you like that?"

"Well, I don't know what to say; this all comes pretty suddenly."

Stan interjected to help his cause, "Actually, now that the cat is out of the bag, Kerry kind of <u>has</u> to come to work for us, <u>don't</u> you Kerry? We couldn't expect Tom to keep quiet about you now that he knows; unless he was to come to work here instead."

"They've offered to double <u>my</u> salary too," Kerry added.

"I can kind of tell by the way you are <u>looking</u> at Kerry, that you probably care too <u>much</u> for her, to rat her out . . ." Stan argued.

Tommy thought for a few seconds, and decided that this was a less important issue right at the moment. He thought to make the pitch he had initially planned, "Could we possibly get both you and Atlas to build beaming stations?"

"That may be out of the question," Stan answered, "They'd steal half our market share, and we can't have that . . ."

"Well, what if you did a marketing study and discovered that there is enough business for this to be profitable for both companies?"

"We <u>could</u> do that, possibly, but we'd want an early jump on them; say the first year at least before they could come to the market with theirs."

"—And the twenty-five million? Would we still get that?"

"Well, that's if we get the exclusive; it would be less if we have to share the market; but the two-hundred-thousand-dollar offer still stands, if you want to come to work for us instead of Atlas . . ."

"Well, let me talk to Atlas about this development, and see if they are still willing to go ahead with building a beaming station on the basis of a shared market."

Stan shook his head, "We really don't want them to know how we got the <u>information</u> about this. They may bring a lawsuit against us, or even against Kerry personally."

Tommy thought for a few seconds, "I <u>could</u> tell them that I approached you in <u>addition</u> to them. They wouldn't have to know that it was Kerry who leaked the information."

"Yes, I suppose that would <u>work</u>. Why don't you go back to them and tell them about our offer, and maybe we could meet again next week?"

"They're not going to be happy about this; and I don't look forward to being the one to break it to them."

"Well, I guess you're a little young yet; but you'll see, it's just business. Besides, if it was half-way successful, we were bound to build a beaming station and get into the market eventually anyway."

"Yeah, I guess you're right; I just have to roll up my sleeves and get my hands dirty, and see what I can work out."

Stan smiled and nodded, "Why don't you Skype me after you've spoken with Atlas again, and then maybe we could meet again next week."

Kerry walked with Tommy out to the parking lot, and they spoke on the way, "God, Kerry! How did you ever get involved with Centurion? I thought your allegiance would be to Atlas. After all, they hired and trained you, right out of school, didn't you say? . . ."

"It was actually my boyfriend's idea. Mike works for Centurion. He's on the new product development team. He originally said he could get me a job at Centurion, but then he told me that management would offer me an extra thirty-thousand a year if I could go to work for Atlas, and just report what was said at weekly staff meetings, back to Centurion."

"What if you have to give it all back in a lawsuit?"

"That's why you can't mention my name in connection with all of this. I mean there's no reason why you have to, is there?"

"Centurion should be paying you a lot more than thirty thousand if you are stealing this level of secrets from them . . ."

"I didn't plan for this to happen; it's just that when I started going out with you, Mike had a lot of questions about you; so I told him what you told me over dinner; that your sister was the inventor of a process where you can beam a person's mind into an android; and you told me that you were in talks with Ron Goldstein about building a beaming station here on planet P. Mike then mentioned it in a staff meeting, and it got back to Stan . . ."

"You mean you wouldn't have told Centurion about this on your own?"

"Yeah, you got me there; of course I would have reported it; it's big news!"

"That's what I'm saying; Centurion should have been paying you a lot more to provide them with inside information; and you should have thought twice before agreeing to be a mole for them."

"So what, are you going to tell Ron Goldstein that I leaked the information to Centurion?"

"No, I wouldn't do that to you; besides, I don't want to start a big scandal. I'm going to suggest that neither company get an exclusive, because if we get into a bidding war, the price may be driven up so high that it offsets all the profits that could be made from people signing up to be beamed, for years!"

"Yes; I guess that would be defeating, wouldn't it?"

"Yes; and I want this to be a profitable enterprise, if only so that I can continue to make visits to earth, over the course of my lifetime . . ."

Dismissing his own selfishness, Tommy realized that he had an even bigger question on his mind, "Do you know?—Are there any other android manufacturers on the planet that we should be talking to about this, just to get all the cards out on the table?"

"No, I don't think so; I've never heard of any others besides Atlas and Centurion . . ."

"Good; well at least maybe I don't have any more surprises in store for me then."

"Tommy; there is one other thing; you know how you told me about your sister's current work developing androids that, when you beam your mind into, you can taste and feel?"

"Yes?"

"Well I told Mike about that too, and he wants to talk to your sister about it. He says, assuming she could actually invent this, Centurion would like to build and market androids with that capability here."

"That's not even close to having been developed yet; but I'm sure that when it is, it will be available for sale to us here on planet P."

"Mike says Centurion may want to invest in the research, if it would help bring it to the market any faster. Can you ask your sister if further financing would help her?"

"I'll ask her; I think they're working off a government grant, but maybe they could use some more money, I don't know." Tommy was just making conversation. He could hardly believe that Kerry was still pitching ideas to him, after she had revealed herself as having behaved like a lying, conniving little bitch!

"Well here's my car," Kerry said, unlocking the door, "I'm heading back to Atlas. As far as they are concerned, I just took a late lunch. Call me when you know what's happening, so I can prepare myself, would you?"

"Sure, I'll be in touch . . ."

Tommy needed a distraction, so he headed back to the Lexus dealership and bought the sports coup after test driving it. The transaction took less than an hour to complete, as Tommy was paying cash, and the registration process on planet P was streamlined. The dealership had its own office of the state DMV there on the premises. All Tommy had to do was to fill out a one page document, in order to get his plates and registration certificate, now that he was officially a resident of Fairhope.

Afterward, Tommy had the salesman follow him in the new car to the airport, where he turned in his rental car. He finally made it back to his hotel a little after four.

Wanting to get it over with, he Skyped Ron Goldstein at Atlas Android to tell him about his dealings with Centurion, "Hi Ron, it's me; I just wanted to let you know that there's been a new development. I've just been talking to Stan Tillman over at Centurion Android, and they want to build a mind beaming station too . . ."

"I see . . . you approached both companies, did you?"

"Yes; there are literally dozens of companies on Earth that are building beaming stations; I'm sure there's room for two companies on planet P to share the market, don't you think?"

"Well we'd really rather have an exclusive, but we've offered twenty million for that privilege, so I suppose we could save ourselves a lot of money if we agree to share the market with Centurion. I suppose they'd get the rights to build a beaming station eventually anyway. Tell me, have they offered you anything in the way of a job?"

"Two hundred thousand a year; they have the same idea about using me for an advertising campaign, only they are asking me to travel at least one week per month. I told them I'd rather not . . ."

"Well we'll match anything they offer you, in terms of salary. We really want you in our camp."

"That's nice to know. I think I'm going to want to visit further with the staff I might be working with, at both companies, in order to make my decision; would that be alright with you?"

"I could have Paul Klein bring you into his weekly meeting with the marketing staff, and introduce you to those you would be working with, how about that?"

"That would be great; I'm glad you're being so flexible."

"Paul's marketing staff meetings are on Monday mornings at nine; can you make it on Monday?"

"Yes, I'll be there."

"Well good then, it's settled. After the meeting, why don't you stop in and see me; I'd like a chance to tell you a little more about our company. I think when you see all we're doing here, you'll want to come join us; but that's your decision."

"Thanks; I'd be happy to stop in after the meeting; I'll see you Monday morning."

Tommy hung up and Skyped Stan Tillman right away, "Hi Stan, I just talked with Ron Goldstein over at Atlas; he took it pretty well; I mean that there's another company that wants to build a beaming station. His feeling was that you could both possibly save yourselves twenty million if neither company got an exclusive on building a beaming station; and eventually you'd both get the rights to build one anyway probably."

"Well in that case, I guess whoever gets you in their corner will have the edge, at least initially.—Sure! We'd be willing to do it without an exclusive; there's only two of us android manufacturers on the planet."

"Ron said he would match whatever you would pay me in salary, so I've decided that I'd like to meet with the staff I'd be working with at both companies a little more, and get a feel for which company I'd rather come to work for; would that be alright with you?"

"Well why don't you come in and meet with Sam Shapiro first; he's our marketing director. I believe he will be in all week next week; what day would you like to come in?"

"I could come in Tuesday; would that work?"

"Sure; why don't you come in around noon. We could have lunch, and then Sam could introduce you to some of our marketing staff members afterward; those who are in the office, anyway."

"Sure; I'd like that. I'll see you on Tuesday."

After hanging up, Tommy sat back in his chair, relieved that he had averted a scandal, and that both companies were willing to share the advent of mind beaming technology. He decided to Skype Alyssa and tell her the news, "Hi Alyssa; how's it going?"

"I'm fine; what's happening up there?"

"Actually, I've got good news; it looks like Centurion and Atlas both want to go forward with plans to build beaming stations. The only downside is that, if neither is going to pay you for an exclusive, you're out twenty million. Did I do something wrong?—Because I could try to arrange for one of the companies to get an exclusive if you'd rather."

"No, that's alright; we'll get a residual on the use of the beaming stations. We've arranged it so that each time someone signs up to have their mind beamed, we get a portion of the fee."

"So you'll recover a lot of that money over time, huh?"

"Exactly; besides, I don't really need the money. Albert and I are making millions selling the rights to build mind beaming stations around the world; and if we can finalize development of the new androids, we'll make more yet, on selling the plans to android manufacturers."

"Well that's good news for me, because both companies are in a bidding war over hiring me, and it looks like I'll be making over two hundred thousand dollars a year working with whichever company I choose! They both want to use me for an advertising campaign. How do you like that? Because of you, I'm a celebrity here!"

"That's great news! I'm happy for you."

"Now, if I can just get married and start a family, I will have achieved all my dreams."

"How are things with your married girlfriend?"

"She's coming over in a bit. I'm going to ask her if she wants to go with me to get a new Skype mobile phone. I don't know how I've gone so long with the old one I have. At this point, I think I'm going to need the newer satellite version, so I can be reached, visually, at any time, no matter where I am.—I'll call you and give you the number once I get it."

"Okay; well if you'll excuse me, I have to get back to work. We have an android expert at the lab today, and we have to pick his brain, if you'll excuse the expression, and tap his extensive knowledge; because he seems to know most, about a certain type of fiber-optic wiring we've been trying to use, to send signals from the synthetic sex organs to the electronic brain. We seem to be stuck on that phase of development."

"Okay; then I'll let you go; Good luck sis; talk to you later . . ."

Sally arrived promptly again, at five-thirty, and accompanied Tommy to the phone store, where he bought the latest model Skype phone. It had a screen that either unfolded, to become a four-inch square screen, or you could use it with its two-inch square screen when it was all folded up. They stopped at a Chinese take-out place on the way back to the hotel and ordered four of their most expensive dishes. Once back at the hotel, they ate voraciously, and made love passionately afterward.

Laying in afterglow, Sally finally revisited the eternal subject, "So are you going to tell me about your meeting with Stan Tillman?"

"Yeah, I'm trying to get both Centurion and Atlas to build a beaming station. I think Stan and Ron Goldstein are going to be amenable; isn't <u>that</u> a surprise!"

"How about the job offer? Are you thinking you want to come to work for Centurion?"

"I'm not sure yet. Centurion and Atlas are both offering me an incredible sum of money to come to work for them."

"I'm not surprised; from my standpoint, it's almost better if you go to work for Atlas. It would be easier to hide our affair."

"I'll take that into consideration, but I'm going to meet with the marketing staff at both companies next week."

"Well in that case, you're going to meet with my husband; are you ready for that?"

"Yeah, I think I can handle it."

"He knows that we've met, but he doesn't know anything else. I hope you'll keep it that way."

"Don't worry about that; I think we have plenty of other issues to talk about."

"Yes, I guess you do . . . How about if we watch a movie together? There's one I want to see, about a hospital where all the nurses and doctors are androids. Something goes wrong with their programming, and they start connecting the patients psychically to one android who has superior intelligence, and develops a plot to wipe out all human life in Clarion DC, and gain political control over the planet!"

"That sounds interesting. Yeah, maybe it will take my mind off the stress of my situation.

CHAPTER TWENTY

MONDAY MORNING FELL, AND Tommy entered the Atlas Android building at a quarter of nine, and headed for Paul Klein's office. Paul led them to a large conference room down the hall from his office.

There were over a dozen men and women seated around the long table. Paul addressed the group, "Good morning everyone, I want to introduce you to Tom Symms. He came here from Earth recently. He is the brother of Alyssa Symms who invented mind beaming, which, for those of you who aren't as familiar, is a process where a person's mind is transferred into an android, so that you are effectively living inside a different body. A few of you know that we have offered Tom a position with us. We are planning to build a mind beaming station, now that Tom has brought us the plans, and we'd also like Tom to help us advertise it to the general public."

A hand went up, and a young attractive woman was called upon by Paul, "That's quite fascinating! How expensive will this be; could it possibly fit in with our plans to market androids to lower income individuals?"

More questions were raised by the staff during the meeting, and afterward Paul took Tommy around to their offices to introduce him individually, to each staff member.

When they came to the office of the attractive young woman who first shot her hand up at the staff meeting, Paul introduced her as Kim Tomlin, and she invited them to come in and sit down, "Paul has asked me to head up the initiative to bring the mind beaming station to the market. Ron and Paul have suggested that you might work directly with me.—Now Ron has made me aware of the fact that you are not too keen on traveling, in your work, so we would try to minimize the amount of traveling you might do, in this capacity; but at the times you might be asked to, we would probably be traveling together, should you come to work for us."

Tommy regarded her more closely as she continued to speak. He couldn't help noticing the clarity of her eyes, and he also found himself somewhat distracted by her long flowing red hair. Tommy guessed she was about his age, groping for words. Finally, she seemed to have finished communicating the thoughts which had seemed to be most important to her to get across, and he had the opportunity to get a word in edgewise, "Those are some interesting ideas, you seem to be very much up to speed. Just how long have you been with the company?"

"I came here right out of college, about four years ago."

Paul spoke up, "She is our prodigy; she received her Master's, at the young age of fourteen, and we recruited her right away."

"That's pretty impressive. You seem to be a little like my sister."

Kim disregarded the compliment, "I've been working with banks, to put together financing, for our initiatives to market to lower income workers, and I'd like to know more about the cost of mind beaming, so I can add that into the equation as we develop our financing arrangements, if it's going to be somewhat expensive."

Paul took the opportunity to bow out, "Well I'll leave you two to get to know each other," he said cordially, as he turned and walked out.

Tommy picked up the conversation, where they had left off, "I really don't know much about the cost. At this point, you would have to ask Alyssa about that."

"I'd like to get her Skype number if I could."

Tommy was quite captivated by Kim, and he stared into her magnetic green eyes, as they talked for another ten minutes or so. He couldn't help noticing that she wasn't wearing a wedding ring.

He figured she was probably married to her job, and didn't have much of a social life, but his wishful thinking seemed to kick in, and he began to picture the idea of possibly being with her, as a lover.

When they were done talking, she stood, and they parted with a handshake, before Tommy headed down to Ron Goldstein's office. He had to wait five minutes for Ron to finish up his meeting with the rep from the Lockwood Synthetic Skeleton company, but he was eventually ushered into Ron's office, "Hi Tom; how was the staff meeting?"

"It was interesting; you have quite an energetic marketing staff."

"What did you think of Kim?" He smiled as he made the comment, "She's pretty attractive, isn't she?"

"Yes, very; she's also very sharp. I told he that she reminds me a little of my sister."

"She is quite the prodigy, indeed. She handles herself well, in her meetings with top executives at the banks we are negotiating with. With her as the point person, we're having a lot of success at working toward securing good terms, and a low financing rate. She has done studies which have convinced at least a few of these banks, that there will be a lot of business coming their way if they get involved."

"Is she working on the bank financing for the beaming station?"

"No; I'm working directly with Clarion Capital on that, at this point. So far, I've only asked her to put together some projections I can use in my negotiations."

"I see," Tommy said as he nodded his understanding.

Ron filled him in further, "I had a Skype conversation with Jim

Stevens, the president at Clarion, this morning. He wasn't pleased to hear that Centurion may also purchase the rights to build a beaming station, but I told him that I'd have Kim do a market study on our potential profitability of the venture, assuming a shared market with Centurion.

"I sure hope that getting Centurion involved doesn't derail your efforts to secure financing . . ."

"Me too," Ron echoed nervously, "Clarion Capital is going to have to lend us a lot of money to complete the project, and he's worried about our ability to pay back the loan, if we have to share the market. He needs us to demonstrate that there is a large enough potential market for mind beaming, considering the cost, and the apparent inclinations of those who might be considering trying it.

"Oh? What's involved with determining that? How time consuming do you think that process is going to be?"

"It may take several weeks. Kim plans to do a survey of most of the major metropolitan areas. She has to locate lists of residents and send a massive emailing as well, and we'll just have to hope that we'll get a good response."

"I see; so that's why she has to get some idea of the cost to have yourself beamed into an android, so she can include it in the survey you will be conducting, and in the emails she will be sending out."

"Exactly; but we're expecting a good response. We think it's a great new development that a lot of people will be interested in."

"So you'd hire me on, on that basis, and pay me the two hundred thousand a year?"

Ron nodded affirmatively, "We have no doubt that this is just a formality, to do the survey. I'm quite confident that we'll get the financing eventually, and probably in pretty short order."

"Well, I can see that you have a lot of confidence in Kim."

"Yes, she's been highly effective, and of course she's very attractive, to boot!" Ron knew that this could be a real plus in dealing with the executives at the banks they were dealing with, who were mostly all men.

"I might like to come back and meet with Kim again, maybe toward the end of the week."

"I'm sure we could arrange that. Let me talk to her, and I'm sure she'll find the time. Would you like to come back on Friday afternoon? I could see if she would be available to have lunch with you."

"Well it would actually have to be in the morning; I'm catching the one o'clock shuttle to Chilton on Friday."

"Oh; you're going to visit your stepfather this weekend, are you?"

"Yes; I'll be away until the following Monday afternoon. I have an appointment with Bill's lawyer on Monday morning."

"Okay; I'll see if I can work you into Kim's schedule for Friday morning. Shall I Skype you later this afternoon?"

"Yes; let me give you my new mobile Skype number." Ron reached into his pocket and pulled out his mobile Skype phone. "Are you ready?"

"Okay, shoot," Ron confirmed.

"It's one two one, five two three, six three four six seven."

"Let me also put that into my computer."

With the afternoon to kill, Tommy found his way to the Alderon Sports Shop, and bought himself a set of golf clubs. Then he headed out to the Brantwood Country Club in Fairhope. He arrived there shortly after noon, and found the pro shop, "Hi, I'd like to sign up for a tee time. Can you get me out this afternoon?"

The attractive young teenage girl behind the desk smiled at him as she looked up the schedule, "Let me check." She punched a few keys on the computer terminal, and gently bit her lip, "I have a one-fifteen tee time available. You'd be playing with a twosome . . ."

"That's fine; I'll have some lunch while I wait.—I'll need some balls and some tees, and a cart. Shall I pay you now?"

Tommy signed up and paid, and then found his way to the restaurant in the next building. He noticed that there were two more young attractive girls working with two older women behind the bar.

"Can I get you something to drink?" asked the pretty, scantily clad girl waiting on him.

"Yes; I'll have a cranberry and tonic."

"Sure; I just have to deliver an order to that table," she pointed, "I'll be right back, and then I'll bring you your drink."

She disappeared into the kitchen behind them, and Tommy addressed the older woman re-stocking the drink cooler, "Are these girls old enough to work here?" he asked.

She smiled back at him, "They're androids."

"Really; I've never seen androids that young."

Yes, the owner, Mr. Brantwood, likes young teenage girls. He hires us women who are willing to connect to them, and they serve customers with us. He has over thirty android girls, working around the club."

"Where did he get them from?"

"Oh; from Centurion Android."

"Centurion; is that right? Do they manufacture them there?"

"No, they don't have to make child androids. There were literally thousands of them that were confiscated from Earth and sent here. They just put in new computer brains to update them, and recirculate them into the market."

Tommy suddenly realized why Centurion's factory was so much smaller that Atlas's. He resumed his conversation, "Like I say, I've never seen androids that young looking."

"Most of the ones Centurion has put into service are modeled after well-developed thirteen and fourteen year old girls. That's also the age Mr. Brantwood likes them. He goes to their factory and picks them out a few times per year, and he finds women who agree to connect to them, because he pays us pretty good money to do it."

"Do you know, are there even younger looking androids than these available?"

"Yes, I think the youngest ones are modeled after four year olds. The young child androids are mostly bought up by sex offenders who have been released from prison, on parole and probation. The government considers it to be safer for our children if sex offenders released into the community who are attracted to children, own a child android. It's supposedly lowered the rate of re-offenders to almost nil, since they started allowing people to own child androids about fifteen years ago; that's when they were confiscated on Earth, and were sent here in droves."

"No kidding?—And they allow men to have sex with them?"

"I know; it sounds pretty sickening; but it works to keep the crime rate way down."

"God! I wonder if Atlas Android is in this business too."

"No; I think it's just Centurion; at least that's the only place us women have gone to get the programming done, in order to get connected."

"God! That's pretty sickening!"

"Hey; that's why they call this place planet P; it's for pedophiles, of course. Somebody has to deal with them, if Earth is going to exile them and send them here. The government is just doing its best to protect the population from them. The prison system is pretty lax here. They let some prisoners out once they have completed a treatment program, if they aren't violent offenders."

"I guess that's why the ratio of men to women is so high; they must let a lot of prisoners out into the community."

The pretty android girl came back with Tommy's drink, "Here you are sir; would you like to order lunch?"

Tommy played golf on the sunny afternoon. The weather was perfect. He barely broke a sweat, and he scored well; much better than in his first few rounds at the Stafford Club.

After he put his clubs in the car afterward, he Skyped Ron Goldstein from his cell, "Hi Ron, how are you?"

"Just fine; what's up?"

"I'm out at Brantwood Country Club, and they've got young teenage android girl servants working here!"

"Yes; I'm quite well-aware of that . . ."

"Well I understand they were supplied by Centurion, and I was wondering; is Atlas also involved with sales of child androids?"

"No, we didn't get into that market. There are android holding companies out there that still have thousands of those things, which, as I'm sure you know, were confiscated from Earth. We polled our customers at the time they first arrived sixteen years ago, and found that we were favored over Centurion because we didn't get involved with child androids. Many of our customers said they would never consider becoming a customer of Centurion, because this was a huge focal point of their business. As a result of their relative popularity, they've turned out to make the majority of their profits from re-working and selling child androids, although there are a few other smaller companies that do that as well; and we have dominated the market for adult androids. All of our androids are modeled after adults; mostly in their twenties."

"That's comforting to hear, because I don't think I want to go to work for a company that markets child androids."

"I purposely avoided talking about that, because I didn't know how you might feel about it; and if you weren't bothered by it, I didn't want to emphasize our disdain, as it might have turned you off; but I'm glad to hear you're in our camp."

"Is the two hundred thousand dollar offer still good?"

"Yes it is . . ."

"Well then I've made my decision; I'd like to come to work for Atlas."

"That's great news! We're delighted to have you! When do you think you might want to start?"

Tommy took several seconds to think carefully before answering, "Why don't we plan for two weeks from Monday? "-That will probably give me enough time to settle into my new house."

"That's fine; I know you are also working on getting your stepfather out of prison. We'll be flexible, at the times that you may have to be in court for that; and you'll also have weekends off, if you want to visit him. You did say, that the visiting hours are on weekends, didn't you?"

"Yes; Saturday and Sunday mornings."

Ron moved on, "I set up an appointment for you to meet with Kim again on Friday morning at ten; do you still want to keep it, or should we wait until two weeks from Monday to see you?"

Tommy remembered Kim's pretty face, and her captivating manner, "No, I'll keep the appointment. I'm curious to hear more about how she plans to conduct the survey. It will give me something to think about for the next two weeks."

"Fine; well I'll tell her the news that you've decided to come to <u>work</u> for us, and that you'll see her on Friday. I'm sure she'll be pleased."

Tommy drove back to the hotel and Skyped Alyssa. When her face finally appeared, he especially enjoyed that she looked quite life-like, on the big screen over his desk, "Hi Alyssa; I've got some more news for you."

"Okay, what's up?"

"I found out today that Centurion re-programs and sells some of the child androids that were confiscated from Earth. They've apparently bought up quite a few . . ."

"Well, that doesn't <u>surprise</u> me, I imagine there must be several companies there that are in that market. I believe there were several <u>million</u> android children confiscated and shipped there."

"Yeah but don't you find that creepy, that people are allowed to own them here?—And a large part of the market for them is apparently to sex offenders who were released from prison! I find that particularly disturbing . . ."

"Well you know that at <u>one</u> point, you could also own them here on Earth, before they became outlawed," Alyssa reminded him.

"Yeah, well I don't want to go to work for a company that sells child androids. In fact, I don't know if we should even let them build a beaming station?"

"Look; don't be so <u>hard</u> on them. They were <u>shipped</u> there, they're <u>legal</u> and there's a <u>market</u> for them. Besides, Albert and I already signed, and sent out the contracts for Atlas and Centurion, along with about ten other companies, both here, and on Earth-2, just this morning; so we've already sold them the rights to build a mind beaming station. It's too late to back out, now. Who knows, you may even want to beam yourself into the body of a child to see what that's like. That's something we can't do here."

"I don't know about that."

"So go to work for Atlas, and forget about Centurion."

"I already agreed to; I called Ron Goldstein and told him I'd start in a couple of weeks."

"Congratulations! You're doing well up there!"

"Yes, I am making progress; now if I can only get Bill out of prison . . ."

"Tommy," she interrupted, "I'm sorry, but I have to go; Albert is waiting for me. Can we talk about this later? . . ."

"Okay; Skype me back when you get the chance; bye sis."

Tommy thought for a few minutes, and then he Skyped Stan Tillman. He answered cheerily, "Hi Tom, nice to hear from you. What can I do for you?"

"I just discovered the most disturbing news about your company; I found out that you are selling child androids."

"Yes; we've been in that market for over fifteen years now.—We're just responding to the needs of the public; there's quite a demand for them, you know."

"Yeah, well I can't be involved with that. I want to cancel my appointment tomorrow; I just accepted a position with Atlas."

"That's very disturbing news to me . . . You're sure there's nothing we can do to change your mind?"

"No; I'm absolutely certain about this."

"Well I'm sorry to hear that."

"You can build a beaming station if you want; Alyssa and Dr. Freudenthal have already signed the contract and sent you the rest of the plans, so there's nothing I can do about that, but I won't help you advertise; you're going to have to do that on your own."

"Well I'm sorry you won't be joining us, but I'm relieved to hear that we've been cleared to build a beaming station.—I guess I can understand your sentiment; there's lots of folks who are against ownership of child androids, but as I say, we're just responding to the needs of the public. There's a lot of men in particular who like young teenage girl androids, and there are also quite a few sex offenders released from prison, who realize it is in their best interest, and indeed in the interest of the public for protection against reoffending, for them to own a child android; and we feel it important to meet these needs."

"I understand; I just don't want to take part in it."

"Well okay; if that's the way you feel; but I'm very disappointed to *hear* this. I believe we're on the forefront of android development, here at Centurion, and you *could* have had a great career with us."

"Well I've made my decision; I'm going to hang up now."

It was late Wednesday night before Tommy saw Sally again. She knocked on his door at ten-thirty. When he let her in, she hugged him and kissed him as though she was very glad to finally be with him, "I've *missed* you," she said very convincingly, "It's so great to *see* you again!"

"I've missed you too; it's been about a *week* since I saw you last . . ."

"Sam talked with Stan Tillman, and he told me about your aversion to child android sales, and your decision to go to work for Atlas . . ."

"Yes; I'm sorry, but that's the way I feel. I hope you'll understand . . ."

"Don't worry, I'm *okay* with it. I kind of have an aversion to it myself, but I have to support my husband in his work. He makes a lot of money, and he spends a lot on *me*. I have a fabulous wardrobe, and he buys me a new car every year. I have an android woman servant, and we live in a big mansion with a pool and an exercise room with all the latest equipment and everything. All I have to do is be his assistant, and be home with him in the early evenings when he's in town."

"—And he lets you have affairs . . . Does he know yet, that you're having an affair with me?"

"No; he says he doesn't want to know about any affairs; it would just *upset* him. He usually goes to bed around ten; and as long as I'm there in bed with him when he wakes up in the morning, he can tolerate it if I'm out 'till the wee hours of the morning."

"I see. Then why haven't you come to visit me for the last several days?"

"Well, Sam's been sick, so I've stayed with him all night, to take care of him, since he came home last Friday; and it was also our anniversary yesterday, and I didn't feel I could leave him."

"So you have feelings for him . . ."

"He treats me well, and I've grown accustomed to being with him over the last three years since we've been married. I don't want to hurt him; I just have needs he can't fulfill."

"Well I miss your loving, and your company, and your scent; and you are so beautiful!"

They kissed passionately. "Why don't I give you a massage with a happy ending?" she suggested.

"That would be great!"

She gave him a back massage for about half an hour, and then she rolled him over and slipped out of her dress. She wasn't wearing anything underneath. Her sudden nakedness turned him on intensely, and they made love for another half-an-hour. She collapsed on his chest afterward, and he held her tenderly, the scent of her hair intoxicating him.

"Can you stay and sleep with me for a while? I want to feel your warm body against mine," Tommy pleaded.

"If you set your alarm for four o'clock, I can get home before Sam wakes up . . ."

Tommy set the alarm and crawled back into bed to snuggle with her. Sally fell asleep within a few minutes, but Tommy was enjoying her lovely scent, and her warm, sleepy body pressing up against him, too much to go to sleep right away. He held her for probably about an hour before drifting off to sleep himself.

They slept for a while together until the alarm went off in the middle of the night. Sally dragged herself out of bed, pulled her dress back on, and kissed Tommy goodbye. She slipped out of the room as Tommy fell back asleep.

Friday morning, Tommy awoke early and went down to soak in the Jacuzzi. He planned to check out at nine-thirty, before heading to Atlas to meet with Kim.

As he sat there, the jets blasting away at his back, he thought to himself, "I'm going to have to get one of these things installed at my new house; this is such a great luxury!"

He reviewed his plans, and felt satisfied that he had thought of everything in order to make the transition to living at his new house.

He would catch the one o'clock shuttle to Chilton and stay at the Stafford club for the weekend, visiting with Bill on Saturday and Sunday mornings. He had a nine o'clock appointment with Phil Pierson on Monday morning, to review the progress on Bill's upcoming sentence modification hearing, and then he would catch the noon flight back to Alderon.

He had arranged to close on the house at three o'clock at Tony Romano's office, and he had scheduled the movers to meet him at the house at four-thirty, to move his new bed, and the furniture he had bought, from the garage into the house, and help set it up.

The kitchen appliances were coming Tuesday morning, so he'd have to eat out on Monday night, but otherwise, everything was arranged perfectly, he thought to himself.

Tommy arrived at Kim Tomlin's office promptly at ten o'clock, and found her sitting at her desk, typing on her computer, "Come on in Tom; I'll be with you in a minute; I'm just sending an email to Clarion National Bank. They're one of the banks we are seeking financing with."

A few minutes went by while Tommy sat waiting patiently, and she finally turned from her computer screen, "There; that's finished. Clarion National has just approved financing for our new marketing initiative, you know; marketing our androids to blue collar workers. My contact at the bank says they are not inclined, however, to give us additional financing so that we can offer loans to customers who want to try mind beaming; so I was explaining the potential profit of the mind beaming services which we will now be offering . . ."

"Oh? Have you already gathered enough information to project profits from potential mind beaming sales?"

"Well no; but I explained, to my contact at the bank, that your sister has informed me, mind beaming prices range between approximately ten-thousand and eighty-thousand dollars on earth, depending on your location and the length of time you wish to exist in an android's body. She says most places will only do it for up to a month. The beaming station we're planning to build has ten beds, so at ten at a time, with a conservative price of twenty-thousand per person per week, say, that's ten-million in gross revenue in the first year; and it could be double or <u>triple</u> that, if it's really popular."

"Ten-thousand at a minimum, huh? I didn't realize it would be that expensive. What does ten thousand <u>buy</u> you?—One day?"

"Yes, and eighty-thousand buys you a month; but there's two-million people living in the metropolitan area here in Alderon alone, and I believe that something like, over ten percent of them earn in excess of two-hundred-thousand a year; and, of course, some entrepreneurs are millionaires several times <u>over</u>."

"Yeah I guess it's a drop in the bucket for them; but it seems it's going to be way out of <u>reach</u> for blue collar workers."

"Not <u>necessarily</u>; some blue collar workers may take out a loan for ten thousand for the novelty of living in another body for a day . . ."

Tommy considered her supposition, "I suppose the price will come down as more beaming stations are built around the <u>planet</u> . . ."

"Yes, but our revenue should also increase as we build more beaming stations, regardless of a dramatic price decrease, perhaps, over <u>time</u>. We'll probably more than make up the difference on <u>volume</u>. This <u>could</u> be a hugely profitable venture for us."

"Yes, I can see that.—So how are you going to go about taking a survey? It seems like you only have to reach the top ten percent, income-wise, in order to get an indication of interest and sales volume."

"Exactly; although it's somewhat difficult to identify <u>just</u> the wealthy individuals, so we'll do a mass emailing to business owners and anyone who owns a house. We can target residential neighborhoods, as opposed to apartment complexes where blue collar workers are more prevalent."

"Alright; well good luck with that. I'd better go; I have to catch a plane to Chilton at noon, but I wanted to meet with you again, to quickly get some information on how you are moving forward."

"Well now you <u>know</u>!" Kim looked at the clock on her computer, "Yes, I guess you had better get on your way, if you're going to catch a one o'clock flight. When are you coming to work for us?—two weeks from Monday, was it?"

"Yeah, I'm probably going to need some time to settle into my new house."

"Yes, well I hope you don't find it too tedious of an undertaking; moving can be so stressful!"

"Well, I'm actually looking forward to it; I've bought a bunch of new furniture, and everything . . ."

"That's nice; well I won't hold you up; good luck on your trip.—I'll see you in a couple of weeks . . ."

Tommy drove to the airport and checked his suitcase and his golf clubs, and then went to grab a quick bite to eat before going out to the gate.

He Skyped Kerry at work, and found out she had taken the day off, so he tried Skyping her at home, and found her still in her bathrobe, as he greeted her, "Hi Kerry, I just wanted to catch you before I headed to Chilton for the weekend.—Are you feeling okay?"

"Yes, I'm fine physically; are you going to visit Bill?"

"Yes, and I have an appointment with his lawyer on Monday morning. I hope to hear that things are falling in place for his sentence modification hearing."

"Are you going to stay at that sports club?"

"Yes, the Stafford Club. Listen, I wanted to let you know that I accepted the position at Atlas. I mainly made my decision based on the fact that I discovered Centurion is selling child androids, and I don't want to be involved in any company that does that."

"Okay; I can understand that. I only got involved, myself, because Mike works there; but the truth is, I don't really much care that they are involved in that market. They're just machines; I don't think it's hurting anyone for people to own them. What a person does behind closed doors is their business, as far as I'm concerned."

"Well I don't want to be involved with it. I'm just letting you know my decision, and I also wanted to tell you I avoided telling Ron Goldstein that you've been acting as a mole for Centurion; but I'm also advising you that if you are going to stay with Atlas, you'd better break off your arrangement with Centurion."

"I will . . ."

"I think you'd better break it off with Mike as well. He's the one who got you involved as a double agent, and in my opinion he's really not good for you."

Kerry instantly felt distressed, "But I've been dating him for well over a year! I like him, and he's asked me to marry him; I can't do that . . ."

"Well my allegiance is to Atlas now, and I've decided that I'm not going to keep quiet about your double role unless you stop seeing him. Besides, I want you to be with me! Won't you stop spending time with him and start spending time with me instead?"

There was more silence while Kerry mulled over what Tommy was asking. She raised her eyebrows, "You're asking for a lot . . ."

"I'm asking you to get out of a bad relationship, that's all."

"Well, he has been verbally abusive to me lately . . ."

"That's even more good reason to leave him."

"You won't report me if I break off my arrangement with Centurion and leave Mike?"

"Yes; on that I give you my word; but would you just give me a chance to get to know you better? I want to see you next week when I get back."

Kerry hesitated for a moment, "Okay, call me when you get back, and we'll go out."

"Great! Well listen, I've got to go; my flight is boarding; I'll be in touch . . ."

Chapter Twenty-One

THE WEEKEND HAD GONE fine. Tommy played golf twice, and visited Bill on both Saturday and Sunday mornings. He had checked out of the Stafford Club hotel, and after fighting traffic, he arrived at Phil Pierson's office a little after nine.

"It didn't seem to matter much that he was late. Phil's assistant ushered him onto the conference room to wait for him, and it took a good twenty minutes for Phil to join Tommy.

He finally entered the conference room, "Good morning Tom; I'm sorry I had to make you wait. I was on a Skype call with the judge."

"That's alright; tell me how things are progressing with Bill's sentence modification. Do we have a hearing date yet?"

"Yes; the hearing is scheduled for September seventh, at ten o'clock. Can you be there?"

"Yes, I can be there; that's about two weeks away, isn't it?"

Phil nodded silently in response.

"Okay; is there anything else we have to do before then to prepare?"

"No, I don't think so. I'm just waiting for the private investigator's report. I should have it by later this week. He tells me that your sister Alyssa is in a relationship with a man she has been seeing for well over a year now."

"Yes, he is a physicist, who works at her lab."

"That's good for us, because the prosecutor won't be able to show significant hardship and damages to the victim. She continues to work, obviously in a very effective capacity, with her associate, Dr. Albert Freudenthal, and as far as we can tell, she seems fairly well adjusted."

"Good; the private investigator seems to have helped our case."

"It will help somewhat, but I talked with the prosecutor last week, and she has dug up a transcript of Alyssa's interview with the former prosecutor, showing that, at least at that point, she was cognizant of her online memories of Bill's sexual thoughts, and of some of his sexual acts with his android woman Shayna; which he, of course, was sent to prison for."

"So she'll fight our motion for a sentence reduction, in the modification hearing?"

"Undoubtedly, but the judge seems to be more on our side, at this point. He's almost certain to reduce Bill's sentence, but we don't know by how much."

"That is all decided in court?"

"Yes; each side will present their case, and the judge will make his decision on the spot. The only thing that could delay it is if the prosecutor says she needs more time in light of information she wasn't aware of, which gets introduced at the hearing."

"Are you planning to give her all of the information that you get from the private investigator?"

"Yes; I think it would be a good idea. We don't want any surprises at the hearing."

"How about my statement? Will you tell her what I plan to say on Bill's behalf?"

"Well no; I think that's better left unsaid. We'll want to establish that you will provide a stable home environment for Bill. That will help sway the judge's decision to let him out on probation."

"Well, as I told you last week, I bought a home in Fairhope, just outside of Alderon; and I've just taken a job with Atlas Android in their marketing department."

"Good; that will help. One other thing; Bill is used to having an android; if we can get him out on probation, do you suppose you could afford to buy him an android?"

"I don't think that will be a problem. Atlas actually wants to give me an android as a signing bonus, and I don't think I want one myself. I don't see any reason why they wouldn't connect it to Bill instead."

"Okay, then we've got that covered, it looks like."

"Is there anything else I can do to help?" Tommy asked, attempting to prompt Phil to think of any other details.

"Well, there is one thing you could do, although I don't know if you could arrange this, but if you could get a letter from your sister saying that she doesn't object to Bill getting released, that would be helpful."

"I can ask. I don't know if she would be willing or not."

"Well, why don't you work on that, and arrange to be here on the seventh. We can go over your statement via Skype later in the week. Why don't you put together what you'd like to say at the hearing, and I'll let you know if there's anything you should change."

"Okay, I'll do that; I'll Skype you later in the week."

Tommy returned the rental car at the airport, and checked his suitcase and golf clubs. He had an hour to kill, so he had a leisurely breakfast, and read the local paper.

The flight was right on time. At the other end, he picked up his bags and took a shuttle to the long term parking lot, where he picked up his car. From there, he drove to the First National Bank and had a bank check drawn up for four-hundred-and-fifty-thousand, and another one for nine-thousand to cover the closing costs on the house.

He got to Tony Romano's office early in case there were any problems to work out before the closing. He found Tony in his office, working on the contracts, "Hi Tony; is everything ready for the closing?"

"Yes; I'm just finishing up on the paperwork. Did you bring the checks?"

"Whoops! I left them in the car. I'll go get them and be right back."

The closing went smoothly, and afterward, Tommy headed to the house. It was an hour before rush hour traffic would begin, so he made the trip in less than twenty minutes.

It was a good thing he got there right away, because the movers were already there waiting for him. He unlocked the garage, and they started moving the furniture in.

Tommy instructed them as they worked, "The bed and the dressers and the nightstands go into the master bedroom in the far side of the house on the second level."

He had bought a sofa and two easy chairs, and a big screen TV that they set up in the living room. He had a gas grill and some outdoor furniture set up on the back deck.

He had bought a large desk, a floor lamp, a rolling chair and a filing cabinet which were set up in one of the spare bedrooms. The new computer was set up on the desk, and Tommy connected it while they brought in the rest of the furniture.

They worked until after nine-thirty. When they were done, the house was basically all set up, except for the empty two remaining bedrooms. He gave the four movers a hundred dollar tip, and as they pulled away, Tommy realized he was famished, not having eaten since breakfast, at the Chilton airport. He ordered dinner, which he had delivered; and he sat and ate in front of the big screen TV; then he put the sheets on his king size bed, put the pillow cases on his new pillows, spread out his new down comforter and went to bed early.

He slept well in his new pillow-top bed, and awoke refreshed at a little after eight a.m. He got dressed, made a pot of coffee and sat out on the deck with a cup, the morning sun warming him pleasantly.

He stared out at the lake, and resolved to go shopping for a boat. After twenty minutes or so, he went inside and booted his computer. He searched online for a marine contractor to build him a dock. After getting a few names, he Skyped Rex Marine Contracting, "Good morning; I'm interested in having a dock built. I live in Fairhope, and my property borders on Mead Lake. I was wondering if you could come out and give me an estimate."

"Sure; I'll give you to John Peterson, and you can schedule a time for him to come out to your place. Just a moment . . ."

The receptionist transferred Tommy, and a middle aged gruff—looking man appeared on the Skype screen, "John Peterson; can I help you?"

"Yes; my name is Tom Symms, and I live out on Mead Lake in Fairhope. I was wondering if you could come out and give me an estimate on building a dock?"

"I can do that; let's see, I could come out tomorrow morning; would that work for you?"

"Yes; I could <u>be</u> here; what time were you thinking?"

"How about nine o'clock?"

"That will be fine; let me give you directions . . ."

Tommy went boat shopping at Chessy Marine, on the outskirts of Fairhope, and found a thirty-six foot hydrogen powered boat with a cabin that he really liked. It was too big to fit in the boathouse, but Tommy figured maybe he would convert the boathouse into a cottage on the water eventually anyway.

The boat had two bedrooms with queen size beds that Tommy found were very comfortable. The boat would sleep four, and he dreamed about spending the night with Kerry on the boat, out on the lake. Maybe they could leave Kerry's android in the other bedroom, to serve them and cook and clean for them.

He Skyped Kerry at work to tell her about the boat, and to set up a date for later in the week, "Hi Kerry; do you have a minute to talk?"

"Sure; how was your trip to Chilton?"

"It went well. I saw Bill, and I met with his lawyer yesterday morning. We have a sentence modification hearing in two weeks. We're hoping to get him off on probation."

"Well, I wish you good luck."

"Are you alone? Can we talk?"

"Let me close my door, and I'll be right back."

She came back, and spoke in a low voice, so no-one would hear her, "Let me tell you what's going on; I went to visit Stan Tillman on Friday morning after you and I talked, and I broke off our arrangement."

"That's <u>good</u>!"

"I also went out to lunch with Mike, and broke it to him that I was going to stop seeing him."

"What did he say?"

"He took it hard; he figured out that you were behind this, even though I tried to deny it at first, and he got very angry; but I calmed him down, and explained that I have a hard <u>time</u> with his anger, and I thought it was best if we stopped seeing each other; at least for a while."

"I'm glad to hear that; did he back off?"

"He finally said he was very upset with my decision, but if that's what I wanted, he would honor my request."

"That's <u>good</u>! Are we still on for a <u>date</u> later this week?—Like maybe Friday night?"

"What; did you want to go out to dinner or something?"

"Dinner would be fine; what time do you want me to pick you up?"

"How about eight o'clock?"

"Eight it is; I'll see you then . . ."

Tommy felt exhilarated; Kerry was quickly becoming the girl of his dreams. He sat out on the deck again for a bit; and then realized he was starting to feel a bit bored.

He Skyped Ron Goldstein, "Hi Ron, how are you?"

"Fine; how was your weekend in Chilton?"

"It was good. Listen; I <u>thought</u> I would need more time to get settled into my new house, but I'm actually <u>all moved in</u> and set up, and I think I'm ready to come to work earlier than we planned."

"Oh? When did you want to start?"

"How about if I come in on Friday?"

"That's fine; your new desk isn't coming in until next week, but I can arrange for you to work with Kim Tomlin on Friday, and you can probably be in your own office by mid-week next week."

"Will you have a space for me to work in, if I begin a week early?"

"Sure; you can use the conference room until your new office is ready. There will be a staff meeting in there on Monday morning, but otherwise I think it will be free. You'll be at the staff meeting anyway, so it shouldn't be a problem."

"Okay; one more thing; I need to be in Chilton for my stepfather's hearing on September seventh. Would it be okay if I took a few days off? I'd like to leave on Friday afternoon; that's the fourth; and I can be back in the office, as soon as Tuesday, the eighth . . ."

"Sure; that will be fine."

Tommy was pleased to have given himself something to do. Realizing that they had worked everything out, he made his parting comment, "Good; I'll see you Friday morning then; nine o'clock?—Or do you start earlier?"

"No, we work nine to five around here."

"Alright, I'll see you Friday morning then . . ."

The afternoon passed by pleasantly. Tommy took a long walk in his new neighborhood. Then, at two o'clock, his new kitchen appliances were delivered. He sat out on the deck while they unpacked and installed the dishwasher, stove, and refrigerator. Then they brought in the washer and dryer and set them up in the laundry room. He felt pretty pleased that his house was, the rest of the way, being set up that afternoon.

Later, he found himself standing in the doorway of the slider going out onto the back deck. The workers had just left, and he was admiring his fully functional kitchen, when his Skype phone rang. It was Sally, "Hi Tommy; I <u>miss</u> you! How was your weekend in Chilton?"

"It went fine; how was <u>your</u> weekend?"

"Fine, except I missed you alot. Did you move into your new house yet?"

"Yep; I moved in yesterday. Thanks for helping me shop for furniture and everything. Thanks to our efforts in the last couple of weeks, everything is moved in and set up already. I never realized it would happen so quickly."

"I want to see you. I could come over later, like around ten . . ."

"Sure! Come on over; I'll give you a tour of the house."

"Okay; maybe we could try out your new bed!" she suggested, seductively.

"I sure miss your pretty face and your sexy body . . ."

"Oh?—Are you ready for some more <u>loving</u> tonight?"

"I sure am; I'm just going to do some food shopping, and then I'm going to make myself dinner. I'll be waiting for you later."

"Fine; you'll have to give me directions."

"You mean later tonight, or did you mean how to get here?" he joked back, seductively.

Sally arrived a little after ten, and Tommy greeted her at the door with a big kiss, "Welcome to my new place! Come in, let me show you around!"

They walked through the spacious house, and out onto the back deck. They could see the lights bouncing off the water on the lake in the distance.

Next, he took her upstairs to see the bedrooms, one of which he had converted into an office.

Tommy had saved the master bedroom suite for last. Standing in the doorway of the upstairs office, he turned to her and smiled at her, "Do you want to see the master bedroom? There's no TV in there yet, but I'll bet we can think of something else to do in there," he turned seductive again.

He led her into the room and out onto the upstairs deck which also overlooked the lake. "The master bedroom is beautiful, Tom!" she complimented, "—And so is the whole house! You should be very happy here."

He smiled, and took her in his arms and kissed her, in the warm night air, "Are you ready to go in and try out my new bed?"

"Yeah!" Sally whispered excitedly. She disappeared into the bathroom with her overnight bag, and emerged a few minutes later in a sexy nighty, "Nice bathroom; it's big!" she remarked.

"Maybe we can soak later in the double tub . . ." Tommy suggested.

"You mean after we tire ourselves out?"

Tommy noticed her eyes looked a little funny, "What did you <u>do</u> in there?"

"Oh, I just took a little something to enhance the <u>sexual</u> experience; do you want some?"

"No, I don't do <u>drugs</u>," he answered flatly.

"Okay, whatever; but I <u>swear</u>, it moves everything up a notch."

Tommy made no comment; he wasn't the slightest bit interested. He had been waiting in bed for her, and she climbed on top of him. She kissed his ear and blew into it, and shivers ran up his spine.

They made love for the longest time; Sally had been right about her heightened sense of sexual pleasure, as a result of her little trip into the bathroom before they started. They eventually wore each other out, Sally having had multiple orgasms, and they finally collapsed and fell asleep in each other's arms, as usual after late night sex.

Tommy awoke to sunlight streaming in the upper windows, at the peak of the cathedral ceiling in his bedroom. It was just eight-thirty. He rolled out of bed and made his way to the bathroom. When he came back to bed, Sally was awake, "Good morning handsome," she greeted.

"Good morning; we forgot to set the alarm."

"Yeah, Sam will be upset with me that I wasn't there when he woke up this morning."

"Where will you tell him you were?"

"I don't know; it doesn't much matter; he'll suspect that I've been with another man. I hate to hurt him this way."

"You know what? I love being with you sexually and everything, but we probably shouldn't be doing this, I'm thinking. I'm starting to go out with Kerry, and if I want a real shot at a good relationship with her, I can't be having an affair with a married woman at the same time."

"Why not!? Why don't you at least wait to see if things start to get serious between you two, before breaking it off with me?"

"Well, I'm going out with Kerry tomorrow night, and I plan to tell her about our affair. I want to be open and honest with her about what's going on in my life. If I can't say that I've broken it off with you, that can cause me some complications, and obstacles to our getting to know each other better."

"I guess I can respect that; but can we resume seeing each other again if it doesn't work out with Kerry?"

"Well normally I'd say no, to a married woman, but I'm kind of addicted to you; I'd probably get back together with you again in a heartbeat, if I was unattached."

"I may go to Kerry and offer to buy her out of agreeing to see you . . ."

"You would do that!?"

"No," she smiled, "I'm just kidding. I won't try to stand in the way of what might develop between you two. I suppose you told me from the beginning, that you want to get married and have kids ideally."

"I do; and Kerry is so beautiful and so sweet; she just got involved with Mike, and he convinced her to become a spy for Centurion. I don't know if you heard, but she broke off that arrangement."

"No, I didn't know that; but it seems she's been hugely helpful to us already, so it won't be as much of a loss going forward."

"Well she's broken it off with Mike as well, and she's agreed to start seeing me, and I don't want anything to get in the way of my having a successful relationship with her, if it's as rewarding as I think it might be."

"Okay; I'll back off for now, but as I say, if things don't work out for you and Kerry, I want us to start seeing each other again."

"You got it; and meanwhile, we can stay in touch as friends if you want . . ."

"I don't know; we'll see. It might be easier for me if we just break it off altogether, at least for a while."

"I can understand that," Tommy said sadly. He really hated to let Sally go, she was so warm and friendly and sexy, and she smelled so nice; he loved sleeping with her; but he believed it was best for him to break it off, if he wanted to pursue his dream of becoming married and having children.

They got dressed and he walked her to the door. They had a last embrace. Sally had tears in her eyes.

"I'm sorry if I hurt you," Tommy said as they looked into each other's eyes one last time.

"No, don't worry about it; Sam worships me and adores me, and he gives me whatever I want; and I won't have any trouble finding another man to fill the void between us romantically and sexually."

Tommy eyed her up and down; she really was gorgeous, "No, I suppose not; still, don't you ever wish you had married someone who you were really in love with, instead of Sam?"

"Yeah, I'm thinking that right now, about you; but I have to live with the decisions I've made, and life's not too bad this way. It can be kind of exciting at times, and I get to have a variety of sexual partners," she argued weakly.

Tommy tried to strengthen her, "I'll bet you do; there's so many hungry men on this planet; well, at least the ones who can't be satisfied sexually by an android, like me."

"Don't knock it 'till you try it; an android can give you a pretty satisfying sexual experience; at least that's what several men have told me."

"I can't see making love to a machine . . . Well, I wish you good luck. I don't know when we might see each other again . . ."

"Good luck to you too; it's been real . . ." Sally turned and walked away.

Tommy sat in a daze out on the back deck. He was second-guessing himself; he really felt conflicted about turning Sally away.

The doorbell rang, and he went to answer it. "Hi, Mr. Symms?—Fred Prince with Central Pools and Spas; you had called us for an estimate on putting in a Jacuzzi?"

"Oh, yes; I forgot you were coming this morning. Come on in and I'll take you out to the back deck, where I'd like to have it put in."

Tommy led him through the living room and out the slider onto the deck. "Can you cut into the deck, and install it so that the top of the Jacuzzi is level with the floor of the deck?"

"Sure! Would you like something square or round?"

"Square is good; something that will seat like four, or maybe even eight people, in case I have guests."

Fred showed Tommy catalogues of different style Jacuzzis. He took measurements, and checked out the electrical box in the basement, to make sure there was ample room to handle the large pump Tommy wanted for the jets.

When Fred finally left, almost two hours later, Tommy had given him a deposit check for five-thousand; the balance due on completion of the installation, which would begin the following week.

Tommy felt exhilarated again. It was really fun buying things for his new home. He was going to have such an exciting and relaxing life there, he thought.

He loaded his golf clubs in the car and headed to the Brantwood Country Club for a round of golf. He was getting used to the teenage girl androids working everywhere around the club; from behind the desk at the pro shop, to in the restaurant. Even the starter and the ranger on the course were teenage android girls. They're really pretty cute, he thought, as he recollected fond memories of some of his interactions with them, during his drive to the course.

He had another good round of golf again, that afternoon. This time, he was put with a threesome, and he rode in a cart with whom he would discover, was a retired prison guard. He projected into his own future, and had fond thoughts, picturing himself being as fit and healthy looking as this golf partner, when he was over two-hundred years old himself.

When he got home, he sat at his computer and worked on his statement for Bill's hearing, and emailed his draft to Phil Pierson.

When he was done, it was almost six, so he made himself dinner and ate in front of the TV. He was watching the top stories when a report came on about Atlas Android and Centurion android's plans, to build mind beaming stations. Tommy's name was mentioned in connection with the plans being brought to planet P, and made available to the two companies.

"I made the news; I'm a celebrity!" He thought to himself. The report said both companies planned to have a beaming station ready for use by sometime next summer.

Tommy knew that Atlas had not even secured the financing yet. He figured Atlas was trying to keep up with the competition, so they were making an optimistic projection.

Afterward, he watched two movies before going to bed. He set his alarm for seven-thirty, so he'd be up in plenty of time to get to work by 9am.

Tommy slept restlessly, but he finally fell asleep around one-thirty. He awoke to his alarm going off, and got right up. He took a shower and got dressed in a new suit, with a fancy red tie. He wanted to make a good impression on his first day of work for Atlas.

Traffic was heavy, and he just made it into the building at five of nine, and headed for Kim Tomlin's office. Kim greeted him with a smile. She looked especially pretty when she smiled. It was going to be fun working with such a pretty young woman, he thought.

"Good morning; I see you're right on time. How was the traffic coming in from Fairhope?" she asked.

"The highway was kind of slow. I had to race through the city streets to get here on time. I'll have to leave a little earlier."

She just smiled, "I'll get you set up in the conference room. I just got a verbal commitment from Clarion Capital on the financing for the beaming station, so I want you to work on a press release about it."

"I'd be <u>happy</u> to work on that; that's great news that you have secured financing!"

"Well, we haven't secured it quite yet; we have to finish the written proposal and draw up the contract. We won't really have secured the financing until they sign it."

"The company will probably have to start making payments on the loan long before the station will start generating revenue, won't they?—I <u>know</u> that new android sales are down; will you be able to afford to start making these payments?"

"Well that's just it; we're trying to set up a payment schedule where our payments will initially be low; and then they will step up once we have the beaming station in use."

"That makes sense; I hope the financing company will go for it."

"Well, the reason I want you to work on a press release today is that I want to send it with the proposal to Clarion, showing them our starting strategy for marketing the beaming service."

"Why don't we offer a discount to those who sign up early? Maybe it could be first come, first serve, as far as who gets a price break, for the first people signing up to have their mind beamed into an android . . ."

Kim was impressed, "That sounds like good <u>idea</u>! Why don't you write up a pitch, and then maybe we could get video footage of you announcing our proposed initial cost of the service to the public, later today."

"Fine; I brought my laptop, as Ron informed me that my office furniture and my new computer won't arrive until sometime next week."

"Good thinking. Well, you know where the conference room is; you could bring your laptop in there and get started."

Tommy sat and wrote everything he could think of about the way mind beaming works, and the potential uses and benefits of having your mind beamed into an android.

Kim joined him in the conference room at around eleven o'clock, reviewed what Tommy had written, and added her own thoughts and perspective.

Together, they hammered out a script which Tommy would read on the teleprompter, and deliver his address into the camera, which Kim said might well be used to introduce the idea to the public the following week, assuming Clarion Capital would sign the contract to provide the financing by then.

Tommy and Kim had lunch in the company cafeteria, where they joined a few other marketing executives and some clerical staff members. It was an informal setting that Tommy found pleasant, as he got to know a few more of his fellow staff workers there.

After lunch, they went up to the third floor where there was a sound booth set up with a camera and a teleprompter, and Tommy tried several takes, as they revised the wording in-between takes, until Kim was satisfied that they had filmed a good presentation.

They went back down to Kim's office, and she Skyped Ron Goldstein to report on their progress, "Hi Ron; I just wanted to let you know that I've been working with Tom Symms most of the day, and I think we have put together a good press release, which I also plan to send to Jim Smith at Clarion Capital today, along with the final proposal and the contract terms we are bargaining for."

"That's superb! I'm glad to hear you are making progress. Is the legal department done reviewing your draft yet?"

"I was just about to go down there and see where they are on that. I was hoping to send a courier over to Clarion Capital with the package, including Tom Symms's planned public address, by late this afternoon; which reminds me;—Would you like to <u>hear</u> the address?"

"Yes; why don't you give the disc to Tom, and tell him I would like to see him in my office."

Tommy arrived at Ron Goldstein's office a few minutes later with the disc of his presentation in his hand, and they watched it together. When the five minute address was over, Ron turned to Tommy, "I like it! You're actually very photogenic, which is a plus since we plan to make you the point person in our advertising campaign about the beaming station."

"I'm glad you're happy with it; I enjoy working with Kim."

"Good; I'm glad the two of you are getting along well. Tom, I wanted to talk to you about our apprentice program. Normally, we get kids right out of college, and hire and train them in our one year marketing apprentice program at a forty thousand dollar starting salary. You're obviously making a lot more than that, and of course we plan to utilize you in our advertising schemes as we talked about; but I want you to go through the marketing apprentice program too."

"Sure; I have no objection to that. I really don't know anything about marketing, I mean at least I have no training in that field."

"Exactly; we want our marketing employees to have a strong underpinning in the fundamentals of marketing before beginning work with us as a staff member. It will also help add to the value of your work in advertising for us."

"What does the apprenticeship entail? Will I have to go to classes? Attend extra meetings?"

"Well there is a daily meeting at 9am Monday thru Friday, but we'll arrange it so you can complete everything else on the computer at your desk. We have tutorials you can watch, and footage of speakers at seminars and such."

"—And this lasts for a year?"

"You'll be working on your own, so you may complete the program in less than a year. It all depends on how much time and effort you put into it."

"Sounds good; when do I start?"

"Why don't you start attending morning meetings on Monday, and you can begin with the tutorials as soon as your office is set up, with your new computer."

"Okay; is there anything more I should do this afternoon?"

No; Kim is going to be working with the legal department for the rest of the day; why don't you take the rest of the day off; and we'll see you bright and early on Monday morning."

Tommy hit the cigar store on the way home. He bought a humidor and some more good cigars. When he got home, he sat out back, on the deck, and smoked a cigar. Afterward, he took a long walk, and had a nap before picking up Kerry for their dinner date.

He arrived at Kerry's apartment at eight, and she greeted him at the door, "Hi Tom; come on in. I'll be ready in a few minutes; I just have to put on some makeup."

"Where would you like to go to dinner?"

"I thought we could go to the Pierpont Inn; it's close by, and I think you'll like the food there. It's American cuisine, so it's something you'll be familiar with."

When they got to the car, Tommy opened her door for her, and she thanked him and climbed in, "<u>Nice</u> new car!"

"Yes, I just bought it last week. It's a little small, but it just fits my golf clubs in the trunk."

"Have you been playing golf?"

"I played on Wednesday, at Brantwood; it's a nice course, and it's only about fifteen minutes from my house."

"It is a nice course; I've played there myself."

"Oh? You are a golfer?"

"My father started giving me lessons a couple of years ago. I don't play that well, but I go out with my father about once a month."

"Does your father live around here?"

"He lives in Palmetto; it's about twenty minutes away, just north of Clarion DC."

"Is that close to where your sister is? Where did you say she's from again?"

"Rockland; it's about half an hour from Palmetto where my father lives. We all get together in Clarion for dinner sometimes; it's about a twenty minute drive for each of us."

"I forget; did you tell me your sister's name?"

"Tammy; she's twenty-six, and Doug is twenty-nine."

"How often do you see your brother?"

"He comes with his wife and the two girls a few times a year. They stay at my father's house, and I get to see him a few times while they're in the area. They usually stay for about a week when they come."

"That's nice, that you all get to see each other."

"So what did you do today?"

"I actually started work at Atlas today. I was going to stop and see you, but I figured we were going out tonight . . ."

"How was your first day? What did you do?"

"I spent most of the day working with Kim Tomlin. They want me to announce the mind beaming service Atlas plans to start offering next summer, to the public. I guess they think I am some kind of celebrity, being the brother of the inventor."

"Yes, I guess you are."

"Well anyway, we videotaped me making a pitch, which Kim plans to air next week, as soon as Atlas has a signed contract with Clarion Capital to provide the financing."

"Sounds exciting!"

"Yes, and Alyssa and Dr. Freudenthal are making good headway, working on developing the new strain of androids that people can have their mind beamed into, which will make it possible to eat and taste, and feel sense, such as touch, and even sexual response."

"That would be fantastic! There's probably a lot of people that would like to try it."

"Well, it's going to be kind of expensive initially, but I'm hoping the cost will come down as more beaming stations are built, so the average Joe will be able to try it."

"How much will it cost, when it first gets up and running?"

"Kim says it's going to cost about ten thousand for a day, and up to eighty thousand for a month of living in an android body."

"Wow! That is a lot. I don't know if I will try it at that price."

"Yeah, probably only wealthy people will try it at first; but there's half-a-million people in the Alderon area alone who could probably afford it."

"Yes, I guess that will be quite a novelty for them."

"Yes, especially when you figure that they will be able to travel to Earth and beyond."

They talked on over dinner, for another hour or so, and then Kerry said she was tired; she had been getting up early all week, and she just wanted to go back home and go to sleep.

Tommy drove her home and walked her to her door, and kissed her goodnight. She was such a pretty young thing, and she gave him a nice warm kiss. As he kissed her, Tommy could smell her lovely body scent, which kind of put him in a lingering trance. He drove home, dreaming of sleeping with her someday soon, if things kept progressing as well as they were so far.

Chapter Twenty-Two

Two weeks seemed to pass by quickly, and Tommy found himself at the airport, waiting to board the shuttle to Chilton. He had some time to kill, so he Skyped Alyssa, "Hi sis; how's it going?"

"Just fine; how are you doing? How is everything going at your new job?"

"Everything is going along fine. I started on the apprentice program last week. I've been working for hours on the computer every day. I find it somewhat interesting, working under Kim, and learning about marketing."

"Where are you? I hear people in the background."

"Yes, I'm at Alderon Airport, waiting to get on the shuttle to Chilton. Bill's hearing is on Monday. We're hoping for the best, but I don't want to get too optimistic. He may still have a lot of years in prison ahead of him."

"Did you get my letter?"

"Yes, and I'm sure Bill will be thrilled to hear that you are not objecting to his release into the community here. Phil Pierson says it may well improve his chances at getting released right away, but we'll have to see on Monday."

"Well, he might as well be free, and living with you, if that's what you want."

"I would be greatly relieved if I could get him out of prison. It's a tough existence for him, after putting in twelve years with US Android, having a very useful and productive lifestyle. He's used to being busy and active, and now he just sits in a cell most of the day."

"Yes, it must be difficult; and he's gone through a lot of humiliation."

"That's true; he used to be an upstanding member of the community, and now he's been stripped of all standing and respect, and banished."

"Mom says he deserved it, but I felt kind of badly for him when it happened. I always liked Bill, and I never wanted anything this bad to happen to him."

"I'm glad you feel that way; that's the way I feel about it too. I don't think he should have ever been convicted; or I guess he was able to plead nolo contendere, which, I've learned from Phil Pierson, means you're not contending the charges against you. Personally, I don't think he did anything so wrong; he's just a victim of society's ultra-conservative view on sexual exchange between an adult and a minor. The laws are supposed to protect kids from getting exposed to sexuality at under the age of eighteen; but probably in many cases, the punishment doesn't fit the crime, and it seems quite overbearing and unnecessary, to me."

"Well don't say that to Mom; she'll just get angry and start spouting off at you. She's hoping they keep Bill locked up for life."

"I suppose she doesn't want to realize that you turned out alright regardless of what happened."

Alyssa tried to cast perspective on their mother's position, "Well, she knows that the trial was hard on me, and she also reminds me constantly, whenever we get onto the subject, that I should feel angry with Bill for having sex with Shayna, when they had a pact not to, as this was what was responsible for me ending up with the bleedthrough sexual memories."

"If you want, I won't mention to Mom that you sent a letter saying you don't object to Bill's release."

"Thanks, I'd appreciate that. I have to live with her; we see each other a couple of times a month; and it's a sore subject, if you know what I mean."

"Yeah, I've only talked to her once since I've been here, and she hung up on me."

"That's just the way she is; I guess we have to accept it."

"Have you had any more developments on the new strain of androids?"

"Yes, we're making a lot of progress on mastering sexual sensation. Hopefully, when people beam themselves into an android they will be able to intensely enjoy sexual activity, assuming this new strain can be mass produced at a reasonable cost."

"So, you still think it will be a couple of years before the new strain might be released into the public?"

"Yes, I'm thinking that it's probably going to be quite a while before android manufacturers can tool up to make the new strain of androids, but maybe the first ones will be coming off the assembly line as soon as next year some time, who knows?"

"That's great news! I'll come back to visit you, and we can go out to dinner together, and have a night out on the town!"

"I'd look forward to that; I miss you Tommy!"

"I miss you too Alyssa.—Well, I'm going to go out to the gate, so I'll sign off; I'll talk to you soon; I'll call you after the hearing."

Tommy hung up and Skyped Kerry, "Hi there gorgeous; I'm at the airport waiting to get on the shuttle, and I had a few minutes, so I thought I'd call and see how your day is going."

"It's going okay; I'm just finishing up on my second programming of the week; this one's going to a retired prison guard. He came here from Earth thirty-one years ago, but he was already well over one hundred years old, and he took an early retirement last year. It must be nice; he has like three hundred and fifty years of retirement ahead of him."

"What, does he have a rich relative or something?"

"No, as I said, he got an early retirement package; that's what he bargained for when he came to planet P. He worked a lot of overtime in his job on Earth, and chose to have it apply to his pension instead of taking it as extra income."

"How did you come to know all this?"

"It came out in the interview, when we were gathering information for the programming."

"I guess he is a lucky guy if he has enough money to retire that early, from working as a prison guard."

"Yeah, well it's not a high paying job, but it comes with benefits."

"Well, I'm sorry I won't be able to see you this weekend, sweety, but I'm visiting Bill tomorrow and Sunday; and Monday is the big day; we'll see if we can get Bill out of prison."

"Oh, I hope things go well; it would be great if you didn't have to fly to Chilton every other weekend to visit Bill in prison anymore."

"You said it sister! I don't fly well; I get sinus headaches from the altitude."

"Well when you get back, I'll have that android you liked, Becky, ready for programming."

"No, not for me; I don't think I want an android, at least not now. I only wanted you to reserve her for Bill, in case he is let out of prison on Monday."

"Oh, I see; that's why you were asking about her the other day . . ."

"Yeah, if Bill gets out, I'm going to see if I can get him a job at Atlas. He used to work in the marketing department at US Android. He actually worked there for twelve years."

"Yes, I know; you told me."

"Oh, I did? I forgot; I'm sure Atlas isn't hiring right now, but maybe Ron will cut me a break."

"Well, first things first; you have to get Bill out of prison."

"Yeah, that's true; I'm jumping the gun."

"Well, I've got to get back to work. The retired prison guard, whom I'm programming this android for, is coming in later this afternoon to pick up her up, and I've still got a couple of hours' work to do before she is ready."

"Okay, I'll let you get back to work. I'll talk to you later . . ."

Saturday morning, Tommy arrived at Chilton Prison a little before 8am. He took off his shoes and his belt, to go through the metal detector as usual.

Putting them back on, he greeted Bill, who was just arriving from the prison block, "Hi Bill! It's good to see you! How are you doing?"

"I'm alright; I'm bored. There's nothing newsworthy in the Chilton paper you sent me a subscription to, and I ran out of good books to read, so it's been difficult passing the time."

"I'll bet you are excited about your hearing on Monday . . ."

"Yeah, that too; I've had some anxiety over that. One of the guys I know on the block, told me they almost never grant probation to a sex offender unless they have taken the sex offender treatment program, and they haven't even offered it here for over a year."

"Do they offer it at other prisons, do you know?"

"I'm told they offer it at Northbrook, but I'm not sure whether they would transfer me there."

"Well let's see what happens Monday, and if they won't grant parole or probation, I'll work on trying to get you transferred. How long is the course?"

"It's a year, but some sex offenders can't even get out after they've taken the course. Apparently, you have to demonstrate beyond a shadow of a doubt, that you have rehabilitated yourself; and some of us just can't seem to do that . . ."

"Well let's hope they at least substantially shorten your sentence. Who knows? They may only keep you here for another couple of years, if that."

"I don't know if I can take another couple of years here, but I guess I may <u>have</u> to."

"I guess we'll find out on Monday."

"So how's life in Alderon?"

"Fine; I just bought the house in Fairhope, which I think I told you about. It's just outside of Alderon. It's about a twenty minute commute to work; maybe a little longer when the traffic is heavy."

"Are you still seeing the married woman?"

"Sally? No, I actually broke it off with her. I started dating Kerry a couple of weeks ago; she's the one who I told you gave me a tour of Atlas's facilities when I first visited there."

"I thought she told you she's seeing someone else pretty seriously; you said he asked her to marry him . . ."

"Well, it's an interesting story; you know how I told you Kerry was a mole at Atlas, and she was feeding Centurion Android information about Atlas's plans and endeavors?"

"Yeah, I remember you told me she was going to quit, and go to work for Centurion."

"She was thinking about it; but when I joined Atlas, I told her I wouldn't keep it a secret that she's been spying on us, unless she ended her arrangement with Centurion."

"I don't get it; what does that have to do with her relationship with this other guy?"

"That's just it; her boyfriend was the one who talked her into being a spy for Centurion; he's worked there for years. I told her she has to stop seeing him too, in order to keep me quiet about her being a mole!"

"You didn't!—And did she agree to that?"

"Yeah, it turns out he has been verbally abusive to her more recently, so that helped make her decision to break it off with him alot easier."

"So she's seeing you now?"

"I told her I wanted to start seeing her, and we've been out on four dates in the last two weeks. I really think she is beginning to like me."

"That's great news! I hear it's hard to find an attractive woman on this planet. They're mostly taken by wealthy men."

"I'm pretty wealthy!" Tommy reminded Bill.

"Yeah, but she doesn't know that, does she?"

"No, I haven't told her what I'm worth yet. She probably assumes I took out a big mortgage to buy the house; which is fine. I want her to like me for who I am. Sally married her husband for money, and I'm sure he's not happy she's having affairs because they don't have natural chemistry between them."

"I see your point. Does she know you're getting two hundred grand a year to help advertise the mind beaming machine?"

"No; but she'll know by the end of the year, because Atlas publishes the salaries of their key people in their annual report."

"Oh, and you think you are a key person there?"

"Well I will be if their mind beaming station gets off the ground; at least I may be."

"I think your advertising campaign would have to generate a lot of success for that to happen; and you're young; you're just starting out."

"That's true; that reminds me, I started the apprentice program at Atlas last week. I'm probably learning a bunch of things you already know, having been in android marketing for twelve years."

"Yeah, if I do get out of here, I probably can't go into that business as a sex offender; no one would hire me."

"Well, we'll see about that. Alyssa and I are both in the android business, and we might be able to pull some strings."

"Listen, I'd be happy to flip burgers if I could just get out of here!"

"Yeah, I know what you mean. Hey, I got a new car!"

"Oh yeah? What'd you get?"

"It's a Lexus sports car; it's hydrogen powered?—It goes from zero to ninety in six seconds!"

"Wow! That's fast! You've got to watch out you don't kill yourself in a car like that."

"No, I drive reasonably; it's mainly the style and the luxury I bought it for. It's a really cool looking car."

"I'm sure it is; I hope I'll get a chance to ride in it soon."

"I'll keep my fingers and toes crossed for you on Monday."

"So are you staying at that club nearby? Are you playing any golf or tennis?"

"Yes, the Stafford Club; I've got a round of golf scheduled for later this afternoon. I'm supposedly playing with a guy who shoots par. I hope he doesn't show me up too badly."

"Are you coming back to visit me again tomorrow morning?"

"Yes; I can't count on your being let out on Monday; I want to visit you every chance I get when I come to Chilton."

"I appreciate that Tommy; it's good to get a glimpse of the outside world, from talking with you. In here, it's the same old boring thing, day after day."

"Well, we hope that will end soon, and you will be back out in the free world!—In many ways, living here on planet P is very similar to living in the United States. I didn't know what to expect before I moved here. Nobody talks much about planet P on Earth, and there wasn't anybody I could ask questions of, because nobody that comes here ever returns to Earth!"

"Well I'm glad you are finding it comfortable living here. It was a real surprise when you showed up to visit me; I thought I was a goner, and I'd be stuck here in prison for forty years. Now, I am hopeful that my sentence might get vastly reduced, and also that I may live a reasonable existence after I get out of here!"

"I hope that is the case, although not even Phil Pierson knows what to expect. There aren't very many cases of this kind that have been brought to a sentence modification hearing, and I think the results have varied widely."

"I understand. I'll try not to get my hopes up too much, so I won't be let down too badly, but it's hard not to feel optimistic at this point."

"What do your cellmate and your friends on the block say about this?"

"Several of them have said I'm lucky to have a family member here fighting for my release. Not many prisoners' family members are willing to come to planet P because they don't want to get stuck here."

"Well I'm glad to be here helping you out, and I hope our efforts are successful."

Just then, the prison guard announced that the visiting session was over. They said their goodbyes as they embraced over the table.

Chapter Twenty-Three

"All rise!" the bailiff commanded. Tommy had arrived at the courthouse promptly at ten, and he sat nervously fidgeting for about twenty minutes before the judge came out of his chambers to start the hearing.

"This is a hearing for the motion of sentence modification for William Symms. The honorable judge Joseph Thompson will preside over this hearing."

Judge Thompson turned to the prosecutor, "Will you please read the charges against Mr. Symms?"

"Yes, your honor; Mr. Symms was charged with sexual assault in the fourth degree. The victim was Alyssa Symms, his stepdaughter. He was sentenced to exile from Earth to planet P, and to life imprisonment, suspended after forty years in a federal penitentiary. It should be pointed out that Mr. Symms had made a pact with Mrs. Symms, to refrain from sexual activity with the family androids which they were psychically connected to, for the duration of the ten-year test period; and he violated this agreement. The State believes this is a significant basis to recommend that Mr. Symms remain incarcerated for the full duration of his sentence. "

There was a pause while Judge Thompson wrote himself a few notes. Then he turned to Phil Pierson, "Mr. Pierson, we will now hear the arguments for the defense. You may tell the court what you have to say about this case, on your client's behalf."

"Thank you Judge," Phil Pierson started off, "Mr. Symms was an upstanding member in the community on Earth, in Natick, just outside of Boston, Massachusetts. He worked as a marketing executive for US Android at their Boston Office for over twelve years, after going through their apprentice program initially. Mr. Symms was asked by his employer to participate in a family-android prototype test program, and he complied with this request, connecting his wife and two stepchildren to a pair of family androids for what was to be a ten year test period. In the ninth year, it was discovered that the victim, his stepdaughter Alyssa, had experienced bleedthrough sexual memories of sexual activity between Mr. Symms and his female android, who was also psychically connected to the victim. She was a minor at age six when she was first connected to the android. Chinese wall software was supposed to protect her from experiencing any sense of sexual activity between Mr. Symms and his android, but the software malfunctioned, and sexual memories were discovered in the victim's online memory file. Mr. Symms did not sexually assault the victim directly, and he had no inkling that she may have been significantly harmed, by these bleedthrough memories of sexual thoughts and acts considered to be very disturbing to his stepdaughter, so we submit that he shouldn't have been convicted of sexual assault on this basis. The victim has written a letter to the court, stating she has no objection to Mr. Symms being released into the community, and her brother, Mr. Symms' stepson, has a statement to make on Mr. Symms' behalf as well."

The judge nodded, "Let's hear what his stepson has to say."

Tommy stood, and the judge addressed him, "Please state your full name, for the record."

"Thomas Symms, your honor. I just have to say that my stepfather Bill has always been a good father to me and Alyssa.

He took his family responsibilities very seriously. He had steady employment with US Android during the whole time we were growing up. He was a good, steady wage earner, and he provided for our every need, from counseling us and educating us, to consoling us at times when we were upset over problems we faced, within our family relations, and in our relationships with our friends and classmates over the years. In addition, Bill provided for us by fulfilling other responsibilities, from taking us clothes shopping, to helping us with our school projects, and providing us with the latest computers and Skype stations to keep in contact with our friends. He and our mother decided to take part in the family-android test project, connecting us to the pair of family-androids after doing much research on how this might affect me and Alyssa. The androids did perform well in almost every aspect. They taught us a lot that our friends didn't know about, helping us to become more mature at a young age, and exposing us to the latest technological advancements. We excelled at our schoolwork, and Alyssa and I also believe that being connected to the androids helped us to become very popular with our classmates. Alyssa was elected class president three times during our junior high and high school years, and she took an early interest in science, developing at a genius level with the help of the noted Dr. Albert Freudenthal during and after college. As a result, she was instrumental in developing mind beaming, which has become a worldwide miracle experienced by millions. I want to again emphasize that my stepfather was completely unaware of any significant disturbance which may have been caused by the bleedthrough sexual thoughts and feelings my sister was exposed to, and we believe he was wrongly convicted of sexual assault. At this time, we request that the court let him out on probation. I have told Bill that he is welcome to come live with me at my house in Fairhope, near Clarion DC, and that I would provide him with an isolated psychic connection to a personal female android, to satisfy his sexual needs, in order to further reduce any risk of reoffending."

Judge Thompson responded, "Thank you Mr. Symms; is there anything else you would like to add, Mr. Pierson, before the court evaluates your client for a sentence modification?"

"Yes, your honor. We wanted to add that Misses Symms had a serious drinking problem which kept her from fulfilling her responsibilities as mother of the victim, pretty much all throughout the period they were connected to the family-androids. We hired Mr. James Pope, a private investigator in the Boston area, and he has provided us with a report of his findings, showing that Misses Symms went to a drug rehab, and has sought alcohol counseling in the last three years; to further substantiate our claim. Mr. Symms has been incarcerated for eleven months, and we ask that you consider this as time served, and grant him probation at this time."

"Thank you Mr. Pierson. Unless the prosecution has anything to add, we will adjourn while we talk this over in my chambers, after which we will reconvene to hear the court's decision on this matter."

The judge, Phil Pierson, and the prosecutor disappeared to discuss the issue. There was a fifteen minute interval before they returned to the courtroom.

The bailiff announced that court was back in session, and Judge Thompson spoke as he looked at Phil Pierson, "I have reviewed the evidence in this case, and determined that there is no reason why Mr. Symms should have been deemed responsible for the sexual bleedthrough memories, and in our legal system's definition he did not commit sexual assault on the victim. The cause seems to have been a software malfunction which nobody involved was aware of until after the fact."

The judge now turned to address Bill, "Mr. Symms, It is therefore my decision to release you on probation effective immediately, provided that Mr. Pierson can show, that you have a residence within the Alderon area where your son will have responsibility for your supervision. Your release is further conditional, pursuant to the laws governing this planet, that given your permanent status as a registered sex offender, you must actively participate in the sex offender treatment program. Probation requirements are that you be prohibited from contact with minors and the victim, you are barred from going to malls and shopping centers, beaches and parks, and you must remain drug and alcohol-free, including E-Tox, for the duration of your ten year probation. I am also stipulating that you maintain full time employment for the duration of your probation. Violation of any of these conditions will subject you to further incarceration for all, or part of the remaining thirty-nine years of your original sentence. Do you understand and agree to these terms, Mr. Symms?"

"Yes, your honor," Bill uttered somewhat woefully, upon hearing the litany of conditions and stipulations.

"Then this hearing is hereby adjourned." The judge banged his gavel, "Next case, Miss Adams?"

Before they could leave the courthouse, Bill had to visit the probation office, where he was given his probation officer's name, and a Skype number to contact her.

He was also told that he had to return to the prison in order to return his state-owned prison clothes, and pick up his personal belongings.

Bill objected, "But I don't <u>want</u> any of my personal belongings! My <u>cellmate</u> can keep them."

The probation officer thought for a few seconds, "Well, if you don't want any of your belongings, there <u>is</u> a way you could circumvent returning to the prison, but you would have to pay a fifty dollar charge to buy the prison clothes you are wearing."

Tommy spoke up, "I'll pay the fifty dollars."

Tommy took a fifty out of his wallet, and once the charge was paid, they left the courthouse together. Once outside, Bill spun around and did a little dance, "I'm free! I can't tell you how good this feels!"

Tommy smiled back at him, "Yes, and it feels great that I have accomplished my mission in coming here! Come on; my rental car is parked this way. Let's get you some clothes, so you can get out of those prison tans."

"Yes, I can't wait to throw them out; that, and these sneakers that I've been wearing for the last year every day."

It turned out to be a chore to find a clothing store that wasn't located in a mall or a shopping center, but they finally found the Burlington Coat Factory store located on the outskirts of Stafford. Tommy bought Bill several outfits and shoes and sneakers, and a suitcase to put them in, to travel back to Alderon. Bill changed into a new outfit and left his prison clothes and his old sneakers in the dressing room.

Tommy had checked out of the Stafford Club hotel facility that morning, and he had his suitcase and golf clubs in the car, so they packed Bill suitcase, loaded it into the back seat, and headed for the airport.

After returning his rental car, they entered the airport terminal building and Tommy sauntered up to the desk, with Bill in tow. The clerk greeted them, "Welcome to global Airlines; what can I do for you?"

Tommy handed the clerk his ticket, "I'm booked on the three-thirty flight to Alderon, but that's almost four hours from now. I'd like to exchange it for a ticket on the next flight you have to Alderon, if possible, and I'd like to buy another ticket as well, for my stepfather who will be traveling with me."

"Okay; let me check to see when the next flight leaves." She punched a few keys, standing at her terminal, and responded after about thirty seconds, "There is a flight which leaves at noon, but you'll have to hurry; it's boarding already."

Tommy nodded, "That's fine."

She turned to Bill, "I'll need to see some identification, sir."

Bill reached into his pocket and pulled out his prison I.D., "This is all I have; will this do?" He handed it to her.

"Have you recently been released from prison?"

"Yes, just today actually," Tommy responded, before Bill could get the words out of his mouth.

"Congratulations!" the clerk said with a friendly smile, "I'll bet you must be happy to be back out in the free world!"

"I sure am!—So is the ID valid for travel?"

"Sure, this is fine. Give me a minute and I'll print out your tickets."

They arrived at Alderon Airport a little after two. After picking up their bags, they took a shuttle bus to Tommy's car, which was parked in the long-term parking lot. "Wow! This is a pretty snazzy car, Tommy; but it's kind of small. Will it fit all our things?"

"Sure; my golf clubs just fit in the trunk, and our suitcases will fit in the back seat."

When they left the airport exit, Tommy headed toward downtown Alderon on the Beltway. "Is this the way to Fairhope?" Bill asked.

"Well, I <u>will</u> take us to the house in Fairhope, but first, I thought we'd stop at a furniture store in Alderon, and buy you a bed and some bedroom furniture."

"Oh, that's a thought. Where will I sleep, until the furniture arrives?"

"We'll see how soon we can get it delivered, but you can sleep on the sofa in the living room until then."

"Okay; anything's more comfortable than those prison beds. It's a three inch thick mattress on a steel plate!"

"I'm so glad we got you out of there. The next thing we have to do is find you a job. You heard the judge; you have to have full time employment."

"Yes, that will be a good trick; nobody wants to hire an ex-felon."

"Well, I've thought of that. I seem to have the in's with Atlas Android; maybe I can get you a job working in the marketing department there."

"Do you think? That would be great!"

"I go into work tomorrow, and I'll try to get an appointment with Ron Goldstein; he's the president. I'll try to convince him to at least give you an interview."

"How is Atlas doing with android sales anyway?"

"Well, the market is pretty well saturated. Most of those who can afford it already have one. However, they're starting a new campaign to offer low cost financing, so that lower income people can afford to buy an android, too. Apparently, a large percentage of the population consists of blue collar workers, either working at, or supporting services to the prisons. There's apparently something like three hundred prisons on the planet. All of the countries on Earth, Earth 2, and Earth 3 currently exile their sex offenders here; that's over five hundred countries altogether, which is why the prison population here is so large."

"Wow! I had heard that there's a lot of prisons on planet P, but I had no idea there were that many."

"There's something like three-hundred-thousand blue collar workers connected with providing direct prison services, and at least another three-hundred-thousand who provide indirect services, like meal service, recreational sports equipment and weight lifting equipment, facility remodeling contractors, and so on, who will be Atlas's target market in the next several years; and then there are something like six-million other blue collar workers on the planet to market to as well."

"Wow! That ought to keep them busy for a good long time. What's the total population of the planet?"

"I think it's a little over twenty million, and rising. There's a fair number of new births every year these days."

"Then if mind beaming takes off and becomes popular, Atlas ought to have a huge potential profit there too."

"Well, the trouble is, it costs a lot to set up a mind beaming station, so I don't know how fast that business will grow."

They reached the city limits of Alderon, and they could see the tall buildings in the center of the city in the distance. "Wow!" Bill remarked, "This looks to be a pretty good sized city in itself!"

"Yes, Alderon is by far the largest city on the planet. There's over two million people living here, including in Clarion DC, which is a district of Alderon, just north of the downtown section. Just like Washington, Clarion DC is the central hub of the government. There are representatives of all the thirty-six states on the planet either visiting or residing here. I think the population of that district is close to a half a million alone."

"That's interesting; how many countries are there on planet P?" Bill asked, his curiosity piqued.

"There's only one; I thought you knew that." Tommy said, looking out of the corner of his eye as he drove.

"Nah, they don't tell us anything in prison; well at least not in protective custody. You can sign up for courses, and actually get an education, if you're in the general population at the prison, but they don't let sex offenders into general pop, because they keep getting shanked. In protective custody, you're just fed and housed, and that's it . . ." A minute of silence went by before Bill spoke again, "About how long a drive is it from here to Fairhope where the house is?"

Tommy answered as they began entering the downtown section of Alderon, "It's about twenty minutes. Barnum Furniture is here on the left; that's where I got most of my furniture. They have a nice selection. We <u>should</u> find something you like."

"How big is the bedroom I'll be staying in?"

"I think it's twelve by sixteen."

Bill's eyes widened, "That's pretty spacious."

"Yeah, I think there's plenty of room for a king size bed with a night table on either side, and a dresser and a desk."

"A king size bed; boy that will be nice."

They picked out the furniture and a bed, and scheduled delivery for Wednesday afternoon, two days away. Next, they bought a computer and a Skype phone for Bill before heading out to the house. When they arrived, Bill took a first look at the house, "Wow! This is a really nice house; it's big!"

"It's right on the lake; I'm having a dock built, and I bought a thirty-six foot boat with an inboard engine and a cabin that sleeps four!"

"Well, I'd say you're living in the lap of luxury, young man."

"I figured if we're stuck on this planet for life, we might as well be comfortable. Come on in and I'll show you around."

Tommy gave Bill a tour of the house, after which they fixed dinner and ate in front of the TV. Afterward, while Bill cleaned up and loaded the dishes into the dishwasher, Tommy excused himself and went upstairs to Skype Alyssa and give her the news, “Hi Alyssa, how are you?”

“I’m fine; I just got back from having dinner with Mom. She’s staying here in Philadelphia for a few days. She’s attending a three day conference at the Sheraton in downtown.”

“Okay; listen, I wanted to give you the news; Bill got let out on probation today! He’s going to live with me here in Fairhope.”

“Isn’t that something! I’ll bet you’re relieved that he’s finally out of prison.”

“I sure am; it makes it all worthwhile that I came to planet P; however I have to find him a job; he has lots of restrictions and stipulations, and one of them is that he be employed full time for the duration of his ten year probation.—Oh, and that reminds me; One of his restrictions is that he can’t have any contact with you, as the victim.”

Alyssa shook her head at the ridiculousness of it all, “He’s probably not going to find a decent job, as a sex offender and an ex-felon.”

“Well, that may be true, but I’m going to try and get him a job in the marketing department at Atlas.”

“I don’t know if they will <u>hire</u> him, but I wish you luck in trying.”

“I’m going to approach Ron Goldstein tomorrow about it. We’ll see what he says.”

“I suppose you have plenty of room for him in that big house of yours.”

“Yes; I’m sure he’ll be very comfortable here. We just bought furniture for his room this afternoon, and it will be here in a couple of days.”

“I hope you’re not going through your money too quickly.”

Tommy shook his head, “No, not at all; I’ve still got well over twenty-four million, and I’m making sixteen-thousand a month; so I won’t even have to dip into the principal.”

“I guess you’re in pretty good shape financially.”

“Yes I am. They’re starting work on putting in my new Jacuzzi next Monday, and the dock on the lake should be built by the end of the month.”

"—And you said you bought a boat; will it be too cold to go out in it by then?"

"I don't know how quickly it turns cold here in the fall, but I'll probably get a few boat rides in before I have to take the boat out of the water for the winter."

"Speaking of leisure time, I'm going to Mexico for two weeks next month with Ed."

"The physicist?"

"Yes; we're all taking time off next month. We're kind of burned out. Albert says if we take a little break and rest up a bit, he's projected that we may be able to complete development of the new generation of androids by early next year. Then it will be in the hands of the android companies to tool up to mass-produce them and release them into the public as soon as possible."

"That's great! I know you've been working around the clock for several months straight on that project."

"Yeah, it will be nice to take a break."

"I'm sure it will; you certainly deserve it; and with all the money you're going to be making, maybe you <u>too</u> could find a new house soon, and maybe get an android servant or two, to wait on you."

"Yeah, I might do that too."

"Well, I just wanted to give you the news, and see how you were. I guess I'll sign off and go back down to visit with Bill."

"Okay; it's always good to talk to you, Tommy; I love you!"

Bill and Tommy watched TV and talked until eleven, when Tommy said he had to get to bed in order to get up for work in the morning.

Bill slept on the couch, with his clothes on, like he had in prison for the last eleven months.

Tommy entered Kim Tomlin's office a little before nine the next morning. Kim looked up from her work to greet him, "Hi; I see you're right on time again; how did things go in Chilton?"

"They went great! They let Bill off on probation, and he came back to Alderon with me yesterday afternoon."

"That <u>is</u> great; I'm happy for you. I know you've been looking forward to getting him out of prison since you arrived here."

"Yeah, mission accomplished; but he has all sorts of restrictions, and he has to find full time employment. I'm going to ask Ron if he could come to work for Atlas; he has a background in marketing; he worked for US Android for about twelve years."

"Good luck with that; Atlas doesn't usually hire ex-felons."

"Well maybe Ron would be willing to make an exception; it can't hurt to ask . . ."

"You're right; it can't hurt to ask. Listen, I've got good news; Clarion Capital signed the <u>contracts</u> yesterday afternoon! It looks like we have financing not only for building the beaming station, but also for low interest financing on sales of new androids to lower income workers."

"Wow! That's wonderful! So now we can begin advertising?"

"Yes we can. Ron has decided he's going to make the pitch himself; we're going to be filming a commercial later this week, which should begin airing next <u>week</u>!"

"Wow! He's not wasting any time!"

"Yes, we have to get going on this right away; the company is in financial straits; which is also why your stepfather may have difficulty landing a position here in the near future."

"We'll see; maybe I could take a pay cut, to bring him on."

"That's a thought; I'll tell Ron you'd like to see him, and you two can discuss it."

"Thanks;—if you don't have anything more pressing for me to do, I'll be in my office, working on my apprenticeship studies."

Tommy worked on his computer until about three o'clock, when he got a Skype call from Ron Goldstein, "Hi Tom, how are your studies going?"

"Good; I'm most of the way through the sales presentation section of the course. Maybe by next week I'll be starting on the market analysis tutorial."

"I'd say you're making good progress. Kim said you wanted to see me?"

"Yes; do you have a few minutes for me this afternoon?"

"I've got another appointment in about twenty minutes. Why don't you take a break from your studies, and come and see me now."

"Sure; I'll be right up."

Tommy left his desk right away, and took the elevator up one floor. Sarah greeted him as he entered Ron Goldstein's outer office, "Hi Tom; go right in. I just sent in some checks for him to sign while you are talking!" She said with a sarcastic grin.

Tommy walked in and found Ron sitting behind his desk, with paperwork spread out all around him, "Hi Ron, this shouldn't take long; I can see you're busy."

"Sure; why don't you have a seat, and I'll be with you in a minute." A couple of minutes passed by, and then he looked up from his work, "Okay, that's finished; what's up?"

"Well I don't know if Kim told you, but my stepfather was released yesterday on probation . . ."

"Oh! Congratulations; I know you were hoping to get him out of prison."

"Yes, well now that he's out, one of his probation requirements is that he be employed full time, and I was wondering if you would consider hiring him here; he was a marketing executive for US Android for twelve years, and I think he may be able to help us with our new advertising campaign."

"Well?—I don't know where we're going to get the money to pay him, for one thing; there's no money in the budget, in fact I have to lay off workers in the next few months."

"Kim mentioned to me that we are at low ebb financially right now, but with these new marketing initiatives coming on board, who knows; you may be hiring people <u>back</u> in the next several months. However, I had an idea; I could forfeit some of my salary this year in order to provide cash to pay him; what do you think?"

"It would mean that much to you, huh?"

"To be honest with you, he's going to have a very hard time finding a decent job. There's only two android companies on the planet, that I know of, and I've heard that most companies won't hire an ex-felon."

"Well, that's usually our position too;" Ron paused briefly, as he considered this obstacle, "But why don't you bring him in on Friday morning and introduce us. I'll send him down to marketing for an interview, and maybe I'll make an exception, as a favor to you."

"That would be great! I'd really appreciate it; and he would probably be a worthy addition to staff around here, with all of his knowledge and experience."

"I'll look forward to meeting him then; shall we say nine o'clock?"

"I'm sure that will be fine; I'll tell him."

Tommy went back to his office. He was too excited to work, so he Skyped Kerry, "Hi Kerry; did you hear the news?"

"What news?"

"My stepfather Bill got out of prison on probation, and he came back here with me yesterday afternoon!"

"Wow, that's fantastic! Where is he now? At your house in Fairhope?"

"Yeah, when I left for work this morning, he was hooking up his new computer on the kitchen table. His new furniture arrives tomorrow."

"Wow, that's fast."

"Yeah, when you're buying four thousand dollars' worth of furniture, they bend over backwards for you!"

"What did you get him?"

"A bed with a carved wooden headboard, and a top-of-the-line king size mattress, as well as a matching dresser and nightstands for either side of the bed.—I also got him a computer desk, and a rolling chair. Then, as we were walking out, we saw an electric easy chair that looked great, so I bought him that, and a floor lamp for reading."

"Sounds like you're taking really good care of him."

"Well, he took really good care of me and my sister, the whole time we were growing up."

"I suppose that's true; I guess he deserves it. Hey, by the way, you mentioned that he might want your android, Becky; the one we set aside for you but you didn't want?"

"Yeah, I was telling him about that last night."

"Well, he can come in any time, and I'll schedule him to begin the interview process with the intake division. As soon as he's finished with the opening interviews, I can begin Becky's programming."

"Great! He'll actually be here on Friday; he has a job interview at nine. Would someone in intake have time to work with him after that?"

"Sure; new android sales have been really slow these days. There's no one on the schedule even, until next Tuesday. I've been spending time going through inventory; it's pretty boring . . . —I'll tell you what; just buzz me on my cell when he's finished with his job interview; and I'll see that he gets in to meet with an intake interviewer in short order."

"Aren't you going to comment on the fact that Bill is applying here for work?"

"Yes, that does sound strange, since they just announced at the Monday morning staff meeting that there are going to be some layoffs."

"Get this; I told Ron that I'd forfeit some of my pay, to provide cash, so they can afford to pay Bill."

"You didn't!"

"Yes, I did; you have no idea how hard it is to gain employment as a sex offender; nobody wants to hire you, unless you find a special situation like this."

"But how are you going to make your house payments?"

"I don't have any house payments; I bought the house with cash."

"Cash? Where did you get the money for that?"

"My mother gave me some money. Don't worry, I'll have plenty of money to survive. Bill needs full time employment in order to avoid violating his probation; they'll send him back to jail!"

"Oh; I didn't realize it was that serious."

"Yeah, well anyway, Ron's going to have him meet with Paul Klein; and Bill might also get to meet with some of the marketing staff.—You know Paul Klien, don't you?"

"Yes, I know Paul; I see him at the Monday morning staff meetings; he's always after me to have lunch with him."

"What can I say; you're a very pretty girl; or young woman, I should say."

"Thanks . . ."

"That reminds me; would you like to have dinner with me Friday night?"

"Alright; where should we go; Valley's again?"

"Sure, I like that place. I'll pick you up at eight?"
"Okay, it's a date!"

Tommy breezed through the rest of his work day. He couldn't remember Bill's Skype number, and he didn't write it down and bring it with him to work, and so breaking the news to Bill about the job interview which Ron Goldstein had granted, as well as the first interview scheduled with the intake department, as a first step in customizing Becky's programming to serve Bill as his personal android, would have to wait until he got home.

The traffic on the Beltway was unusually slow, but Tommy made it home a little after five-thirty. Bill was sitting at the kitchen table, glued to his computer, "Oh hi Tommy, I've been on this computer all day; I've mostly been looking for work, but I'm not having any luck. How was your day?"

"It was great! I have good news for you; Ron Goldstein, the president of Atlas Android, invited you to come in for a job interview on Friday morning! He wants me to introduce you, and then he's going to have you meet with Paul Klein, the head of marketing afterward."

"That's my boy! That's really great, because I've been striking out all day. As soon as I disclose that I am a sex offender, they all say, I'm sorry, but there are no positions available for you here."

"Well, I'm pretty sure that once the folks at Atlas get to meet you and talk with you about your experience in android marketing, they will want to hire you. Besides," Tommy said with a grin, "I actually offered to take a salary cut in order to provide the money to pay you, because otherwise, there's no money in the <u>budget</u>, and they're actually laying off workers, at this point."

"Tommy, I can't thank you enough!—But I <u>don't</u> want to take money out of your pocket . . ."

"I don't need it; and you need a job. Besides, it's only temporary. The largest venture capital firm in the state just signed contracts to provide financing for lower income workers to buy androids on credit!—And they are also providing funding for Atlas to build a mind beaming station. I can only figure that their financial troubles will be behind them within a matter of months!"

"Then maybe they'll raise your salary back to the level it was, or higher in the future." Bill was catching up with Tommy's exuberance.

"Right; the way I see it, you are a shoe-in, if they can get past the sex offender status."

"Yeah, that's a big "if" . . ."

Tommy knocked on Kerry's door promptly at eight on Friday night, and she opened the door and greeted him with a hug and a kiss, "I missed you last weekend, and I know we Skyped a couple of times this week, but I haven't seen you in over a week. I've missed having you around!—I suppose you've been spending a lot of time with your stepfather, huh?"

"Yeah, we've had dinner and spent the evenings together, every night this week."

"That's good; I'm glad you two are close. It's nice to have family around you, isn't it?"

"I wish I could have more of my family and friends around me, but yes, it's been nice spending time with Bill."

"That's nice; I'm ready, shall we go?"

"Sure; how is the interview process going with Bill, as far as creating the profile for Becky's programming?"

"Tina says that your stepfather was a perfect gentleman; whereas she's used to men flirting with her all during the interview process."

"Yeah, I've met Tina; she's pretty good-looking, too . . ."

"Watch it, Mister!" Kerry gave him a fake frown.

"She doesn't begin to measure up to your beauty, babe . . ." Tommy complimented.

Kerry smiled, "Some people would argue with you on that!" she said modestly, toning down his comment.

Tommy got back to the subject, "Has Bill seen Becky yet?"

Kerry raised her eyebrows while nodding her head up and down, "When he saw Becky, he almost flipped! He said she's absolutely gorgeous!"

"She is really beautiful. It will be nice to have her around the house; especially if I don't have to take care of her."

"I think you have it backwards, silly; an android takes care of you!"

"Yeah, well I don't want one; I want the real thing!"

"Lucky thing I have Abby; because I won't cook or clean for you!" she joked.

They had a nice dinner at Valley's, and afterward Tommy invited Kerry to come back to the house with him.

When they arrived at the house, they found Bill watching TV in the living room. "Hi Tommy, hi Kerry! I was just watching a documentary on the hydrogen-powered engine. Do you want to join me?"

Kerry spoke up, "I'm afraid I don't have much interest in watching <u>that</u>."

Tommy chimed in, "I'm just going to give Kerry a tour of the house, and then we might sit out on the back deck for a while; it's a warm night. You're welcome to join us if you want."

"No, that's alright; I'm involved in this program. You two go ahead; don't let me interrupt you."

"Okay; suit yourself," Tommy said nonchalantly, preferring to spend some time with her alone anyway, "Kerry, shall I show you the house?"

"Yes, please do; I'm anxious to get the tour."

Tommy walked her through the house. As he had done with Sally, he saved his bedroom for last. When they entered it, she took one look around and noticed how spacious it was, and how well decorated, "Wow, this is really nice! You have quite a nice house; it must have been quite expensive."

"I paid over half-a-million for it, actually. What's really nice is that it is right on the lake."

"Yeah, you told me you are having a dock built, and you bought a boat."

"Yes, if the weather is still nice enough after the dock is built and the boat is in the water, I'll take you out for a ride."

"I'd like that. I haven't been on a boat since I was about eleven. One of my uncles had a motorboat, but he found he couldn't afford all of the expenses associated with it, so he sold it several years ago."

"That's too bad; well anyway the boat I bought is a thirty-six footer, and it has a cabin with a galley in it, so we could even cook dinner on it if we wanted."

"Sure! If there's room for Abby to come, we could have her cook for us! I see you even have a wet bar in the corner over here."

"Yeah, it came with the house. I don't drink, so there's no booze in it, but I have the small refrigerator stocked with juice and soft drinks. There's a small deck just beyond the slider on the back wall here; how about if I fix us some drinks and we can sit out there for a bit?"

"Sure, that would be nice."

They sat for a few minutes, sipping their drinks and chatting, and then Kerry got up and walked to the railing and looked out into the lighted back yard. She could see a few lights out on the water in the distance.

Tommy walked up silently behind her, close enough that he could smell her heavenly scent. She turned around, sensing his presence, and the two met eye to eye, inches apart.

He leaned over and kissed her gently on the lips. When he pulled back, she smiled at him, so he kissed her again. They embraced each other and kissed passionately for a long time. "Stay with me tonight," Tommy coaxed.

"Okay," she said brightly.

They went in and fell on the big, soft bed together, making love in heated passion for quite some time. Afterward, Tommy waited until she fell asleep, and then he cuddled up to her and held her until he fell asleep too. They slept blissfully until past ten, the next morning.

They awoke at about the same time, and Tommy invited Kerry to take a bath with him in the big double tub in the spacious master bathroom.

She sat behind him and held him as they soaked. He laid back against her, enjoying her soft, warm body, and her gentle touch. At that moment, he wished she might be his woman for life.

Chapter Twenty-Four

THE FOLLOWING FRIDAY, TOMMY took the day off. Bill had been hired by Atlas Android, and was to start work on the following Monday.

They slept in a little bit, and were both up around nine-thirty. Bill fixed breakfast for them while they talked in the kitchen, "So did Kerry tell me it's today that she will have finished programming Becky for you?" Tommy asked.

"Yes, she told me I can come in to pick Becky up any time after noon."

"That's great! I've decided I'm going to give you some money, for you to get set up with whatever you need to start out. When's the next time you will see your probation officer?"

"She wants me to come in every Thursday morning at ten, and then the sex offender treatment group meets afterward until noon."

"Well it's a good thing you got your driver's license yesterday, so you can get around for these things. Did you arrange to get the time off from work every week, to see your probation officer and go to group?"

"Yes, Paul Klein is being very flexible and supportive. I explained the background of what happened to me, and he doesn't believe I'm any kind of a risk; in fact he thinks it's pretty ridiculous, all the restrictions and requirements imposed on me, given what happened."

"Yeah, me too, of course. How about if we go downtown after breakfast and open you a bank account, and put some money in it. That way you can go shopping for a car and whatever else you need. The back seat of my car is so small that I don't even know if Becky will fit in there with us. Maybe you could buy yourself a car and pick her up in it yourself this afternoon."

"That's quite generous of you; I really appreciate all you are doing for me."

"It's the least I could do, considering that Mom set me and Alyssa up with some money, even though she took all of yours. Besides,

I'm very thankful to you for taking care of us so well, the whole time we were growing up."

After breakfast was finished, and the dishes were cleaned up, Tommy took Bill downtown to the main branch of the Bank of Alderon, where he drew up a check for five-hundred-thousand, and handed it to Bill.

"Wow! This is an incredibly large sum of money! Are you sure you want to give me this much? I mean I can probably buy even a <u>new</u> car for under thirty-thousand . . ."

"As I said earlier, it's the least I can do, considering all you have done for me and Alyssa; and in light of the fact that I have twenty-five million, due to the fact that you took the initiative to talk Mom into signing us up for the family-android test project; which I think went remarkably well, personally."

"Well alright, if you insist.—But I may be buying you some pretty expensive birthday gifts!" Bill joked.

Tommy smiled, "I'm just going to walk down the street to the cigar store while you open an account. You may actually want to open a savings, and a checking account."

"Yes, I certainly do, with this much money."

After Bill opened his accounts and made his deposits, Tommy took Bill to "auto dealership row," and they drove through the lots, eyeing the new cars. After driving around a bit, they pulled up to one of the dealerships. Bill got out of the car first, and walked up to an attractive four door model. A salesman was quick to approach, "Can I help you sir?"

"Yes; how much does one of these new Alpha's cost?"

"Well first, let me tell you that this is a hydrogen powered sedan, with an eight speed automatic transmission, air conditioning, power windows, and a multi-media stereo system. This one also has a sunroof. It sells for thirty-three-ten. Would you like to take it for a spin?"

"Thirty-three thousand, huh . . . Yeah, sure; Tommy? You wanna come?"

The three of them piled into the deep blue Alpha and pulled out of the lot. Bill took it out onto the beltway and accelerated to highway speed, "These hydrogen powered cars really do get up and go!" he commented, "And it rides nice and smooth."

When they got back to the dealership, Bill parked the car, got out, and walked around it. The salesman started to speak, but Bill cut him off, "I'll give you thirty-thousand cash for it right now; do we have a deal?"

The salesman shook his head, "I can't approve of that kind of deal myself, but let me speak to the manager and we'll see what he says."

Bill drove away from the dealership in his new Alpha about two hours later, after haggling with the manager over the price, and going through a tedious registration process.

Tommy had left as soon as Bill had hammered out a deal and signed the paperwork. He had packed his golf clubs in the trunk, so he headed straight to Brantwood Country Club for a round of golf.

Bill had butterflies in the stomach, as he pulled into the parking garage at the Atlas Android building. It was almost four o'clock. Feeling both tired from his long ordeal of purchasing and registering a new car, and excited with the anticipation of picking up Becky, set the stage for a peculiar state of mind indeed. Collecting himself somewhat, as he emerged from his car, he straightened his clothes, and made his way to the android pickup area; once there, giving the clerk his name.

She pulled up his information on the screen in front of her, "Oh yes; you're here to pick up Becky one-sixty-four."

"I never heard a number after her name before. Does that mean there are a hundred-and-sixty-three other Becky's?"

"Well there's thirty-six states, and eighteen million other people on the planet, outside of Alderon. You'll probably never see another Becky model, but if you do, she'll tell you that she's not yours right away, if you ask her to do something for you."

"That's fair enough, I suppose."

"I'll see if she's ready. Who is the programmer?"

"Kerry Arnold."

"Kerry; okay," She punched the intercom, "Kerry, there's a William Symms out here to pick up Becky one-sixty-four."

"Okay, I'll bring her right out."

A minute later, Kerry and Becky came out walking side by side. Kerry gave Bill a friendly wave, "Here she is!"

"Hi Bill, I'm Becky; it's nice to meet you," she stuck out her hand for him to shake, "Or would you prefer a kiss?"

Bill raised his eyebrows at Kerry, and then turned back to Becky, "No, we can wait for that until when we get home."

Kerry beamed a proud smile, "I think you'll find her to your liking; but if you have any problems or questions, just Skype me. If I don't answer, leave me a message and I promise to get back to you as soon as I can."

Bill smiled back, "I've got your Skype number programmed into my cell, but I hope I won't have to bother you."

"Well, you've owned an android before, so you probably know what to do. Shall I leave you two to get acquainted?"

"Yes, I'm a bit worn out; I've been all over town today, and I just finished the experience of buying a car," Bill said as he rolled his eyes.

Kerry commiserated, "Oh; I know how long and drawn out, and stressful that can be."

"So we'll just be going along, and I'll catch up to you later."

Bill took Becky's hand and led her out to his car. As they approached it, Becky broke the silence, "Shall I drive?"

"Not on your life, sister; I just bought this car and I'm driving us home!"

Okay, that's fine. I'm programmed to serve you in every way; just tell me what you want."

"Well why don't you climb into the passenger's seat."

As they had approached the car from the rear, Becky sat in the nearest passenger seat, which was the back seat. "Hey! What are you doing?! No, always sit in the front passenger's seat when I'm driving, unless I tell you otherwise."

Silently, without a word, Becky moved to the front seat, as ordered, and they pulled out of the parking garage. When they reached the entrance to the Beltway, Bill could see it was stopped-up with rush hour traffic, "Oh man; it's probably going to be a long ride home."

"What is the address of your destination, if I may ask?"

"Twelve Evergreen Street, Fairhope; why do you ask?"

"If you want to get there as quickly as possible, don't get on the Beltway; go past the underpass, and take a right on Algonquin Road at the next light."

"Oh, what, do you have GPS or something?"

"I have Internet access to a satellite overview of all the streets in the area, including the average speed travelers are driving at on those roads at any given time."

"So you've computed us a route, on the back roads, that will take us less time?"

"We should reach our destination in approximately twenty-three minutes, using the route I suggest."

"Wow, that's great! It would take us almost an hour I think, if we took the beltway."

"Fifty-six minutes is my projection, using that route."

"You can be pretty handy to have around!"

He turned to her and she was smiling at him. She was so pretty; like a goddess. "You smell really nice; what, did Kerry put some perfume on you?"

"No, I actually have scent glands, and I emit a scent like a natural woman."

"No kidding! What will they think of next?"

"The scent lasts three months. You'd have to take me to any Atlas outlet to recharge my scent, and there's now over two dozen different scents to choose from; so if you ever don't like my scent, you can change it at any time; for an additional charge, of course."

"So if I don't want to spend any more money, you'll be scent-free, like a dryer sheet, in about three months, Huh?"

"Turn left up ahead on Mystic Street," Becky interrupted.

Becky's route was much less tedious than sitting in traffic, and it got them home in about twenty-five minutes. She followed him into the kitchen, "I'm hungry; can you fix me something to eat?"

"Sure; what would you like?"

"I'd like some soup, and a ham sandwich with cheese, lettuce and mayonnaise. "

"Okay, will you show me where the ingredients are?"

"Bill familiarized her with where the refrigerator and the pantry were, and she made him lunch. Afterward, she cleaned up, "The kitchen is dirty; shall I clean it for you?" she asked.

He stepped up to her and kissed her. She had soft, warm, full lips, and her scent intoxicated him, "Not now," he said, " Follow me up to my bedroom; let's see what kind of lover you are."

She followed him upstairs silently. Bill closed his bedroom door behind them, and locked it in case Tommy returned. He turned to her and kissed her again. This time, she responded passionately, which excited Bill all the more.

"Oh yes!" he said to himself with excitement, "This going to be fun!"

He took off the rest of her clothes, and he was very aroused by her naked body. She was anatomically correct in every way. He laid her down on the bed, and climbed on top of her. He made love to her until he had a very satisfying orgasm, and then he rolled off of her, "Come snuggle up to me; I want to take a nap with you."

They got under the covers, and he held her, content with her warmth, as he fell asleep. She felt good, and he thoroughly enjoyed her lovely scent as he buried his head into her neck, her long blonde hair falling all around him. Life was going to be great with her, he thought.

Bill awoke to the sound of Tommy calling his name. He got up and put on a robe, "Let's get you dressed, and then I'll take you downstairs to meet Tommy," he said to Becky while she was still lying in bed." He's my stepson."

She got up and dressed herself, and they went downstairs. Bill found Tommy in the kitchen, "Hi Tommy; how was your golf game?"

"It was fine; it was a beautiful afternoon to be outside." Tommy had seen Bill's new car in the driveway, and now he spied a pair of women's underwear laying on the floor, "I see you picked up Becky," he said with a smile.

Bill realized how Tommy surmised this, and smiled back, "Yes, I finally got to Atlas Android around four."

"Oh, and are you enjoying her company?"

"Very much so; she made me a late lunch, and I took her up to my bedroom for a roll in the hay."

"Yeah, I guess it's been a year or more, since you've had any sexual activity; you must have been pretty horny!"

"Yeah, well she was really good in bed!"

"Good; I'm glad things are working out well with her so far."

"They sure are! I'm going to take her clothes-shopping tomorrow."

"You'll have to go into the dressing room with her, of course; she can't function without someone else's eyes to guide her."

"What a shame!" Bill said sarcastically, "I'll have to watch as she changes into her new outfits!"

"She <u>is</u> absolutely gorgeous, and she <u>does</u> have a lovely body," Tommy commented.

"Yeah, well I suppose you prefer the real thing."

"Yes; that reminds me; I invited Kerry to come over tonight. She'll be here around eight. Will you have Becky make dinner for us?"

"It would be my pleasure," Becky responded, entering the room.

"I just went shopping, and I got us a roast beef," Tommy informed.

"Mm; my favorite!" Bill replied enthusiastically.

"What time would you like me to have dinner ready?" Becky asked.

Tommy thought for a second, "Maybe around eight-thirty or so."

"Well then maybe I'd better get the roast into the oven; it's prime rib?" she asked.

"Yes, it's about four pounds," Tommy replied.

"It may not be ready until near nine o'clock," she said knowingly.

"That's fine; we'll have a drink, and talk out on the deck, if it's warm enough."

They all ended up having a lovely evening together. After dinner, they watched a movie on TV together. Tommy and Kerry turned in early, and Bill stayed up late, with Becky to keep him company, until he was ready to go to bed around midnight.

CHAPTER TWENTY-FIVE

AS ANOTHER TWO YEARS and eight months passed, Bill and Tommy and Kerry continued to work for Atlas Android. Atlas and Centurion had both brought mind beaming services to the market, and were sharing in the success and popularity of the new development.

Android sales had picked up considerably for Atlas, as a result of their marketing initiative to sell androids to lower income workers via long range, low cost financing.

Seeing Atlas's success, Centurion Android started offering similar financing, and the two companies continued to compete for market share in new android sales, which was booming.

Tommy and Kerry had gotten married, and Kerry had given birth to boy and girl twins, just as they had planned to have.

Neither Tommy or Bill had tried mind beaming yet, because they were waiting for the new strain of androids, which Alyssa and Dr. Freudenthal had developed, to come to the market.

The Real-Life Android Company of America was the first to release the newly mass-produced model of androids specifically designed for people to have their mind beamed into, affording taste and sensory perception.

Alyssa Skyped Tommy as soon as she read the article posted online, announcing the good reviews on the new line of receptor androids, which several android manufacturers releasing them in the U.S. and abroad had been testing, as far as the effects of mind beaming.

"Hi Tommy; I haven't talked to you in a while; how are you?"

"I'm doing well, thank you; I just got back from a three day business trip to Terracotta, which is a state that's about a seven hour plane ride away from here. Of course, the trip was a bit tedious, but I am actually enjoying traveling when I have to for work. I was initially convinced I wouldn't enjoy this at all."

"That's good! How are Kerry and the twins?"

"They are doing just fine. Kerry returned to work last month. She takes Sarah and Jesse with her, and leaves them at the day care center while she works. She says it gives her a nice break from full-time, around the clock attention to the twins."

"Well, if you remember, a few months ago, in January I think, I had called and told you, when I heard, on the news, that several android companies around the world have tooled up, and are manufacturing the new strain of receptor androids that you can beam into and have sensory perception."

"Yeah, I remember that," Tommy confirmed.

"Well, now a slew of them have gone into service; and the reports are consistently saying that the results, when polling the first users, are that it is a very satisfying and trouble-free experience. I just heard another news special on it last night!"

"That's great news! We've been waiting for this to happen for a long time."

"Yes; and it means that you all can beam yourselves back to Earth and come for a visit!"

"Yeah, isn't that great?!"

"Well, when do you think you might come?"

"I don't know;" Tommy scratched his chin as he thought, "Maybe we can get some time off next month; I'll see if I can arrange it."

"That would be super! I can't wait to see you in person."

"Yeah, I hope it won't be too weird for you, you know, when we come and visit in a different body."

"I'm sure I'll get used to it. It will be <u>you</u> inside, and that's what counts."

"I suppose so. Well, I've got to get ready for work, so I'll sign off for now, but I'll Skype you later and we can talk some more."

Tommy got dressed and went downstairs. He found Bill and Kerry in the kitchen. Becky was making breakfast for them.

"Where's Abby?" he asked.

"Oh, I left her upstairs in the twins' room. I woke up early this morning and I didn't want to disturb you, so we left the bedroom quietly."

"Thanks, that was considerate of you. I didn't wake up until about twenty minutes ago. Alyssa just Skyped me to inform me that the new strain of androids, being manufactured in mass quantities now back on earth, have passed the initial tests with flying colors! Apparently, almost everyone trying it is having a wonderful experience! She invited us to come visit with her and try out the "beamed experience!" What do you think? Do you want to come to Earth with me, and meet Alyssa in person?"

Kerry was a little apprehensive, "I don't know; I may not want to be one of the first ones to try beaming into these new androids."

"Oh? You think we should wait a while until others have had successful journeys, being beamed from here into the new androids?"

"Well it would be safer . . ."

"I suppose you're right." Tommy turned to Bill, "How about you, Bill? Are you going to beam yourself back to Earth for a visit?"

"Sure! I think it would be a novel idea; I'd look forward to seeing my old stomping grounds!"

Tommy got more excited, thinking about it, "Me too! I miss seeing Alyssa, and I miss Boston. Maybe I could see a few old friends . . ."

Bill nodded, "I've been Skyping with some of the people I used to work with at US Android. Some of them have moved out of the area, but I could visit with Barry and Kathleen; and John Posthauer is still in the area. He's working with a company by the name of Real-Life Android now."

"Isn't that something! Alyssa told me that's company which first <u>manufactured</u> the new strain of androids . . ."

"Huh! I haven't spoken with John in almost a year, and he never mentioned that they were working on developing mass production of them. I wonder if last time I talked to him, he was even aware that his company was working on that initiative . . ."

Tommy continued selling the idea of accompanying him to Earth, "Well I'm pretty sure Alyssa would see you, but we'd have to ask her not to tell Mom."

Kerry's curiosity peaked, "How come your mother couldn't know?"

Tommy gave her a wry smile, "Because technically, Bill isn't supposed to have any contact with Alyssa, and Mom might try to make some trouble for him if she caught wind of his visiting her."

Kerry began to understand, "Oh, Bill can't have direct contact with Alyssa, but if his mind is beamed into an android on earth, would that be considered a violation?—Is it his body or his mind, that can't have contact with her?"

"That's a good question," Tommy said ethereally, as he contemplated it.

Kerry took advantage of their new resource, "Becky, are there any laws preventing a person beamed into an android from acts which they might not be able to do while living in their own body?"

Becky was silent; this question was beyond her; it did not compute.

Tommy fielded the question to the best of his ability, "Well no, not yet, at least not that I know of, but I'm thinking that Mom could go to the authorities, and I don't know how they would look upon this; they might disallow him from being beamed into an android back on Earth, at least eventually if not right away . . ."

Bill piped up, "Yeah, I don't know if I could even go; I'd have to clear it with my probation officer. I think there may be some new restrictions on mind beaming, for those on parole or probation."

Tommy thought for a second, "I know you have to report to your probation officer every week, but couldn't you beam yourself to Earth in between? She'd probably never even know . . ."

Bill shook his head, "No, I wouldn't want to chance it; if I violate my probation, they'll send me back to prison, and I can't have that happen!"

"Yeah, you're right; you're better off asking your probation officer and hoping she'll say yes," Tommy replied, changing his mind.

Becky was flipping eggs with her back to them. She looked over her shoulder at them, "I just checked on the internet while you guys were talking, and there is a new law that was just passed preventing sex offenders from beaming anywhere without written permission from their probation officer."

Bill shook his head, "Yeah, I was afraid of that. Well, I see Makeisha tomorrow morning; I'll ask her."

Becky took down three plates from the cupboard, to dish up breakfast, while announcing, "It's eight-ten; you all have about twenty minutes before you have to leave for work."

Kerry looked over at the clock, "Did you feed Sarah and Jesse?"

"No, not yet," Becky replied, "I'll feed them now; but otherwise, they're dressed and ready to go."

Early that afternoon, Tommy was working in his office when Ron Goldstein knocked on the door frame and looked in, "Kim said you wanted to see me?"

"Oh yes; I was talking with my sister this morning. She told me that the new strain of androids are now being manufactured; you know, the ones you can beam your mind into and have taste and sensory perception?"

"Yes, I was reading about that on the internet this morning; that's an exciting new development, isn't it?"

"Yes, it sure is. Well, she invited me and Bill and Kerry to visit next month, and I was wondering if we could take some time off to go?"

"Sure, I don't see why not. Ron took out his pocket computer and looked at the calendar, "Why don't you go on the tenth, after the Monday morning staff meeting; that's four-and-a-half weeks from now."

"That will be great! I'll tell Kerry and Bill. I've been looking forward to this for a long time."

"How long would you be gone?"

"Well, I haven't decided yet; I think for a week or two, if that's alright."

"Well you let me know; I think that will be fine.—Is there anything else?"

"No, except you might want to consider buying some of these androids and having them sent <u>here</u>. It might be very popular for our customers to try beaming into one. It would make a vacation a lot more enjoyable . . ."

"Yes, I'm well-aware of that; in fact I just placed an order for a hundred of the new receptor androids late this morning; I think they'll be a big hit!"

"Absolutely;—boy, you didn't waste any time! They were just released to the public, weren't they?"

"Actually, the first ones were purchased in New York about three months ago. I was waiting for news of the first users' experiences with them, and I just heard about some very favorable results this morning."

"Maybe you read the same internet article that Alyssa read before she Skyped me . . ."

"Well anyway, I Skyped the president of the company mentioned in the article, Real-Life Android, and he agreed to send me a hundred for five-million, including shipping! That's fifty-thousand apiece, and they wholesale for over sixty; not to mention that they retail for over a hundred-thousand; so I saved a bundle on the volume discount."

"That's pretty good! How long until they arrive?"

"They are supposedly in stock, so I was told that I should have them in less than two weeks!"

"Wow, that's great, that you didn't have to pay any shipping charges. It cost almost four thousand for me to fly here from earth!"

"Well, it was a promotional rate; I'll have to pay shipping for the next batch. Maybe I should have ordered more!"

"Maybe so!—Well that's great news, that we'll have them here. Maybe Kerry and I will try beaming into one for a day, before we take our excursion to Philadelphia."

"Is that where your sister lives?"

"Yes, she actually lives in Bryn Mawr; it's a little north of the city. She bought a gorgeous house there last year. We'll be living in luxury!"

"Good, I hope you enjoy. Listen, I've got to get back to my office; I have a meeting with Clarion Capital in about ten minutes."

As soon as Ron left, Tommy Skyped Kerry, "Hi gorgeous; what are you up to this afternoon?"

"Hi Hun, I'm programming like crazy. Even though we've tripled the staff in the last year, I'm having to get about four androids programmed and out the door each week these days."

"Well, I won't take up your time; I just wanted to tell you that I asked Ron, and he said we could beam ourselves to Earth for at least a week or two, next month on the tenth; isn't that great news?"

"I don't know; I'm still a little leery about that. Let's watch the news over the next few weeks, and read more about others' experiences with it.—Hey Listen, I have to go; I just got called; I have to deliver an android I finished programming earlier this morning, to a guy who's out in the waiting room. Can I Skype you back in half-an-hour?"

"Sure, I'll let you go; I love you!"

Chapter Twenty-Six

FOUR WEEKS PASSED BY quickly, and soon, the tenth of June was upon them. Tommy and Kerry both woke up early. As they laid in bed, Tommy put his arms around Kerry and gave her a gentle hug, "Well, this is the big day. Are you ready for this trip?"

"I think so. It was a good thing we tried beaming into androids here first. I'm a lot less apprehensive than I was two weeks ago."

"Yes, it was fun; I especially enjoyed making love in a different body, and the lobster dinner we had was delicious!"

"Yes, I enjoyed it much more than I thought I would."

Tommy changed the subject, "Normally, I'd be up early to pack for a two week journey, but there's nothing to pack!"

"Yeah, I'm going to enjoy clothes shopping in Philadelphia. I hope I have a perfect body to dress."

"I'm sure you will. You know as well as I, that androids are only modeled after the most beautiful and handsome men and women, and I have never seen an android woman who wasn't very shapely and attractive."

'That's true; I'm actually pretty excited to go. I've heard about Earth, but I never thought I'd actually have a chance to visit there."

"I'll take you to Boston where I grew up. You won't believe how big the city is, and there's lots to do. We can go to some museums, and you can learn more about Earth's history."

"Okay! Hey, what do you say we take a Jacuzzi together out on the back deck. It's nice and cool out there at this hour of the morning."

"Sure, we have plenty of time before we have to leave the house."

"Yes, I'm so glad Ron let us out of the Monday morning staff meeting today."

"Yeah I don't know about you, but I don't think I would have been able to concentrate on what was being said in the meeting anyway, I'm so excited about seeing Alyssa."

They put on their bathrobes and went downstairs. Abby made them breakfast, after which they strolled out onto the back deck and slipped into the Jacuzzi. Tommy sighed, "This jet feels good blasting against my back. That's one thing we won't be able to enjoy on our trip."

"Yes, I remember. In the new androids, you have feeling in your hands and arms, mouth and face, and of course in the genital region, but otherwise you can't feel a thing!"

"Alyssa and Dr. Freudenthal are working on the next generation of receptor androids, where you should have sensory perception all over your whole body."

"Yes, that's a huge undertaking; how are they going to fit all of that wiring and brain function into a body with a normal size head?"

"Alyssa says the wiring won't be a problem; they're using fiber-optics which are incredibly thin; but brain size is their main problem. They're going to be challenged to fit all of that brain function into a normal-sized skull."

"She'll figure it out; it's too bad Bill can't join us on our trip back to earth . . ."

"Yeah, his probation officer wouldn't approve it. It's not just him; all sex offenders on parole or probation across the board are now prohibited from mind beaming. Apparently, there were at least a few cases where sex offenders reoffended while they were beamed into an android body."

"That's a shame; a few bad apples spoil the whole bunch."

"Any way, it's just as well; he and Becky can take care of the twins while we are away."

"Actually, I hired someone to stay at the house, and she and Abby will take care of Sarah and Jesse for us."

"Oh? Who did you hire?"

"She's a middle aged mother of two, but her kids are grown and they have their own families now, so she no longer has child-rearing responsibilities."

"Will she stay in our bedroom?"

"No, I've worked it out so she and Abby will stay in Bill's room; it's closer to the twins' room, and that way Bill gets the use of the master bedroom suite while we are away."

"That was thoughtful of you. I gave him the key to the boat yesterday, so he should be living pretty luxuriously for the next couple of weeks!"

Tommy and Kerry arrived at the beaming station on the third floor of the Atlas Android building a few minutes before nine. They were ushered into their individual beds, and fitted with an intravenous feeding tube. They strapped on their mind beaming helmets and were ready to go within twenty minutes' time.

Before they knew it, they were waking up in android bodies at the Rothschild beaming center in downtown Philadelphia. Tommy got up first. He leaned over to the beautiful female android sitting in the chair next to his, "Kerry, I assume?"

"Tommy? Is that you?"

"It's me; what do you think of my new body?"

"Ooh! You look like a very handsome hunk of a man!"

"You look absolutely stunning yourself! I like you as a blonde."

"Is that all that's different about me?"

"Well, you couldn't have gotten much more attractive than you are in real life, to me; but with that long blonde hair and that face, you're absolutely gorgeous, and you have a rockin' bod!"

"Oh good! This is going to be fun!"

"Well if you're ready, let's get out of here! Alyssa said she'd be here in the waiting room when we arrived."

The door to the chamber opened, and there stood Alyssa, "Tommy?"

"Hi Alyssa; yes it's me! It's so great to see you, actually in person, for a change!"

Alyssa felt a little awkward hugging what was physically a stranger, but the psychic connection had been made, and it became very real to her that she was finally with her twin brother again.

Tommy became aware of his limitations within the android body, as he couldn't feel Alyssa pressing up against his chest, but he could feel the warmth of her body in his hands and arms, and he gently squeezed her affectionately, "It's so great to see you again, and it's great to be back on earth!" He stepped back and held a hand out to Kerry, "Alyssa, this is Kerry."

"Tommy's better half, I'm sure!" Alyssa joked.

"It's nice to finally meet you in person; I never realized how slender you are! I don't really get to see much of your body on Skype; mainly your face."

"Yes," Alyssa smiled back, "Maybe I'll have to come out your way and see how you and Tommy look in person as well!"

"We'd welcome a visit any time!" Kerry shot back cordially.

"Thank you; that's nice to know. Well? What would you two like to do, now that you're here?" Alyssa asked nonchalantly.

Tommy responded, "Well, since we are in downtown Philadelphia, why don't we go to a museum? I've been telling Kerry some of what I know about earth's history, and I think she might find it interesting to learn about it firsthand."

Alyssa thought for a second, "Well, we could go to the Museum of Natural History for a while, and maybe have lunch together afterward, what do you think?"

"I'd like that," Kerry answered, "I'd be especially interested to find out more about the history of android development, since I program androids for a living."

"Well, there's the Android Museum on Fourth Street. Would you rather go there?" Alyssa suggested.

Tommy laughed, "That's funny; a couple of androids going to visit the android museum!"

"Sure! Let's go there," Kerry followed Alyssa's lead, "Personally, I think I would find it fascinating!"

"Okay; my car is in the parking garage across the street. Shall we go?"

They spent almost two hours walking through the exhibits, and listening to the pre-recorded monologues explaining the history and development of androids over the centuries.

Afterward, they went to an outdoor café and sat at a large circular table, with an umbrella to shield them from the afternoon sun. The place was somewhat crowded, but the waitress finally came to take their order. She looked at Tommy and Kerry, "You two look too perfect to be human, are you androids?"

"Oh, are we that obvious?" Tommy asked somewhat seriously.

"Well, we get a lot of traffic here; I've learned to spot androids over the years. I assume you two won't be eating then?"

"No," Tommy corrected her, "We're real people who have been mind-beamed into the new receptor androids. We can eat and taste and feel."

"Oh, I'm sorry, I didn't realize; well in that case, let me take your orders. Have you seen the specials?"

"Yes, we were just talking about them," Kerry answered, "I'll have the lobster salad and a large lemonade."

Tommy looked over at Alyssa, "How about you sis, what'll you have?"

"I'll have a cup of the clam chowder and a turkey club on whole wheat, and an iced tea."

The waitress looked over at Tommy, "How about you sir, what would you like?"

"I'll have the Caesar salad with grilled chicken special, and I'll try your tropical punch. Is it canned, or fresh?"

"It's made with real fruit, blended and strained," the waitress answered.

"That sounds fine."

Kerry spoke up, "That sounds good; I think I'll have that too, instead of the lemonade."

When the food came, they dug in, "Mm! This lobster is really tasty; way better than the lobster we get at home," Kerry commented.

"I've had lobster here before," Alyssa said, "I think it's imported from Maine; they have the best lobster in the country, supposedly."

Tommy spoke up, "It's really great to finally eat something; I was hungry."

"It's quite common," Alyssa informed, "It's a syndrome that most people experience in the hospital when they first get put on an I.V. They're getting enough nourishment that their body doesn't need to eat too, but they're used to consuming food."

"Yeah, our real bodies are on I.V.'s back on planet P right now, but it will probably be several days before we stop feeling hungry, or so they told us at the beaming station before we came," Kerry commented.

"It's kind of funny how this food we eat in these android bodies actually satisfies our hunger, I guess because hunger is almost more of a psychological thing; we don't need to eat, if we're getting adequate nourishment otherwise," Tommy added.

Alyssa looked puzzled, "—And how did you come to know this?"

"We beamed into receptor androids a couple of weeks ago, back on planet P. We wanted to see what it would be like before we came on the long trip to Earth," Tommy answered.

"Oh . . . How long were you beamed into them for?" Alyssa asked with interest.

Kerry jumped in, "Just for a day; I was really nervous about coming, until I got familiar with what it's like, living in an android body."

"I see," Alyssa gave Kerry an empathetic smile, "Well I suppose that was the smart thing to do."

"We went to Texarkahna, which is about a six hour plane ride from where we live in Alderon. It's on the equator, so the weather is like Hawaii. We could feel the hot sun on our faces, and the native fruits and vegetables were delicious!" Tommy spouted.

Kerry smiled mischievously, "You told me your favorite part of the experience was when we got back to our posh three room suite and made love!"

"Yes, Alyssa; the sex is great, in these new android bodies! You don't get worn out physically!"

"Yes, I never realized how much having an orgasm is in your mind, until I was living in an android body that couldn't even experience one physically," Kerry added.

Tommy had on a sly smile, "I think she probably knows; or do you sis? Are you still with Ed these days?"

"Yes, he keeps asking me to marry him, but I don't know if I even <u>want</u> to get married; although I may want kids a few more years down the road . . ."

Tommy brought the conversation back to the topic they were discussing, "Yes, but have you and Ed vacationed together in the new receptor android bodies?"

"Oh yes; we were one of the first couples to try them out, about four months ago; and yes, the sex was amazing!"

"Where did you beam yourselves to?" Tommy asked.

"We went to New York City. We had a blast! We stayed at the Four Seasons hotel in downtown. We went clothes shopping on Fifth Avenue, and we saw a play and a musical on Broadway. We went to the Metropolitan Museum; and we rented a car and drove ourselves to the Bronx Zoo; and we ate like royalty. Food never tasted so good!"

"Yeah, me and Kerry were thinking about going to New York. We may, towards the end of our stay. We'll probably rent a car."

"Why bother? You can take the Rolls Royce. I have two other cars in the garage. I bought one for Ed, but he prefers driving his Lexus convertible."

"Tom has one of those," Kerry informed, "It's hydrogen powered, so he only has to fill it up about twice a year."

"Speaking of your garage," Tommy interrupted, "After lunch, why don't we drive back to your new house; I'm anxious to see it."

"Sure, that's fine with me," Alyssa said agreeably, "It's kind of hot today. We could all go swimming in the pool. Wait 'till you see it, it's huge!"

"That reminds me, we have no swim suits; maybe we could stop at Macy's and pick up a couple on the way . . ." Tommy suggested.

"I'm anxious to go clothes shopping," Kerry said in an excited whisper, her eyes lighting up, "Maybe we could buy a few outfits while we're there . . ."

"That reminds me, "Tommy realized, "We have no money! We were going to overnight our debit cards here, but we were told at the beaming station that they wouldn't be honored anywhere."

"I <u>thought</u> of that," Alyssa replied, "I opened two accounts in each of your names, and put ten thousand in each account, so you'll have some spending money. I have your debit cards in my purse."

"Good thinking sis; you think of everything!"

After lunch, they headed to Macy's in North Philadelphia, on the way to Hatboro. First, they went to the women's department and Kerry tried on several dresses and tops and slacks. She also bought two bathing suits, underwear, and a sexy negligee. Then they went to the men's department, and Tommy found clothes he liked in about half the time.

On the way out, they stopped at the shoe department and bought several pairs of stylish shoes. They spent over three thousand dollars altogether, but Alyssa put it all on her charge account, so it wouldn't cut into their spending money.

They arrived at the house a little after four-thirty. As they pulled up the long driveway, Tommy could see that it was nothing short of a mansion, "Wow! This is huge! I like the pillars and the marble steps. It must have cost a fortune! How many bedrooms did you say it has?"

"It has eight bedrooms, and they all have balconies and gas fireplaces; and there's a bathroom adjoined to every one of them."

Kerry's eyes lit up again, "Do we get to pick which one we want to stay in?"

"Sure; they're all different sizes and shapes, including one round one, but that's the master bedroom, so you can't have that one!" Alyssa said humorously. "Also, I have a live-in maid and a butler, and two android servants, but they remain inactive most of the time; so that leaves four bedrooms to choose from."

Alyssa parked the car in the circular driveway, in front of the marble steps. The butler came out to greet them, "Good afternoon madam."

"Good afternoon; James," Alyssa said as she turned to introduce him, "This is my brother Tom, and his wife Kerry."

"How very nice to meet you," James said cordially. "Madam, will you be using the car later, or shall I put it in the garage?"

"Yes, put it in the garage," Alyssa ordered, "I think we've done enough traveling for the day. Oh, and would you bring in our shopping bags? They're in the trunk."

"Very well, madam." James bowed and left them.

Alyssa gave them a tour of the house. First, they went into the living room. It was quite spacious, with a marble fireplace. Tommy noticed the firewood in a brass tray off to one side, "Oh! An old fashion wood burning fireplace, huh?"

Alyssa nodded and smiled, "We like the aroma; we have three kinds of firewood; apple, hickory, and oak. Personally, I like the scent of the apple wood, but Ed prefers the hickory."

"I suppose James keeps the tray stocked," Tommy guessed.

"The furniture is lovely," Kerry complimented.

"Thanks," Alyssa accepted cordially, "I had an interior decorator pick it out. I paid a small fortune for it all, but she did a very nice job, don't you think?"

"I'll say! This place must have cost you some serious bucks; look at it!" Tommy said, flabbergasted.

"They wanted seven million for it, but we talked them down to six."

"Six million! Wow! I suppose you paid cash for it . . ."

"Yes, well it is a little extravagant," Alyssa admitted, "But Albert and I are making so much in royalties for our inventions that it was a mere drop in the bucket."

Next, Alyssa showed them the den, which she had converted into her home office. This time it was Kerry who was flabbergasted, "Wow! A ten screen Skype station, and look at the size of those screens!"

"Bill actually bought us a ten screen Skype station when we were growing up," Tommy informed her, "So we're used to it."

"Albert and I do our Skype conference calls here," Alyssa said as she pointed to the two chairs in front of the main desk, "Once, we gave a speech to ten different audiences at the same time!"

"That's pretty incredible," Kerry said, shaking her head.

They passed through the kitchen on the way to the elevator. It was twice as big as the one in Tommy's house. The maid was already starting to prepare dinner, with the assistance of the two android servants. Alyssa was busy telling them more about the house, so she didn't stop to introduce Tommy and Kerry.

When they got to the second floor, Alyssa first showed them the round shaped master bedroom, and they gawked at the modern furniture and artwork on the walls. "Wow!" Tommy exclaimed, "Is that real gold leaf on the ceiling?"

Alyssa smiled proudly, "It is; if you like that, then you'll like the guest room. Here, let me show you."

They walked about halfway down the long hallway, and entered the guest room. "As you can see, the whole room is wallpapered in gold leaf. The wallpaper cost two hundred thousand!"

Kerry walked dumbfounded into the bathroom, "More marble, I see." She eyed the double Jacuzzi tub with mirrors on all three walls surrounding it, "Well I can see this tub was made for the vain and beautiful . . ."

Alyssa blushed a little, "Shall I show you the other bedrooms?"

"This one is spectacular!" Kerry said as she turned around. She looked at Tommy, "Right, honey?"

"Absolutely," Tommy answered.

"I think we'll stay here, if it's alright. I'm actually feeling kind of worn out from traipsing around all day; I think I'd like to take a nap," Kerry said tiredly.

"Tommy gave her a hug and a kiss, "You go right ahead sweetie; I think I'll take a swim with Alyssa; we'll call you for dinner."

Tommy changed into his bathing suit, and met Alyssa out by the pool, "You weren't kidding when you said the pool was large; this is terrific! You've really outdone yourself sis."

Alyssa adjusted the strap on her bikini, "Yes, well I spent the first twenty years of my life with my nose to the grindstone most of the time; and intend to spend the next twenty enjoying life more, besides working with Albert."

"You certainly deserve it."

"By the way, guess who else is coming to dinner, besides Ed?"

"Albert?"

"Nope; guess again . . ."

"I give up; who?"

"Mom."

"She's coming? You didn't tell me that! I haven't even talked to her in the past year, I don't think . . ."

"I know; she wanted it to be a surprise. She's been working rather intensely with a therapist recently, and she's changed quite a bit. I think you'll like her new attitude and disposition."

"Really? She's changed that much, huh?"

"You'll see; she's not mad at you any more for going to help Bill. In fact she's only staying the night. Tomorrow she's planning to beam herself to planet P and pay a surprise visit to Bill. I told her he couldn't come with you, and she was disappointed. She misses him and wants to see him.

"You're <u>kidding</u>!"

"No, I'm not; she says she can't find a guy she likes half as much as she used to enjoy Bill's company. She says they're all after her for her money . . ."

"I guess that's the one downfall of becoming very rich."

"Well anyway, she realizes she went way off the deep end blaming Bill for all that went wrong with the family-androids we were all hooked up to, and she sees that I am able to have a stable long term relationship, so I obviously haven't been so seriously damaged by the bleedthrough into my online memory file. She plans to apologize to Bill; and she may even want to get back together with him, if he's still willing."

"Wow! That's an amazing transformation; I hope Bill is ready for it."

"She asked us not to Skype Bill and tell him about her visit; she wants it to be a surprise. She's worried that if he knows beforehand, he may find ways to avoid seeing her."

"I don't know Alyssa; what do <u>you</u> think?"

"I tend to agree with her. If I were Bill, I wouldn't want to see her, after all she did against him. Personally, now that I've seen the change in Mom, and she's been sober for several years now, I'd like to see the two of them get back together again, if that's what they both want, so I'm not going to interfere with Mom's plans."

"Yeah, I suppose you're right; let her take him by surprise; it's probably the only way she'll have a chance to apologize to him face to face. We might as well let nature take its course."

"That's what I thought too," Alyssa agreed.

"Wait a minute; say they do want to get back together; how is that possible? Bill can't ever leave planet P, and I doubt Mom would ever want to move there . . ."

"I don't know either, but she wants to go visit him, for whatever reason.—Shall we take a swim?"

"Sure; is the pool heated?"

"Of course; I like it at around eighty degrees."

"It must cost a fortune to heat a pool this size."

Alyssa shrugged, "I don't care, I've got money to burn these days!"

"Keep talking like that and you may not have much left when you get into your hundreds!" Tommy joked.

"Well, you might as well know that I'm already close to a billionaire at the age of twenty-two!"

"Jesus, Alyssa; that's great! I guess you do have money to burn!" With that, Tommy jumped in the deep end. He instantly felt the pleasantly cool water on his face and hands and arms, and of course down below, "Ah, this feels good, are you coming in?"

Alyssa cannonballed right next to Tommy, and came up laughing, "How's that for an entrance!?"

"Careful!" Tommy joked, "With this athletic android body I could probably turn you over my knee and spank you!"

"You probably could!" she giggled, "Android bodies are built with a lot of strength, for doing physical work and endurance."

"Yes, it's no wonder that they don't allow violent criminals to beam into one."

"Come on, I'll race you to the shallow end!" Tommy said, changing the subject. Tommy of course won by several lengths.

"Alright for you, Mister!" Alyssa said laughing, "Just wait 'till I come visit you in an android body, and race you in your pool!"

"I don't have a pool; we'll have to swim in the lake, but you're on!"

After their swim, Tommy took a shower and dressed for dinner before waking Kerry, "Hey sweetie, dinner's almost ready, I thought you might want to get up and get ready."

"Oh, what time is it?" She asked sleepily.

"It's a little after six. Guess what; my Mom's coming to visit; she'll supposedly be arriving any minute."

"Oh, I guess that means you're back on speaking terms . . ."

"Yes, it would seem. Alyssa told me Mom's been in therapy for several months, and she's worked through a lot of issues. She's supposedly not upset with me anymore, can you believe it?"

"Wow! What changed her mind?"

"She supposedly has come to realize that she was just being overly harsh and irrational, putting all the blame on Bill for the family-android problem; you know, the bleedthrough to Alyssa's online memory file?"

"Boy, that <u>is</u> a breakthrough!"

"She'll be staying the night, but she is actually beaming herself into an android on planet P tomorrow, and she's going out to the house to apologize to Bill . . ."

Kerry screwed up her face and just stared at Tommy, "That's <u>quite</u> a change, indeed!"

"Get this; Alyssa says Mom confided in her that she misses the way things used to be between them, and she may even try to get back together with him!"

"Well I'll believe that when I see it . . ." Kerry said doubtfully.

"Well anyway, you may want to throw a little cold water on your face, you obviously don't need to put on makeup; an android woman comes with permanent makeup; but it would be great if you could come downstairs in the next few minutes."

"Sure; I feel refreshed! How was your swim?"

"That was refreshing for me! It's great to be reunited with Alyssa. It's been almost four years since we were together."

Chapter Twenty-Seven

Tommy took the elevator down to the first floor, and when the doors opened, he saw Alyssa, and who he figured must be Ed, standing in the kitchen. He approached them with a smile.

"Hi Tommy!" Alyssa greeted cheerfully, "I like your new outfit! Tommy, this is Ed, the love of my life!"

"Hi Tom, it's nice to meet you; Alyssa has told me so much about you . . ."

"Hi Ed, it's nice to meet you too; and I've heard so much about you that I feel like I know you already!"

Alyssa turned to Ed, "Tommy and his wife Kerry have come to visit from planet P, in the new receptor android bodies. It's almost as good as having them here in person."

Ed nodded, "I understand both you and your wife are in the android business."

"Yes, I actually met Kerry at Atlas Android before I even went to work there."

"Oh, is that so; Alyssa tells me your company has just purchased one hundred of the new androids . . ."

"Yes, Ron Goldstein, the president of our company has been following their development, and he placed his order early, with Real-Life Android. They've been a real hit, and he's just ordered two hundred more."

"That's great, I'm glad they're working out for you."

The elevator doors opened again, and Kerry approached.

"Hi sweetie," Tommy took her by the hand, "This is Ed."

Ed got an eyeful of Kerry's gorgeous android body and pretty face, with her long, flowing blonde hair, "My, don't you look stunning!"

"Thank you; we're really enjoying our new android bodies. This is quite an adventure for us."

"Yes, I'm quite familiar with it; Alyssa and I tried the experience a few months ago ourselves."

"So Alyssa told us," Tommy returned, "Alyssa told us today about your trip to New York City."

"Yes, we had a ball! We were thinking we might beam ourselves to Earth-3 next month, to visit your grandfather."

The swinging door to the kitchen swung open and James appeared. He looked right at Alyssa, "Mrs. Symms has arrived, Madam."

Justina followed him into the kitchen, and Alyssa went to hug her, "Hi Mom! I see you're all dressed up; you look lovely!"

"Hi darling; thank you, it's so good to see you!"

"Mom, Tommy and Kerry are here!" she pointed to the two androids.

"Tommy? Is that you inside that handsome android body?"

"Yes, it's me Mom; I haven't seen you in so long; you look well!" He walked over and gave her a big hug.

"—And I take it this is Kerry . . ." Justina motioned to her.

"Yes, Mrs. Symms, it's nice to finally meet you."

"Oh please, call me Justina; it's nice to meet you too!"

"Alyssa tells me you have boy and girl twins; I suppose you left them at home."

"Yes, we left them in the care of a babysitter and Abby, she's my android servant."

"How old are they now?" Justina asked, out of curiosity.

Kerry answered enthusiastically, "They're going to be <u>three</u> in September . . ."

"My, how time passes," Justina commented as she reflected, "It doesn't seem like that long ago Alyssa told me they had just been born."

"Why don't we go into the dining room, now that we're all here," Alyssa gestured, as she herded them, "Dinner is about to be served."

The five of them made their way into the dining room, as Alyssa suggested the seating arrangement, "Mom, why don't you sit at the head of the table; and Tommy, you and Kerry can sit on this side, and Ed and I will sit on the other side."

The dining room set was made of cherry wood, beautifully crafted. The silverware was freshly polished, and the china-wear was pure white with silver edging. It looked very elegant, set on white silk placemats with matching silk napkins.

"Jeez," Tommy remarked, "I feel like I should have dressed in a tuxedo!"

"You have a beautiful dining room," Kerry echoed his sentiment.

"Why thank you!" Alyssa said cordially. She looked over to the maid who was standing at the doorway in a black uniform with a white apron, "Olga, you can begin serving."

"What are we having for dinner tonight?" Ed asked.

"We're having roast duck with cherry sauce," Alyssa said with a smile.

Olga served them very professionally, and they all heartily enjoyed the meal. After dinner, they sat at the table sipping coffee. Justina looked over at Tommy, "I guess I owe you an apology. I never should have been cross with you for going to help Bill. I know you have a very strong bond with him, and you were deeply upset about all that happened to him. At this point I can't blame you for wanting to go to him and do what you could to help him. I've been working through the past with a therapist this year, and I'm realizing that I played a part in all of the trouble, and I came down overly harsh on Bill. I was overreacting; I was deeply concerned because I was told by the authorities that Alyssa had been badly hurt, and I just wanted to come to the aid of my baby; but Alyssa seems to be doing just fine now."

"She is," Tommy agreed, "She's an amazing genius!"

Alyssa blushed, but kept silent.

"She certainly is!" Justina continued, "—And Ed, you have been just wonderful for her; I'm really glad you two are so happy together!"

They talked on for another hour or so, adjourning to the living room. Tommy and Kerry told Justina, Alyssa and Ed more about their jobs, the twins, and their home environment. Justina described her new home in detail, and told them how she was enjoying teaching again since September.

Finally, Justina hugged Tommy and stared into his eyes, "I don't know if Alyssa has told you, but I am going to visit Bill tomorrow . . ."

"Yes Mom, I know; Alyssa told me this afternoon. You don't want us to Skype him and spoil the surprise, I understand."

"Well I'm just afraid that if he knows I'm coming, he may avoid me, or turn me away before I have a chance to tell him what I have to say to him."

"He may anyway; but we won't spoil your plans, I promise."

"Good; well in that case I'm going to bed. I'm tired from the long trip, and I have to get up early tomorrow; I have to be at the beaming station at eight, which means I have to leave here before seven, with the traffic."

Alyssa nodded, "You know which room you're in tonight, don't you? James put your things in the last room at the end of the hall."

"Yes, thank you dear."

Tommy held her hand, "Mom, it's really great to see you. I really love you, and I'm so glad we can be close again. I wish you luck on your trip tomorrow. I think the best we can do on this earth is to reconcile with each other; to try to understand and accept ourselves and one another; and to try and help each other deal with our human imperfections."

"Yes, I wholeheartedly agree" Alyssa echoed, "I really love you a lot too, Mom. Good luck tomorrow."

Chapter Twenty-Eight

Justina awoke and looked at the clock. It was seven-fifteen, "Oh no! I forgot to set the alarm last night!" she thought to herself.

She got up and threw her clothes on in a hurry. When she went downstairs, no-one was up yet. She hurried out to the car, and set off for downtown Philadelphia, but she got caught in the early morning traffic.

She finally arrived at the beaming station at eight-thirty-five. She parked her car in the parking garage and hurried in.

"Hi, I had an eight o'clock beaming appointment. I got caught in traffic and I'm a little late; is that okay?"

The young man behind the desk addressed her in a business-like manner, "What is your name, Ma'am?"

"Justina Symms . . ."

"Okay, let me see." He typed her name into his computer terminal and there was a short pause, "Okay, I'm sorry Ms.

Symms; we only hold the spot for thirty minutes. I'm afraid someone else has taken your spot."

"Oh no!" She looked at him with sad disappointment in her eyes.

"Let me see what I can do . . ." he punched a few more keys at his terminal while she waited for another thirty seconds, "We have availability at two o'clock; shall I schedule you in?"

"That's the soonest you have available?"

"Yes, I'm afraid we're kind of booked up today."

"Well I guess that's okay then, go ahead and schedule me."

Justina walked back to her car wondering how she was going to kill about five hours. She found her way to the Four Seasons Hotel, and had a leisurely breakfast in their luxurious dining room.

Then, she decided to rent a room. Once she checked in, she Skyped Alyssa and told her about the delay, and they talked for a few minutes. Afterward, she took a nap for a couple of hours, and then she watched a movie on the big screen TV.

She arrived back at the beaming station at one-forty-five, and sat in the waiting room until she was called. Everything went smoothly, and by two-twenty she was waking up in an android body on planet P.

She stood up and eyed herself in the mirror, then she glanced over her shoulder at the attendant, "Boy, they sure do make these things attractive!" she commented. He just smiled back at her. "Can you tell me where I can rent a car?"

"Sure; you can rent one right here; in fact this is the only place you'll be able to rent one without a local credit card. I assume you wired money here to the station before leaving today?"

"Yes, I actually wired it last week."

"Well in that case, you can go out to the concierge desk, and I'm sure they will be able to help you."

Justina walked out to the concierge desk and was greeted by a friendly middle aged man, "Good afternoon, how can I help you?"

'Yes, I'm Justina Symms; I was just beamed from Earth into this very attractive android body, and I'd like to rent a car. What do you have available?"

"Sure, I can help you with that; let me just look up your account. How do you spell your last name?"

"S-Y-M-M-S, Justina."

"Oh yes, I can see that you have ample funds. What kind of car would you like? We have compacts, mid-sized, and full sized sedans . . ."

"I'd like a full size sedan with navigation please."

"Okay, we have a full size Astra touring car for a hundred and twenty a day, would you like to rent that?"

"Yes, that will be fine."

"How long do you wish to rent it for?"

"Well, my appointment to beam back to Earth is in a week, so I might as well rent it until then."

"Okay, the weekly rental with tax and insurance comes to Nine-sixty-eight. I'll need your pin number in order to complete the transaction."

Justina thought for a second, suddenly realizing she would be in big trouble if she couldn't remember it. Then the number came to her in her mind, "Four-eight-nine-six," she said to herself, and typed it into the keypad facing her.

"Thank you; would you like cash back as well?"

"Yes, why don't you give me five thousand in large bills. Actually, let me have two hundred in twenties."

Once in the rental car, Justina looked up Tommy's address using the on-board computer linked to the Internet. Then she turned on the navigator, "What is your destination?" a comfortable female voice asked smoothly.

"Twelve Evergreen Street, Fairhope."

"Okay," the electronic voice spoke again, "As you exit the lot, turn right on Algonquin Street, and then turn right at the Beltway entrance ramp. You'll want to follow signs to ninety-five north," it instructed.

Justina made her way to Fairhope, following the navigation machine's instructions, and pulled in to Tommy's driveway a little after four o'clock.

There was a car in the driveway, and she guessed it was probably Bill's. She swallowed hard, suddenly feeling very nervous, but she strengthened her resolve, getting out of the car and approaching the door.

She stood for a few seconds and collected herself before ringing the bell. After about twenty seconds, the door opened, and there stood Bill. "Can I help you?" he asked, not expecting company.

"Bill, it's me . . . It's Justina; I beamed here into this android body this afternoon, to come and see you . . ."

"Justina?! My God!—I never thought I'd hear from <u>you</u> again; I'm not sure we should be talking . . ."

"I know; I've been really terrible to you, but I've recently been in therapy, and I'm beginning to develop more perspective on everything that's happened between us."

"This is incredible! I don't know if I can deal with this; maybe you'd just better go . . ."

"Bill, please let me finish before you turn me away. I'm very sorry I had the reaction I did, to finding out about the bleedthrough sexual experiences that were committed to Alyssa's memory. In a way, it wasn't really any fault of yours; you were just doing what came natural to you. I know you love Alyssa, and you would never do anything you thought might harm her.—And she never came to either of us and complained of anything uncomfortable going on in her life. It's just that society and the law consider what happened to

Alyssa as sexual assault because she was under a certain age. I just jumped on the bandwagon, and it probably hurt Alyssa even more than if she merely had to live with those memories stored inside her occasionally cropping up to trouble her.—And she is such an exceptional young woman that she has grown and gotten past it, to some extent, and she has been in a healthy long-term relationship, including plenty of sexual satisfaction, she assures me, for over three years now with Ed; so I can no longer believe you are responsible for any serious damages. I <u>miss</u> you Bill, I miss the way we used to be with each other, and no other man seems to satisfy me and give me the sense of fulfillment I used to feel when I was <u>with</u> you. I've traveled all this way, and I was hoping we could spend some time together, if it isn't too weird for you that I'm trapped inside this android body . . ."

Bill stood taking all of this in, and he began to nod, "Well, you have to understand this is quite a shock, this sudden contact with you; but I appreciate your honesty, and all the good work you've obviously done in therapy to come to this change of heart. You're right, it is a little weird with you in that android body; but I definitely have the sense it is really you in there because of the way you talk, and your voice inflections and everything . . . I suppose since you've come all this way, I could invite you to join me for dinner, and show you around Tommy's new house . . ."

"Thank you Bill; I was hoping you wouldn't turn me away flat. I know I've acted abominably, and stripped you of all your stature in the community, and took away all your money and everything, but I'd like to try and make it up to you now, if that's possible."

"Well come on in, let's talk."